WEST END

For my pal Chris,
my most loyal, flattering
and glamourous reader

Crockett White
12/29/15

A NOVEL OF ENVY,
REVENGE AND DIRTY MONEY

WEST
END

CROCKETT
WHITE

θP

OLD HICKORY PRESS

NASHVILLE

ҨP

OLD HICKORY PRESS

Nashville, TN

oldhickorypress@gmail.com

West End is a work of fiction chronicling the passing of a golden age in the intersection of the American institutions of the press and politics. Any similarities between the fictional characters and real people living or dead is the result of coincidence with events occurring in similar time and place. The public figures of the times whose names figure prominently in this story are portrayed accurately and as history will record them.

COVER AND INTERIOR DESIGN BY GKS CREATIVE

cityscape image by Max Lindenthaler/Shutterstock

Printed in the United States of America

Hardcover ISBN: 978-0-9965209-2-8

Trade paperback ISBN: 978-0-9965209-0-4

Ebook ISBN: 978-0-9965209-1-1

For Frank, Seig, George, Cecil and John Jay

BLUFF CITY, 1987

It is hard to believe this is the same man I knew twenty-five years ago when his insanity was still secret. The last to know, he is here now in the offices of the County Election Board costumed as a founding father in powdered wig and frock coat from another century, presenting the signed petitions necessary to get his name on the ballot for public office again. Prospects for his election need no comment beyond the sad truth that despite his long recognition as a public figure, most of the signatures were begged on the streets amidst the rolling eyes and stifled sniggers of dumbstruck strangers unbothered by bizarre festoonery of madness. He is running for chief judge of the State Supreme Court.

He did not always need the colonial garb of his hero Thomas Jefferson to get attention, his natural gifts being more than sufficient, and he might not need such accouterments today if only he realized it. He remains the same tall, dark and angular figure with mischievous eyes and the deep mesmerizing voice of a revival preacher, all coagulating in an extraordinarily magnetic presence barely diminished by age. Now and then he even manages that magical smile that once set women atwitter and men to envy. The only thing missing is that distinctive rarified air of confidence rooted in awareness of the man he used to be.

At a campaign fundraiser in California back in '68, where he was a total stranger, I saw him steal a crowd of five hundred celebrities from both the candidate himself and his movie star host for an entire Sunday afternoon. It was a reception for the vice president of the United States at the hillside ranch of a noted star of television westerns back when they were the morality plays of American cinema and the good guys always won. The vice president was characteristically late and the crowd, mostly high-flying movie moguls and rich and famous actors normally unable to find anyone as interesting as they find themselves, had quickly become bored with self-absorption. As the only stranger in the room, with his leading-man face and regal bearing, Seth Tatum Weston III was a threat to fill any such void. And he had crashed the party.

It was not unusual for Weston to show up uninvited to a swell gathering such as this, or a public event like the Super Bowl in New Orleans or a championship prizefight in Las Vegas without tickets. He arrived without notice or reservations at exclusive restaurants or resort retreats, virtually any place he figured he belonged. Often he came in a limousine or a small motorcade, a helicopter if necessary, whatever fashion might convince stunned hosts, ticket takers, clerks or security people that his lack of proper credentials was their oversight. Most people who try stuff like this come off as buffoons or blowhards whose very appearance betrays their imposture. But Weston's style, charm and grace were such that hosts, even after finally realizing they had not invited him, soon wished they had.

That day in California, he had hired a chauffeured car from the most prominent Beverly Hills service to deliver us to the fundraiser. That neither of us had any idea where the ranch was located was of little consequence once Weston tendered, along with his credit card, a mention of his long friendship with the vice president. The driver knew of the event and delivered us to a sprawling adobe pueblo planted like flora just below the edge of a mountain plateau twenty miles from Rodeo Drive, where a cheery blonde with a Spanish rose in her hair greeted us at the front door. Weston returned her furtive smile with an accompanying intimacy—inside information that "the vice president is only a few minutes behind us. He is a great orator, nonetheless, he does go on and on."

Taken as the candidate's advance guard, we were led through a high-walled courtyard entry with planted beds of cacti on one side and a bubbling stream of water snaking through an indoor gravel garden on the other, up a stone incline to a covered slate patio and out into several acres of irrigated estate greenery beyond which sat a small stable and a fenced paddock where a few horses grazed on scrub pasture. Off to one side of the patio, a section of the lawn had been squared off by gingham-draped tables, along which white-coated caterers were spreading the promised buffet lunch. On the other side, a row of bartenders in rose-pocked sombreros lined a long bar, at its end a flatbed farm wagon serving as a stage for a five-piece band of musicians in cowboy hats playing the final chords of "Cool Water."

Word that "the vice president's man" had arrived spread quickly through the movie stars, dispelling an initial perception that Weston might have been one of their own, perhaps a new rising star they had failed to recognize out of makeup.

Already a candidate for the United States Senate, Weston had dressed that day as if he were a candidate for president himself, which he intended to be one day—dark blue, three-piece, pinstriped suit, sky blue oxford shirt with a gold collar pin and red-and-blue striped tie. He had introduced me, almost sheepishly, to the flirty greeter as a Washington newspaper-man who, up until earlier that day, had been traveling with the national press corps accompanying the vice president, a near accuracy supported by my relatively shabby wardrobe of cowboy boots and cheap corduroy jacket. Back then I still dressed like the country guitar player I had always wanted to be, but that also well-suited an underpaid reporter on a Southern newspaper. My lack of fashion had irritated Weston to the point it had become a joke masquerading a serious issue between us. He considered my wardrobe inappropriate mainly because he had interpreted my job as his hometown newspaper's political reporter to be the engineer of his rise to national political prominence, which I resented—even though true.

He often lectured me on the subject, contending my way of dressing was a subconscious attempt to disguise, for some inex-plicable reason, a fine Vanderbilt and Harvard education. This absurdity he attributed to some lower middle-class inferiority complex due to my upbringing on the wrong side of the River. Not that I didn't suffer one, but the Vanderbilt and Harvard experiences had come to me as miraculous, life-changing gifts that in my own mind were, in fact, a quiet source of pride.

One of Weston's many social assets was a rich baritone that a woman once described to me as "how I imagined God would sound." To my ear, he kept it one notch below heavenly perfection by randomly ignoring certain consonants, mainly the letter "r" in the first syllable or at the end of words—not so much in his speeches, but in casual conversation and then just often enough to produce the soft hint of a Virginia plantation upbringing. Coming on to a Southern female, for example, he might sound like Rhett Butler in *Gone with the Wind*. So Harvard came out of his mouth as "Hahvad," and my last name, Arthur, as "Aahthuh." One day he decreed, "Dave Aahthuh, until you agree to dress like you ah somebody, when we get into these fundrasahs, just move on off and melt away in the crowd."

His egotistical admonition was actually an embellished return of advice I had once given him. The very education he had accused me of trying to obscure had included a study of crowd psychology, one premise of which holds that two strangers in a crowd obviously comfortable together in their own conversation are less likely to be noticed than a lone figure, who immediately becomes an object of curiosity to be set upon by hosts or officials suspicious that he might be an interloper.

If there is anything Weston enjoyed being, it was a curiosity. Abandoning him in a yard populated with celebrities, press agents and beautiful women was akin to chumming sharks. So from a few yards away, alone in the comfort of my lower middle-class skin, I watched Weston become the center of attention in a room full of narcissistic Jimmy Stewart and John Wayne wannabes.

The first to approach him was the silver-haired host, a noted producer of television westerns, who started peppering him with questions about the vice president's policy position on this and that, particularly the Vietnam War, opposition to which had become a cause celébrè in Hollywood. Intimately familiar with Humphrey's politics, Weston could articulate them every bit as persuasively as the vice president. As the circle grew deeper around him, Weston began eyeing the flatbed wagon and microphone before which the famous Sons of Pioneers had been entertaining the crowd. It was warm that day and I could see perspiration beginning to bead at the edges of the ebony hair around his face, a stubborn strand of which generally curled to the right and stuck to his forehead. He took off his jacket and folded it neatly across his arms and with the effortless swing of one long slender leg, he popped up on the wagon bed and tapped the microphone, which was still live.

Weston's spontaneous oratorical prowess was actually rooted in written speech. Along with a sizable paper net worth, he had inherited his grandfather's wealth of words and an uncanny ability to put them together, which he did compulsively almost every minute that he was not reading something. The process might begin in the morning with an idea of his own, or a phrase he'd picked out of the newspaper or heard someone discussing at the next table over lunch the day before. It would set him to reading and thinking out loud about the pros and cons, editing and altering thoughts and finally crafting and rewriting sentences until he had developed an insightful and persuasive position on a current public issue with which he was comfortable. Within a few days, he had stored it in a reservoir of thought where it fit nicely with another and from which he could recall it any time the occasion required.

Such linear reasoning was not surprising from a third-generation lawyer whose father and grandfather were both legends of the law in the South. His maternal grandfather, Hannibal Hancock, was highly regarded for his legal acumen and ethics, and his own father, Seth Tatum Weston Jr., for his courtroom fierceness and jury-swaying oratory. But neither ancestor had possessed the polished silver tongue of their descendant who had developed off-the-cuff verbal persuasion to an art form.

"I am Tate Weston, a friend of the vice president," he announced to the movie people, more than a slight exaggeration of the truth. "He has been delayed and while we are waiting for him, I want to take this opportunity to tell you why we need a man like him in the White House.

"A few yeahs ago when I was thirty years old, I was fortunate enough to be at Vanderbilt University to hear a great speech by President John F. Kennedy...the day he gave his famous advice to the young people of America—'Ask not what your country can do for you...but what you can do for your country.' And hearing those words changed my life forever.

"I was born one of the luckiest people in the world. My fathah is one of America's most celebrated trial lawyers. Along the way he made enough money to send me to Duke University and then to the fine law school at Vanderbilt, and he was such a magnificent role model that I chose to follow in his footsteps. And today my name is on the door of a marvelously successful law firm with a great future. I have a beautiful wife from one of Virginia's most prominent families and we have a little five-year-old girl named Brooke who I cannot look at without tears of joy filling my eyes. But a day does not go by that I don't remember President Kennedy's words and ask myself, what can I do today for my country?

"So I have left my busy law practice down South and my nice house in the West End of a beautiful city on a bluff of the River, my lovely wife Pippa and a baby daughter, and I have come out heah to California at my own expense to be with you and do something important for my country—that is, to help a great man and proven public servant, Hubert Horatio Humphrey, succeed Lyndon Johnson as president of the United States."

Weston took a breath and paused for the swell of applause he knew would follow. Then he went after more, rattling off one by one the great unsettling issues of the time—the legitimacy of the Asian war and the unrest it had caused among the nation's young people; the sinful segregation that still existed in America and on and on, explaining Humphrey's public policy positions on each, deliberately saving until last the one he knew would stir the crowd to a fever pitch, obviously trying to hold their attention to the precise minute that Humphrey would arrive and he would have to give up the microphone. In keeping with the good fortune with which his life had been blessed, about the time Weston was reaching for another anecdote or joke with which to extend his oratory, he saw the first line of Secret Service agents file into the courtyard and begin stationing themselves strategically around the back of the crowd.

Knowing that the candidate would not be far behind, Weston quickly grasped the subject he knew to be closest to Humphrey's heart and the signature issue of his campaign—the inequality that had persisted in America from the day the first African slave was led off a boat in chains.

"I would like to close by raising the issue I am sure the vice president—who, by the way, has just arrived—will surely be talking about—an issue on which no one is more passionate and eloquent—and that is the great gulf that exists between the quality of life enjoyed by people like you and me—the lucky ones—and the tragic existence of those who through no fault of their own but by accident of birth have been trapped in the pits of poverty we find not only in the black ghettos of our great cities but in many areas of white rural America.

"Fulfilling the promise of equality guaranteed in the Constitution more than two hundred years ago has been the wellspring of Hubert Humphrey's long record of public service. It is a goal he shared with President Kennedy, who made it the cornerstone of his presidency and ultimately gave his life for in its pursuit. And after his death, this cause was picked up by the Johnson/Humphrey administration, whose War on Poverty has advanced it beyond anything John Kennedy could have imagined. And through it all, no human being has been more vigorous in this pursuit than the man from whom you are about to hear."

By this time, Secret Service agents were stationing themselves around the stage and the same lovely greeter who had met us at the door was strolling prissily across the lawn with the vice president in tow. At first he appeared perplexed by the speaker on the wagon stage. He had expected to be introduced by his host, who was now a statue in the back of the crowd, apparently as enraptured by

Weston as everyone else. I wasn't sure Humphrey had recognized Weston, even though the two had met during Kennedy's term in office as members of the Tractors for Cuba Committee, a propaganda initiative aimed at mollifying Cuban Americans upset by his administration's failed Bay of Pigs Invasion. But after an exchange of whispers with the female escort, the patented happy warrior's smile returned to his florid cherubic face and he appeared poised to climb the stairs to the podium.

Weston never missed a beat.

"That day at Vanderbilt, President Kennedy concluded that famous speech with the promise of a new day in America that would wipe out the tragic blight of inequality on the consciousness of America. He promised new leadership that would bring about 'a rising tide that lifted all the boats.'

"Long before that day and every day since, there has been a fierce force for equality in America, a man who didn't have to ask himself what he could do for his country—a man who knew instinctively what he could and should do for his country, a man who even before President Kennedy promised it to America, has been a wind driving a rising tide. Ladies and gentlemen, I give you the next president of the United States, Hubert Horatio Humphrey."

The candidate bounded up the stairs and bear-hugged the speaker like he was a long-lost son. And to this day I am not sure Humphrey knew he was hugging an interloper who had crashed his reception. But for certain he would never forget Tate Weston.

What would the old warrior think if he were witnessing the current spectacle at the election office in Bluff City? Where this dowdy klatch of courthouse habitués are grinning at the outlandish figure struggling with a heavy rucksack bulging with yellow legal pads, his white wig teetering atop a shaggy gray mop months past time for a trim, the frock coat ill fitting, too, like something borrowed from a carnival barker with much shorter arms, and in cheap, clunky black cloth shoes with soles thick for street walking. This could not be the same Weston—but it is. If not for the unlimited generosity of a couple of friends and his ex-wife, he could be one of the nation's homeless, his net worth piled in a grocery cart parked outside on the sidewalk.

Shamefully, I have chosen to watch it all from a distance, as discreetly as possible from the courthouse hallway through the election office window, not unlike the way I once watched Weston and other swell West Enders with my nose pressed up to the outside of their world, like some itinerant mongrel dog curiously investigating new food smells in a strange neighborhood and being not dissimilarly received.

Some towns thresh their wheat from the chaff by railroad tracks, chain-link fences and superhighways. Bluff City does it with The RIVER, too deep to walk, too treacherous to swim and with west bank cliffs too steep to climb, restricting to the east regular flooding and stagnant inferiority.

Tate Weston had first come into my life wearing the blatant swagger of exceptionalism endemic to West Enders whose high schools were all preparatory academies with their own flags and coats of arms and hundred-year-old pledges of commitment to excellence. His first impression was inflicted rather than left, stamped most certainly by the nature of the social chasm between us.

A teenager, Weston had crossed the River as captain of West Mont Academy's golf team to play in the state tournament at a country club named after one of my ancestors, Davy Crockett. Some big shots, the Vanderbilts or DuPonts, or some other outfit from Delaware, owned the place along with the surrounding mustard-shade Mill Town houses all in a line and the rayon plant where my father and my grandmother and both of her husbands all made their living at one time or another.

I was a tow-headed kid of twelve in the eighth grade, and among the local caddies assigned to the foursome that included Weston, who was a senior at WMA, where high-falutin' West Enders sent their male children to become scholar athletes before they go to the Ivy League, or Duke or Vanderbilt to become bankers, doctors and lawyers. Superior as golfers, too, the WMA team won the tournament but Weston got skinned by my bag, a blue-collar kid nicknamed "Boots" because he seldom wore shoes of any kind on the course. Played either in work boots or no shoes at all, but barefooted or booted, he was Crockett Springs Club's best player and grew up to make his living as a gambler. He was also a cheapskate, so Weston's caddy got the bigger tip that day even though they lost. Still, years later, when I witnessed Boots being arrested in a gambling raid, out of neighborhood loyalty and the recollection of him skinning Weston, I didn't put his name in the paper.

I saw Weston one other time when we were young, from behind a cheap guitar I was mistreating as a last-minute fill-in for a rock 'n roll band hired to play at a dance at Winthrop Hall, the all-girls high school where the rich send daughters they hope will marry the WMA scholar athletes who become doctors or lawyers. By this time, Weston was already a Duke University underclassman and a prime target for well-to-do lays. As a young man, he was so damn handsome, charming and confident, most people liked him right off. But for me, he has been a slow and still incompletely acquired taste.

Taking Weston long term called for conditioning, like learning to swallow castor oil because it is good for you, or appreciating caviar because it is affluent. Such lessons—in fact all but life's simplest—sometimes require a teacher. And finally appreciating Weston is something I must attribute to our mutual friend, Jack Hickenlooper, the *Bluff City Clarion*'s celebrated editor and publisher. At some point, every adolescent male needs to be believed in by some man he admires. In my case, it was Hickenlooper.

Not that I didn't have some male role models in my family. My father was a World War II veteran who at age twenty fought in the Battle of the Bulge and came home forever emotionally scarred by harrowing service to his country. He taught me only two things: Go to work every day whether you feel like it or not and "don't ride the clutch" on his '56 Ford.

The father of my mother was a rough-handed cop from whom I learned how to drive a boat and a car, how to shoot a gun, how to really see that at which you are looking, and how to fight dirty when necessary. My other grandfather was a moonshiner who farmed a hundred acres of mountain corn and once put me up on the back of a Jersey cow. He died when I was about five, before he could teach me anything other than not to eat rancid ground beef, which is what killed him. Also along the way, I had a step-grandfather, a decent man who led the singing in a fundamentalist church and flirted with every good-looking female he ever came across. He taught me how to tie a necktie and that I should grow up to be a Republican.

None of these men met the role model requirements of my mother, Sallie Mae Arthur, who no doubt believed in me before anyone else did and wanted me to "grow up to be somebody." One day when I was about sixteen and still in high school, she showed me the morning *Clarion* with Jack Hickenlooper's picture on the front page with his new wife Deidre, an opera singer from Boston. My mother had several more clippings she had collected and folded up in little squares and held by a rubber band. I liked the way Hicken-looper looked—pleasant, clean cut and serious—and I remember what she told me that day.

"See this man," she said. "This is who you want to be. If you want to be somebody, you can't follow in the footsteps of all these booze-guzzling, slut-chasing assholes you've been around all your life. Your daddy barely graduated high school, and your granddaddies didn't even do that. Your old uncles you don't even know aren't worth a damn either. But if you want to be somebody, you're gonna have be around a man like this Jack Hickenlooper. Why, he knows President Kennedy and all his brothers and is going to Washington with them. Both Father Joe Donnelly and your Granddaddy Crockett told me they know Jack Hickenlooper personally. Someday I'm gonna see that they make sure you get to know him, too."

A couple of years later, Jack Hickenlooper made the front page of the *Clarion* again, this time with a big headline announcing that he was coming home from Washington to be its new editor and publisher. By this time I had developed a newspaper reading habit myself by pitching either the *Clarion* every morning or the *Defender* in the afternoon—sometimes both—onto the porches of damn near every Mill Town bungalow east of the river. But a paper route, Sallie Mae Arthur declared, would never pay my way through college so I could become that somebody she wanted me to be. I needed a better job, which she came up with.

A big Chicago drugstore chain where she worked off and on over the years would pay your way through pharmacy school, she said, if, upon graduation, you would agree to long-term employment in one of the most stable, important but boring jobs on earth— deciphering the illegible prescriptions of physicians and making sure the sick get the right pills in the bottle. My career path to becoming a pharmacist was not negotiable. If there was one thing Sallie Mae Arthur had taught me, it was that you have to do what you have to do.

The Wilson's Drugstore across the river and downtown closed at seven every night, about the time the reporters and editors at the *Clarion* were cranking out the morning edition three blocks away on Board Street.

Captain Morgan Crockett of the county sheriff's patrol, the cop who had been at the top of Sallie Mae's list of booze-guzzling, slut-chasing asshole relatives, obviously knew this because his squad car was sitting at the curb outside when I got off one Saturday night early in the spring of '62. When I opened the passenger door, he said, "Get in," a commandment I had been following since I was a small boy when he began educating me to the ways of the streets, taking me along with tires screeching and siren screaming directly to the scenes of mayhem of all descriptions—stabbings, shootings, rapes and murders—once even to a double shot-gunning of an adulterous couple in a motel bed, from which I had to run outside and vomit. Another time he had me drop to the pavement and hide under a car to watch the fatal ending of a bar fight that had moved outside to an Old West shoot-out, and of course, now and then, made me privy to mysterious meetings I was to later realize were occasional episodes of corruption in progress.

As usual, his black-and-tan cruiser had the strong, clean smell of Old Spice aftershave, which among other attributes had clearly distinguished him from all the other booze-guzzling, slut-chasing assholes from whom Sallie Mae Arthur claimed I had descended. It had to be my cop-granddad the Old Spice marketers had in mind when they came up with the slogan—"If your grandfather hadn't smelled like Old Spice, you wouldn't be here."

On duty or off, Captain Crockett was a dandy, as strong and clean as his aftershave, and Irish as Paddy's pig; not the squatty, freckled, red-haired variety Irish with featureless faces. The other kind, the "black Irish," of his mother who was a Sullivan, tall and angular with sharp cheekbones, hollow cheeks and eyes that moved from soft warm gray to cold beady black with an anger strike or an adrenaline rush. Unless going fishing or bird-hunting, Captain Crockett wore a uniform suited for all kinds of business—a gold-laden navy blue gabardine with starched pristine white shirts, shiny black boots and a Sam Browne belt, and armed to the teeth with at least two nickel-plated pistols, one of them hidden in an ankle holster. He carried a blackjack and a flashlight long enough to make a good truncheon.

"Where we going?" I asked, a question he had heard from me a thousand times.

"To see the most important man in town," he said.

The morning *Clarion* and the afternoon *Defender* were housed in the same office building and printing plant on Board Street, adjacent to the tracks of a railroad yard that marked the end of the downtown shopping district and the beginning of the West End. Though bitter rivals for generations, modern economic realities had driven their owners to wall off their competing editorial departments like fortresses, each forbidding their employees to enter the domain of the other, and to take refuge in a cost-saving, joint-operating agreement that merged redundant advertising, production and circulation departments. It was a fragile and unholy alliance. In fact, the two families had hated each other since the Civil War and were still fighting it.

In the winter of '61, however, the temperature of the long feud had cooled somewhat when the last Perry on the *Clarion* masthead, Luther Wainscott Perry IV, died in what the *Clarion* reported as "a hunting accident abroad." The considerably more specific *Defender*'s account said the twenty-nine-year-old publisher died "in an alcoholic stupor while playing Russian roulette with a Buenos Aries showgirl." Overlapping readers of the two Bluff

City papers—and there were only a few—would tell you that such sharp contrast between their accounts of the same incident was not all that unusual.

The Perry's *Clarion* ownership automatically passed to a care-taker trust in the iron grip of a lone trustee, who was the sole owner of Bluff City's largest bank, the Community Southern, which is how Jack Hickenlooper got to be the most important man in town.

Splendid in his gold-splashed uniform, Captain Crockett marched me into the *Clarion* offices like he owned the place and tipped his peaked cap to the secretary guarding the entrance to a small rectangular office in the front of the "City Room." She was about fifty, frog-shaped and wore her gray hair like a helmet.

"Here to see Jack," he announced, in the same tone he might have said, "Police...open up."

Through the cracked door, we could see one arm and the rolled-up sleeve of a man in a blue shirt resting on a typewriter. An old stern face shifted her perusal from the captain to me. I was wearing my drugstore work outfit—khakis, white shirt and a tie. Decent. Not a delinquent being returned to his parents by a cop.

"Mr. Hickenlooper is about to have his news meeting," she replied, a bit snooty. "You'll have wait."

"That's okay, I see Jack's in there by himself," the captain said, "and we won't be but a minute."

He pushed me right past her and through the door.

Hickenlooper looked up from his typewriter, casually, like people broke into his office all the time. His face, that of movie leading man with pale blue eyes and a five o'clock shadow, broke into a wide grin. My mother had told me she thought Hickenlooper looked a little like Paul Newman and he did.

"Morgan Crockett, I'll be damned," he said, and jumped up to greet my granddad like he was an old buddy.

His loosened tie hung from the open collar of a buttoned-down oxford cloth shirt, the tail of which was having trouble staying inside a pair of gray suit pants that, missing a belt, looked like they might drop any minute down around his scuffed cordovan loafers. He was shorter than I expected and somewhat dwarfed by the square captain whose glistening gun belt, midnight blue, padded-shoulders uniform and tall cap made him loom larger than he was.

"And who you got here, Morgan?" Hickenlooper asked, giving me a once over with his pale blues.

"This is my grandson, Dave Arthur, Sallie Mae's boy," he told Hickenlooper. "He's taking classes at the junior college in the mornings, and he needs a job."

Not that "Dave's interested in journalism" or "wants to be a newspaperman" but that the boy "needs a job," the three-word essence of how politics at every level has always worked, a principle once candidly defined by a famous mayor of Chicago, who, when criticized for cronyism in office, marveled, "If you can't help your friends, who can you help?"

"Needs a job" is the signature lament of Irish neighborhood politics from which the captain of the county highway patrol had risen to be Sheriff Lermon's right-hand man and precisely the repeated plea of my political animal mother from the same zoo, whose nagging had produced this meeting. And however German-sounding the name Hickenlooper, the new editor and publisher of the *Clarion* had just spent two years in the political trenches with the most famous Irish family in American history, so all my granddad had to say was "Dave needs a job." Message sent.

Hickenlooper looked at me and asked, "What can you do, Dave?"

Having no specific skill on the tip of my tongue and scared I was about to stammer, I said, "Anything you want done."

Hickenlooper gave Captain Morgan a look that said "like grandfather, like grandson" and I thought I saw a hint of amusement in his eyes that never crossed his lips. Instead, he said to me, "What kind of work you been doing?"

I told him about the free ride I had been getting from Walgreen's, taking pre-pharmacy classes at the junior college, working part time at the drugstore uptown on weekends and afternoons filling orders at the warehouse—but that it was about to end and that I needed full-time work. I wanted to tell him that I had delivered the *Clarion* and the *Defender* during my last two years at Father McKinley High, where he had gone, too, but a side door to the office opened abruptly admitting old guys in bowties and eye-shades carrying legal pads and reams of wire machine paper, and I never got the chance.

The *Clarion* newsroom of 1962 was the best place I have ever been before or since. Before being obliterated by time and technology, newspaper city rooms where the reporters and editors practiced their craft were the nuggets of the golden age of "The Press," then considered a "fourth estate" even more important to democracy than the other three because it served as a watchdog on their behavior. Now "The Press" is called "The Media," which is not the same thing.

Often shabby, and thick with the barroom aroma of smoke and alcohol, newspaper city rooms were open pits of passion, creativity and idealism, usually with a cast of characters befitting the dramas—silly or serious—they were hired to chronicle. The *Clarion's* room was a typical cauldron teeming with excitement, energy and sense of high purpose, and newly invigorated by a young editor/publisher home fresh from "Camelot."

Despite the *Clarion's* reputation for slave wages, Hickenlooper had attracted aspiring young journalists from the best schools, including former editors of the *Harvard Crimson*, and sons of U.S. senators and Kennedy administration cabinet members. Also among the newly hired were a few West Enders my age who had attended Vanderbilt, Duke and Emory. Some had been awarded reporter openings. Others filled summer internships. But my job was not in that glorious city room. It was in a large wire cage called "the Morgue" located in a dungeon on the low-ceilinged floor below, the place where dead newspapers were cut up with scissors, folded and stuffed into dated manila envelopes and filed away in green metal drawers for posterity.

The morgue's four-to-midnight shift, Mr. Hickenlooper told me, was perfect for a kid who needed a job and was taking morning classes at a junior college. To my ear, he might as well have added "somebody whose cheap khaki work pants, short-sleeved white shirt and clip-on necktie do not fully offset his East-of-the-River hoodlum swagger, his slicked-back haircut or the souped-up, hot rod Ford convertible he drives to work—a kid better suited for sweeping up behind the printers or loading bundles on the dock at two in the morning. Whether I was hearing empathy, disdain or the subconscious soliloquy of my own inferiority complex would remain a mystery to me for some years to come.

Hickenlooper was right that the holder of the night morgue job might even find time to study, which I did now and then—when I couldn't find a reason to hang out upstairs in the newsroom that for me quickly became a roller coaster of emotion. The pace of the place, the glamour of the star reporters, the confidence of the Ivy League imports and the mere sight of the young West Enders had kindled in me the first signs of ominous feelings that Sallie Mae Arthur had repeatedly warned me about. "Envy and resentment," my mother often complained, "live deep in the heart of anybody with an ounce of Scotch-Irish blood, which you have. But then, you know, every family is cursed with something."

Physically, the newsroom was a mess: Old metal desks, World War II Army green in color and jammed three together in a line; their tops scattered with paper coffee cups, some empty and overturned, others with contents cold and growing green slime. Protruding from the debris like sentinels were dozens of sharp metal spikes set into lead bases, now the spines of false starts, deceased or rejected prose. In the desks' center wells were vintage black Underwood typewriters, a few later model Royals, and one electric IBM that belonged to the only female hard news reporter. The desk chairs were objects to covet, barter and even sell according to their level of usability. But mainly they constituted a collection of junk that, along with waist-high trash baskets, served to narrow and cockeye the thin walking aisles, making going from front to back in the newsroom an obstacle course.

Only the west wall had windows and they all looked out on a narrow alley-like passageway shielded from light day or night by the height of the buildings it separated. The rear of the room, or north wall, was the busiest part, especially in the late afternoons and evenings when people outnumbered both desks and chairs. A long pipe coat rack took up the center, and to one side was a table holding stainless steel coffee urns that dribbled out an endless supply of something the color and texture of motor oil that needed changing. Conveniently located on the east wall, appropriately according to some, was the place where you could dribble it out—the entrance to a pisser shared with the *Defender*'s newsroom. The only access one side had to the other, it was truly a "men's room" only. If the lone female on the *Clarion* news staff, ancient court reporter Miss Shirley Keeton, needed to dribble, she had to dribble in the Society Department, the other end of a passageway from the newsroom to an adjacent building. Conventional wisdom held, however, that since Miss Shirley was only at her electric typewriter for a short time between court closing and deadlines, she just held it.

Carved out between the coat rack and west windows was the exclusive "back row"—the room's only two-in-a-line desk arrangement. Seating there was traditionally awarded the *Clarion*'s two most senior and currently highest regarded and best-paid reporters. Hickenlooper had been so honored before going off to Washington. In addition to being the farthest away from any level of management or supervision, these desks came with the best chairs, situated so the occupants could lean back against a giant wall map of the world with a unique geographical feature. There in the sea green Caribbean was a dark cranium-shaped stain left by the oily head of a famous former star reporter who had only recently been hired away by the *New York Times*, and that had been designated by some ballpoint-wielding vandal as "The Bermuda Triangle."

In retrospect, my perfect world would have been spending my entire career there with my head up against the Triangle, surrounded as the occupants of the back row were by the usual admiring and envious younger wannabes and engaging in the most common pursuit of that time and place—speculating about what the boss was up to. Great journalism by any news organization is usually the result of a great leader and whether Hickenlooper was one or not, we believed him to be and he had our undivided attention.

If he was not in the building, he remained in constant two-way radio contact with the city desk for everyone to hear. When he was there, you could tell which of his two jobs—editor or publisher— he was doing that day simply by which office he was using. Mostly he was in and out of the newsroom cubicle, talking to one reporter and then another, transferring caffeine motor oil from the urn table to the pisser, and stopping to see what the back row was up to.

What required more insight and experience was guessing what was going on in the big, swanky, remote publisher's office behind the unmarked door you didn't even notice when you entered the *Clarion* side of the building. It was there where four Perry generations had rendered judgment on all goings-on worth mentioning and waged war against the May family's *Defender* over whose paper was going to decide public policy. The Perrys had always retained both the editor and publisher titles but seldom frequented the newsroom, spending their working hours out of sight in the big front office, preoccupied with greeting personal friends, politicians, celebrities, moguls of all descriptions and dealing with matters demanding discretion such as commerce, personal embarrassments or joint business decisions that required face-to-face meetings with the Mays. For years, they left the editor's role and the small newsroom cubicle to trusted underlings whose qualifications were following orders and keeping their mouths shut.

It was Hickenlooper's nature to straddle both offices, even though their often-conflicting interests bucked against each other like tethered horses headed in opposite directions. Over the next forty years, he came to be regarded by critics and admirers alike as a consummate man of dual purpose, wrestling with a set of the most antagonistic of all principles—good and evil. Committed journalists of that era were always suspect of what goes on behind closed doors, so along the back row the question of whether good or evil had the upper hand was usually answered by how much time Jack Hickenlooper spent in which office.

Long before such esoteric workplace issues ever crossed my mind, even before I knew the meaning of the word "esoteric," the morgue phone rang and the voice of the dour old schoolmarm door guardian with the helmet hair, said: "David, Mr. HICKENLOOPER would like to see you in the PUBLISHER'S OFFICE right away." By now, I not only knew her name, but that when Mrs. Earnhart spoke in CAPITAL LETTERS, she meant business.

Now I faced my own conflict of interest, though relatively petty in light of some to come later. That Mr. Hickenlooper wanted to see me in any office was on the one hand a welcome and legitimate reason to troop through the newsroom in the late afternoon when it was boiling with action. But on the other hand, I knew that any traffic through that unmarked door that time of day would send sinister smoke signals of Machiavellian craftiness and political string pulling, and that my involvement, while most certainly dismissed as a routine delivery of morgue research, would make me a target of searing interrogatories about some mysterious goings-on behind closed doors about which I could not breath a word. And what if my being summoned held sinister implications for my own employment?

Perhaps Mr. Hickenlooper had heard how much time I spent hanging around the newsroom. Hell, editors and reporters wanting something from the morgue did not have to telephone me. All they had to do was summon me over and tell me in person. One old guy took me for a copy boy and kept sending me to the back wall for coffee or across the street to the liquor store for a half pint.

I didn't get to see any of the swanky publisher's office that day because Mr. Hickenlooper was standing in front of Mrs. Earnhart's guard post in a foyer just inside, tie loosened, beltless suit pants dragging the ground again. He had a sheaf of papers in hand. Were they my walking papers? He handed me the one on top.

"Oh, David, good. I was just coming down to see you," he said. Then he put his arm around my shoulder, walked me a few steps back toward the door and with our backs to Mrs. Earnhart, spoke in a near whisper:

"On this list are the names of forty people. One of them is a member of the state highway patrol who lives out in your neck of the woods, somewhere in Mill Town. See if you can find out which one is the cop, and bring this list back to me as soon as you find out. If I am not here, don't give the list to anyone else but Mrs. Earnhart, and tell the city desk to call me on the radio and let me know you have the answer to my question. I'll be back in touch with you, okay?"

I took the sheet, said, "Yes, sir," and headed for the door. He reached out and put his hand on my shoulder, "Oh, and David, by the way..." and crossed his lips with his index finger in admonition that you didn't need to be an Ivy Leaguer or a West Ender to understand.

On my way out of the publisher's office, I ran headlong into the arrival of Tate Weston and an entourage of three well-suited young men and two beautiful women. Weston flashed his movie star smile and held the door for me to leave, and with a slight bow and sweeping motion of his left arm, ushered his group into the office, which kept him poised in the doorway long enough to be recognized by every gaper in the newsroom. Next morning the *Clarion*'s business page spread the news that the newly formed law firm of Weston and Clark had been hired as the newspaper's general counsel.

The next time I saw Weston's smile, it was on the *Clarion*'s front page, in a headshot accompanying a story that he had been selected to chair a State Bar Association Ethics Committee disbarment proceeding against a federal judge who was already serving time for bribery and who had recently been accused of jury tampering at his original trial. According to the old morgue clips, which I had quickly become efficient at finding and perusing, it was reporting by Jack Hickenlooper four years earlier that had put U.S. District Judge Martin Collins in the slammer. Tate's father, Tatum Weston Jr., had served as the special prosecutor in the original trial. The afternoon *Defender*'s follow-up version of the story added a detail that an unidentified inmate was claiming that the imprisoned judge had admitted to him that there had been jury tampering during his trial.

I remember the next morning as among the most exciting of my life up to that point—the first of one "Holy Shit" moment after another after being given the job I needed by the most important man in Bluff City. The lead story on the front page of the *Clarion* identified the juror allegedly tampered with as the former member of the state highway patrol from my neck of the woods, Edgar Barton, whose name I had been able to come up with, thanks to a single phone conversation with an old cop I had known all my life. There was this Edgar Barton full bore on the front page, up close and personal, somehow found and interviewed by the paper's esteemed back row resident and Capitol columnist, Weldon "Red" Whitmore. Indeed, he had been tampered with, Barton told Whitmore, but because he might be called as a witness in any future investigation, his lawyer, Tate Weston, had advised him to say nothing more.

Whitmore's byline was on the story, but it might as well have been mine.

Turned out Barton had been located and set upon by FBI agents a few hours after the list with his name circled on it had been handed over to Mrs. Earnhart while the Weston entourage was still in the publisher's office.

Whitmore later told me that the list Hickenlooper had given me contained the names of all the male prospective jurors in the original bribery case. He knew that because...well...because he knew people in the right places and had procured the list for Hickenlooper. That was the first, but hardly the last, bit of good information I received over the years from listening to Whitmore, which I did any time I got the chance for the rest of his life. No one knew more inside stuff than Red, apparently nicknamed for fire-engine-colored hair he no longer had. The only thing red about him by the time we met was a banana nose bulbous from booze and high-blood pressure. Physically, he was a rumpled Ichabod Crane of a man, long and gangly, stooped and bent in more than one direction. Slow moving, he looked ten years older than the fifty he was at the time. But his face was fixed in a shit-eating grin that said he knew something really juicy that you didn't and that he would never tell you. Frequently, for no apparent reason, he giggled like a hyena, leading you to believe that whatever it was that you didn't know, you were better off not knowing.

Professionally, Whitmore's mind was a machine gun with a laser sight, and he had the fastest typewriter, the best contacts on the paper and a seemingly encyclopedic history of everything anyone in the state had ever done, good or bad. Most valuable of all was his work ethic—an "iron ass" they called it—that enabled him to sit and pound a typewriter for six hours straight without even stretching. People swore they had seen this—and that Red would pursue, catch and sit on a tidbit of a story until it hatched no matter how long it took, believing all the while the most interesting stories he could tell might be about his own exploits.

The first day on my new job, Whitmore was the only person who initiated a conversation with me, something you don't forget. Not surprisingly, he knew Captain Morgan Crockett of the county highway patrol and our family's three-generation history in small ball politics east of the river, and there was something vaguely familiar about him I couldn't quite put my finger on, so I asked my granddad about him.

"He's okay," the captain said. "Only got a couple of barnacles I know of—Old John Barleycorn and whores. Red will get a snootful every now and then in the middle of the day and I'll see that old Plymouth in one of the hot-sheet motel parking lots. Never married, you know. Always buys it. Says that's the cheapest kind. I guess you don't remember seeing him at Colony Court. He was the guy in the cowboy hat."

Then I remembered. Colony Court was a motel one cut above a hot sheet on Highway 41 South and owned by the county sheriff, my granddad's political patron. When Sheriff Lermon was out of office, so was his captain and they hung out at the motel plotting their return to power. As a boy, I used to spend weekends there and when business was booming on Saturday nights they would

31

let me deliver ice to the rooms and keep the tips. One night when I was about eight, I delivered a pitcher to a red-haired drunk who answered the door wearing only a kid's cowboy hat and brandishing a toy pistol. Behind him on the bed was somebody covered with a sheet head to ankles, her only visible parts ten painted toenails. The guy said, "Stick 'em up," took the pitcher, gave me a silver dollar and shut the door, behind which I heard him singing, "Yippie-yi-yo-ki-yay."

It was early April when the Barton story broke and a cold snap had hit Bluff City. I know because I remember wearing a winter coat on my birthday. As usual, I was spending the three hours between my last morning class at junior college and my night morgue shift hanging around the city room. Red Whitmore saw me and waved me over to the back row. "Hey Dave, you doing anything?"

Had I been performing brain surgery on the queen of England, I would have quit immediately when he said, "Let's take a ride, I need some help."

Out in the parking lot that butted up against the railroad tracks of Union Station, he led me to a two-tone, four-door, late fifties Plymouth that had seen better days, the front seat featuring an unopened fifth of Crown Royal peeking from underneath a pile of newspapers.

"You drive," he said, and shifted the whisky to his lap, mumbling, "we aren't going to drink this now. I just keep it in here in case I run into something and have time to get laid during the day."

Red directed me east from the newspaper on Board Street toward the river for a couple of miles to where the road made a sharp turn south along its bank. On that corner was a turn-of-the-century three-story mill that produced feed for farm animals and had small lawn tractors and carts lined up on the sidewalk. Along the side of the building across from the River was a loading dock where a guy he knew grinned and asked, "How many today, Red?"

"Many as we can get in this Plymouth. Six usually, maybe eight, depending on how big they are and how good my new helper can load."

In a minute, the guy came back with three bales of lovely green hay turned sideways on a dolly, which he slipped out from under them and went back for three more. Meanwhile, Red had raised the trunk lid and opened the car's four doors. He pointed at the hay and then held up both hands in front of his face. It was the first time I noticed he had been born missing both thumbs and had only nubs for middle fingers.

We headed north for a few blocks, crossed the river and then followed it eastward for about a dozen miles to where it became a horseshoe and we had to cross it again from the high bluff side. I cracked the window on the driver's side a little, not for a breath of crisp autumn air like you might think, but just to catch the smell of Mill Town hitting the water, an acrid compound of coal train smoke, harsh chemicals from the yarn plant and the damp fishy odor of a river bottom. It was putrid, but it was home. At the bottom of the bridge, Red directed me off the road to a fenced pasture in the river bottom not far from a spot where I had fished and skipped stones as a kid. "Been here before, I bet," he said, and let out one of his little hee-hee giggles.

At the sight and sound of our car, Jersey cows started emerging from the trees along the riverbank and by the time we stopped, there were a dozen by Red's count. Right away they started crowding the rear of the Plymouth trying to mouth the three bales stashed in the trunk, protruding from under the open lid we had secured to the bumper with baling twine.

Red got out and started waving his arms to shoo them away. They would back off for a while, bellowing and staring at him with big soft brown eyes from low-slung heads. "Just pitch these bales out here pretty close together in a circle around the car," he ordered, "while I keep these sonsabitches at bay."

But not all the sonsabitches. Some cows he let eat. Others he ran off, yelling and waving his suit coat at them and then giggling when they stopped and began bawling and pawing. Between hee-hees, he would talk back. "Hey, you're hungry, are you? Well, tell that old cheap-ass sonofabitch Winston Perry to bring you some hay. I ain't feedin' no rich man's cows. All I can do to feed my own." Then he would giggle some more and run and wave his coat at the cows he didn't own that were trying to eat.

How Red could tell the six he owned from the six owned by Winston Perry I had no idea. They all looked the same to me, so I asked him how he knew.

"Hellfire, boy, look at 'em. Mine are fat. Perry's are poor cause he's too damn tight to feed him." And then he giggled, "Hee-hee, that's the difference between Democrats and Republicans."

Winston Perry, Red explained, was one of his closest friends, an uncle of the late Wainscott and one of the beneficiaries of the family trust that owned the *Clarion*. "A goddamn Republican at heart, too," he said, "who claims he's a Democrat, but he's a damn wolf in sheep's clothing like the rest of the bastards. He might as well be a May. He'd be a lot more comfortable on the other side of the building."

On the way back to the paper, without my bringing up what I was dying to bring up, Red told me he had interviewed Edgar Barton in the offices of the paper's lawyers, and that the story was sure to re-ignite the decades-old battle between the *Clarion* and the *Defender*.

"The Perrys and the Mays have fought about everything for nearly a hundred years, every damn public issue you can imagine," he said. "But the fight has always really been about the same thing—the niggers. We are still fighting the Civil War. And now that the Kennedy brothers have control of the federal government, Abe Lincoln might as well be back. The feds are going to march through Georgia again and they are going to start from here. That's why Hickenlooper is back in Bluff City. He wouldn't be back just to run the *Clarion*. He's back to help the Kennedys integrate the South and he can get more done here than there. Old Judge Collins is the first shot in the war. For Chrissakes, he and Colonel May are thick as thieves. They served together in the Pentagon during World War II. This Barton business is like punching the colonel in the nose. Read your clips down in the morgue. You'll see. Hell, that's why Tate Weston is involved. The Kennedys are rubbing salt in the wound, letting him pick up where his old man left off. And this is just the beginning. It's combustible."

The papers had called the bribery case against the judge "a labor dispute" because it centered on an attempt by the Teamsters Union to organize county government garbage handlers in a little hamlet two hundred miles east on the Virginia border, a suburb of Bristol. But most of the drivers and workers at the county dump were Negroes or poor whites easily branded as the dupes of subversive elements of the labor movement bent on undermining what the *Defender* often referred to as "the Southern Way of Life," a phrase Red said had been a staple of the colonel's signed editorials ever since "those Vanderbilt poets published their famous ode to the Agrarian tradition."

Having never heard of John Crowe Ransom and the "Fugitives," I didn't know what he was talking about, making me ashamed of that and of my own ignorance about things in general. But whatever it was must have been simmering inside Red because it set him off on a diatribe about Colonel May and his regular *Defender* column that he called "Straight from the Heart."

"It is straight from the heart all right," Red said. "Straight out of the heart of Jim Crow Dixie. To papers like the *Defender*, anybody trying to elevate the Negro beyond indenture is a communist bent on destroying capitalism and the fucking 'Southern Way of Life.' That damn phrase has been one of the fundamentals of the segregationist code. Using it is how the colonel tries to pass himself off as some kind of intellectual philosopher. All he's doing is trying to put a cap and gown on his racism, which is what a lot of people thought the poets were doing to start with, though that is probably not the case. But that's neither here nor there when it comes to the colonel and Judge Collins. Straight from the heart, hell! This comes straight out of the colonel's ass.

"Hellfire, the *Defender* doesn't sell a half dozen papers in Richmond County. Can't even get there same day it's published and half the town is in Virginia anyway, but the colonel flew the American flag over this story like he was fighting for an orphan in the West End. And why is that?

"I'll tell you why: Richmond County fought for Lincoln instead of Jefferson Davis. Wherever that happened in the South, there is a little nest of folks still ready to wave the Republican flag as the party of the great Abraham Lincoln like they are ready to resume the shooting argument over slavery. Well, that's hiding their hearts under bullshit. Lincoln would be ashamed of 'em. Their ancestors owned as many slaves as anybody else and there is no difference between them and the Jim Crow Democrats. Hellfire, everybody's granddaddy was either in the Klan or afraid to stand up to it all these years. Only reason we got a one-party South is that now we got electricity shooting up the mountains and across the hollows from the coal-fired generators of the Tennessee Valley Authority, and it's all the work of a Democrat. Franklin Roosevelt put the lights on in the country and put the hillbillies in Appalachia to work mining coal. He didn't do that for niggers. He did it for white votes. We got a solid South all right...when it comes to niggers. The party of Lincoln, my ass! Old Colonel May has a big Civil War sword on the wall in his office. You can see it every time the *Defender* runs his fucking picture. You know whose it was? General Nathan Bedford Fucking Forrest, that's who, the founder of the Ku Klux Klan."

Red only took hay to his cows on the coldest days of the winter, before the river bottom grass became so tall and luscious and spring rains turned the pasture into a soft bed that would have swallowed the Plymouth. I chauffeured Red and his hay on many more trips that year and picked up the chore the following winter and the one after, always returning to the *Clarion* wiser than I left.

The next chapter in my early journalism education was not long in coming, and it, too, involved Red. In a congressional primary election the first week in May, the *Clarion*'s candidate, a dry goods storeowner from just east of the river named Billy Andrews, lost by thirteen absentee votes. The ward voting most absentee in proportion to its number of registered voters was an inner-city district that was densely populated, not particularly elderly and had voting precincts conveniently located—not the kind of district that normally has a high percentage of absentees. It had voted heavily for the four-term incumbent, Rep. Elmer Kyle, a toady of the colonel's *Defender* and leader of the party's delegation that supported Lyndon Johnson in the 1960 convention.

Winning spring and summer Democratic primaries in those days was tantamount to election. In the fall, Republican nominees for the most part were just going through the motions. Primary election night in the *Clarion* newsroom was a three-ring circus populated by entertaining clowns, angry lions and lazy elephants taking up space. Hickenlooper was all over, chairing news meetings in his cubicle, looking over shoulders in the back row and huddling behind the publisher's door with Tate Weston and his legal entourage. The next day the *Clarion* cried foul, Weston filed suit against the State Democratic Party demanding a recount and Red Whitmore showed up in the morgue looking for me.

"You been sprung, kid," he said. "I need a leg man and Hickenlooper said you're it. Considering what we have to do, you just might be the right man for the job. Hee, hee."

There was no "we" involved. He gave me another list of names belonging to fifty-six absentee voters in the congressional primary election, and as we left the parking lot, through the rear window of the Plymouth I saw the last glimmer of daylight disappear in the West End.

"Guess Hickenlooper figured you having spent so much of your life around the high sheriff's funeral home, you're not afraid of the dead...hee, hee," Red giggled. He had that right. Since I learned to walk, I had been following one member of my family or another around the Lermon Family Funeral Home, whose inner sanctum was the heart of the sheriff's political machine. I'm told that even before I could stand up, my mother would park me atop the casket she was pitching to the bereaved. Mostly, she worked at a drugstore part time while we were growing up, but no matter what your other job or responsibilities, the sheriff's political inner-circle family members were expected to work a few hours a week at the mortuary converting survivors and guestbook signers into lists of target voters. So looking for the names of absentee voters among those on moss-stained headstones and crumbling monuments of the poor white and deceased residents of the Seventh Ward was definitely in my genetic wheelhouse.

When Red dropped me off in front of the cankered cement angel guarding the entrance to Mount Sinai Cemetery, it was already so dark I could barely make out my hand in front of my face, and then only by the glow from the City General Hospital a mile away, on the other side of the new elevated federal four-lane that had effectively blocked the residents of shabby row houses from the closest emergency room. This was work definitely better done in the daylight, which I dared mention to Red and then wished I hadn't.

"Yeah, but hey, this is a city-owned graveyard, part of the hospital property. Place is full of pauper's graves with little flat stones you can barely see," he said. "Do this in the morning and in five minutes there will be some nosy caretaker over here with a cop and we'll need a court order to finish." he said. "By then the *Defender* and TV will be covering us and I'll be explaining to Hickenlooper why we waited until daylight. That sonofabitch would be over here trying to read these stones with a big box of matches if that's all he had. He ain't the kind to wait for morning. Remember, the Perrys are dead. The *Clarion* is now on a Hickenlooper deadline. So you're gonna need this."

Red handed me a foot-long flashlight like the cops carried. "I'll be back in little while with some coffee."

Fortunately, my voter list was alphabetical so most of the searching for matching names consisted of one swipe of the flashlight. But there were dozens of last name-only matches. These I either had to scribble in the dark holding my notebook in my other hand, or come up with a third hand, which was why the *Clarion* had figured this was a two-man job in the first place. Red had learned how to take notes with a pen wedged between his index finger and the middle digit nub, but he was supposed to be holding the damn flashlight. Most of the markers were flat and half buried, with etching that could be made out by bending and looking straight down, so I tried squatting and placing the notebook on the stone and holding the flashlight with one hand and my pen in the other. But the notebook always covered part of the etching, and even on perfectly flat stones was unstable, and would squirm away from the pen. I tried putting the light down on the stone and trying to write in the notebook in front of the beam, but the flashlight would roll around, emitting a moving beam or fall off an uneven surface entirely.

Finally, after pausing to take a leak upon the clearly marked resting spot of Reverend Frank Peters, 1907-1957, God Rest His Soul, the resolution of my quandary became readily apparent. Though wedded in nature and now years later in my own mind with Diogenes wandering around in the dark with a lantern in search of an honest man, my search for fraudulent dead voters in the Seventh Ward assumed the stooped image of a crouching, humpbacked man randomly pissing a stream of light on grave-stones from a large-headed, metallic ten-inch penis protruding from between his legs.

It was almost midnight when the Plymouth's headlamps again fell upon the cracked skirts of the ancient angel of Mt. Sinai. By then I had worked my way through about half of what must have been a thousand graves. From my list of fifty-six absentees, seven had matched up perfectly with dead residents of the Seventh Ward, including two that Red believed to be long-gone relatives of the current alderman. He had not brought back any coffee, but we celebrated the seven with swigs of the Crown Royal that, when retrieved from the back seat, was no longer unopened.

The next day, brash young lawyers in three-piece suits and French cuff shirts from Weston's law firm found a few more suspected dead voters, all eventually confirmed as fraudulent by the court and enough evidence to overturn the election and order a new one. The following weekend when I reported for work, one of the copy kids, an attractive female named Lucy, was sitting at my desk in the morgue.

"David, they want you upstairs," she said. "There is a rumor you have been promoted to the police beat."

My new job was weekend police reporter, perfect for somebody trying to go to college and work full time—three twelve-hour shifts, Friday and Saturday nights when there was too much police action to jam into the Sunday morning edition and Sunday night when it was so scarce you could mine the leftovers for follow-ups.

Beginning reporters often started on this shift because it entailed very little writing. You just called the news in to a rewrite man who knew all the questions that needed to be answered about whatever you were reporting. The *Clarion*'s was Francois Fontaine, an aging former foreign correspondent for the *New York Herald Tribune* who could speak and write French and Chinese but wore leopard-skin vests and practiced karate in the newsroom by high-kicking over trash cans and threatening fire extinguishers with throat thrusts. If you didn't know the answers to his questions you got an erudite but humiliating and educational ass chewing.

If Fontaine were busy or away from his phone, your call was switched to a dictation machine. My first report, a traffic fatality, went to the machine. A few minutes later, Fontaine called me back at the police station to check the spelling of the victim's name.

Was everything else all right? I asked. "Yes," he replied, "once we wiped away the grits. Listen." He played it back for me. I had never eaten grits in my life, nor could I remember ever hearing the sound of my own voice from anywhere but inside my own head. It was the sound of how grits had always appeared to me, a sloppy mess in bad need of both taste and substance—but not in the least unfamiliar. I sounded like everyone else in Mill Town. That was the day I decided to learn to talk like the man on the six o'clock news.

Reading the stories Fontaine facilely constructed from your barely coherent babbling was a learning experience equally invaluable. Newspaper writing was merely a craft easily learned, like how to build a brick wall. But trying to write a story on deadline before you got the craft down? That's another story indeed.

My second Saturday night shift was over and I was hanging around the newsroom when a boon dock cop called in the news that some redneck had cashed in when his demolition derby car crashed on a dirt track north of Bluff City. The driver had reportedly yelled, "Watch this," out the window before he missed a planned T-bone and splattered against a concrete wall.

I took all the vital information and looked around for Fontaine, but he had already packed his thermos in his big lunch box and gone home. There was no one else in the room but Herman, the late-night copy desk chief with ASAP on his face, and "200 words" on his lips. At least that is what I first believed. I had already learned the first lesson of golden age journalism: "If your mother tells you she loves you, check it out." This was the night I learned the second: "When you think you see something, look again."

Herman nodded for me to sit down at Fontaine's empty desk and said, "You'll have to write it yourself. Slug it, derby." Did he not know I had never written a story for the newspaper? He might as well have said, "Here, take one of those long sharp copy spikes and jab it into your jugular."

After a few false starts that I tossed into the trashcan, not unnoticed by a scowling Herman, I sat frozen as if waiting for Fontaine's typewriter to work his magic. I tried to summon up the brick-laying lessons of the past week, but under the pressure of my first deadline, sat staring at my blank page.

Then I felt, or imagined or heard a noise that suggested the presence of someone else nearby. I looked around and looming behind me was cherub-faced Rhodes Newbold III, the most smug and enviable of all the West Enders. A two-term editor of the *Harvard Crimson* back for his second *Clarion* summer internship, he was referred to as either ubiquitous or obsequious depending on which of his Ivy League rivals was applying the label, and known by those of us who had never before encountered those words simply as Newbold the Turd. Whatever else he was, he was an accomplished writer, acknowledged by that fact that he was the lone late-night shift reporter on Saturday and had been in the can when I looked around earlier. Now he, too, was staring at my blank page.

God, Rhodes Newbold, don't do that, I wished. Please God, don't let him do that. Though I would have enjoyed decking him, I was considering simply standing up and politely asking him to move. Before I could, he began whispering Fontaine-like questions: What is the dead guy's name? What happened to him and where?

I turned around to confess nervousness and ask him to go away, but before I could, Newbold nodded at the blank sheet. "Just type," he said authoritatively and began asking the questions over again in the same order Fontaine might. As I typed the answers on the page, the story emerged:

Rodney Hayes of Springfield died early this morning when his demolition derby car flipped and hit the wall at Hilltop Raceway in Portland County, police said.

A spokesman for the county patrol said the 27-year-old volunteer fireman was driving one of the last two vehicles still mobile in the contest when he attempted a T-bone crash that would have wiped out his remaining opponent. But he reportedly averted his eyes and yelled out his window to an already wrecked competitor, "Hey y'all, watch this." Those were his last words. The target he believed immobile in his path had managed a final escape and Hayes hit the wall. He was pronounced dead on arrival at Portland's St. Mary's Hospital...blah...blah. Survivors, name of mortuary, etc.

I typed answers until Newbold's whispered questions stopped coming and for the first time, turned around, expecting another. He was already walking away toward the back of the newsroom. I rushed the copy over to Herman who gave it a quick once over and flashed me a thumbs up that passed for him as a smile of approval. No one had ever seen Herman really smile.

I looked around the room for Newbold. But he had gone as ghostly as he had appeared. I figured he had to be in the men's room, so I waited, dreading what I knew had to be done. Asking someone for help does not come as easy for some people as it does for others. Never would I have asked Newbold to help me write that story.

By nature I would have found failure easier to take. There were a lot of people like that east of the river, born too proud or too shy to ask for help and too poor or stupid not to need it. Some Scotch-Irish fit into one category or the other—sometimes both—but not the Crocketts, who were not always poor or stupid.

Before the Depression, my great-grandpa Will Crockett had grown accustomed to being thanked for favors eagerly done for the less fortunate. He knew both the satisfaction of being thanked and the embarrassment some felt for having to thank. The lessons had come down to me through his son and granddaughter and ground up into the meal of the Irish politics that sustained us. I knew I had to look Rhodes Newbold in the eye and sincerely offer the gratitude he deserved.

I watched Herman waddle back there for his ritual washing of the printer's ink off his hands from handling the fresh early edition copies, and expected Newbold to come out with him, but he didn't.

"Is Newbold still in there?" I asked

"Nope," he replied. "Nobody in there. Little fucker must have gone out through the *Defender*."

It was two days before I encountered Rhodes Newbold at the coffee table to thank him for his help. Among other things, Newbold was a wise ass with a keen sense of humor. He blew the whole affair off as needless deadline drama and ended up apologizing for sneaking up behind.

"Herman had plenty of time before deadline," he said. "That little brief was not going to make the first edition. He was just in a hurry to get across the street for his Jim Beam. And I was actually only practicing my Francois impersonation. You had your back to

me, of course, so you couldn't see, but all the while I was practicing my martial arts moves. Once I even kicked high over your
head and you were so intense you didn't notice."

By the time I made it into Vanderbilt a year later, the Newbold I
had seen as an arrogant turd and I had become fast friends, room-
mates in a West End apartment owned by his family, and at the
same time, arch-but-forever-cordial rivals. I taught him how to
catch fish and he introduced me to tennis. I taught him the value
of moving quickly and he had taught me patience. When he died
tragically ten years later, we were close enough that I was one of
his honorary pallbearers. By then, I understood why his fellow
Ivy Leaguers had been so mocking and derisive and why I had so
resented his presence the night he wrote my first story. Envy is so
often at the heart of so much evil in the world. And I was quite sure
that in a way, Newbold had taken his own life.

3

A t each end of the congregation, police cruisers had blocked off the street. I call it a congregation because of the way it looked, somber people sitting huddled together in a bunch, elbow to elbow, no room in between, heads bowed, eyes fixed straight ahead like this might be a Sunday morning and they were in a church waiting for the preacher to stop praying to the Lord. But this was a Saturday and they were sitting in the middle of Main Street blocking traffic and the entrance to the Crisscross Cafeteria, so named because it was the busiest business at the busiest intersection in Bluff City. Four months into my new job as weekend police reporter, Martin Luther King's Student Non-Violent Coordinating Committee had opened up a new chapter in the Civil Rights Movement—on my beat. And the event was standing room only.

The *Clarion* must have known it was going to happen because the city desk woke me from a sound sleep and warned me to get in ASAP. When I got downtown, the regular police reporter, Larry

Timmons, who should have been off, was already there. So was
Red Whitmore and Rhodes Newbold, each accompanied by a
Clarion photographer. I didn't find them all at first because they
were up on the sidewalks in the middle of a couple hundred or so
angry white people milling around and yelling at the mostly brown
and young congregation on the pavement.

Lining the curbs between the sitters and the yellers were single
rows of cops in slightly different shades of blue gabardine, the
city police in their dark shirts and white-shirted sheriff's patrol on
the other. All were wielding shiny-lacquered, two-and-half-foot-
long billy clubs, mostly gripped in their white-knuckled hands and
being waved at the white agitators who kept trying to slip through
the lines into the street to take a swing at the protestors. Whether
agitator, cop or mere bystander, every face I looked into among
those standing erect reflected the tension, fear and uncertainty of
the moment—except one, the cherubic mug of Rhodes Newbold,
the only person around cool and relaxed enough to smile.

"Better late than never, David," he said. "Some bad shit is about
to happen. These people are not going to move this time."

Police had already arrested two young white men who had gotten
through the line and taken a swipe at the students, he said, and
while we were talking a white man about twenty in a motorcycle
jacket and a crew cut brushed past us but his throat ran into a billy
club barrier in the hands of a city cop. "Try again, buster," the cop
said, "and they'll be taking you out to General to get stitches."

Standing at the open door of one of the police cruisers that had
blocked off the street was the familiar figure of the gold-and-brass
emblazoned captain of the sheriff's patrol, sunglasses in place and

the creases in his pants as sharp as ever. In one hand was his old metal flashlight, which I knew had dents from being used on heads in similar situations, and in the other was the microphone attached to his car radio. On the opposite side of the congregation, posed by and similarly connected to his squad car, was city Police Chief Baxter Brown, a six-and-a-half foot behemoth whose size belied a soft heart and gentle nature. Newbold said that for the last half hour Brown had been out in the street quietly—and quite literally—begging the students to willingly abandon their protest and had only moments before returned to his car and the radio microphone, which he now held up to his mouth, just as Captain Morgan was doing. This juxtaposition I had seen a few times in the past while an adolescent passenger in the captain's car. Whatever was about to happen, good or bad, would have to be a joint decision by the mayor and sheriff, whose departments shared jurisdiction over downtown crime.

It was not long in coming. Chief Brown pitched his microphone onto the seat of his squad car, retrieved his bullhorn from the back seat and nodded at Captain Morgan. Now he bellowed through the horn what he termed his final warning: "Young people blocking the street. You are in violation of a city ordinance. If you do not move immediately, we will have no choice but to physically remove you. You will be arrested, loaded into paddy wagons and taken to the city jail."

No one on the ground moved a hair. Newbold leaned over and whispered in my ear. "Get ready," he said. "In the past they have always left willingly and submitted to being arrested. But this is a new ball game."

He pointed out a boy at one end and then to a lighter-skinned girl with straight hair in the middle. I had seen them both before, as well as two of the others. "That's John Lewis and she's Diane Nash. They are deliberately getting arrested for the first time. They want to take this bunch to Alabama and Mississippi to ride the buses and block streets down there. Like basic training in the Army."

Army stuff was foremost in the minds of Hickenlooper's young reporting staff. The new president, Lyndon Johnson, was already cranking up the Vietnam War and draft notices were landing all over the newsroom.

The cops stepped off the curbs and stood over the students as if the pointed end of a billy club in the face would encourage them to stand and willingly march into the two paddy wagons that had suddenly replaced the cruisers blocking the street. None of the students resisted violently but none got up willingly either. Instead, they grabbed hold of each other, becoming little Gordian knots that had to forcibly be pulled apart. The leaders had all been well-trained in stoic resistance and set perfect examples of the art, becoming silent, dead weight with arms and legs coupled so tightly police had trouble finding hand holds. Some were lifted up by their coat collars and dragged away. Others more tightly curled were moved like you might move a carpet, rolled over and over down the street toward the wagons.

Now and then, usually when white policemen had put their hands on the wrong part of a black female, there was a testosterone eruption. One young black man took a swing at a county patrolman and got, in return, a billy club in the groin. A not-so-well-trained and foul-mouthed young woman in an auburn-colored Afro hairdo began kicking, screaming, scratching, flailing her arms and cursing with every breath. It took three of the "motha-fuckin' poe-lice" to tow her to the wagon.

I was so busy watching and trying to take notes amidst the bedlam that I lost track of Captain Morgan. His cruiser was gone and I assumed he had driven it. But as the last paddy wagon pulled away, I saw him on the curb trying to grab a handhold and catch a ride on the narrow running board across the back. Sixty years old now and with a leg long crippled in a motorcycle accident, he was no longer quick and agile enough to succeed. When the driver hit the gas pedal, Captain Morgan hit the concrete—knees first. A full block away I could only watch people from the medical emergency section of the fire department hustle him into their vehicle.

Larry Timmons, the regular police reporter, had caught a ride to the jail with the cops, and Newbold had headed for the paper. I found my car three blocks away and drove out to General Hospital. In those days reporters were allowed to frequent wherever they had made friends and I had made a few in the emergency room. One of them led me to a curtained-off gurney where I found Captain Morgan sitting in his undershorts while a nurse worked on skinned and bleeding knees that his sharply pressed uniform pants had failed to protect.

"What the hell are you doing here, boy? Wanna put a picture of my knees in Jack Hickenlooper's paper?"

Later that afternoon I was outside the city police court when the demonstration leaders were released on bond. I recognized John Lewis, Lester McKinnie, Diane Nash and the mean girl with the Afro as the four students for whom I had drawn cokes. "Dave Arthur of the *Clarion*," I said, a declaration I had come to like hearing in my own voice.

Lewis, an intense man not easy to smile, said, "The *Clarion*? Don't I know you from somewhere else?"

"Yeah, Wilson's Drug Store up on Ninth Avenue," I said. "In my previous life."

A decade later when he had been elected to Congress and I was working for another newspaper, I accompanied him back to Alabama to cover the anniversary of his historic confrontation on the bridge at Selma. I would be the one mugged on the street and arrested.

When I got back to the *Clarion*, Hickenlooper's front-page news meeting was just breaking up. Fat old Herman came out of the cubicle with his list of assignments. Red Whitmore had been somewhere at the scene and was writing the main story. Larry Timmons was writing about the hurt and the arrested and I was to feed them my information about the court proceedings and what John Lewis and Lester McKinnie had to say about it all. We were gathered around Whitmore's back row seat when Hickenlooper wandered by on his way to the men's room, shirttail half out of beltless pants. For a while, he looked over Whitmore's shoulder the way Newbold had looked over mine. Obviously this was an editor/writer juxtaposition with which I had better get more comfortable. He turned around right into my face.

"What are you writing tonight, Dave?" he wanted to know.

"Uh" was my first answer, followed by "Nothing, I guess. I gave all my stuff to Larry and Red."

"Did you see anything you didn't tell them?"

I told him I had been to the hospital to see Captain Crockett, what all he had said to me about what was going on and that I had seen him fall from the paddy wagon on Temple Street and what I had overheard John Lewis's people talking about at the courthouse.

"Sounds like a sidebar to me," he said. "Put something down on paper and bring it to me. I'm going to be around here for a while."

"You mean write about my granddad?"

"Maybe. This is tough time for the police. They deserve equal justice, too. That's our job, isn't it? Shine the light down both sides of the street. You think Morgan wouldn't like that?"

"I don't know. He asked me if I was going to put his picture in the paper."

"Try it," he said. "It doesn't have to be long. Just something that catches the mood of the day. You can write a little, can't you?"

"Yes, sir," I said, with only doubt and hope in my mind.

I did know a little more about writing than my dead dickhead, frozen-on-deadline performance indicated. English had been my best subject all the way through school. I could diagram sentences, knew the difference between active and passive voice, adjectives and adverbs. My best grades had come in composition. And thankfully, I was halfway through a creative writing course slipped into my free pre-pharmacy junior college education. The grand old professor had even said that I had promise.

On matters of race, I was not as ignorant as on most other things. Parochial schools were integrated and Catholics were way ahead of the times when it came to the equality of human beings. And as a group, the Crocketts were a soft-hearted bunch. My mother was a Good Samaritan and natural rescuer of underdogs of any stripe, and my great grandfather Will was the fairest man I ever knew. Apparently he had turned colorblind fighting the Spanish in the Philippines when he fell in love with a black nun, an American Negro Army nurse from Kentucky and never got over it. He had a black tom-cat named "Nigger," that he loved so much that he fixed him up a collar lined with thumb-tacks to keep dogs from killing him and wept when the cat finally died of old age. Naïve as I was, I took that as a sign of egalitarian nature. And maybe it was.

Captain Morgan took after his father, the word "nigger" slipping casually and regularly off his tongue, out of ignorance more than intended rancor or disrespect. Next to Sheriff Lermon, his best friend was a black barbecue man named Titus, whose smoking pit at the end of the alley behind the Crockett's boarding house kept our Mill Town neighborhood hickory flavored year round. When the captain wasn't policing with Sheriff Lermon, he was hanging out with Titus, just the two of them standing in the alley toe-to-toe, trading bullshit and dance moves, laughing like hyenas over a kill.

When the river was dammed up, the lake became their getaway for fishing and an excuse for other endeavors, in the captain's case a love affair with Titus's sister Edna, whom he impregnated. She was struck by a pickup truck while crossing a Bluff City street and died carrying his child. He mourned her for months and once told me she was the love of his life. "I would've married her if I could have," he said. "You know, I would've made a good nigger myself. They have more fun than most people. Truth is, I prefer to be around 'em."

I went down to the morgue where I knew there was a vacant typewriter and no one to look over my shoulder, and came up with this:

He was sitting on a gurney in the emergency room at City General, his uniform pants torn open at both knees, watching a medic pick debris out of the bleeding gashes.

"What the hell you doing here?" he said. "And what are you looking at? You want to put a picture of my old knees in your newspaper?"

"What happened to you?" I asked.

He pulled an answer from the past that instantly reversed our roles.

"I ran my bicycle into a telephone pole and fell in the gravel," he said, flashing a familiar grin.

When I was six years old, he and I lived on the same street and he had come to the rescue when my first bike ride ended up at the base of a pole in front of his house. He was the cop who lived in the neighborhood that everybody called when they had a problem.

He was very good at rescue.

While he was having his knees sewn back together, an assessment of the day's bumps and bruises was underway at the county jail, outside the courtroom where some of the arrested students were being bailed out.

A reporter asked a female leader of the group how many people had gone to the hospital. "Sixteen of us and two of them," she said. "One black police and that ole [bleep-bleeping] white police that fell off the paddy wagon and busted his a—."

They all laughed at the mental image of an American symbol of their oppression being humbled to his knees, a metaphor for the crumbling of racial barriers they hope to see before their fight is over. But not everyone they perceive to be an oppressor is one.

The aging cop with the busted knees had answered a sit-in call at a local drugstore a few months back only to find that he was not needed. The proprietor had willingly served the unwanted and unexpected visitors who left without incident, apparently successful and satisfied.

"You did the right thing," he told the proprietor that day. "Serving `em is better than fighting `em."

Yesterday he grumbled from his hospital gurney perch, "Now how's that gonna look? I fell down on my knees in the street in front of hundreds of people. I guess I'm gettin' too old, to fight in the street."

He is sixty years old now, a superior officer who was just doing his job today, enforcing a law he didn't write, supervising the police trying to clear Temple Street of the young black students protesting segregation in America. He didn't have to pull his revolver or swing his billy club like he has had to do hundreds of times before. He sent no one to the hospital and never put his hand on a demonstrator all day. He simply slipped and fell trying to climb aboard a paddy wagon, embarrassing himself and becoming an object of derision among those who had no reason to appreciate the dilemma they had presented him.

I could see Hickenlooper was on the telephone in his cubicle, reared back in his chair. Everybody could see that. Both of his doors were open and the place wasn't big enough to curse a cat without getting hair in your mouth. But Mrs. Earnhart had to tell me anyway—"He's on the phone." She held out her hand for the sheets of paper that were in mine. She took them and marched off to drop them on his desk. Everybody saw that, too, or at least I believed they did—half knew I was turning in my first story to Hickenlooper. The other half didn't give a damn.

My stomach was churning. The morgue had been cold, but I could feel sweat dribbling from under my arms. I headed for the coffee tables and hung around the back row for a few minutes, exhausted from my effort but exhilarated by its conclusion. I had made the first Sunday paper deadlines, without blank sheeting, without Francois Fontaine or Rhodes Newbold whispering questions in my ear. I was trying to decide whether to wait for Hickenlooper's response, which conventional wisdom suggested might never come in my lifetime, or head out for my regular monitoring of Saturday night police mayhem. Then, as if on cue, Hickenlooper emerged from the side door of his cubicle with copy in hand—my copy I hoped. He walked over, dropped it on Herman's desk and said something that I didn't know whether I wanted to hear or not. When he had disappeared back into the cubicle, I called the city desk from Red Whitmore's phone.

"Was that my sidebar piece Mr. Hickenlooper just dropped on you?" I asked.

"Yep," he said. "Front page, too, if we have room. Top of page two if we don't. Jack liked it, said, 'The kid can write a little.' You're getting your first byline."

Now and then, I worked as a "leg man" for the full-time day beat reporters and on this particular day in the spring of 1964, was once again in the service of Red Whitmore, who invited me along when Tate Weston telephoned him with a surprise luncheon invitation.

"Come on, let's go. Weston is taking us to the Woodmont Club. When you ever been there, or will ever go again? Besides, he's a character worth getting to know, not exactly what he's cracked to be. He has something up his sleeve that will make news or he wouldn't be calling. I ain't exactly one of his country club pals, you know. He's always got a reason."

We were standing on the curb like two sailors waiting for a bus when Weston showed up in front of the newspaper driving a new Pontiac sedan, a Bonneville Brougham, glistening black with a vinyl roof, which was the rage of Detroit in those days. If a man six feet four can lounge behind the wheel of an automobile, that's what Tate Weston was doing, lounging, slumped against the door, left leg cocked high like you see some women drivers do in summer time, apparently as a concession to heat of one kind or another.

On the way to lunch, he made a stop at a West End tailor shop "to pick up a couple of suits and a half dozen new shirts," which launched him into a philosophical assessment of men's attire, specifically his own habit of dressing the same every day—the blue pinstripe three-piece, light blue shirt, and red-and-navy striped necktie—and explaining in detail how his daddy, Tate Jr., had taught him, "the best way to lose ten pounds is go get yahself a finely tailhed new suit."

"All you need are three good ones the same color—just three hundah a piece. You just keep one on your back...one in the dry cleaners...one in the closet...and you're always ready to go."

He had his shirts tailored, too, twenty bucks each, and the ties about the same. Both Red and I could look as good as he does, he said. We should go in with him and see Tony the tailor, get measured that day and the suits would be ready in a couple of weeks.

Red said, "And tell him to send you the bill, right?"

Weston grinned. "No, to Hickenlooper."

Fat chance on either count. But we did go inside and watch him get measured by Tony.

Weston kept up the suit sermon all the way to Woodmont. More than once, he diverted his attention from the traffic to check out how we were dressed, looking over at Whitmore in the front seat beside him and through his rearview mirror to catch me in the back. Notorious for spending his salary on prostitutes and hot-sheet motels, the slickness of Whitmore's shiny, baggy gray polyester was glaring evidence that he was already a devotee of Weston's same-look-every-day philosophy. At twenty-one, already married and divorced—actually annulled—and caught in a hair-and-eyeballs struggle between my college tuition and the 1964 minimum wage of a buck and a quarter an hour, I did not have a real suit of clothes to my name. Weston had just rung up 600 in suits, 120 in shirts and nearly that much in neckties—about a third of my annual take home. The only "suit" coat in my wardrobe was on my back—a weathered, green polyester hand-me-down from a step-grandfather, to wear when the occasion demanded something other than short-sleeve shirts and a zippered denim jacket.

At that very moment I was reassessing how my pathetic sport coat might fit into the dress code at the Woodmont, hallowed center of the West Enders' universe, beyond not only the reach of a *Clarion* reporter's pay, but also the stretch of my imagination. Suits were so scarce among the newsroom crowd that when given an assignment demanding at least the appearance of social acceptability, we relied on the "community coats"—a sorry array of ugly sport jackets that hung sadly on a rack of an iron water pipe outside the men's room, purchased not by our cheap-ass *Clarion* employer, of course, but with some pass-the-hat collection by a staff long dead or departed. The Ivy Leaguers and West Enders, of course, had their own sport coats that were also objects of envy.

The Woodmont is every bit as snazzy as it was cracked up to be. A sprawling white-winged colonial set in a bush garden of bright, elegantly trimmed green boxwoods and drooping, flowering magnolias. Inside, the clubhouse bursts with enough fresh flowers to serve five funerals at a Lermon Mortuary. They are flown in daily from all over the country, Weston explains. "Just like the fruit, wait 'til you taste the cantaloupe and the kiwi...." I'd never tasted or even heard of a kiwi.

Our table is in the center of the room in front of a huge bay window framing a stunning view of a golf course said to have still been virgin forest when they cut the fairways through the oaks and hickories not long after the Scots invented the game. In opulence, it is the equal of any country club in New York, California or Chicago and even more exclusive, according to Weston, a fact he supports with the disclosure that Kentucky Fried Chicken would be headquartered in Bluff City had it not been for his failure to get its founder admitted as a member.

"Gentlemen, you should know that our presence heah at the best table in the room is due entirely to the bloodlines and propah behavior of two generations of Westons before me," he declares. "It is part of my inheritance. Accomplishments of my own would not even qualify me to mow the grass, much less command this spot in the centah. A new member needs two sponsors and I could not even talk my own fatheh into signing the nomination form."

This is my first inkling that Weston is not a complete asshole. I never figured him capable of emitting an ounce of self-awareness or self-deprecation, or a drop of sweat for that matter. But he had just begun a soliloquy that was the antithesis of his wardrobe ramblings on the trip over, and while I didn't recognize it at the time, a sign that there was at least two Tate Westons, or more.

"I seriously doubt that if the father of the deceased president applied today, he would be admitted to Woodmont, certainly not if I was his sponsor," he said. "I could not find ten membahs who agree with me or Joe Kennedy—on issues of public policy. Most of them get up every morning, hold their nose and curse the *Clarion*, then stand up and salute the colonel's flag atop the *Defender* in the afternoon. Woodmont Club is more than a place in West End, fellas. It is the centah of a state of mind. No matter how hot the world gets, its membahs rest comfortably in the shade of privilege. And I am here to tell you they are in store for a rude awakening."

Weston talked as eloquently with his hands as he did his voice and laid his evidence on the table by lifting pieces of the silverware from his place setting and pointing it at Red or me before resetting it in the center of the table, one by one.

The knife: "The Supreme Court decision establishing the legal principle of one man, one vote. Every precinct in America is about to be reapportioned. This means, among other things, a two-party South in which Republicans can quit masquerading as Democrats and have their own party."

The fork: "Passage of the Civil Rights Bill. The assassination of John Kennedy assures it. Lyndon Johnson will get it passed. Along with that comes voting rights for Southern Negroes. The black vote will become a big factor in every election from now on."

The spoon: "A national epiphany is coming: A complete change in the makeup of every city council, state legislature and the United States Congress. Republicans will get elected in the South. Negroes will become office holders at every level of government and Congress is going to be filled with progressive Kennedy Democrats—like me."

The spoon he retrieved and then touched to his lips. "One way or another, eventually we all can sup the sweet nectar of change."

"Eventually" was when Tate Weston said he expected to be running for president of the United States, a bomb he dropped as casually as he spread the linen napkin on his lap. "Nineteen seventy-six, probably the earliest." First, he planned, he had to get elected to "the most exclusive club in the world"—the United States Senate. He had the path to Pennsylvania Avenue laid out in "stepping stones just like those we followed up from the parking lot to this luncheon room."

"I am standing on square one at the moment," he declared. "That is why I brought you here today. I want to take you with me."

Square one, it turned out, was the much-anticipated public prosecution of Judge Martin Collins for jury tampering at his own bribery trial.

"The main obstacle in our path, of course, is the colonel, the single most powerful of those who lunch here—by the way I suggest you try the Cobb salad. It's world class—the colonel is probably the reason I can't even get the founder of Kentucky Fried Chicken in the place—and he will use his goddamn newspaper to oppose me to the end of time."

"Our" path? Tate's, Red Whitmore's—and mine? Who was he kidding? While Weston was replacing his silverware—precisely as he had found it—I studied the smirk on Red's face. Weston kept going.

"Judge Collins is the colonel's man. For all we know—and might even be able to prove—the colonel could have been involved in trying to fix that jury. This is going to be a helluva fight between the *Clarion* and the *Defendah* and a lot more is at stake than whether Judge Collins serves a few more years in that country club prison. This is about what kind of town and state and country we are going to have—reactionary or progressive. We have already kicked their ass getting that crooked election overturned. Billy Andrews will beat hell out of Elmer Kyle this fall. No contest. So the colonel will be on his high horse about Judge Collins. But this is a federal case and Jack is home now. We're in for a helluva fight. And we're going to win it."

When the waiter, a graying Negro with a towel of white linen folded over his arm in a *Gone with the Wind* tradition, arrived, Weston introduced him as "My man Jesse Combs," inquired how his son liked his job with the city, and ordered three Cobb salads, all in the space of a few seconds—a mere pause in a campaign speech to touch the hand of a voter.

"My next stepping stone is some business experience. Jack Hickenlooper said the biggest campaign problem for the Kennedy brothers is that they are all lawyers who never ran a business. Their old man did, of course, and they have ridden along a little on that. But all my ancestors are lawyers. I'm going to start a business, a food franchise maybe like KFC. And once that is up and flying, I want to join the only club in the world more exclusive that this one—the United States Senate. I've got the perfect wife, the perfect family, and, best of all the perfect, opportunity."

Surprisingly, Weston had spread his words evenly between Red and me, his eyes moving back and forth between us, honing in, making you feel like the most important person in the room and he is talking only to you—the same way the motivational speakers make a living doing it. That he and I had met before as teenagers on the golf course and the dance floor never came up; he claimed no recollection of either many years later when I finally brought them up in a petty fit of anger over his continuing wardrobe nagging.

But it was becoming clear now why a finely tailored appearance was so important to his long-range goals and had been the overriding topic of discussion in the Pontiac. It was part of the brand he was building: The Weston brand, like the shape of a Coke bottle, or the starred circle hood insignia of a Mercedes. Stopping at the tailor shop on the way had been no coincidence, and I was beginning to realize that maybe neither was I.

"Jack Hickenlooper told me that when he gave you a job, he didn't believe you had a chance of making it in the *Clarion* newsroom," Weston announced, as nonchalantly as he picked at the blackberry cobbler before him.

That was not exactly a surprise. I had suspected as much, but only as a natural manifestation of the insecurity with which I was sure I had been genetically afflicted—a gift from the Arthurs no doubt, since the Crocketts brimmed with confidence and were perpetually full of piss and vinegar. But Woody Arthur had spent his whole life in a ditch of low expectations and I had been born like father, like son, a kid who went to school every day praying to not be called on in class and too shy to look an adult in the eye unless forced to do so by my mother or granddaddy. I had spent the first six years of my life looking down at my own shoes.

Even when Captain Morgan took me job hunting at the *Clarion*, I never expected Jack Hickenlooper to hire me. And hearing his reservations about me now from Weston's lips there in front of Red and a whole passel of West Enders who I absurdly believed miraculously overheard his every word, had the emotional impact of stripping me naked. I wanted to get up and leave, but surely my flesh was hot pink with embarrassment, and by remaining seated, at least most of me was still hidden by a tablecloth of white linen. And wasn't that what they used to wrap the carcasses of dead paupers?

"But Jack is of a different mind now," Weston told me. "Says you are a natural…a good investigator and politically astute. Best of all, you can be trusted implicitly, which is the reason I asked Red to bring you along. We might be going places together…eventually."

4

The day after Billy Andrews was elected to Congress, validating the *Clarion*'s challenge of the fraudulent absentee ballots in the primary a few months earlier, I was hanging around the back row with Red Whitmore when Billy and a small entourage showed up in the newsroom.

"Well, lookee here, Billy certainly didn't waste any time before coming down here," Red said. "I hope Earnhart is on her toes today and puts them into the big office up front."

"Why?" I asked. Red's bait was often small enough to swallow.

"'Cause Jack's cubicle is not big enough for him to bend over in front of that many witnesses to kiss Hickenlooper's ass. Hell, Jack's not even here this early anyway, least his car wasn't when I came in, so they're in for a wait I expect."

As usual, Red was right on all counts. Earnhart deposited the visitors up front and Hickenlooper was late—as he was notoriously—which Red attributed to hanging out with the Kennedys. So Billy and his bunch waited and waited and waited.

"You are witnessing first-hand why Billy Andrews is the perfect *Clarion* candidate," Red explained. "Persistent and loyal. By God, he came down here to thank Jack Hickenlooper, and by God, he wasn't leaving until he did it. Count him in the fold. And now that he's in Congress, we can set about putting Tate Weston in the Senate."

The prescience of the man was phenomenal, or was it just experience. I didn't know then, but I do now. That you don't realize the value of experience until you've had it is a great human tragedy. It was nearly lunchtime before Hickenlooper showed up, beltless and hair wet and gnarly from a shower. Later that afternoon, he summoned me to the cubicle and inquired whether I had college classes the next morning.

I was not yet in hock financially to the *Clarion*, and as it happened, I had no Friday classes. But considering the correspondingly high levels of my ignorance, and fascination with Hickenlooper and newspapering at the time, I would have told him "no" anyway and opted for whatever he had in mind. Screw the classes.

"Good," he said. "How'd you like to take a plane ride?"

I had never been off the ground except for a brief run in a state police helicopter for a story surveying a stretch of twisting highway west of Bluff City that Hickenlooper believed the most dangerous in the Southeast, a conclusion he'd reached after a careening motorist ran him off the road. The day I flew over, the road was nearly barren of traffic and the only danger was that of wetting my pants when the copter lifted off backwards, a sensation you don't feel every day.

"Sure," I said, as if I was looking forward to it.

"Okay, then, Tate Weston is in his office and says he has time for an interview about a franchise venture he's planning. It's only a business story now but the guy's going places politically, or believes he is. So it will be helpful for us to keep up with what he's doing."

The offices of Weston & Clark were on the ground floor of the city's tallest building, a thirty-story phallic symbol owned by Equitable Life, Weston's father-in-law's insurance company. The law firm was less than a year old but the door looked to be a hundred, old oak with a brass nameplate that a black guy was polishing like his own name was on it.

Tate was in his office, literally sprawled in a big high-backed, leather chair the color of rich mahogany—vest unbuttoned, striped tie relaxed from an open collar and one leg propped on the corner of a desk the size of a junior baby grand. From behind a pair of serious dark-rimmed reading glasses perched low on his nose, he flashed his signature smile and bellowed a pleasant "What about you, young David Aahthuh? Come in this house and take a load off."

He did not move a muscle or bother to right himself. However, a good-looking, kind-faced guy about Weston's age, around thirty I guessed, with wavy blond hair and a linebacker's chest, got up from the chair he was occupying in front of Weston's desk, and stuck out his hand.

"You know my partner Miller Clark," the reclining Weston bellowed again, not a question. No, I had never met Miller Clark, but he smiled and offered me the chair beside him. When I sat down, I noticed we were both looking straight up at the sole of

Weston's long sleek black wingtip—way up. The desk on which it was propped rested on a platform of some sort, assuring that anybody else in the room would be dealing with an occupant that already commanded the high ground. Miller Clark caught me looking at the shoe.

"Don't be offended," he said in a raised voice. "Weston doesn't know that showing everybody the bottom of his goddamn shoe is a frigging insult."

"Fuck you, Miller Clark," Tate yelled, without moving. "Dave Aahthuh's from the same side of the river you are and probably doesn't know it is an insult. You wouldn't either if you hadn't gone to See-wanee before you came to law school. See-wanee's the only place they teach shit like that."

Clark turned to me and smiled, "He doesn't think much of Sewanee College. We graduated Vanderbilt Law together—and believe me—our partnership is a trial every day."

I liked this Clark guy right off and later found out he had graduated at the top of his class at Sewanee and at Vanderbilt law where Weston had been somewhere near the bottom.

Weston finally sat up at his desk and got to the reason I was there.

"You ever heard of the Packer brothers?"

I had not.

"Terrific guys. Judd Packer is a close friend of mine. Pippa and I are going up there tomorrow just to say hello and be seen a few places with them. Hickenlooper wants you to go with us. Our deal with them is already done. They're gonna put up most of the launch money for Tennessee Ham and Biscuits, or whatever we decide to call our new franchise business—probably that, right

Miller Clark? Miller Clark is putting up a few dollars, too, aren't you, Miller Clark."

Clark did not respond, instead pulling some change from his pocket, two quarters, a dime and a nickel which he showed me in an open hand, low between our chairs, then whispered, "About this much."

Weston heard him, righted himself for the first time and peeked over his glasses to take a look at the low-down communication. "What? Pocket change? That's his damn lunch money. Cheap bastard eats out of vending machines in the lobby. Don't let him kid you, Dave Aahthuh," Weston said. "Miller Clark is unbuckling for Tennessee Ham and Biscuits. A founding stockholder, right, Miller Clark? He knows a good deal when he sees one."

Clark shook his head in dismay. Not angry or impatient dismay, but rather the chagrin of a loving father amused by an incorrigible child, who was still going on and on about how Kentucky Fried Chicken had plowed the ground for new fast food franchises. People were even beginning to deliver pizza to homes, which might work for ham and biscuits as well, but he wasn't sure. Anyway, the really profitable restaurant businesses all had licenses to sell alcohol and being able to at least sell beer with the ham was a critical part of his plan. Tennessee ham is salty and makes most people thirsty, which would mean bigger beer sales. I didn't know it at the time, but this was about the limit to his business model planning.

Having learned enough by now to know that misquoting my newspaper's lawyer was not a good idea, I had begun to take notes assiduously.

"Launch early next spring…first unit company owned…right off the Vanderbilt campus on Twenty-first Avenue in Nashville…first of March (he hopes)…That is my target anyway."

Early in his spiel, Weston had begun to twirl the gold key chain that normally dangled from the vests of his pinstripes. At its end was a small gold pocket watch that belonged to his grandfather, Hannibal Hancock, and somewhere between plowed ground and launch, it flew from his fingers and landed on the thickest carpet I had ever felt under my feet. Naturally, my eyes went to the thud and my instinct was to stop taking notes, pick it up and hand it back to him.

But Miller Clark must have seen this movie before. Gently, surreptitiously, he took hold of my coat sleeve and held on to it firmly. A brief glance at his eyes told me: No, do not do that. So I left the watch and chain in its resting spot and went back to note taking. Every time I looked up, Weston was staring straight into my eyes while he talked. Now and then, he would look down at the watch, then back at me. After a couple of those taunts, I fixed my eyes on my notebook and never looked up again. After a while, he shut up and stood up. Meeting over.

"Well, thanks for coming down, Dave Aahthuh. See you in the morning at six at Bluff City Air. Better bring something warm. I am a little worried about the weather." Little worried was a slight understatement.

The mere sight of the perfect wife freed memories from my adolescence that rushed back and brushed my lips like a sweet kiss, before kicking me in the stomach and reminding me of something precious I had only recently lost. I am not talking here about Pippa Weston, the perfect wife of Weston who was going to help him win the White House eventually, though she was along on the trip and stunningly elegant as always. I mean the perfect wife of Dave Arthur—or the woman that would have made a perfect wife—had it ever worked out.

Even at six in the morning with daylight still in hiding behind clouds of dark winter that spit little ice darts in our faces and threatened our purpose, Allston was her perpetually sexy, effervescent self, giving off the faint hint of something fresh as spring honeysuckle.

"Why hello, Vic," she said, causing the Westons to exchange quick quizzical looks like maybe I had an alias, before breaking into their greeting smiles for which either could have obtained a federal patent.

Seeing the two beautiful women across the counter at Bluff City's private aviation terminal was like watching a taller, slimmer Elizabeth Taylor talking to Annette Funicello, the most fetching member of early television's *Mickey Mouse Club* with whom I fell in love at age four. It was the colorful, cherry-cheeked Allston who stole my heart from the black-and-white Annette when we were in the first grade—or the second. We could never agree on which, or much else, but that never mattered.

If oil and water ever made a perfect mix, we were it. Had the Bard known our story—Allston's and mine—he would never have bothered with Romeo and Juliet, our tragedy being so much tawdrier and a lot funnier. But the best part of our story was already behind us then, in the winter of 1965, or I believed it was—because even though we were barely twenty-one, Allston had married a thuggish night crawler, borne his child and was seemingly lost to me forever.

Her presence there at the terminal that morning was neither coincidental nor superfluous to the fact that I was about to take my first airplane ride. Her mother, Henri, a woman I was convinced had ruined my life already, had married the owner of the aviation terminal, who happened to be Pippa's father, old Brownlee Caldwell Stokes. Now stepdaughter to a multimillionaire, Allston was running the place. Except for me, this was sort of a family affair.

The Westons were headed for an early morning meeting and lunch with the Packer brothers, prominent investment bankers in a part of the state where Weston was not well known and had been chosen by him for that specific reason to finance the business experience he believed helpful in his planned run for the U.S. Senate two years hence. Lunching with the board of First Trust Savings and Loan, Bristol City's largest, would be tantamount to their endorsement and an introduction to the region's business establishment.

Once we had settled into the little plane and I was seated knee to knee across from the actual perfect wife and she had slipped the scarf of many colors down around her shoulders and shook her long, rich ebony mane and I saw her face to face, I concluded that even if Tate Weston never got elected to anything, he was still the luckiest man on earth.

What I had first taken as a scarf was actually a lightly crocheted shawl that she then folded and carefully arranged across the lap of an elegant beige designer traveling suit so that it draped below and between her knees and mine, preventing them from touching even accidentally. Then she directed a violet gaze at me as bewitching as those Elizabeth Taylor cast from the movie screens, and proved that no amount of heavenly beauty, swell blue blood, Winthrop Hall finishing school and Wellesley fine arts degrees can stem one lovely woman's interest in the personal life of another.

"I had no idea that you and Allston were friends," Pippa Weston said, smiling. "I thought she had mistaken you for someone else. What was that she called you, Dick?"

"Vic," I said. "A childhood nickname. We grew up together, sort of."

"Oh, I didn't know she was from Mill Town."

Coming from the mouth of some other West Ender, the words "Mill Town" could have landed with a coat of disdain, whether by the tongue of the speaker or the inner sanctum of my ear I was never sure. But not so from the lips of Pippa Stokes Weston, who reeked of caring and sincerity. She never uttered a hateful word in my presence.

"Allston is not from Mill Town," I told her. "She lived closer in—in Belair where we went to grammar school in the first and second grade. That's when we met."

"Oh, that's right. I knew that. Her mother Henri—my stepmother now I guess you know—told me they moved here from Charleston when Allston was a tot."

I laughed. "Allston once told me they moved there because her mom had heard that Elvis's manager lived there and figured it must be a really good neighborhood. She should have called a realtor. But Belair is okay, one twist of the river closer to downtown."

The fabulous Pippa proved as perceptive as she was curious and bold. She had topped off her education with a Master of Law and Diplomacy degree from Tufts, so she was not just a pretty flower. She fixed those Liz Taylor eyes on mine, and said, "David, even though she called you by a name I didn't recognize, after I watched the way you two looked at each other, I got the feeling you were... well...close. There was something almost intimate about the way she said Vic."

There was no way that at our first meeting, I was going to tell the wife of the *Clarion*'s candidate for the U.S. Senate how I got to be "Vic." I would let Allston do that, in her hilarious monologue that she was prone to deliver anytime the subject came up, just for the enjoyment of my embarrassment.

I got to be "Vic" when Allston and I were seventeen and discovered "IT." Or at least when I discovered IT. IT is what teenagers of my generation called sexual intercourse, a phase that never was uttered in mixed company, even among those mixing at the time. Adolescent females only used the word "fuck" in the presence of other girls and adolescent males never used it in the presence of the girls they were trying to. So the neuter pronoun of the objective sense became the synonym of choice, as in "Let's do IT," "I can't do IT. It's my period," "I can't do IT with my leg caught in the steering wheel" or "We can't do IT yet, my mother is still in the kitchen."

I was never quite sure whether Allston had discovered IT before I did. But that didn't matter once we got IT done together, on prom night our junior year in high school, in the back seat of Captain Morgan's 1957 Chevrolet. Then we did IT in the back seat of my car, in the front seat of her mother's car, stark naked on the sofa in her den with her mother not ten yards away in another room and anywhere we figured we could and not get caught. We got very good at doing IT, too, or so we thought, so we did IT over and over and over until we were exhausted. And then we tried to do IT again, even if we couldn't.

One night when we were trying to do IT again, in Captain Morgan Crockett's doublewide when I was ready but she was too dry, I reached over and grabbed a jar of Vaseline, which turned out to be something else entirely—Vick's VapoRub—which set us both on fire and ended IT—for that night anyway. But the moment lived on in infamy and in Allston's frequent retelling: "You think I was in heat already...damn...now I was really on fire...hottest pussy Dave Arthur will ever have, you can count on that."

From then on, I was "Vic." She never called me anything else, and promised that if we ever had a son, Vic would be his name.

That she never became pregnant as a result of our excess is a miracle. Or maybe my theory that the Crocketts have offsetting genetic hormonal deficiencies that worked in our behalf has some validity, which could mean that all my seed spilt on her belly need not have been spilt. God knows, she was fertile enough to bear child and later proved it. But I have come to believe that all males carrying Crockett blood from their maternal side, though cursed with an overload of testosterone, were blessed with a balancing dearth of live motile sperm, a cause of considerable difficulty in reproducing.

I once proposed this possibility to my mother Sallie Mae, citing as supporting evidence myself and reports of several distant cousins I'd never met who were said to be the sole offspring of their parents' union. She dismissed it, cavalierly: "Well, you are only 25 percent Crockett. You are also 25 percent Cherokee from your grandmother and mostly Scotch-Irish from your father. And there must be a reason there aren't many Indians anymore. And your daddy is more Scotch than Irish. I know his old sorry family and those Arthurs were all tight as bark on a tree about everything. They probably skimped on live sperm, too."

The flight to meet the Packer brothers took only an hour or so, but flying conditions, which Weston kept referring to as "problematic," clearly justified his apprehension. From the moment of takeoff, Weston closed his eyes and sat inexplicably trance-like and inanimate except for an occasional sigh, or was it a gasp for a deeper breath? I couldn't tell.

Prior to take off, I had seen him in what appeared to be an unusually serious conversation with Allston and the pilot, which Pippa said had something to do with the possibility of ice forming on the wings or the propeller at high altitude, but that the pilot had concluded the temperature was rising quickly and that it was entirely safe to fly.

I had no way of knowing one way or another, but I must admit Weston's concern mirrored my own. The little plane, a four-passenger Cessna with only one engine, bounced around like one of those balls attached by rubber band to a ping-pong paddle, going this way and that, up and down, in whatever direction the wind took us. One gyration was so swift and sudden that Weston banged his head on the roof of the cabin, breaking his trance and evoking in vane-name taking two members of the Holy Trinity. Only Pippa made the entire trip without a single white-knuckle, and she tried her best to lighten the angst around her.

"Better get used to it, darlings," she said. "Don't all politicians blow in the wind? Just hold up your finger, Weston, to see which direction and then just go with it."

I expected a typical Weston retort, something reflective of his usual supreme confidence and ebullient spirit. But he just stared at her glumly and said nothing, a reaction that Pippa tried to blanket with amusement.

"Oh, Tate just does not like small planes," she said. "We were in a really bad storm in one of these once and I thought he was going to eat the window curtains. Allston had to get them re-attached after we landed."

Weston gave his wife a killing look, but finally broke into his patented smile.

"She's a piece of work, isn't she? Dave Aahthuh," he said, shaking his head and placing his hand high on her thigh. "Be sure to include in your story that Tate Weston is married to a wise ass."

The Westons charmed the Community South bank board into complete surrender. Together they conjured up a vision of royalty that rivaled that of the White House Kennedys when they were the most watched and admired couple in the world. Weston was nearly a half a foot taller than the late president, moved around like a cat and was smooth as silk from any view. Kennedy was not his equal as an orator and was usually speaking other men's words. Weston was always summoning his own feelings and rationing them in verbal and body language concert that reeked passion and sincerity. Even if you disagreed with what he was saying, you had to listen and consider the possibility that the man knew what he was talking about.

The luncheon guests, a dozen or so, were all middle-aged or older white men, mostly dyed-in-the-wool Republicans—at least at heart—and hardly in tune with Weston's progressive liberal politics. Not many in the room that day had voted for Kennedy. But Weston's talk was of business, not politics. He was campaigning for financial support, not votes, so the words about the exciting new world of franchise enterprise, landing on their ears as it did in the soft rich accent of a plantation master's voice, resonated in their hearts.

Although the bank's boardroom offered a splendid view of the Tennessee River and some rising parkland behind it, most of the men couldn't take their eyes off Pippa, the only female in the room. Unlike Jacqueline Kennedy, whose noble horse face and command of French and fashion were the foundation of her attraction, Pippa Stokes Weston was a natural beauty and an emblem of something closer to home, a gorgeous Southern iron magnolia.

When the lunch crowd had gone, the five of us moved to Judd Packer's office, which looked like it belonged at the King Ranch or maybe downtown Fort Worth. The Packers were native Texans and Judd had brought a lot of Texas with him, I guess to remind him of home or his visitors of what he considered home. Furniture surfaces were adorned with Remingtons and on the walls, tiny Russell watercolors had been expertly situated as accouterments to oil paintings of cows grazing and horses bucking by Frank McCarthy and Tenney Johnson, sweeping landscapes by Wilson Hurley and the striking Old West town scenes of G. Harvey.

A few years older than Weston, Judd was good-looking, prematurely silver haired and nearly as charismatic and he, too, had affected a brand. I never saw him wear anything but expensive-looking, finely tailored Western-cut suits, usually in shades of shiny sharkskin ranging from nearly black to nickel silver. Whatever image he intended, what came to my mind was a cobra, and not simply due to the high-heeled, snakeskin cowboy boots he favored to offset his short stature. There was something about him that looked ready to strike. Nearly two decades after meeting him that day with the Westons, before he had gone to jail and when I was still running a big newspaper in New York, I came to work to find him already coiled in a chair in my office. The mere sight of him was unsettling. Be it a soft smooth approach to a target of seduction, or a vicious thrust at a male rival, Judd seemed perpetually poised for an attack of some kind on something.

His brother J. W. was another story. However uncouth, tacky and amateurish it is to resort to describing human beings by relating them to another of God's creatures—as I have already done to Judd—doing so is quicker to the point. And it is possible that the omnipotent creator deliberately developed so many variations in design just so she could keep them straight in her own mind and we could tell ourselves apart. If so, the Lord had a bullfrog in mind when she made J. W. Packer. Only one thing he said that day rated a scribble in my notebook. When Weston wondered aloud about how much the Packers might be willing to put up behind his franchise idea, J. W. grunted, "million." Yes, however, uncouth and, probably due to my growing up close to the river, I felt myself in the presence of a snake and a bullfrog.

Later, on the plane ride back to Bluff City, Pippa Weston told me that Weston's decision to drop off our traveling party and opt for an overnight trip with the Packers up to Blackberry Farm in the mountains had been his own idea, not J. W.'s like he had claimed. Flying back home without him left me riding knee to knee across from the perfect wife, which I must admit was intimidating and exhilarating at the same time. Never had I ever been alone with a woman like her.

Among many charms, I discovered, was candor. She had not bought the explanation that her husband's overnight in the Smoky Mountains was necessary to hammer out details of the franchise financing.

"That was not a reason," she said. "It was an excuse. All the fine print was worked out before we ever came up here. Tate carried the written agreement around with him for days. I think he just didn't want to fly back today in this little plane. He hates them. The Packers are going to send him home tomorrow in their bank's jet."

"I don't blame him," I confessed. "I was a little nervous myself. This was my first plane ride."

"No kidding?" She seemed legitimately surprised. I guess so. She had taken dozens of plane rides. "I got used to it as child," she said. "We went to Europe or somewhere at least once a year. Daddy loves airplanes. That's why he bought Bluff Air.

"The big planes are a lot different. Tate is a lot more comfortable on them. He wants something with more than one engine and room to stretch out. I think being cramped up has a lot to do with his apprehension about the little ones. I've never been on one with anyone as nervous as my husband. That time I mentioned that he almost ate the curtains. It wasn't really on Bluff City Air. I was just kidding about that. It was on our honeymoon, on a little commuter jump from Miami to the Bahamas. We got into some thunder and lightning and Tate was soaked through with sweat by the time we landed. He's went into therapy for it."

Pippa was not someone from whom you had to wring conversation. The mention of the honeymoon led her directly into the story of how they had met and how one way or another the *Clarion* had always been part of their lives.

"You probably don't know this but Wainscott Perry—God rest his soul—introduced us. He and Tate went to West Mont Academy together and played on the Duke golf team. I met them both the same night at my coming out at the Woodmont Debutante. Almost everyone there went to Winthrop Hall and WMA. Wainscott was a nerd but Tate was irresistible. If he is interested in you, he comes into your life like a hurricane and blows you away. I never met anyone like him. And sometimes I say, thank God for that. One is enough."

Suddenly, she put her hand to her mouth. "God, I forgot I was talking to a newspaperman," she said. "You aren't going to write that, I hope."

So new at the game and so enthralled with the suddenly comfortable companionship of a real West End debutante, I hadn't even considered it.

I said, "Mr. Hickenlooper probably would not like me writing anything like that about the paper's lawyer."

Pippa smiled, a look of relief maybe, but then said, "I don't know about that. Tate says Jack Hickenlooper would hang his own brother in the newspaper if he had a brother that needed hanging. But he and Tate have become really close friends, which surprises me, I mean, for two men so different."

She looked at me and smiled again, like I was supposed to say something, but I didn't know whether to agree or not, so I just sat there like a dunce and nodded. The dumbass must have shown on my face because she went on to explain.

"I mean, Jack's so low key and calm no matter what and Tate is... well...so...so dramatic and outgoing. You know, when Jack did all that good reporting on the labor unions, neither one of them knew the Kennedys. So one day Tate just made one of those lawyer-to-lawyer calls to Bob Kennedy in Washington and told him that the *Clarion* had an expert on union corruption that his Senate investigating committee ought to talk to. Next thing you know they're both off to Washington and come home pals of the brother to the next president."

"And Hickenlooper ends up running the *Clarion*," I said.

"Well, Tate's grandmother is responsible for that. Hasn't he told you that story? He's told everybody else, including me so many times I know it by heart. You have met Clara by now, haven't you."

I had. Clara Hancock Weston was seventy-eight years old and a social aberration of the times, a powerhouse female in a man's world. A beauty in her day, she had contested aging with diet, exercise and enough facial tissue tightening to qualify her for a witness protection program. She was still fit and trim enough to ride a jumping horse twice a week and to accentuate a lovely widow's peak in hair the color of blue gun metal, pulled straight back tight against her skull and either twisted into a bun and or flowing to her shoulders, depending on the occasion.

The other big bankers in town were all buttoned-down native sons who had gone away to Ivy League schools and returned to Bluff City to look down their noses and run things. A native of Richmond, Mrs. Weston had inherited her wealth and influence, but had earned her respect by matching her dead husband's prowess in business and personal relations. Seth T. Weston had been the town's most successful lawyer and rich enough to own controlling interest in Community Southern Federal, one of the city's three largest banks. His spitting image and the apple of his widow's eye was their grandson she saw slouched in a chair across from her desk, according to Pippa's recollection of the story.

She said, "Tate always refers to that meeting as 'The Grand Entreaty.' Even before he was born, Clara decreed that he should call her 'Grand'—no way was she going to be a Grandma. Not her. So he looked into those azure blues of hers—they have the same eyes you know—and told her how gorgeous she looked that day, and she was beautiful and still is, and said, 'Grand' there is no othah man alive more equipped to run the *Clarion* than Jack Hickenloopah. You must bring him back from Washington immediately and rescue the papah from the hands of the Perrys' drones before the colonel's *Defendah* eats them alive.'"

Pippa had Weston's affected Southern planter accent down pat. I had no doubt these were close to his exact words because among Weston's many genetic assets I came to appreciate were total recall, a keen ear for the subtleties of diction and a facility for precise replication of anything he heard. His legendary great grandfather Hannibal Hancock was said to have swayed juries with a mesmerizing voice that "dripped warm honey" and people said that by the time Weston left for Duke, he had it down pat. So Grand no doubt heard his appeal that day in a voice that was an uncannily accurate replication of her father's.

According to Pippa's account, "Grand" offered only feeble resistance, "that Jack being only thirty-five and had never run anything," to which Weston had replied, "Hell, Grand, Wainscott Perry was six years youngah than that and a moron to boot. His passing is a blessing in disguise for the papah and the town."

The final obstacle Weston had overcome, she said, was the opposition of his father, who preferred making some interim appointment, and waiting to see how it turned out. Both visits had taken place in Grand's office suite atop the Community Southern Building, the only edifice in town not dwarfed by the two mammoth insurance company headquarters that dominated the Bluff City skyline, which Pippa said gave Weston the opening he had been waiting for and quickly seized.

Picking up her husband's affected Virginia drawl again, Pippa quoted his response that she said was pretty close to verbatim.

"'Grand, you know how much I love my fawthah,' he told her.

'He is the best trial lawyah practicing today and you of all people know how smart he is. But he and I do not agree on all mattahs, which is why I am out on my own with my new firm. Criminal law is neither my interest nor my forte. Fact is that our differences of opinion on this mattah are clearly generational. If this office looked west instead of east we would be looking at the buildings of Equitable Life and National Accident. Both are run by rich, educated men of my fathah's generation. Both are dyed-in-the wool Republicans at heart—no mattah what they say in public— and to my way of thinking no more than tools of Colonel May and the *Defendah*.'"

Pippa Stokes Weston obviously enjoyed mimicking her husband, not in any way belittling, but simply having fun, acting out his part.

"This is the part I like best," she said, raising her voice an octave. "Tate said Clara admonished him for speaking harshly about his new father-in-law—who, by the way, owned Equitable Life lock, stock and barrel—but he said he told her, 'Well, old Brownlee nevah disagreed with one of the colonel's Straight from the Hearts in his life. For God's sakes, in nineteen twenty, the *Defendah* gushed over the Vanderbilt poets trying to hang on to slavery forevah and in fifty-six, it endorsed the Southern Manifesto and praised the courage of every racist asshole that signed it. Pippa's old man cheered and toasted them both.'"

Now she was talking with her hands, too, as Tate did, lifting them in cadence, as an orchestra leader might, conducting her own words, just as was Weston's practiced technique of point making.

"'But radical change is upon us, Grand,' Tate said. 'Camelot is here, and the great issue of our time certain to be taken on immediately by the Kennedys is segregation. That will mean a big fight heah and across the South. Whatever else the *Clarion* has been, it has been the voice of progress standing up against Jim Crowism and the racist colonel at every turn. I doubt Wainscott would have been up to the challenge and his minions clearly are not. But Jack Hickenloopah is joined at the hip with Bob Kennedy and he is just as intelligent, tough and passionate in this great cause. Believe me, Grand, putting him in charge of the *Clarion* is the right thing to do. And I know how you always want to do the right thing.'"

By the conclusion of her soliloquy, Pippa had risen a half foot higher in her seat, and was laughing out loud, her hands above her head applauding her own performance.

"And he had convinced her that Jack Hickenlooper was her man," she said.

A grandmother taking the advice of a grandson over that of his father is as convincing evidence as I ever came across in support of the theory of genes skipping generations. Weston and Grand Hancock Weston were two peas in a pod. While Seth Jr. had a face like mashed potatoes and was a little chunky, Weston and Grand were tall and lean, with the same high cheekbones and widow's peaks. She folded and unfolded in and out of chairs and cars the same way he did. Though I never witnessed it, I suspect she also lounged around in private with her legs spread, crotch exposed and her feet above her head the same as Weston did in public.

There's some scientific evidence that a male inherits the social part of his brain—where decision-making about right and wrong is done—from the female side of his family. It is also this part of the brain that most often goes haywire. People from my side of the river usually have to deal with their own haywire, but West Enders could take theirs to the couch of a celebrity shrink, a well-born Austrian who collected neurotics like rare birds, including both Grand and Weston, the latter I suspect being the rarest, most intriguing and therefore most analyzed of all the enigmas in the Austrian's aviary. Having gotten to know both Weston and his therapist, I have come to wonder if a psychiatrist ever drove a patient insane, or vice versa.

Whether Jack Hickenlooper was party to Weston's Grand Entreaty is something neither man ever saw fit to share with me, and I never summoned up the nerve to ask. Hickenlooper was the more accomplished Machiavellian but both were chess players and you could never be quite sure who made the first move or had the last. At the time, Hickenlooper was still in Washington with Bob Kennedy, and Tate made a habit of acting on behalf of people without their knowledge. Some of their previous joint maneuvers had been mutually beneficial, but not all. But the threat of the union of these young men and their goals had energized their worst enemy and would levy debt neither would ever be able to discharge.

Pippa had settled back in her seat, a smile of satisfaction evident on her lovely face.

"When Tate sees something he likes," she sighed, "he just grabs it and runs with it."

All day I had been calling her Mrs. Weston and trying to remember what meager bits of etiquette Sallie Mae had known to teach me, acting like I was in the presence of the queen of England, so I don't know what got into me. But alone with her in that little plane, watching her gradually become more at ease in my presence, had finally given me confidence enough to say something that came to my mind instead of letting it pass, so I blurted out, "I guess that's how he got you, huh, Pippa?"

She flashed me one of those glorious Liz expressions that I had seen so many times in the movies, that sort of furtive, come hither look of vulnerability they said could turn a thousand ships or melt an iceberg, the one that probably snagged Tate Weston. "I believe you're right," she said, "that is exactly what he did."

Not that she was the least bit flirty with me. I never thought that for a minute. It was more of a "Hey, I like you" sort of thing, "we could be friends," which is exactly what we became for many years after that.

It was easy to see why Pippa Stokes Weston would be a political asset. She was a confidence builder. She had just referred to me as "a newspaperman" even before I had begun to think like one. In fact, if memory serves me, no female other than my mother had ever referred to me as a man before, I mean, calling me a man to my face. That may have been the day I became one. Being around Pippa Stokes Weston could make a man of you.

I had not been back in the *Clarion* newsroom ten minutes before Hickenlooper came out of the side door of the cubicle, motioned me to come in. He didn't sit down or invite me to either. We were standing just inside the doorway talking.

"How'd it go?" he asked.

I tried to recount the trip in detail, including my own first flight nervousness and how it was not helped by Weston's behavior, which amused Hickenlooper.

"He gets pretty uptight. I've seen it. How were the Packer brothers?"

"Okay, I guess. I didn't get much chance to do anything but watch them in action." I said. "They put on a good show for Weston. Big crowd, all movers and shakers apparently. Weston probably made some friends. He's pretty convincing on the stump, isn't he."

"The best I ever saw or heard," Hickenlooper said. "Man can sell ice to Eskimos. All off the cuff, too, I bet."

I nodded. "Never varied a word from what he said to me in his office when you sent me down there."

"If there is such a thing as a photographic memory, he has one," Hickenlooper said. "Once he writes down a phrase, thinks about it until he is sure he likes it, then anytime he wants, spews it out just as he wrote it."

"His wife is impressive, too," I said. "Those bank guys couldn't take their eyes off of her."

"Tough and smart," Hickenlooper said. "Won't take any of Weston's bullshit either. You know the saying...behind every great man...she's got his number. I suspect he tries those good lines out on her. By the way, did you get to meet Miller Clark? He's the real working lawyer. In court, Weston's usually spouting a catchy version of something Miller researched."

This opened an opportunity to mention the strange incident of Weston dropping his watch at my feet and Clark preventing me from retrieving it. Hickenlooper shook his head and smiled, knowingly, as if already familiar with the episode. And as it turns out, he was.

"I know about it," Hickenlooper said. "The asshole told me about that himself, and I shouldn't have been surprised that he did it to you. But I was. He does that to people all the time, new clients especially. He was testing you and you passed."

"Testing me?"

"Yes," he said, "sit down."

What had been a casual conversation suddenly became deliberate and to the point. He began to move quickly like a man on a mission with little time to do it.

I took a chair across from his desk. He closed the side door and stuck his head out of the door in front and told Mrs. Earnhart to hold his calls. Then he shut that door, too, which was disconcerting. He didn't seem angry with me, but I had heard that people closeted like that with him were getting an ass chewing. And even if I wasn't, people in the newsroom might believe I was.

His tone of voice and body language became casual again when he took his seat at his desk and twisted around so he could rear back and rest his foot on a small trash basket. The movement caught my eye and he saw me looking at his perched foot. He had on his normal unpolished penny loafers—but no sock. I had seen women wearing low-cut shoes and no socks, men in tennis shoes with no socks and men on the beach in Florida with loafers and no socks. But this was early 40-degree winter in late November.

Hickenlooper looked at his own foot and then at me. "I left home in tennis clothes this morning and wearing thick white athletic socks," he said. "I changed into my work clothes afterward and I'm always in such a damn hurry I forget something... my belt...my necktie. Today it was my socks. I figured a bare foot would be less a spectacle than white socks and a suit.

"Anyway, back to Weston. Let me tell you about Weston and his goddamn do-it-yourself personality test. He pulls that watch trick all the time, mainly on new clients. First of all, that watch is not a granddaddy antique. It's some kind of new shockproof fake or he wouldn't be throwing it around like that. He believes that trick tells him up front right away what kind of person he's dealing with. Somebody that is likely to be pushed around by opposing lawyers at a deposition or easily led on the stand in cross-examination. He was trying to find out how much of a patsy you are."

"I figured something crazy was going on the minute Miller Clark grabbed my coat sleeve," I said. "But just because a person picks up something somebody else drops doesn't mean he's a patsy."

"No. You're right about that," Hickenlooper agreed. "And Miller was actually there just to meet you, but somebody in that office is always playing that role in Weston's test. See, he is up on that goddamn platform because it naturally puts him in an intimidating position, like a lawyer or a judge is in a courtroom. By catching your eye and then looking at the watch, Weston was trying to intimidate you into picking it up. I bet Miller only grabbed your arm once and then left you to your own notion."

The scheme sounded whacky to me. Hearing it explained by Hickenlooper made me more than a little skeptical about whether he had been in on it from the beginning. I said, "I guess that scenario works in political meetings or business deals, too. But it tells me more about him than it told him about me. Is he nuts or what?"

Hickenlooper looked amused again and went silent for a minute—and so did I, me still stewing inside about the whole business. Then he said, "Well, you know what they say about the line between genius and insanity," and told me where Weston came up with the idea.

"Right out of the book of one of our ancestors, yours and mine, a legendary newspaperman...Old Colonel Robert McCormick, owner of the *Chicago Tribune*. Back in the thirties, Henry Ford sued the *Tribune* for libel. Weston's grandfather, Hannibal Hancock, was one of the most celebrated trial lawyers in the country. The *Tribune*'s lawyers wanted to bring him in to argue the case on appeal. A meeting was arranged in the colonel's office atop the Tribune Tower because McCormick, who owned the law firm, too, wanted to interview him alone. When the meeting was over, old Hannibal got up to leave but couldn't find the door to leave. He turned this way and that but found only walnut walls. No doorway. No knobs. Finally, he had to turn back to the colonel, who without a word of explanation or even acknowledging the lawyer's helplessness, didn't even bother to look up from his desk. But he apparently had pushed a button somewhere and Hannibal heard a noise behind. One of those wooden panels had disappeared under the one next to it. I can't imagine that he left intimidated, from what I've heard of him, but he did come home wondering exactly what you just asked: Is this guy nuts? He never joined the defense team but he told the story with relish to everybody he met, including his grandson."

All I knew about McCormick and the *Tribune* then was that it was one of the biggest and most powerful newspapers in country, and the strongest newspaper voice in the Republican Party. I had never been to Chicago but imagined it a hellish place I never wanted to go. I expected Hickenlooper was about finished with me and was on the edge of my seat ready to leave, but he kept on going.

"McCormick hated Franklin Roosevelt—as did our colonel next door by the way," he said. "President Roosevelt went to Chicago for a speech on the lakefront once and was greeted by a billboard-size sign McCormick had made and hung on the Tribune Tower that Roosevelt couldn't help but see while he was speaking. It said, 'The *Chicago Tribune*—Undaunted,' which was a word from the paper's morning editorial protesting Roosevelt's speech as an intimidation tactic. He didn't even want Roosevelt in his town."

I was getting a lecture on politics unlike anything I ever heard in my classes at Vanderbilt, where the political science professors were supposedly among the best in the country. Hickenlooper had never finished college, but he had given me a paperback copy of *All the King's Men* written by the Robert Penn Warren, who'd taught at Vanderbilt and was one of the famous literary "Fugitives."

"You finished Penn Warren's book yet?" Hickenlooper wanted to know.

I had.

"Best book I ever read," I said, which wasn't saying much. "Thank you for turning me on to it."

"Lot of intimidation in there, Dave," Hickenlooper said. "Intimidation is a staple of governance of any kind. Kings and dictators intimidate with guns. In this experiment in democracy, we do it less violently. Politics is a combination of money, imagery, personal relationships—all three of which can be intimidation tactics of one kind or another.

"Weston is a political animal. He may be nuts or he may be a genius—or both. All I know is that the guy is as smart as a tree full of owls and for all his eccentricity would make one helluva an elected official. He's so damn persuasive he can build a consensus, which is what the system is all about.

"And as long as I've known him, he has come down on the right side of every issue and squarely on the side of the *Clarion*. What I like most about him is what I liked about the Kennedys and Teddy Roosevelt—no sense of entitlement to their privilege. They take advantage of their inherited wealth to make things better for people born without it. Tate is not so much a friend of mine, as he is a friend of the *Clarion*. We don't really have anything in common except a passionate belief in the main tenant of the paper's editorial policy—equal justice and opportunity for everybody no matter their color, race or politics, which is good enough for me.

"But he comes with some barnacles. We all do. You know Red Whitmore is the most highly skilled and experienced reporter on this newspaper. Normally I would have somebody like that on Weston because he is tough to deal with, which you have found out, and he's going to be hard to cover when and if he runs for the Senate. But Red Whitmore would have picked up that watch, called Weston a rich, snobbish little asshole and thrown it in his face. I am glad you didn't do that. If you keep making progress learning this craft, by the time he runs, you'll be the *Clarion*'s reporter on his campaign. He likes you but he knows now that he can't intimidate you and you've got the energy and the feel for politics to do it."

He got up from his desk and slid the side door open. A meeting I never wanted to end was over, as was the conversation that set me in Hickenlooper's stead for many years to come, the place I most wanted to be, and at the same time fixed me as a satellite in Weston's orbit, sometimes at a tolerable distance and often up too close for the comfort of either of us.

The retirement of the *Clarion*'s ancient religion writer created a succession of musical chairs in the newsroom that resulted in a vacant desk in the next to last row in front of Red Whitmore. He decided I should get it, I guess so I would be handy to haul hay to cows or wander through graveyards at midnight.

Sitting next to him for the next year was an education in itself and unlike anything I was struggling to pay for in the grove of academe. When something happened that I did not understand, Red either knew the illuminating factual details or had figured out the most likely explanation. He was a rumpled course in deductive and inductive reasoning. And nothing seemed to surprise him.

He knew, for instance, before I ever mentioned it, that Weston had pulled his watch trick on me and that Hickenlooper had me in line to cover his pending campaign. He even knew why.

"The real reason Jack wants you on that story is that you are acceptable to Weston," he said. "You're a good-looking young guy with a feel for politics. You won't spoil his image."

"Spoil his image?" I had no idea what Red was talking about. "How?"

"You wouldn't spoil the picture."

I was still confused.

"Look at me," he said. "I'm old and pleasure bent and have worn my old suits until they're slick. My fucked up hands are enough to attract attention away from Weston when we walk in anywhere. I'd spoil the picture. And you, well, I don't mean this as any slight to you, but you are not the only good young gun on this newspaper."

Then he pointed across the city room at Rhodes Newbold, bent over his typewriter, hair askew, thick glasses low on his nose and a cigarette dangling from his mouth.

"Take Mr. Cool over there," he said. "He is a little older than you, better educated, more experienced and a West Ender to boot. Why wouldn't he be the guy to cover Weston?"

Red let that question hang in the air, like he was waiting for me to answer it. I didn't. I had no idea why.

"Well, look at him," Red said. "He's an ugly little fucker and dresses like he just turned the laundry basket upside down and put on what fell out," he said. "Weston is pretty and wants everything around him to be good-looking like Pippa—and you."

That conversation took me back to the day Weston had taken us to see Tony the tailor and blathered on and on about his wardrobe. I had assumed it was Red's idea that I go along, just a kind mentor's gesture to an understudy. Now I wondered if that encounter had been Weston's idea all along—or Hickenlooper's— or both? Who's idea was it? What's going on here? My first thought was to ask Red directly. His loquacious nature had raised doubts in my mind about Weston, Hickenlooper and even Red himself. These guys were already intimately familiar with Machiavelli and I had barely touched him in the Cliffs Notes.

But then I remembered a pithy lesson from my childhood taught me by my street cop granddad. One day when I was about ten, and we were cruising a rough neighborhood in an unmarked sheriff's patrol car, he kept returning to the same block containing a stretch of small businesses—grocery stores, dry cleaners, a barber shop and such, where people were milling about. He would drive by slowly, leave the area for a few minutes and then go back and circle the block again from a different direction. I was full of whys back then, just as I still am, so I wanted to know why we were going around in circles.

He said something that confused me even more. "Son, you need to look at something until you know what you are seeing."

And then, he explained, "Look at those three boys over there. Everybody else is walking by them, but they are stopped in front of that alley. They're up to something. I'm not sure what. Two of 'em are giving the other one a hard time. I can tell by the way they're standing. Two are standing tall, hovering over the other who has his head down, cowering. If I go over now, flash my badge and start asking what's going on, I'll never know. If I watch and wait long enough I might find out. I want to see what happens, how this meeting turns out. I'll come across them again one day. Maybe catch them one at a time later. You're better off asking your questions when you are pretty sure that you already know the answers. In this world, that's the best way to find out the truth."

A couple of circles later, the bigger boys had moved on. The captain cruised up beside the smaller one and interrogated him. The kid said he didn't know the other two, who were new in the neighborhood looking for a friend and he was just trying to come up with directions on how to find him. His posture was natural to the order on the streets, the silent signal of the smaller and weaker saying that they want no trouble from a more imposing stranger. Had the two older boys been asking an adult for directions, the picture in the captain's eye would have been a mirror image.

At this point in my life, all these many years later, the truth about Red, Weston and Hickenlooper is clear in my mind. But it had to emerge over time, as the truth usually does and what I was concerned about then—whether I was being manipulated—was merely the insecurity about my place in the herd. But considering the direction I was headed on the street—into journalism and politics—those early days of suspicion and self-doubt were blessings in my life. Yet from that day to this, my first view of anything has been through the prism of the Florentine schemer, Machiavelli: that what I am looking at might be something other than it appears to be.

Take, for instance, the short little blurb in the afternoon *Defender* that no special prosecutor would be appointed for the jury tampering trial of disbarred federal Judge Martin Collins, a spot Tate Weston had been counting on to keep his name fresh in the public mind. The *Defender* said that current U.S. Attorney Fletcher Maddux planned to handle the case himself. The next morning the *Clarion* editorial page roared "Conflict of Interest" in big type and urged Maddux to recuse himself because he and the judge had once worked for the same Bluff City law firm. Although the word "resignation" was not used, the editorial concluded with a not too thinly veiled suggestion that Maddux's eight years in the job had fulfilled his public service obligation.

Red Whitmore added the insight that Hickenlooper had personally written the editorial and that underlying the *Clarion*'s anger was the fact that Maddux, an appointee of President Eisenhower, had not submitted his resignation when Kennedy was elected. Federal district attorneys appointed by one president routinely submit their resignations upon the inauguration of a new one. Rumors were that Maddux had been willing to resign but that pressure from Colonel May and the *Defender* had kept him from doing so.

A week later, Maddux abruptly resigned, citing the need for more time with his family and an opportunity to earn money in private practice. It was many years later before I came to know that both Red and I—me innocently and Red not so—were intimately involved in the how. And it was not until then that I finally understood Red Whitmore's value at the *Clarion* was calculated on more than journalistic skills.

One of the recurring stories during my time on the police beat were routine raids on uptown taverns and pool halls where gambling was the main enterprise. Though forbidden for over a century by the state's constitution, gambling was routinely ignored by both city police and the sheriff's patrol, as were liquor laws prohibiting its sale by the drink over the counter. Every now and then, usually following some prominent fundamentalist preacher's Sunday morning rant, Captain Crockett's men would target the back room of a night club, take sledge hammers to the backroom roulette tables—it made good pictures—and haul the illegal whisky home in the trunks of their personal cars.

Daytime raids were usually carried out by city cops and invariably aimed at the healthy numbers racket, a significant underground economy controlled and run by the "Negro elements." The only white man I ever saw arrested in a black numbers raid was the Mill Town gambling addict, Boots, who had bested Tate Weston at golf when we were young. But the black numbers were also sold in the white pool halls, which doubled as bookie joints for interstate betting on baseball and football. If charged under state statutes, the violations were misdemeanors, with small fines and short jail sentences time written off as the cost of doing business. But because these numbers bets were laid off by phone to bigger numbers banks in other cities, the local numbers bosses were instantly susceptible to federal crimes of conspiracy and violations of interstate commerce laws. They could be put away for a long time, which no doubt was in the back of my mind when I didn't list Boots in the paper among those arrested.

It was against this backdrop that the *Clarion* hotline rang on my desk in the police station pressroom one night and it was not the city editor, but my mentor Whitmore on the line. He sent me out to the heart of "nigger town" with a specific order to find a prominent parking spot on Lincoln Avenue as close as possible to a house believed owned by P. J. Culverhouse, the lone minority member of the city council. "Don't try to park on his goddamn front porch now," he said. "Just somewhere you see it when something happens."

I knew Culverhouse to be also the prominent lawyer who invariably represented the black numbers bosses, so I assumed Red had prior knowledge of some kind of raid about to happen. There was no raid. What happened was that a car I recognized from the radio aerial on the roof as belonging to a *Clarion* photographer stopped beside me in the road. Red Whitmore jumped out and into the passenger seat of mine.

"What the hell is going on?" I wanted to know.

"You don't want to know," Red said. "Believe me, you do not want to know. You were never here. Neither was I. You ever breathe a word of this, I'll call you a liar."

I wish I could say now that my reporter's intuition was already so well-honed that I instantly connected my bizarre assignment to the sudden resignation of Fletcher Maddux shortly after, or that as an accomplished investigative reporter, I was able to ferret out the story on my own. I must confess that the entire episode remained a mystery to me until Red explained it a few days before he died in the nursing home. I always planned to raise the issue with Hickenlooper but never summoned the courage. It would have been like asking your best friend if he beat his wife.

5

Vic's notice to register with Uncle Sam came the same day he and Allston started up again. They had been at IT for the second time on a sofa in an apartment near Vanderbilt that belonged to Rhodes Newbold, from whom he had rented room-mate privileges, and afterwards were giddy as usual. He decided to read her the draft notice, which had been ambiguous as to the length of time and the age that college students would lose their college deferment. Vic got up to retrieve it from his jacket.

"I'm getting pretty dry down there, Vic," Allston said, seriously, like it was something she really wanted him to consider. "While you're up, see if your buddy Rhodes has any of that stuff that gave us such a hot time in your granddaddy's house trailer. Or maybe something even hotter like that stuff that comes out of the flame-throwers they're using to...what is it...defoliate Vietnam. That's where you're headed, right?"

"Well, not right away," Vic said. "And I don't know where Rhodes keeps his napalm. I bet he keeps it locked up."

"Damn," Allston said. "I'll just have to use this cigarette I just lit up. When is it you have to go to the Army?"

"I'm not sure. My student deferment ought to keep me out at least another year and half, or that's what this letter says. That's why I want you to read it. See what you think? Besides, I'm not going to the damn Army."

"Well, what are you going to do, hotshot? Run off to Canada. I'm not coming all the way up there just to fuck a draft dodger."

"I'll tell you what I'm going to do. I'm going down to the Navy recruiting office right away and volunteer," Vic said. "If I have to go to war, I want it to be in one of those jets that take off and land on aircraft carriers and drop bombs on the little bastards. I'd rather not crawl around in a rice paddy."

"You're nuts," she said. "I wouldn't ride in a plane with you. Not on your life...or my life, I guess. Whatever."

This was typical of Vic and Allston's conversations. Even subjects as serious as a draft notice were couched in some kind of an improvisational comedy routine hatched in Allston's mind on the spot. He served as the straight man, setting her up for the next joke. She was a perpetual entertainer, which is what drew people to her like bees to honey, especially men or boys as Vic was when they fell in love—or whatever it was into which they fell.

Vic says it all started in the second grade, and it did in a way, because that is when he first saw her, a short friend of tall Gladys, who obviously liked him the best of the boys in the class because he was the only one tall as her. He caught this blonde making eyes at him on the second day in arithmetic and again at lunch. After-wards, when he had marched in line outside to the playground,

Gladys came up, told him her name and asked him his. Allston was with her. "This is Allston," she said, first time he ever knew her name. A couple of nights later, he dreamed about it, only Allston wasn't Allston. She was Annette wearing Mickey Mouse ears. This went on all through the second grade. Gladys flirting and Allston talking only with her television eyes. He couldn't remember ever hearing her say a word, even when she watched Gladys kiss him goodbye on the cheek on the last day of school.

The next year his mother bolted from the Church of Christ and had him baptized Catholic, a "little mackerel snapper" according to his pissed-off grandmother. Entered in the Holy Eucharist Parochial School, well past Belair and nearly to the bridge that crossed the last crook in the river before Bluff City, he would not see Allston again for nine years, when a fractured ankle cost him his football scholarship to Father McKinley and he transferred back to Belair High. His first day in English class, there was something familiar about the girl sitting in front of him, who turned around and gave him a smirk-draped once over.

"You're new here," she said. "Who are you and where did you come from? I don't want a stranger sitting behind me. When someone is poking me in the back I want to know who it is."

"I'm not going to poke you in the back," he said. "Why would I poke you in the back? And who are you anyway?"

"You will poke me in the back," she said. "Because you are a boy. Boys are always poking me in the back. My name is Allston."

He knew immediately. It was her. Annette Funicello without the ears, now a cheerleader for Belair High instead of the *Mickey Mouse Club*. That night he went to the football game just to watch her cheer, and never took his eyes off her the whole night. The next morning, a Saturday, after he got his paper routes supervised, he went by her house in the pea green 1949 Ford with the busted muffler and the bald tires that Captain Crockett had bought for him to drive to his work instead of his more dangerous motorbike. He was barely sixteen.

Allston was standing in the driveway with her mother's Pomeranian on an orange plastic leash.

"I heard the Everly Brothers moved down here from Kentucky and live around here somewhere," he said. "The *Clarion* wants me to get 'em to take the paper. You know where?"

"Yeah, down the street," she said. "I'll show you."

She and the Pomeranian got in the Ford, though he had to open the passenger door from the inside because the outside handle had rusted frozen, and they rode around the block so she could show him the house, which he already knew about. But he never let on and acted like it was something new, which is how he felt every time he saw Allston for the rest of his life.

She must have felt that way, too, or he never quit believing that she did, because for years afterward she always seemed deliriously happy to see him and started showing up with little gifts, which prompted him to do the same. Their ardor for each other never seemed to cool, maybe because they were never together long enough to run out of things to say, or for touches to be taken for granted. Something always happened that kept them apart: His military obligation, her becoming pregnant and eventually married, his newspaper or political jobs in other cities. But they never lost track of one another, and when they could they met and made love. Each time they were as hungry for each other as they had been on prom night, their rendezvous little birthday parties with intimacy as presents to open, celebrating the anniversary of their ill-fated attempt to get married when they were eighteen.

That happened the weekend after the Belair junior prom and after the old pea green Ford had been swapped for a 1955 Chevy with a new two-tone silver-and-green paint job, a souped-up V-8 and recapped tires that would make it all 150-plus miles across the Georgia line to Rossville, where Vic had heard that anybody any age could get married if they found the right guy. That bit of information and the telephone number of the right guy had come from B. J., one of Vic's newspaper carriers, a kid about his age who had dropped out of high school in favor of becoming a petty criminal.

They took off on a Friday night after the basketball game, each with a single change of clothes they had smuggled out the house, his in a backpack and hers in a cleaning bag with the cheerleader's outfit that had a big pleated skirt just like the one Anne Funicello wore on the *Mickey Mouse Club*. Vic called B.J.'s guy from a pay phone in Chattanooga that Allston then used to call home and tell her mother she was not dead or kidnapped. Vic could still hear her mother screaming from the other end of the line before Allston hung up.

Sallie Mae Arthur was calmer, but warned her runaway son there would be hell to pay if and when he came home. His having a job always prominent in her thinking, she said he would be damn lucky if the newspapers didn't fire him for turning his route supervising duties over to that no-good B. J. for a day and half.

By the time they got to Rossville on Saturday morning, the right guy had produced their phony marriage license on the printing equipment in his garage. It was already signed and notarized by a magistrate, who lived two blocks away and was waiting to pronounce them man and wife and collect his ten dollars. B. J.'s guy and his wife Mildred were the witnesses. The whole deal cost Vic sixty-three George Washingtons, which was about two weeks take after taxes from his newspaper job.

It was high noon when Vic carried Allston across the threshold of room 212 of the new Holiday Inn in her cheerleader's skirt. She had jerked the key out of his hand and insisted on unlocking the door herself from the resting position in his arms, an adventure so difficult and comedic that Allston made it the subject of a hilarious monologue—"Vic was so damn tired he couldn't get it up when we got in bed"—which was not true. But before leaving Bluff City, they had agreed not to do IT or even touch each other in a sensitive place until after they were married.

"We ought to save ourselves for each other until after we get married," Allston had declared.

"But what about all the times already we haven't saved," Vic protested. He would have done IT in the driveway of the magistrate on the way to the ceremony.

"Oh, they don't count," Allston said. "My mother wanted me to still be a virgin when I got married, but you ruined all that. So tomorrow, I will just pretend to be one. Don't be alarmed when I squeal like it hurts. By the way, I hope you brought the hot stuff because I am likely to go dry on my wedding night, or afternoon. Whatever."

Where and how they were going to live as a married couple—previously of only passing concern—was the major subject of conversation on the trip back. Allston was certain they could start out at her house because her mother was divorced and worked long hours at the private air terminal. Anyways, her house was bigger and in a better neighborhood—all of which made sense to Vic, who would have been happy to live with Allston in a tree house or in the back seat of the Chevy.

They stopped again at the same pay phone in Chattanooga to report their decision to Allston's mom, Henri, whose last name was then Williams, from her marriage to Allston's father from whom she was divorced. But Henri was from one of South Carolina's finest families, the Charleston Ravenels, who for generations had built a swell public reputation for erudition and decorum. Neither that nor Henri's Wellesley finishing education was any more evident in the second call than during the first. The screaming had been toned down to shouts and curses, but still loud enough that Vic overheard himself being referred to as "a little no-good sonofabitch" before the receiver got back onto its cradle.

"Oh well," Allston said. "She'll get over it."

It did not look that way to Vic when he had to park the Chevy out on the roadway, partially in a ditch, in front of Allston's house because so many cars were bumper to bumper in the driveway. Behind Henri's big Buick was Sallie Mae Arthur's plain white Ford Fairlane, and behind it a Cadillac that Allston did not recognize. The last vehicle in line, however, was very familiar to Vic—a county sheriff's patrol car.

Inside the house, sitting side by side on the very sofa where he and Allston had done IT many times—with Henri in another part of the house—were two very unhappy mothers. In the two chairs across sat a little bespectacled, bald-headed guy Allston knew to be the lawyer for the flying service and Captain Morgan Crockett, who carried a warrant for kidnapping and taking Allston across state lines that Henri Ravenel's lawyer had obtained from a federal court, and that the U.S. marshal's office had turned over to his grandfather out of courtesy.

To make a long, arduous story short and less painful, the jig was up. The marriage was annulled by a Bluff City court— and the Catholic Church—which Henri and Sallie Mae had insisted on. Captain Crockett had Vic's —or rather David Arthur's—driver license restricted to "work purposes only" inside the geographic boundaries of his newspaper route supervision district. Allston was grounded by Henri for some period to be determined by her behavior, and forever forbidden to see her "kidnapper" again— except incidentally on the grounds of Belair High where they were about to be seniors.

In Vic's mind forever was how long Henri Ravenel Williams Stokes would be blamed for ruining his life.

The Bluff City recruiter for the United States Navy was a smiling, middle-aged guy with receding hair, an easy job and a salesman's mastery of bullshit. He scanned all the test results pertaining to my application to enlist and fight in the Vietnam War and gleefully announced, "Son, we'll be glad to have you. You're certainly smart enough. You could make officer. But you will never be a pilot."

"Why not?" I demanded, summoning all the military bearing I could muster.

"Because pilots need to be able to see and hear," he said. "You can't do either. What the hell happened to your ears? You can't hear an elephant fart. Your depth perception sucks, too. You wouldn't know it if you were landing on top of a building. What you can do is think and write for the admirals and believe me they need help and you can become one of them just doing no more than that in this man's branch of service."

If ever I could hear high-pitched sounds, I didn't that day and cannot to this one. And since I never got the opportunity to land an airplane I have no reason to believe I could. But unless they were going to let me take off and land one of those F-17s on an aircraft carrier, I had no interest in a sailor's career. So back to square one.

The Walgreen pre-pharmacy tuition subsidy had run its course and the *Clarion* was not paying me enough to live on my own. The only way I was going to come up with four hundred a quarter was to drop out, try to save enough to go back, then drop out and save and then go back again. Moving back home with Sallie Mae Arthur was no option considering she had just divorced Woody for the first time and their house was up for sale as part of the settlement. She was renting a little old apartment not big enough for a cat and dog.

Anyway, once you fly the coup, you better have figured out a place to land. I had learned that lesson from running off with Allston. What was I thinking? That we were going to live off Henri Williams or Sallie Mae? That's not what a man is supposed to do. I could never have looked my daddy in the eye, even if I ever saw him again which I didn't expect to. I didn't even know where his old tormented self was laid up at the time. I would have had to intercept him going or coming through the rayon plant gate, a sure thing because that's all the man ever did was work his shifts and drink a lot a beer when he was off. He never missed a day doing either. A born Scot, tight as a drum, he took care of himself and paid his bills, and was never one to ask for help from another living soul. Didn't believe in it, which was one of the things between him and Sallie Mae. She was all for help, giving it and getting it. It was the Irish in her, the way they did politics. No shame in taking care of their own. I could walk back in her door busted anytime, but never in his. And all I had was a low-paying job and the prospect of falling further behind when I had to give it up and go to the damn Army. Thus, the brainstorm that swept me into a chair in the editor's cubicle across the desk from Jack Hickenlooper.

"Yeah, what is it," he said, barely looking up for a second from whatever my Earnhart-arranged appointment had interrupted, annoyed, it seemed to me.

"Well, I just wanted you to know that I am not registering for school this quarter because I can't afford to. And since I won't be going, I was wondering if I could work some more hours for the paper. I can work seven days. I love what I've been doing and want to do it for the rest of my life. I've already had to register for the draft but before my deferment runs out in about a year and a half and I have to go to the military, I'd like to get as much experience as I can and move up here. Maybe I could save enough to go back to school part time when Uncle Sam gets through with me."

Hickenlooper looked up, but again just for second.

"That won't work," he said.

"No?" I said, the deflation so great I could feel myself shrinking in the chair. "Why is that?

"Because if you quit school, you won't have a job?"

"I won't have a job?" What the hell was he talking about? "Why not?"

"Because if you quit school, I'll fire you. I never finished college and that's the dumbest thing I ever did."

My brain and my mouth atrophied simultaneously. I sat there like a mute, having no idea what to say even if the atrophy subsided.

"Okay," I finally muttered, and got up to leave.

He finally quit looking down at his desk and looked directly at me.

"Well, what are you going to do?" he asked.

"I don't know," I told him. "Nothing, I guess."

"Come back to see me tomorrow," he said. "Let me think about it."

Then he went back to perusing whatever was so damn important.

After work that night, I went across the street with Rhodes Newbold where he bought a half pint of Jack Daniels. We sat in my car until after midnight while I mostly watched him drink it. A genteel son of the South, Rhodes offered me the first sip, but I turned it down. Growing up I had seen Captain Crockett and my daddy, who through two divorces and several separations was never around all that much, consume enough "hooch" to float that '57 Ford down Board Street. All the while, Sallie Mae Arthur and the nuns were convincing me it was the devil's brew. They might have been wasting their breath had not the love of my life, a chain smoker in her teens whose bar owner father had died early of liver failure, set me against it, too, just about the time I was old enough to imbibe. "Lips that touch liquor will never touch mine," Allston Williams declared in one of her comedic soliloquies, "even though I do tolerate them sometimes in another place you are familiar with."

Newbold offered me the last little swig of Jack. It was the first time I'd ever tasted whisky.

Naturally, Hickenlooper was not on time with the outcome of whatever it was he wanted me to let him think about. At that point—and maybe never in our relationship—was I as high on his agenda as I wanted to be. But he was always high on mine and always came through—eventually. His critics wanted to believe that his perpetual tardiness was part of the chess game he played with everybody, as was his frequent impulsiveness, both moves calculated to anger or intimidate or whatever ulterior motive was on his mind. Maybe so, I was still trying to figure him out even after he had gone to glory or wherever.

It was three days before he and I ran into each other passing in the *Clarion* lobby. I was headed out and he in.

"Come on with me," he ordered. "I've got some ideas for you."

This time he led me through the door into the darkened publisher's office. When I'd left the newsroom, Earnhart had been at her post outside the cubicle, only a few feet from the publisher's door. At the sight of us, she was up and off like a beagle after a passing rabbit, and was upon us in a heartbeat, turning on the lights. The inner sanctum I had expected to be some sort of Shangri-La was hardly more than an upscale version of Sallie Mae Arthur's living room. The Perrys were reputed to be lavish-spending Texans who owned sprawling estates, Cadillacs and even their own riverboat. But you couldn't tell it from the furnishings of the office where they conferred with politicians and advertisers and sometimes, even unhappy readers if they were heavyweight enough. The carpets were lush and handsome oils of ranch scenes and cattle herds and imposing Hereford bulls decorated the walls, but otherwise it was Main Street America, a deliberately modest setting, I was later to realize. The last thing the old newspaper proprietor-entrepreneurs wanted was for advertisers and politicians to see their wealth. So they met them at the office, not in their homes.

Hickenlooper parked himself in a chair of black leather behind a big walnut desk, and as was habit in his cubicle, pulled out a bottom drawer and perched his right foot in a scuffed loafer on it, and though it was a cold December day—a sockless foot. According to Red Whitmore, the no-sock business was an acquired Kennedy affectation—"What is it with them...they all got yachts and airplanes and can't afford socks? Jack always wore socks before he went to Hyannisport."

The publisher again caught me glancing at his foot. "Forgot 'em again," he said. "Played tennis at noon with the new U. S. attorney. I've been running late all day."

Then he began grilling me about my pathetic finances and feeble career plans. How much did I make—as if he didn't know? Where was I living? How much was my rent? How many more credit hours did I need before I could get my degree? What was my grade point average for the first three years? What specific courses did I need to complete my major in political science?

Finally filled in, he said, "Okay, what do you think of this? Looks like all you have left are those political science courses over at Vanderbilt. John Crowe Ransom is still teaching over there. And Alex Heard is a new star, probably be running the place before he's done. Why not register over there for your last year. I'll talk to Alex about it."

I had never even considered getting into Vanderbilt. You don't go to Vanderbilt on Mr. Walgreen's pre-pharmacy tab. The money wouldn't go far enough.

"They won't let me in," I said, my Mill Town upbringing of low expectations slipping out. "Besides I can't afford it."

"You can get in," Hickenlooper said. "Your grade point is good enough, and Vanderbilt has a reciprocal agreement with your place. They send their athletes over there to get physical education credits. You can take political science under the same deal."

"Yeah, but what about the cost? I'm having trouble paying where I am."

"Here's what you do. We got a credit union here. You borrow enough to register for the first quarter. The paper will take it out of your check a little at a time. I'll give you enough raise to cover it. By the time the next semester rolls around I think I can get you a stipend from the *Wall Street Journal* that will take you right to the end. They got a program for guys just like you. All I have to do is tell them you have some promise. I don't mind a little white lie."

It took a second for what Hickenlooper had said to sink through my numb skull. When it did, I looked hopefully for some sign on his face that he had been joking. Surely he was. There was none. The incident bothered me for years. Hickenlooper had hired me, moved me up to a reporting job and was trying to keep me in college until I got a degree—all without any confidence I would make the grade as a journalist? It made no sense.

I once brought it up to Miller Clark, Hickenlooper's neighbor after both were semi-retired and playing golf. Hickenlooper and Weston were never best friends, but he and Clark eventually were.

"I think back then Jack might have been half serious," Clark confided. "Something to do with your grandfather, I think. But I don't know what."

By that time, Captain Crockett was in the death grip of Alzheimer's. He didn't even know me. He would stand by the dog kennel in his backyard that had grown over with weeds and talk to an English setter five years dead. I never brought up to Hickenlooper what there was between he and the captain until we were both senior citizens, no longer mentor and protégé, but veteran soldiers from the foxholes of one kind of war after another and had watched our beloved printed press die before our eyes. Jack laughed out loud, a kind of shrill hoot that he had developed with the comfort and irrelevance of age.

"That's right," he hooted. "I thought you were too much Mill Town to ever go anywhere, but I owed your granddaddy for my Pulitzer. That guy I found who had scammed his insurance company by faking his own death…well…I didn't exactly find him first. Morgan did. You know the cover story had been that he fell off his boat and drowned. They even found some deteriorating carcass believed to be his.

"Morgan had arrested him one time for a DUI and like everybody else, thought he was really dead. Then years later Morgan gets on a fishing boat in Pensacola and there is my missing man, big as life. His wife was with him. Morgan couldn't wait until he got off the boat to call me. Hell, I just went down there, found out what name he was using and went to see him with a photog in tow. Just like in politics. It's who you know and what they know about somebody else."

That's how I got Vanderbilt on my resume, from somebody who knew somebody else—a quick Hickenlooper boost up from mediocrity to swell, which happened again and again for me early when I needed it, just like it had for Hickenlooper, coming up fast the way he did once discovered by the Kennedys. They were big on finding the best and the brightest, even in the lowest of places, and old Joe was as familiar with the lowest of places as he was the highest. Like life-hardened Red Whitmore told me once, "Not wearing socks didn't make a Kennedy out of Hickenlooper. He was just a loyal talent they could use. Sometimes, all you need to cross over the river is a leg up into a passing boat. If you are willing to do the hard rowing once you're aboard, they will take you with them as long as you can grip the oars and grunt."

Sallie Mae Arthur did not want me to go to Vietnam, not after seeing what war had done to the grinning, hawk-nosed country boy whose baby she had taken to the new military camp near Edinburgh, Indiana, so he could see his son before leaving for the Battle of the Bulge. Her journey by train through the dire straits of an economy on war footing had been the worst days of a never-easy life. Both she and the baby might have starved to death while waiting to see her corporal, had it not been for free eggs from her landlord's chickens and the empathy of an old milkman who kept leaving quarts on her doorstep even though he knew she could not pay.

And then her soldier boy finally came home visibly in one piece, but skinnier than ever, with both tolerance and hope for the future in shreds, to work and drink his life away, giving up a smile only when three sheets to the wind, which he wanted to be anytime not up to his waist in the water pit of Mr. DuPont's textile mill. Together they never saw one day of the privilege Roosevelt's GI Bill had promised and might have provided—had he the energy and ambition to reach for it. That had been all the patriotic sacrifice she figured was due her country.

The day I got my draft notice, she declared, "Why don't you just go to Canada with the others?"

Because Allston said she wouldn't go to Canada to fuck a draft dodger I wanted to say—and might have— had we not been in public where someone might overhear me using the F word in front of my mother, which would have embarrassed me more than her. Sallie Mae had a bawdy streak in her, a gift from Captain Morgan's mother who'd run a boarding house and ruled it with rough language that Sallie Mae had never shied away from using in front of me. Whatever I knew about the birds and bees as a kid had come from her in graphic terms, the country boy soldier having been either too shy or disinterested to let on what he knew about the subject.

I had driven back across the river to see her where she was working in a drugstore two blocks away from Belair High. Only in her forties then and still attractive in a plain Irish, Paddy's pig sort of way—with alabaster skin and dyed auburn hair, she was dressed more for going honky-tonking than selling cosmetics. Mill Town girls liked to dress up in ways West End women considered dressing down, you know, leopard skin scarves, feather boas, too much hair, and too little skirt, a layer too many of lip and eye icing.

When I ran off with Allston, Sallie Mae had assumed part of the blame: "Dave, you've been infatuated with a woman's twat ever since you saw mine the day I climbed that fence after old Mrs. Kilgore."

Maybe so. The first female pubic hair I ever saw was hers. I was ten years old and had just suffered a head cut and swollen lip in a losing fight with an older neighbor boy, who had ended it by hitting me in the forehead with the hinged end of a slat from an infant's playpen. The fracas had occurred in the Kilgore backyard, which was encircled by a wire fence. I was bleeding like a stuck pig when Sallie Mae and Mrs. Kilgore came of their houses to investigate. Mrs. Kilgore started yelling at me. "Get your ass home, you little shit. What are you doing over here starting trouble with my Billy?"

This ignited Sallie Mae's short fuse. "Damn, Ethel, it's my boy bleeding, and he's two years younger and a lot smaller than that lummox of yours."

One word led to another, and Sallie Mae, barefooted and wearing nothing but the thin summer shift she slept in, and about half the size of Mrs. Kilgore, didn't bother finding the gate.

"Well, I think I'll just come over there and kick your big fat ass," she threatened, and grabbed the top of a fence post and started over. Made it, too, but the shift didn't. It caught on the wire and when my mother hit the ground on the other side, she was buck naked from the waist down and Mrs. Kilgore was slamming the door behind a rapid retreat.

Had I injected Allston's name in our draft dodging discussion that day in the drugstore, it would have would set off a Sallie Mae rant about how Henri Williams had gone overboard charging me with kidnapping since she knew Allston was every bit as responsible for that escapade as I was. She believed Henri had looked down her nose at us—the Arthurs and the Crocketts—through the whole affair. Sallie Mae had found infuriating the potential that Henri's term "white trash" might be applicable. Though Sallie Mae never read McCourt's *Angela's Ashes*, she could have written the profanity for his characters.

"That Henri Williams thinks her shit don't stink. If you'd been a West Ender and your daddy a big lawyer, it would've been a different story. She just thinks they're better'n us and you weren't good enough for her daughter. Hell, your ass would make that little bitch a good Sunday face. Look what she went out and did. If she hadn't turned up her twat to you, you wouldn't have been so hot after it."

If I had heard that once, I'd heard it fifty times during the years since our failed elopement. Class-consciousness was in the water in Mill Town and the degree of inferiority complex infection was greater on some than others. My mother had contracted a terminal case and had been the driving force behind us moving out of Mill Town to Belair before I started school, even though it gave my daddy a longer commute to work. He didn't want the increased debt either, or the fact that she believed I needed a better environment than he'd already provided. He would have preferred the less expensive expansion just over the first bend in the river where they had moved Mill Town houses on trailers and set them down on new foundations alongside dirt roads, a subdivision that had already been imprinted as "DogPatch," the neighborhood roamed by Lil' Abner in the comic strips. Sallie Mae contended that if left to his own devices, her husband would have lived up over the store in the railroad gulch the rest of his life.

Whatever anguish Haywood "Woody" Arthur had endured out there alone dodging German patrols and the lethal incoming ordinance of Allied artillery had drained his spirit on to the frozen terrain of the Argonne Forest, and with it, in Sally Mae's mind at least, some of the high expectations she had for her future and mine, and would not let die.

"Well, you're not going to Vietnam," she declared. "I'll see to that." And indeed she tried her best.

Letters from Home:

January 21, 1964

My Dear David,

I hope you get this letter because I was not sure where to send it, since I haven't heard from you since I put you on the bus to Texas. Surely Uncle Sam will give you time to write your mother, for Chrissakes. It's very cold here and I guess there. I know Lackland is in Texas. Is Texas cold too? Please stay warm if you can.

I am glad you didn't have to go until after Xmas. We had such a good time. Of course, Woody and your granddaddy had to louse it up by getting snookered. I had to run Woody off after you and Daddy left. He wouldn't leave me alone. Beer just made him sleepy but whisky always turned him into a red-hot lover—in his own mind anyway. I never really thought so and finally told him. He left here with his tail between his legs like the dog he is.

That will probably be the last Xmas we have in this house. We are getting a lot of lookers for it being the dead of winter. Surely it will sell when spring comes. I already miss seeing your name in the Clarion. *It made me proud every time I saw it. Everybody that comes in the drugstore and knows how I felt about you having to go tells me they are sorry and hope you come home safely. At least you are not going to be gone that long and probably won't have to fight the North Viet Cong, or whatever you call them. Anyway, you're so smart and such a good writer they will probably let you write speeches for the generals. At least that's what that Jack Hickenlooper told me the last time I talked to him.*

He's such a nice man. I knew he would help us out. That's where I got this address. Mr. Hickenlooper said your friend Red Whitmore got it for me from the Air National Guard office. I hope it is the right one.

Well, that's about all there is to tell this time. Write me, damn it.

Love,
Your mother

Feb. 10, 1964
Dear Dave,

Thank the Lord you finally wrote your mother. She was on my ass for the first three weeks you were gone trying to get me to get your address. She thinks the police can do anything at the drop of a hat. Red Whitmore finally got it for us.

She said you told her you were having trouble with blisters on your feet. Well, so did I when I went to Fort Hood, Texas. Hell, I was thirty-seven years old when Roosevelt came after me and smoking two packs of Homeruns a day. For a while, I thought Uncle Sam was going to kill me before the Germans got a chance to. And my feet came apart the first week. They never made one of them damn combat boots that would fit a foot.

Here's what you do. First, you show the drill sergeant your blisters and see if he can get you a pair that fits better. He probably won't but you can go the PX and get you some powder, maybe sulphur if they got it, and mix it up with some Vaseline and coat those blisters before you put your boots on—and wear two pairs of socks. That's what I had to do. They'll probably still hurt like hell but it will be better.

I know you are down there with a bunch of jigaboos and Mexicans. Stay away from them as much as possible. They are more dangerous than the Nazis. I've had to arrest a half dozen of them over the years and their heads are hard as rocks. Lot of jigaboos and Mexicans in there, they'll cut you in a minute.

I saw Red Whitmore's old Plymouth at that hot sheet he frequents out on the Huntsville Road and pulled him over when he left. Damned if he didn't have that good-looking Culverhouse girl in the car with him. He's got to be buying it.

He told me Sallie Mae has become a regular telephone buddy with Jack Hickenlooper since you've been gone and he got her tied in with Tate Weston, who is going to run for governor sure as God made little apples. You know Sallie Mae can run a headquarters good as anybody. And she loves doing it.

Well, you know I am more a talker than a writer. This is about it. Take care of yourself.

Granddaddy

April 1, 1964

Dear Vic,

Startling news from the home front. And this is not April Fools. Thought I better tell you before your mother or somebody else did. I'm pregnant. But don't worry, it is not yours. I was already pregnant and just didn't know it the last time we did IT. This was from when I was still living with Randy before we separated. Far as I know, he doesn't even know it yet and I am sure as hell not going to tell him. He can read it in the paper if somebody would put it in there. I would myself except you are the only person I know at the Clarion *and you are off playing soldier boy.*

At least you didn't go to Canada—just because of what I said I bet—that I wouldn't do IT if you did.

I don't know what I am going to do about being pregnant. Mother is all for me going to Charleston and have it fixed. She said this happens all the time down there and she knows somebody safe there that will do it, a real doctor I mean, not one of those guys in an alley with a coat hanger.

She always hated Randy from the beginning and so do I—now. But I'm thinking about having it, its daddy is a no-good sonofa-bitch. I can always name him Vic and nobody will ever know the difference.

What do YOU think I should do? I wish this baby was yours and I am really sorry it turned out like this. But I don't have anybody to blame but myself.

When Mother stopped me from seeing you, I must have gone crazy. I don't even know what I saw in Randy to start with. He was just older and well, so good-looking. Mother is sorry, too. She knows she was wrong in what she did, just like I was wrong. She even told your mother that when she called to get your address. But like the song says, it is too late to be sorry now.

I hope you like the military and at least can stomach it for a while. If you get a chance, write me at Mother's. You know the address on Idlewild Drive. You were our paperboy.

Love you,

Allston

April 30, 1964

My Dear David,

Guess what I just heard. Allston Williams is pregnant. You might know it already because old high-toned Henri called me up to get your address. The bitch didn't say a word about it. I heard it in the drugstore from one of their neighbors, old

Mrs. Murray. You remember her girl Anne you used to ride to school with.

Henri said the baby is not yours. Thank God. It belongs to some thug she was supposed to have married. But I'm sure as hell not sure of that. They always claim they were married when they are about to have a bastard.

That Allston has been nothing but trouble in your life since the day you met her. If whoever this baby belongs to won't take care of it, Henri Williams will go around blaming it on you before it's over. And I'll have to go over there and pull all of her damn hair out.

She didn't even have enough starch to tell me why she wanted your address, and yet you wasn't good enough for her little girl who was turning it up to anybody she got in the car with. Class, my ass! Neither one of them have an ounce of it. When I found out Allston was pregnant, first thing I thought was that Henri was trying to pin it on you. I hope you have been smart enough not to have had anything to do with that little bitch.

How much longer are you going to be up there, honey? It seems like you been gone a year already.

Love you,

Your mother

6

THE week I returned home from Lackland, a full-fledged, certified Airman 4 clerk for the Air National Guard, the federal jury tampering case against Judge Martin Collins was in full bloom. Miss Shirley Keeton was covering for the *Clarion* but Red Whitmore and I went up the street to the courthouse to hear Miller Clark's final prosecution witness. We found Tate Weston already seated—sprawled is more like it—in the last row of benches. He made us climb over him to sit.

"The judge is going away for a lot longer than he thought," Weston said. "My client—yo' man Edgar Barton—is going to nail him in his testimony."

"My man!" I said. "How did Edgar Barton get to be 'my man'?" "Just a figah of speech, David. But Jack told me that you came up with his name. That not right?"

"No, that's right. I did, or the truth is, my grandfather did."

"Mohgan Crockett. He grew up with my fathah, David. Did you know that? They used to shoot mahbles togethah on the squah in

Huntsville until Grand Hancock put a stop to it."

Red Whitmore let out one of his high-pitched hee-hees.

"This keeps up, Dave, you and Weston gonna be kin."

"We ah kin, Red," Weston quipped. "Brothahs under the skin, both striding to gloreh, right, David Aahthuh?"

"Whatever you say, Tate. What's Barton gonna say?"

"The truth, David, the Almighty Goddamn truth. Just you wait and see."

I had never seen Martin Collins except in *Clarion* morgue pictures. He was a huge man, six foot five or better, 250 maybe, with a barrel chest. He had not come to court looking like some jailbird in an orange jumpsuit. Better dressed than his lawyer in a dark blue suit, white shirt and crimson tie, he looked healthy and well-tanned, like he was fresh from a Florida country club, which is what they called the white-collar prison where he was doing time.

When his former peer on the federal bench entered and we all rose in tribute, Collins fit perfectly in my mind's eye the power-brokers from the eastern part of the state, many of whom I had seen around the Capitol during sessions of the state legislature. They traveled in big black Cadillacs, Lincolns and Mercedes, with "Friends of Coal" bumper stickers and dark-tinted windows that hid the occupants.

"I think the guy was a One Star in World War II," Red Whitmore said, "Colonel May followed him up the ladder. I'll tell you one thing. The guy that pulls you up the ladder behind him in the goddamn Army is one of the greatest soldiers that ever put on a uniform."

Edgar Barton, bald, rotund and red-faced with jowls like a blood-hound, was Miller Clark's only witness for the day. He wore a tan suit and a white shirt, open at the collar, and black half-boots, "chuckas" they used to be called, popular footwear for police and other people in uniform.

Miller Clark was six foot two, blond, with the face of a television anchorman. He led Barton through an introduction for the jury: Mill Town born, son of one of Woody Arthur's fellow workers at DuPont's textile mill, married and the father of four, concluding with his most important qualification for the task ahead—deacon and song leader at the East River Church of Christ.

"Mr. Barton, you were at your home on the night of September fourth, nineteen fifty-nine when your phone rang and you answered. Who was it calling you that night?"

"I don't know. It was a man's voice. He never gave me his name."

"Why did he call?"

"Said he was calling to tell me that if I wanted to be rich, all I had to do was vote Judge Martin not guilty in the bribery trial where I was a juror."

"What did you say?" Clark asked.

"I didn't answer. I said, 'Who is this?'"

"What did the caller say then?"

"He said, 'Never mind,' but that he was from the *Defender* and he knew I had taken his newspaper for years, so I could believe him."

Clark walked up close to the witness stand and stood next to Barton, his back to the crowd and his face to the jury.

"Do you recall his exact words?"

I felt a sharp elbow in my side.

"Heah it comes," Tate Weston whispered. "Thundah and lightnin.'"

Edgar Barton looked at the jury, too, he and the prosecutor, heads turned in unison, so they could see into their eyes.

"I believe I do," Barton said. "He said, 'I'm from the *Defender*, and I know you have been taking my newspaper for years, so you can believe what I say.'"

"His newspaper?" Clark repeated. "He said, 'his newspaper?'"

"Yes, sir. That's what I remember."

"Sonofabitch," Red Whitmore whispered. "They're going after the colonel."

"You bet yoh ass, we ah," Weston said. "You bet yoh ass. Listen to this."

Miller Clark walked around for a minute or so, letting all that sink in. Then he asked Barton, "What did you do the next day?"

"I reported the call to the Highway Patrol Investigative Division and asked them to see if they could get Southern Bell to tell where the call came from."

"The telephone company. And did they?"

"Yes, sir. A couple of days later, they said all they could tell us was that the call was made from the main number at the *Defender*. All the calls that come from the newspaper register to that main number."

"So we don't know from which specific telephone that call came?"

"No, sir."

"Mr. Barton, do you know who owns the Bluff City *Defender*?"

Judge Martin's lawyer leapt from his seat.

"Objection, Your Honor. Objection. That question is irrelevant and immaterial."

"Sustained," whispered Weston, "That's Harley Binkley. Binkley and Norman represent the *Defender*. The colonel would have cut off his nuts if he hadn't objected to that question. Sustained today, Harley, but the jury heard it and so will all of Bluff City tomorrow."

The court disallowed Clark's question and Harley Binkley declined to cross-examine Barton. The next day, the *Clarion* devoted most of its front page to the story—"gloated it" might be the more accurate description—including the facts that Colonel Hiram May had declined to return Shirley Keeton's call requesting a response to Edgar Barton's testimony and that Judge Martin was being represented by the same firm that regularly served as counsel to the *Defender*.

News photographers had been barred from shooting in the courtroom and even from the hallway outside. But a *Clarion* photographer captured the star witness and his lanky pinstriped attorney for the center of page one, the focal point of which was Tate Weston's patented smile showing his perfect Chiclet teeth, the front-page picture having been personally selected by Hickenlooper.

That afternoon in a Straight from the Heart editorial placed directly under its eagle and American flag masthead on the front page, Colonel May denied that anyone from the newspaper had made the phone call to Barton and lamented that they had not been given the opportunity to deny the same in court, a slam at his own legal representation.

"Edgar Barton's allegations are a put-up job designed to muster distrust of the *Defender*'s strong voice of protest to the way the Democrats are running the federal government, specifically Attorney General Robert Kennedy at the Department of Justice," the colonel said. "We consider this a direct attack by Washington on the integrity of this newspaper in an effort to silence or undermine expressions of opinion under the rights guaranteed by the First Amendment of the United States Constitution. Thomas Jefferson must be spinning in his grave. But we will not be silenced. We will defend our trusted good name."

A second front-page editorial led the *Defender* the following day, alleging that Judge Martin Collins had been the "victim of a federal government railroading pure and simple." Red Whitmore read it aloud on the back row to a klatch of admirers.

"Whooooh weee, boys, we have set the colonel on fire," he whooped. "Jack Hickenlooper has lit his fuse and the old fart has exploded...two days in a row. I can't ever remember the Perrys doing that. Man the bucket brigades."

The curse of violence was clearly in my genes. The Crocketts became famous in history for fighting, first Indians and then the Mexicans at the Alamo and everyone knows how that turned out for Davy. I grew up watching his great-great-grandson Captain Morgan settle his arguments with fists, blackjacks and pistol butts, and he seemed even to enjoy smashing gambling tables with sledgehammers. And of course, there was Woody in the Battle of the Bulge and Sallie Mae Arthur climbing fences to get at the neighbor lady. But I surprised even myself that summer day when I sucker punched Allston's husband.

I was working weekend police, no longer a permanent assignment, but a one-time shot as fill-in for my successor. On the way down to the public square where both the city police and the county sheriff had headquarters, I stopped by the Andrew Johnson Hotel where my mother was setting up the early headquarters for the inevitable Weston for U.S. Senate campaign headquarters a full year and half before the primary. As usual, Sallie Mae Arthur was full of news from east of the river, the most depressing of which was that Allston Williams had gone to the hospital to have her baby earlier than usual because of reported difficulty. That would be the baby resulting from her doing IT with the husband from whom she claimed to be estranged, Randy somebody. I didn't even know his last name, only the car he drove because I had seen Allston in it with him more than once before I left for Lackland.

"Randy Sikes," Sallie Mae Arthur said. "He's from that rough area just across the river from Bluff City, and not very nice from what I've heard."

"Allston flew all around the pretty flowers and landed in a shit pile," she said. "You should have known better."

Late that Saturday afternoon, the police radio reported an officer in trouble and requesting assistance at Hickory Beach Lodge, a public picnic area on the reservoir around a new TVA dam in the north end of the county. It was way the hell out, but having nothing else to do, I drove out. By the time I got there, the officer was no longer in trouble and I saw what appeared to be the last county patrol car leaving the scene. But there among the cars in the parking lot was the one I recognized as belonging to Randy Sikes.

In retrospect, I don't believe I would have done this had I not been only a couple of weeks out of basic military training, which leaves you with a fundamental grasp of judo-based self-defense and the feeling that you are in good enough physical condition to climb a thorn tree with a wildcat under each arm. But I went strolling among the beachgoers spread out on the sand in recliner chairs and blankets with no particular mission in mind, and there among them was a tall, dark and handsome young guy with a lot of black hair shaped just like the head I had seen with the reasonable facsimile of Annette Funicello nestled beside him in that snazzy 1955 Chevy out in the parking lot. Lying on a blanket at his feet was a tawny blonde with the long, lean body of a high-fashion model. He glanced at me as I approached. Two questions burned streaks in my brain, like one fast snake chasing another. First, if you can attract a woman like that, why did you even bother stealing my girl? And second, why the hell aren't you at the hospital with her having your baby with difficulty?

"Are you Randy Sikes?" I asked pleasantly.

"Yeah," he replied, and sort of slinked to his feet and assumed an aggressive stance. "Who the hell wants to know?"

The tone of his voice was all it took to ignite whatever flammable substance simmers in the blood of young male fools. I hit him in the throat, not with the judo chop I was taught at Lackland, but with my fist like I had learned in Mill Town. He went tumbling over the blonde and tried to speak and get up. I kicked him in the head. He went down again, face in the sand and did not move. As I walked away, I could hear the blonde calling me a motherfucker, and screaming for someone to call the cops. Someone obviously did, maybe the same meddling Good Samaritan that took down my license number. I was only a few miles away from the beach when the county patrol car screamed its siren and pulled me over. Naturally, it was someone who worked for my granddaddy. "Well, what the hell is Captain Morgan going to think about this?" he wondered aloud. "You know, that guy is claiming you broke his jaw...or his girl is. He can't talk."

Captain Morgan was publicly mortified and angry, but privately amused.

"You're lucky you didn't kill the prick. But you better be careful. He's the kind that gets even."

I kept expecting him to do so. But he never filed charges and I never saw him alive again.

A few weeks later, however, a city police homicide detective assigned to the state attorney general's office that served Bluff City and the surrounding county met me in the parking lot of the *Clarion* when I reported for work. I figured he was bringing me a story. "All I got for you is a subpoena," he said. "Somebody killed Randy Sikes last night. And they want to talk to you downtown."

Randy had been ambushed, literally. Someone hiding in the parking garage at his apartment building emerged from behind a car with a shotgun and blew Randy into pieces next to his Chevy. Fortunately I had been sitting in my Ford on the street outside the *Clarion* drinking Jack Daniels with Rhodes Newbold at precisely the time it happened. After taking my statement, the detective's last question was, "Do you know anyone that would like to see Randy Sikes dead?"

"You mean, besides me?"

"Yeah. Other than you."

"No," I said. But that was a lie. I had no doubt Henri Ravenel Williams hated him as bad as I did.

It was a long time before the murder was solved. Some rowdy former friend from the rough neighborhood finally admitted it, probably someone whose girl Randy had stolen.

7

The best and the brightest are there gathered around the swimming pool at Hickory Hill, the sprawling estate of U.S. Senator Robert F. Kennedy from New York. These are the men who had engineered his campaign and the election of his brother as president: The Irishmen O'Donnell and O'Brien, the wordsmiths Sorenson and Goodwin, and the brothers-in-law Smith and Shriver. The Kennedy brain trust is readying for another run at the White House. The only people missing are the old patriarch Joe, who is ailing, and the senator himself, already on the campaign trail to run in 1968 and on the way home from an early fundraiser in California.

What the hell is somebody from Mill Town doing here in the late August swelter watching the cast of Camelot dodge soccer balls being kicked into the big pool by the older golden-haired Kennedy boys and sidestepping doting nannies dipping the youngest of Ethel's brood in the wading pool? Because I have become the *Clarion*'s appendage to Tate Weston, that's why, who is sprawled among them on a pool lounge in his seersucker suit and Duke blue golf shirt, as if he owns the place and as if it were he, and not Jack Hickenlooper, who had called them all together to hear him talk about his campaign for the Senate. And like all his audiences, they are listening intently, as if he might be the one who follows Bobby into the White House in 1976. The guy is amazing. Once he starts talking, you cannot help but listen, even Hickenlooper appears to be enthralled and he'd heard the spiel all the way up on the airplane.

"The Baker vs. Carr decision has revolutionized politics in America, gentlemen," Weston lectures. "The senator can take a completely revamped Congress into office on his coattails. Disenfranchised America will finally have a government that is truly representative. Blacks in Memphis...poor whites of Appalachia, the young people that President Kennedy energized and who are out in the streets today still giving Lyndon Johnson hell over this stupid war—they will all have a voice now. The one-man, one-vote principle and the Voting Rights Act that you all ah responsible for has given it resonance and finally the promise of the United States Constitution to delivah equal justice to all will be fulfilled."

Some of those words are mine, now being played back in an Old Virginia accent by a modern-day Henry Clay, without notes, without a pause that was not programmed, without an uh...or I mean... or a you know or any of the crutches most speakers lean on when they are trying to find their next thought. I would not have been surprised had the Kennedy brain trust broken into the applause I had heard time and again as Weston polished his pitch in the ghettos and mountains in our home state. That he was doing it now for the most unlikely of audiences was all Hickenlooper's doing, just casually bringing Weston along to the gathering of the Kennedy inner circle, as if for Weston's education as well as mine.

"I see it as a win-win, especially with Sorenson and Goodwin," Hickenlooper told me later. "His message is a helluva lot clearer than Bob's. They'll recognize that. I wanted to give Weston a test run before experts. And what better group? Their feedback can be very helpful and they might even learn something from hearing Weston. You know, Weston introduced me to Bob. He knows him as well as I do and he is a helluva lot more at ease with that crowd than I ever was. Didn't he look like he belonged there? First time Bob took me home with him and I saw the Kennedy lifestyle, I felt like a bastard at a family reunion."

That trip to Hickory Hill was a moment of recognition for me as well, an introduction to the classic Hickenlooper chess game, a friendlier term for what you readily call manipulation or exploitation in the other guy. Rather than tell his friend Bob Kennedy that his message needed refining, the chess player takes an already-refined message to Kennedy's speechwriters, knowing they are astute enough to pick up on it. That a Hickenlooper even found himself in a position to influence a Kennedy using a Weston as a pawn and that I am here to watch is proof the dream is still alive in America for anybody to live.

Both Weston and Hickenlooper had been drawn to the Kennedys by a common guiding principle that all men are created equal, but the group around the pool, all accomplished Caucasian males, were a contradiction, living, glaring evidence of just how temporary that newborn juxtaposition can be. Where you land upon arrival from the womb makes all the difference. By birthright alone, Weston had more in common with the Kennedys. They were born with their luck, slipping out of the vagina coated in it, landing softly on the soft cloud of privilege into dreams already being lived.

Hickenlooper, whose father was a carpenter, had to find the door to his luck somewhere along the way, and finding Hickenlooper had become the crack through which I would slip toward mine—both our dreams at that moment only works in progress. I never discussed this sort of thing with him. He and I were always all business—the business of newspapering—or politics. I was never quite sure of which, or even if a difference really existed. Personal feelings about someone seemed like gossip, and Hickenlooper had never seemed like a gossipy kind of guy. The conversation we'd had after the Weston watch-dropping trick had been the lone occasion, and I had assumed to be in the interest of my education.

His admiration for the Kennedys and the peculiarly attractive Weston, I figured, was rooted in the same pot. Inherited wealth often produces socially conscious offspring who devote their lives to improving the lot of others. Eventually a good-hearted Roosevelt or Rockefeller comes along and invigorates public service. But these particular scions of the *nouveau-riche* somehow arrived free of the sense of entitlement that usually comes with the territory. Old Joe Kennedy had not started out rich. But he was all about money and moving up in the world. His sons, born on the move, seemed to have grown up looking down at the rungs below through a prism of empathy. Freed from the burden of mere existence, money seemed less of a concern if they did not have to worry about it as their father had.

I finally put Weston in this same boat. Back then, medical science was only beginning to develop the ability to determine what part of the brain controls one particular behavior as opposed to another, and how this might be genetically passed on through generations and which parent's chromosomes determine who got what. But one of the theories derived from early research was that the emotional side of an offspring—the non-blooding pumping "heart" that determined feelings like kindness and empathy for others—came from the female. When applied to the Kennedy family, this would suggest that the Kennedy boys had gotten their drive and ambition from old Joe—and their "hearts" from Rose.

The day Red and I rode with Weston to his tailor shop and swanky country club, I had booked him simply as a guy already rolling in dough. But a year or so later, as he was gearing up to run for the Senate and the *Clarion* had attached me to him like the sidecar on a motorcycle, I was watching him finally gaining appreciation of something he had always taken for granted—a need for money.

We had just come back from California where Weston had delivered that virtuoso performance on a test stage in front of a group of donors important to any aspiring president, the Democratic Party elite of Hollywood, where he had seized Vice President Hubert Humphrey's audience and held it in his hand for nearly an hour. Back home now, we were in a Pontiac again—another brand new one—when Bluff City radio news reported how the founders of Kentucky Fried Chicken had become overnight multimillionaires after their initial stock offering hit Wall Street. It was the beginning of the franchise mania in American business and the launch of the air balloon Weston believed would eventually land him on the White House lawn.

Up to this point, the success of the ham and biscuits business venture that was to secure his qualifications for public office had scarcely moved beyond the idea stage he had first pitched to me in his office and had outlined to the board of the Packer brothers' bank. The Packers' promise of million-dollar backing had not progressed beyond a figment of his imagination and the scheme was still so sketchy that Hickenlooper had advised Weston not to even mention it to the congregation at Hickory Hill.

"These guys are about government, not business and they're all from Boston," Hickenlooper had told him. "They don't give a damn about biscuits."

Looking back on that advice now, I can see Hickenlooper was all about using Weston to educate the Kennedy brain trust on how to sell Bob to America—not about selling Weston to the best and the brightest. I was beginning to understand the sophistication of his cleverness. Killing two birds with one stone was a way of life with Hickenlooper and the key to his effectiveness as a Svengali of good intentions. Putting Weston on stage was good for both Weston and his audience.

In describing the Kentucky Fried Chicken stock bonanza, the guy on the Pontiac radio had said the stock was then selling at forty times the company's earnings and used the term PE ratio.

"What the hell is a PE ratio?" Weston asked me.

That I knew it meant stock price to earnings ratio was as startling to me as the fact that he didn't. Unknown to me at the time, both his lifestyle and his new law firm were running on the fumes of unsecured loans from the Bluff City Bank chaired by his beloved Grand. Both he and wife Pippa were in line for sizable inheritances and considered safe risks. The idea that stock in "Country Ham and Biscuits" could not only make him an instant business success story, but pay for Pontiacs, Tony the Tailor and the mortgage on his West End mansion instantly became an obsessive mission of an intensity only a man of Weston's energy and talents could generate.

Like all the other franchise movements spawned by KFC, Weston's ham and biscuits company was a copycat. His first order of business was to find a celebrity whose name could result in instant recognition and branding, just as the former Army Colonel Harland Sanders had done for KFC. Actually dressing up in a white suit and offering succulent chicken breasts from his own hand had been Sanders' idea to begin with. But he had sold it and himself to a Nashville entrepreneur and promoter for a $40,000-a-year-lifetime contract as a pitchman.

After several unsuccessful attempts to seduce big name country music entertainers Roy Acuff and Eddie Arnold into a similar arrangement, Weston scored with a gravel-voiced, former silent movie cowboy with a string of hit records named Tex Willis, who had become a Hollywood and Nashville icon. Willis appeared regularly on the Grand Ole Opry, usually growling his way through a hit version of "Night Riders in the Sky," and was a frequent attraction strolling through the Saturday night crowd outside Ernst

Tubb's Record Shop and hanging around Tootsie's Orchid Lounge, whose back door was directly across the alley from the stage door entrance to the Ryman Auditorium.

Unlike a lot of music celebrities, Tex was family wholesome and free of DUI and disorderly conduct arrest records. The closest he had ever come to a public scandal was my own *Clarion* report of an urgent Sunday night visit to the emergency room at Bluff City General. It was early in my days on the police beat that I got a call from an ER nurse with whom I had gone to Belair High. "You might want to come over and check out a guy from Nashville who just came in here. He might make a good story."

Hers was the smirking face at the entrance desk when I arrived. She aimed a thumb over her right shoulder and said, "Second curtained-cubicle on your right."

The tails of those cubicle curtains hung a couple of feet above the floor and underneath them on the second one down, I could see a pair of garishly painted needle-nosed cowboy boots nestled in a pile of dropped pants, exposing a couple of hairy, blue-veined calves. Behind them, pointing in the same direction, were the cushion-soled shoes and green hospital scrubs of a medic. Obviously, this was a standup meeting not be interrupted. So I just stood there, notebook in hand and ear ready for the news-paper quotes that followed.

"Bend over now, Mr. Willis, this might hurt a bit," the medic said.

"Awright, son," growled the man in the boots. "Go ahead. Just remember you are looking directly up the a--hole of America's Number One Cowboy."

The world's number one cowboy and Weston staged a musical opening of the headquarters for Tex's Ham and Biscuit food chain near Nashville's Music Row and had their pictures taken in the lobby standing in front of a huge oil painting of the "Pardners" clad in Western-cut suits tailored by Tony and hats the size of a long horn. Naturally, I was there to cover it for the *Clarion*. And after the photographers, television crews, and Tex and his band had departed and Weston was about to turn out the lights, he called me over to stand where he and Tex had stood to peruse the portrait he had commissioned by a young female Western artist named Amy Goodnight.

"Look closely at this, David Aahthuh," Weston said. "Tony tailored these cowboy pants pretty tight and the woman that painted us...well, look good now, don't you think she painted Tex's crotch bigger than mine. I mean, the bulge in his pants is a lot bigger, isn't it."

Well, I looked good, and, well, I had to admit that Tex's bulge appeared a little larger than Weston's. "But after all, he is a cowboy," I quipped.

Weston was not amused.

"Okay," he said. "Then it was not my imagination."

A week later, he visited his headquarters again with me in tow. And we paused once more in front of the painting, which hung just outside his office.

"I had Amy come back and do this part over," he said, pointing at the repainted spot. "She got it right this time. They are closer to the same size now. Mine might be even a little bigger."

For all his exceptional attributes—the good looks, the photographic memory and enviable oratorical skills, Weston suffered some of the same banal male afflictions as the rest of us, perhaps even with exceptional intensity considering his overall bigger-than-life existence. I wondered if the uneven blue jean bulge had ever been the subject of a session with his West End celebrity therapist, who showed up at the opening and was beginning to worry me. Not that a concern over the size of another man's bulge should not have been a therapy topic. But I had seen Weston pointing out the crotch painting to Dr. Gunther Goebbels, who had also gone out of his way to let every media type at the event know that he was an early investor in Weston's ham and biscuit franchises. The *Defender* had chosen to contain its coverage of the event in a large photo of Weston wearing the same getup in which he had posed with the artist Amy and Dr. Goebbels, admiring the painting of himself, and Tex dressed up like Butch Cassidy and the Sundance Kid.

Ethical constraints prevented Goebbels from identifying his patients to the news media but the inference was clearly there to be drawn. And Weston had never seen any reason to keep private the fact that he had been a visitor to Goebbels' psychiatrist couch, referred there by his beloved Grand, presumably for no other reason than to cure his fear of flying in small planes. Since becoming his ad hoc political guardian, I had suggested that broadcasting that fact might not be helpful to a career in politics. But he had blown it off.

"Hell, you go to a doctor if you have pneumonia," he told me. "What the hell is the difference? Neurosis or pneumonia?"

If he didn't know, what would be the use of telling him? But I did anyway. "Because every voter can catch pneumonia. Damn few of them believe they need a psychiatrist, even if they do."

"Forget it," he said. "Gunther is not just my therapist. He's my pal. You ought to go see him and find out why you won't wear a suit and tie."

It was not long until Weston began to realize what he was up against. First the *Defender* ran a long series of business stories about how the success of Kentucky Fried Chicken had spawned several dramatic franchise failures, including a dog grooming enterprise in which the founder was jailed for cruelty to man's best friend a week after the first shop opened.

Somewhere in the stories, the *Defender* always mentioned other notable franchise ventures including Tex's Ham and Biscuits, invariably accompanied by a headshot of Weston in his cowboy getup. And the paper's cartoonist took up the cudgel, too, depicting Tex and Weston riding double on a slobbering wild hog decorated with dollar signs and hell bent for the United States Capitol. Somewhere in every cartoon, a goofy bird flew over the Capitol dome tweeting "Bobby Says 'Hello.'" The 1968 Democratic primary for the U.S. Senate was still more than a year off but the character assassination of Tate Weston had already begun.

No matter the year or the elected office at stake, the *Defender* and the *Clarion* backed opposing candidates. No one could ever remember them being on the same side of anything. The *Clarion* had loved Franklin Roosevelt. The *Defender* had hated him. The *Clarion* had backed Truman and Adlai Stevenson, the *Defender* loved Dewey and Eisenhower. Even though the incumbent senator up for re-election, J. Howard Binghamton, was a Democrat, the *Defender* was supporting him. Such was the rivalry of the two papers; had it been Adolf Hitler, the colonel would have gone for him, too, especially in light of what the *Clarion* had just done to his pal Martin Collins.

Binghamton had made it to the U.S. Senate on the back of support curried from road builders he had favored first as state highway department commissioner and later as governor, a post from which he had appointed himself to fill the un-expired term of a notorious drunk who had died in office. That Binghamton was a former Klansman, a confirmed racist and a Democrat, was no deterrent to Colonel May, who knew being a Republican was still a handicap in the South. A war hawk and personal friend of President Lyndon Johnson, Senator Binghamton had once bought one of Johnson's prize Angus bulls at a cattle auction, and now echoed every Johnson pronouncement on the validity of the Vietnam War, usually working in a phrase or two reflecting the *Defender* editorial position that Viet Cong communists were poised just across the river to the north, ready to repeat General Sherman's march through Dixie.

Because Senator Binghamton often said one thing to the bib-overall habitués of one public square in the eastern part of the state, and something contradictory to the tobacco spitters in the west, the *Clarion* had equipped Rhodes Newbold with a tape recorder to follow him everywhere and record every word he said. The senator traveled the state in a giant Winnebago mobile home accompanied by two state highway patrolmen and the *Defender*'s political editor, Dexter White. Rhodes rode behind in a rented

Mustang accompanied by his girlfriend, a leggy tart from Georgia that he had met at Vanderbilt.

For months, Rhodes and I criss-crossed the state following our candidates, his Mustang nestled in the diesel fumes of Binghamton's big motor home, and me in the front seat of a Pontiac with a gregarious young law student driver and Tate sprawled all over the back seat enthralled by the sound of his own voice, as he practiced his lines. Pippa frequently traveled with her husband in the Pontiac and was always along when a leg of the trip demanded a small airplane from Bluff City Air. Weston did not want to fly without her. She was as good a campaigner as he was, the two of them attention getters by stunning appearance alone. They were especially effective in the urban Negro areas where the female occupants and their offspring who populated the ghetto apartment buildings gathered around them like children around a maypole, two tall striking alabaster statues in a sea of chocolate.

Pippa always picked out a sullen young girl in the crowd, maybe a little chubby or otherwise unattractive, to approach and engage in conversation. Next thing you know, she is telling the kid how naturally beautiful she is and special in one way or another. By the time the campaign stop was over, the child was smiling and promising to diet her way to the next Miss Black America pageant.

In the small rural towns where the election would be won or lost, the Westons aimed for the lunchtime crowds of courthouse employees and day laborers. Weston drew the female swoons and Pippa the wolf whistles. I watched construction workers lay down their saws and hammers and follow her into a restaurant they had just exited after lunch. She was a good speaker, too, with a sense of humor and often ended her spiel by saying her husband had many wonderful attributes, not the least of which was his taste in women.

Reading my accounts of her prowess as a campaigner, Hickenlooper decided that Pippa had become a potent political asset being wasted as a tag-along to the candidate. He and Weston arranged for her to take up a separate travel schedule of her own designed to get out the women's vote. She spoke to garden clubs, toured hospitals and schools, and began doing television and radio talk shows and sometimes took their precocious five-year-old daughter Brooke along. The kid had inherited her mother's looks and her father's charisma and attracted attention everywhere she went. Like a lot of well-intentioned political decisions, the one to separate the Westons came with unintended consequences.

Always the pied piper wherever he went, Weston led his followers on strolls down sidewalks, along city bike paths and rural state park trails, necktie loosened and vest unbuttoned, tongue and foot in sync, his Chiclet smile spreading good humor and whatever line of bullshit crossed his mind. He was at his best among the disadvantaged and the young, preaching the Kennedy gospel of a rising tide lifting all the boats. Sometimes he would step up on automobile or truck bumpers and sit down on the hood, or slouch on the top step of a stairwell and hold court, asking questions of those around him, their names, where they lived, how many brothers and sisters, where they worked and what if anything they liked or disliked about their lives, as if he really cared. I could not tell whether he did or not, but I could see that he had made them believe that he did.

Often he appeared ridiculously incongruous with his surroundings, the vested three-piece pinstriped ensembles among blue denim and khaki work clothes in the agricultural communities and the rags of the urban poor. But he resisted any advice to dress down as Senator Binghamton had, who, when outside urban areas, disembarked his motor home in plaid shirts, khakis and work boots.

Weston worked Binghamton's wardrobe habits into his speeches, ridiculing him as "a chameleon that talks out of both sides of his mouth, changing his mind with the change in his clothes."

"This is who I am," he would say, dropping his open hands to frame his vest and watch chain, "a courtroom lawyer from the state capital. These are the work clothes of the job I am asking you to hire me to do. If I try to be anything else, I am a phony and everybody will know it."

The loosened tie and rolled-up shirtsleeves were his only concessions to convention. And for a long time, I believed it was going to work. Our polls suggested that if the urban areas turned out their votes, he was going to unseat J. Howard Binghamton and take that first big step to the White House.

But political campaigns are treacherous journeys rife with unseen potholes, unmarked curves and sometimes, fatal head-on collisions. A month before the primary, Colonel May began to take his revenge. Two thunderbolts came out of nowhere and struck the Weston campaign dead center. Neither Jack Hickenlooper nor I had seen them coming.

The national press had gotten wind of the potential upset and began showing interest in Weston's campaign. Years before Senate and House campaigns became traveling circuses like the presidential elections had already become, a few astute political editors had begun to recognize Weston as the harbinger of a new breed of politicians riding into office on the wake of John F. Kennedy's 1960 election.

Texan Lyndon Johnson, one of the old Dixiecrat rulers of the Senate, where seniority has been the law for two decades, was clinging by fingernails to his inherited presidency, while his old boy buddies on Capitol Hill were being challenged all over the old Confederacy by younger, more progressive and attractive men like Weltner and Carter in Georgia, Bumpers in Arkansas, Askew in Florida and Hollins in South Carolina.

As our primary day drew closer and the South began to leaf and blossom, political correspondents, network anchors and now and then a sultry news babe from local television stations appeared like spring robins to peck around the Weston campaign, all with a sense of entitlement to the seat in the Pontiac that had been abandoned by Pippa's launch as a Weston proxy.

The visiting firemen usually tagged along behind the Pontiac in their own vehicles forming small motorcades that disturbed the peace and tranquility of life in the farm belt and created traffic hazards in the urban areas. I once likened the supposed sight of us hustling through a changing stoplight as a four-car funeral procession; something for which Weston never forgave me but that Hickenlooper and I laughed about for years to come. Occasionally when more than one journalistic big foot showed up needing transportation, a small van would be rented, and I would give up my seat as shotgun rider so both of them could have at Weston at the same time. If there was ever a candidate capable of handling two adversaries at once, it was Tate Weston. They never laid a hand on him.

I began giving up my Pontiac shotgun seat as often as possible after the *Columbia Journalism Review*'s treatment of the Binghamton-Weston campaign slammed the *Clarion* and the *Defender* for ethical misbehavior, depicting Rhodes Newbold's coverage of Binghamton as the work of an "assigned assassin" and my appendage status as a "handler and publicity agent for the *Clarion*'s lawyer." The *Defender* did not get off unscathed. The longhaired Columbia student journalist depicted Dexter White as engaging in "brother-in-law coverage" of the Binghamton campaign and accused the *Defender* of ignoring Weston as if the incumbent was unopposed.

At a joint campaign appearance in Bluff City where our candidates alternated at the podium to take questions from disgruntled secondary school teachers, Newbold and I agreed that the kid from the *Columbia Review* had been dead right about us. But so green behind the ears at the time, we were not certain just how embarrassed we should be. We kept hoping that Hickenlooper would weigh in on that subject, but he never acknowledged the criticism.

Many years later, when that *Review* article was disinterred and read to us at an industry ethics seminar, Hickenlooper blew it off as the result of the author's youthful naiveté concerning the history and function of the American free press. "The country was probably better-served when readers had the choice between newspapers with opposing points of view that aggressively supported one candidate and opposed another," he proclaimed, and never mentioned it again.

I had not felt that way when I read about myself in the *Review* in 1968, but twenty years later, I believed exactly as Hickenlooper. Embarrassment at being accurately portrayed as no more than a Weston stooge was followed in short order by devastating shrapnel from the worst combination of decision and coincidence to which I was ever a party.

When Pippa's seat in the Pontiac first became available as an interview exclusive for selected media types, Weston gave me the job of deciding who got to ride with him. But then he reclaimed it and began granting the up-close-and-personal access to whatever female television news babe suited his fancy that day. Nothing untoward happened, but the man would flirt with a fire hydrant if you put a skirt on it.

Before that could turn into a problem, which in retrospect it probably would have eventually, Amy the crotch painter showed up—in her words—"to chronicle for posterity the color and excitement of the campaign in watercolor sketches." I had no clue that she would turn out to be the excitement.

Amy Goodnight was a dishwater-blonde looker in tight jeans with big hair to her waist and spike heels, not elegant or stunningly beautiful like Pippa, but sexy hot and a little on the trashy side, cool and dry to the look and touch but with a little too much lipstick and rouge and the illusion of steam roiling beneath hidden places. Though slim and taut, her stripper's bosom somehow filled up the back seat of the Pontiac, seemingly so tightly restricted under brassiere and tank top that if loosed it would pin your face to the windshield. Born in Arizona, Amy had affected some guttural Austrian accent that gave her speech an international flavor.

From the minute she showed up on the campaign, I had the feeling hers was the first voice Weston had ever preferred hearing to his own and that he might well have had that crotch bulge of his measured by the touch of hands with artificially long tangerine colored fingernails. The ignition of this visiting stick of dynamite set off a series of implosions that blew Weston's political hopes and dreams to hell.

The Weston campaign had made an overnight stop at Blackberry Farm, a 4,000-acre resort in the foothills of the Smoky Mountains on the Tennessee side. The physical accommodations resembled a mini-sized, rustic version of The Greenbrier in West Virginia— horses, golf and breathtaking views. Weston loved it and had looked for excuses to go there ever since the Packer brothers had hustled him up there after the bank board meeting. We had driven over in the Pontiac following a private fundraiser in Bristol with plans to take the day off for a photo shoot the following day to accommodate a freelance photographer commissioned by *People* magazine.

What could have and should have been an omen knocked on the door of my room at the Blackberry shortly after midnight— the elusive but never far away love of my life—Allston Williams. "SURPRISE!" is what she said when I opened up, "Wanna do IT?"

"What in the hell are you doing here?" I asked her. I had answered the door barefooted, in a T-shirt and gym shorts. She dropped her bag at my feet, put her arms around my neck and pulled my head toward hers. She smelled strongly of something awful I could not immediately identify but that had definitely been disguised by cigarette smoke.

"Damn, what have you been eating?" I said, before she clamped her lips on mine. "Garlic, Vic darling," she said, through the smooch. "Some shrimp dip we stock the airplanes with. Pippa and I have been to New York today for her interview with *People*. She knew you all were here and decided to stop over. I think we landed in a pasture."

I dragged her bag inside and when I looked up she was already shoeless and down to her bra and panties. She flung a jump suit toward a chair and reached out and hugged me again. I turned away from another aimed kiss and played back to her a version of a game we had enjoyed. "My lips will never touch lips that touch garlic," I said, joking of course. I would've eaten her alive wrapped in the stuff.

"Oh, they won't, huh?" she said, leaning back against the door and flicking the deadbolt."

"Vic's little lips don't like garlic. Well, let's see how Vic's little dick likes it."

With that she yanked my shorts down, grabbed my penis and stood there holding it in her warm hand. It responded accordingly. This was not a new experience. IT had begun this way before more than once. I knew precisely what my next move was supposed to be—to back up slowly and sit down on my bed or a chair or whatever I could find without dislodging the guiding hand. She dropped immediately to her knees on the carpet and looked me directly in the eye like I had seen Annette Funicello do a hundred times to the television camera and made an announcement:

"Now, ladies and gentlemen, watch closely. Vic's little dick is about to get its first garlic blow job."

Allston could have made a good living teaching fellatio. But I always pulled away before she could complete the job. It was my turn. She had cultivated a black bush wide, deep and thick enough to hide Randy Sikes's killer. The mere sight of it sent my pulse sprinting and my blood rushing. My face had been buried in it enough to leave an identifiable imprint. She was a moaner, too— the sound of which took me places I never wanted to leave—and left me with graphic nightmares of her moaning to the touch of someone else. She was prone to multiple orgasms, and I always made sure there were multiples before coming up for air. And then the real athleticism began and did not end until one of us ran out of positions—or energy. And then that was IT. It was wine and cigarettes until we could do IT again.

When I regained enough breath and awareness, I finally asked, "Where's Pippa?"

"I don't know," Allston said, "but she was going to get her own room and shower before surprising Weston."

I sat straight up in the bed. "You mean he didn't know you were coming?"

"I don't think so," she said. "We were working off the schedule the campaign had given to *People* magazine. They knew where their photographer would be tonight. Why would it matter?"

"I don't know that it does," I said. "But that crotch artist is around somewhere and I have no idea where she's sleeping."

"Uh-oh," Allston said. "I don't want to think about that."

"Me either," I said. "None of our business anyway."

"Right," Allston said, and reached for me again.

In the morning she would be gone in a hurry, the way it always has been between us, hurrying to get married, hurrying to get unmarried, her hurrying to someone else's bed, me hurrying to Texas and the Air Force and then to Washington briefly before being attached to Weston, one of us invariably left disappointed and angry enough at the other to do something stupid. This time it was a daylight call from Pippa summoning Allston to the Bluff City Air charter headed back home. Pippa would not be aboard, Allston was told, but a car taking her and Amy Goodnight to the airstrip in the pasture would be around shortly.

The elephant in the back seat of the Pontiac was cloying silence. For five solid hours, Weston pretended to be asleep and Pippa hid her mood behind dark glasses aimed at an open novel, the pages of which never changed. My usual posture in the Pontiac was cocked for conversation with Weston, who invariably sat behind the driver, tongue keeping pace with the breakneck speed at which the lead-footed law student moved us from stop to stop. If he wasn't delivering a lecture, Tate was usually peppering me with one question after another, a man hopelessly in love with the sound of his own voice.

The trip to Bluff City was the longest I had ever been in Weston's presence and not left both ear weary and piqued at my predicament as a listening post. Toward the end, from my cocked position where I could detect a raised eyebrow or a clenched jaw, I would say something provocative to the driver, Nate Larson, just to see if I could break the trances in the back seat. Something like, "Nate, that little Amy Goodnight is some artist. Did you see that landscape she turned out of Tate sitting on that boulder in the afternoon sun?"

Larson, a tall, handsome and—as I later learned—brilliant and entertaining law student who went on to become a federal prosecutor and esteemed judge—played along, glancing up at his rearview mirror to catch any reaction.

"Sorry, Dave," Nate said. "I was always too busy ogling Amy's physical attributes. My eyes never dropped low enough to check out her sketch pad."

Nothing from the back seat. Not a twitch or twitter, grunt or groan. Only once during the entire trip did I see any movement from either passenger. When Larson made a sharp turn to the right in an effort to align the Pontiac with a gas pump, Weston's knee swayed like a sleeping man's might do and touched Pippa's leg. She jerked away as if it had been a stick afire. Otherwise, the Westons were two elegantly sculpted life-like mannequins posed in the back seat, emotions in the same state of atrophy as their bodies. What had occurred between them the night before I only learned a week later in the worst way—by reading the *Defender.*

Not having a Sunday paper, the *Defender*'s biggest circulation day was Saturday, when the press time was moved early in the day so the paper, loaded with regular weekend feature packages, landed about noon. I had just arrived on the *Clarion* side of the building as the early *Defender* editions were being delivered to the newsroom. The top of the page was dominated by two photographs, juxtaposed as they might have been, had the lens been capable of catching them as one.

On the left was Weston from the waist up in a strapped under-shirt, his hair wildly askew, and behind him in the background the head and bare shoulders of Amy the crotch painter, a shocked look on her face and her arms folded across her chest. On the right was a side profile shot of Pippa Weston and at her side their daughter Brooke. Pippa had one hand over her open mouth and the other finger—pointing at Tate's face in an accusatory pose if ever I saw one. Underneath was an inch-high, near replication of a now familiar *Defender* editorial cartoon caption, "Pippa Says Hello."

The story underneath was brief and spare of details, much like the 'gotcha' photographs that front British tabloids and grocery store newsstand scandal sheets in the United States: "Mrs. Tate Weston pays a surprise late-night visit to her husband's senatorial campaign at the scenic Blackberry Farm resort in the Smoky Mountains earlier this month. At her side is their five-year-old daughter Brooke."

That was it. Amy Goodnight was neither identified nor explained. She could have been a secretary taking dictation, a sister in the room with her brother, another daughter even, considering she was at least twenty years younger than Weston. This was tabloid reporting and editing at its best, devoid of any details that might have opened up the publication for libel or invasion of privacy lawsuits, but the insinuation was unmistakable. The *Clarion*'s candidate had been caught in an indefensible position, and the defense came to rest in my lap.

Within an hour I was in the cubicle with Hickenlooper and Red Whitmore trying to decide if and how the *Clarion* and the Weston campaign should respond, the two now melded in common cause.

The old adage *if you can't say something nice, say nothing at all* came immediately to mind and I suggested it.

Hickenlooper wasted little time jumping to that conclusion. "Let it just lie there and die," he said. "Follow the advice of our esteemed President Lyndon Johnson: 'Never kick a fresh turd on a hot day.'"

Unfortunately, *People* magazine did not heed the warning of an old Texan experienced with manure piles. A few days later, the magazine "profile" of up-and-coming political star Tate Weston described Pippa Weston's "obviously stunned reaction upon finding her handsome husband in the room with a lovely young sketch artist well after midnight." The *People* photographer, who at the invitation of Mrs. Weston had been along to capture her husband's reaction to the surprise visit, had taken photographs accompanying the piece.

$$\boxed{8}$$

Not that it came without warning. The new federal district attorney had to find a way to warn his old law partner of the impending disaster, the two being as close as the brothers Kennedy. But it could not be done directly. Miller Clark was in tune enough with the ethical protocol of his job to have foregone his planned investment in Tex's Ham and Biscuits and astute enough to know the best way to get the information to Tate Weston would be to have one of his minions leak it to the *Clarion*.

Not surprisingly, the leak did not come to me. This was the kind of sensitive, inside, maybe even lethal, information to be trusted only to a courier with the guile and experience of Red Whitmore. Unbeknownst to me, my job was to be the middleman. The bomb reached me—and the Weston campaign—via a message delivered to the desk of a Memphis hotel, where the candidate was making a luncheon speech. The note said "Call Red at the *Clarion* ASAP."

"Are you sitting down?" he asked. "No," I said. "There are no chairs around the pay phones in Peabody. What's up?"

"A shit storm," he said. "The feds are about to indict the Packer brothers for bank fraud. The million dollars they finally put into Tex's Ham and Biscuits turned out to be marked money."

"Marked money? You mean money that came from a bank robbery?"

"Yeah, but not the kind you're thinking about," Red said. "This robbery was an inside job. Miller Clark is going after the Packer brothers for violating banking laws by hiding bad loans from bank examiners. And the loans were not just bad—they were to themselves. And that ain't all...well, let's just say this ain't gonna be grand for Grand—Community Southern Federal—his grand-mother's bank. What this boils down to—I mean other than a field day for the *Defender*— is that the money now in the Tex's Ham and Biscuit franchise account at Clara Hancock Weston's bank was transferred there from a falsified account in one of their Knoxville branches where it was last used to pretty up an ugly illegal bad loan to the Packer brothers to finance the purchase of quarter horses in Oklahoma."

"Jesus Christ!" I said.

"Better call on somebody that knows you, Dave," Red advised. "And by the way, you get to break this news to Weston. He doesn't know yet, and tell him to call Hickenlooper. Who calls whom and what is discussed about this matter is likely to end up as evidence before a grand jury. You just ask Weston for a response to this news and get back to me. I'm doing the story from here."

"Is this a *Clarion* exclusive?

"Not for long. I think maybe we just got an early break on it. Miller Clark is announcing it at a press conference later today. I had it dropped on me by the FBI this morning like a ton of bricks."

Being the bearer of bad news was the worst part of the job I had come to love. You get the experience early doing obituaries and covering police. Sometimes the person you are calling for information about somebody arrested, injured—or dead—first learns it from you. I did not look forward to taking the news to Weston. So I waited until we were settled in the Pontiac. Fortunately, Weston had not brought along some passenger to entertain in the Pippa seat, which had been devoid of Pippa ever since Blackberry Farm. When I dumped the news on him, it was obvious he already knew but wasn't supposed to know. The animation and anger I expected was as noticeably absent as his wife. My messenger job had obviously been an attempt to mask the fact that somebody had already given him advanced warning.

"I will need some response from you for the paper," I told him.

"Tell the paper I could not be reached for comment," he said.

"I can't tell Hickenlooper that," I said. "He knows I am sitting in the front seat of your car."

"What should I say?" he asked, glumly. "Just make something up. I don't care."

The combination of the news and the speech had taken the starch out of him. He was wilting in the back seat, slipping into the trance-like state I had first witnessed on the trip back to Bluff City after the surprise visit. Our next stop was a small, private gathering at a country club a hundred miles from Memphis. We got there early and while Weston had gone to put on a fresh shirt, I telephoned the *Clarion* to report that Weston had no immediate comment on the Packer brothers' indictment. Herman the deskman said, "You better hold on." He immediately switched me to Earnhart who put Hickenlooper on the line.

"When he gets his damn shirt changed, tell him to call me," Hickenlooper said. "He has to say something. Tell him I will be waiting for the call."

I did and he did but what was said in that conversation I could only deduce from reading Red Whitmore's story in the *Clarion* the next day. Weston was quoted as saying he had no knowledge of the internal workings of either the Packer banks or Community Southern Federal and therefore had no reason to question the source of funds invested in his franchise business.

"They bought a franchise and, like many other investors, paid for it by transferring money from one bank account to the corporate account of Tex's Ham and Biscuits at Community Southern Federal. That is all I know."

That response might well have been sufficient to deflect fallout from the Packer brothers' legal trouble, had Colonel May not been lying in ambush, honing his Civil War sword and hell bent on revenge. The *Defender* took a decidedly different view of the news and included details that had not been leaked to Whitmore or kept out of the paper by Hickenlooper, a quandary I deigned to consider.

"Bluff City and Knoxville Banks Targeted in Federal Probe of Tex's Ham and Biscuit Franchise Scheme," blared the newspaper's headline, followed by the subhead, "Miller Clark goes after former law partner Tate Weston and his banker grandmother."

There were front-page pictures of the so-called federal

"targets"—the Packer brothers, Senate candidate Weston in his cowboy hat, and an aristocratic Clara Hancock Weston, silver-haired, widow-peaked chairwoman of Community Southern. Though U.S. Attorney Miller Clark issued a statement to the *Defender* explaining that technically recipients of bank transferred funds suspected of being the proceeds of a criminal act are not necessarily targets of the grand jury investigation, the lot of them had been all but indicted, convicted and sentenced by the *Defender* for heinous crimes of bank fraud, specifically the transfer of money from one bank to another to hide conflict-of-interest lending to bank insiders.

Seth T. Weston Jr., counsel for Community Southern, was quoted as saying that neither his mother's bank nor his son's franchise business whose account it held could or should be held criminally libel for any actions taken by banks under control of the Packer brothers. He said that both were cooperating with the federal investigation and that a vigorous defense would be mounted against any charges that might result. None ever did, but the damage to Weston's Senate campaign had been inflicted. And the colonel was far from done.

A few days before the May primary, the early edition of the *Defender* resurrected the picture of Weston and his friend, franchise investor and psychiatrist, Gunther Goebbels, and the artist Amy Goodnight admiring her handiwork at the headquarters opening of Tex's Ham and Biscuits, and placed it above another big bold headline:

"WESTON AND THE PACKER BROTHERS ROLLING IN DOUGH"

Beneath it was what the paper termed a "secret transcript of a Tate Weston therapy session with Dr. Gunther Goebbels, a major investor in Tex's Ham and Biscuits, the financing of which is now the subject of federal criminal investigation."

Dr. Goebbels: Tate, tell me about these dreams and sudden stress attacks concerning the financing of the ham and biscuit business. When did they start?

Tate Weston: After I went with the Packers to Blackberry Farm to speak to the board of First Trust. You gotta know these guys to appreciate what I'm about to tell you, Gunther. They are fire and ice. Judd and I are brothers under the skin—outgoing, and lots of energy, fun to be around. Wilbur, now, he's different. Cold as they get, but smart as hell. Well, anyway, they want to go up to Blackberry Farm to work out the details of what they get for putting up the million, the size of their franchise territory, stuff like that. You ever been to Blackberry? Man, it is something. Food is terrific. You'd think they moved the Waldorf out and set it down on 4,000 acres of Smoky Mountains.

Anyway, we're still in the bank building. Judd says, "Wilbur—he doesn't call him J. W. like everybody else does. He says, "Wilbur, what does a million dollars look like?" J. W. says, "A million dollars looks like a million dollars."

"No," Judd says. "I mean in cash. What does a million dollars in hundred bills or fifties look like? Have you ever seen that much cash at one time? Wilbur—I mean J. W.—"

J. W. says, "Hell no. When would I ever?"

Judd says, "Do we have that much in the vault downstairs?"

J. W. says, "I don't know." Then he picks up the phone and calls somebody to ask if they do. They say yeah, and J. W. says in what dominations, and whoever it is must have said, "Any way you want it." J. W. covers up the phone and says, "Yeah, we got it in hundreds, fifties and twenties."

Well, to make a long story short, Judd takes the phone and tells whoever it is to put together a million in cash any way he wants, hundreds only until they run out and then whatever dominations you need to make a million. Put it bags and meet us in the parking garage.

J. W. is the oldest, you know. He says, "Judd, are you crazy? You wanna take out a million dollars in cash out of the bank in bags?"

Judd says, "Yeah, I am. And you are, too. Let's take it up to Blackberry Farm with us and put in the center of the room so we can look at how much money we are about to risk giving it to this other crazy sonofabitch from Bluff City to make biscuits."

I think they are joking. No, they weren't joking. A guy meets us in the basement of the bank where there is a parking garage with a cart full of money. I mean bags of money, not real moneybags, those satchels they use to move it in armored cars. I mean plain old garbage bags, black plastic garbage bags. They fill up the trunk of J. W.'s big Cadillac. So much so we have put our regular luggage inside the car. Judd's even got a big pistol with him, in case somebody tries to rob us, he says. He's got it stuck in his belt under his coat like some cowboy.

When we get to Blackberry Farm, Judd has the bellmen haul all those bags up with our luggage to his suite. They don't have a clue what they're carrying. But they looked heavy. Judd dumps all the bags on the carpet and stacks up the bills that are in packets, you

know with bands around them up. The stack is three or four feet
high. Then we start drinking and talking and looking at the stack.
Before long, Judd's sitting down there with it. Then, he yells, "Hey,
the money is taller than I am sitting down." He picks up a stack.
They didn't have enough wrapped hundreds to make a million, so
there are a lot of stacks of fifties, too. He looks at them until he
finds a stack of hundreds and takes off a wrapper. "You gotta feel
this," he says. "Come on down here and put your ass down on a
million dollars. Feel what it's like to be rolling in dough."

Dr. Goebbels: Stop here a minute, Tate. So Judd is down on the
floor rolling around in the money. Do you and Wilbur, or J. W. or
whatever his name is, get on the floor with the money, too?

Weston: J. W. didn't. He just sat there drinking Jack Daniels and
watched his brother. I hate to tell you this, Gunther. But yes, I did.
I got down on the floor with Judd Packer and a million dollars.
And he opens some of the packets and starts throwing the cash
up in the air and letting it fall down on us like rain, hundreds and
fifties and twenties. It is raining a million dollars on our heads. We
are rolling in it.

Dr. Goebbels: And now you're having dreams about that day?

Weston: Hell yes, nightmares. I wake up in bed looking around
for the money. And sometimes there is J. W. pointing Judd's
gun at me and demanding his million dollars back. Sometimes
during the day, even when I am about to make a speech or riding
in the car someplace, that picture of me and Judd on the floor
in the money just comes back into my mind and I can't think of
anything else but me owing the Packers a million dollars. And I
begin to shake and sweat. And now they tell me the Packers are

up to their ass in trouble and gonna do time. What in the hell was I thinking?"

That was it. No story. No explanation of how the transcript got into the hands of the *Defender.* No comments from the Packers or Weston or Dr. Goebbels. But there was a front-page Straight from the Heart editorial signed by Colonel May endorsing Senator J. Howard Binghamton for re-election, citing his long record of public service and dismissing his un-named opponent as being "unqualified and unfit to hold public office."

Red Whitmore and I were sitting in the back row of the newsroom trying to visualize what a million in cash looks like. Red had a little calculator out on his desk trying to figure out how much a million in cash weighs or how far it would stretch laid in bills end to end when Hickenlooper came out of the publisher's office and headed our way.

Red had already called the Treasury Department in Washington to get the dimensions of a paper bill, which is about six by fifteen centimeters, and the fraction of a pound that a single sheet that size weighs, an amount so tiny we didn't know how to calculate it. And we had no idea how much was in hundreds or if the bank had any thousand dollar or five hundred dollar bills, which they still printed in those days. But if the whole million had been in hundreds, there would have been ten thousand bills that altogether weighed a little over twenty-two pounds. If there were a lot in fifties and twenties, the total weight could have been twice that and if stacked on top of each other, it would have been three-and-half feet high like

Weston was saying in the transcript.

Red, who was ready with the final total when Hickenlooper reached us, looked up from the calculator and said, "Jack, if you came to ask me how much cash it takes to fill up two black garbage bags that barely fit in the trunk of a Cadillac that already has a case of Jack Daniels in it, I have the answer right here."

And he holds the little calculator aloft like he is reading from it, and announces as if awarding a prize, "The answer is: A SHIT-LOAD... heh...heh. Our candidate for the United States Senate was rolling around in a SHITLOAD of dirty money."

"Sonofabitch," says Hickenlooper, shaking his head in disgust. "Timing is perfect, isn't it? Weston's campaign is probably done. Not enough time to defend yourself or for people to forget. Television and radio will be all over this story and it has long legs. Miller Clark just told me the bank examiners expect a dozen banks or more will fail and be shut down before it's over. He said this could be the third or fourth biggest bank failure in history, the biggest since the Depression. Community Federal has a lot of exposure."

Never shy to ask the sensitive question, Red wondered aloud, "Couldn't Miller Clark at least have waited until after the election?"

"Hell, this is not Miller. He didn't have a thing to do with it. This is a Treasury Department deal," Hickenlooper said. "Washington kept Miller in the dark until the last minute, maybe just to protect him if nothing else. If this had leaked prematurely, there would have been a lot of finger-pointing and conflict-of-interest allegations. They didn't come to Miller until they were ready to prosecute. That's his job, but he may even recuse himself if criminal charges are brought against Grandmother Weston's bank. He's still on the start-up loan to the firm and Community's got the mortgage on his house."

Hickenlooper put his hand on Red's shoulder. "What have you picked up this morning?"

"Not a lot," Red said. "But your friend Miller Clark is telling you right about Treasury agents working the bank laws, not the local feebees. They only found out when Treasury showed up with the warrants issued in Washington. Looks like the Packers were lending money to phony corporations and swapping those loans. That's the real nut of this. The money that went to the Tex franchise account was originally a loan to one of the Packer shell companies that is bankrupt. But Mrs. Weston's got some more loans he transferred to Community Federal just to hide it from the bank examiners, so she's got a problem, too."

Hickenlooper had a habit of running a finger back and forth across his upper lip when he was plotting coverage and whatever else he plotted. "Well, that's probably the best angle for us to pursue—how many local banks are going to take a hit. We need to get out front on that part of story, so you grab that and run, Red."

And then he turned to me. "And what about you, Mr. Arthur? Following the federal investigation is what everybody is going to do. But there is another great story here, maybe the best of all. Whatta you think that is?"

Two years earlier, I would have had no clue. And if I had, I would have been loath to risk spitting it out and being dead wrong. But I knew now that Hickenlooper had just thrown me a slow soft ball right down the middle.

"How in the hell did the *Defender* get that transcript?" I said.

The first place I went looking for an answer was in the Pontiac an hour later. Weston was speaking to a luncheon meeting of the Centennial Club, a high-tone women's group with a hundred-year-old history, at which Pippa, a third-generation member, was to introduce him. The badly shaken, toned-downed candidate I expected to encounter did not show up. From all appearances, Weston was his normal, high-energy-full-of-piss-and-vinegar self.

First thing he says to me is, "Do you not own a necktie, Mr. Aahthuh? Couldn't you possibly have dressed for the occasion? This is one of the classiest groups of women in the South. Nothing else close. You are looking at a typical member."

He made a dramatic open-handed swing toward the Pippa seat, its occupant glittering with diamonds and resplendent in some mauve-colored Oscar Dela Somebody business suit and a coal smoke blouse cut low enough to flash a little cleavage, hair pulled straight back showing off the widow's peak. What is it with these West Enders? Are they all born with a widow's peak! She had already lowered her eyes and begun to smile, having heard this sermon before. So had I by now and was weary with it.

"I didn't want to shock you," I said. "I figured you'd had enough for one day."

I was in my cocked position, physically as well as mentally, so I could see Nate Larson duck his head and repress a smile, and

Pippa throw her head back and let out a little howl…"Whoooo?"
"Tate Weston, you asked for that," she said.

I also saw anger flash in Weston's eyes, a scowl that once I would
have cowered under. Immediately I regretted what I had said. But
he was an overbearing sonofabitch and I had never forgotten the
cruel streak in him that had pitched that phony gold watch on the
floor just to see me bend over at his feet and pick it up. Fuck you,
I thought.

Then Weston's face relaxed into that perpetual, piano-key smile
that was his public signature.

"My, how quickly your friends turn on you and pile on when
you're down," he said. "What did you have for breakfast that made
you so ornery, David Aahthuh?"

"A big dose of the *Defender*, I guess, just like you got," I said.

"Screw the goddamn colonel," Weston said. "I'm gonna beat
Binghamton's ass anyway and Tex's Ham and Biscuits will make
us all rich. Tex called me an hour ago and I had to talk him out of
physical violence. Said he was going to rope and hog-tie that little
dwarf and drag him down Board Street.

"Tex is okay. He's been in bar fights before. But I am worried
about Grand. She is old and tired and not taking this too well.
Couldn't come to the phone when I called. My daddy said she had
taken to her bed."

Weston and Pippa wowed them at the Centennial Club. He
left them all believing that John Kennedy's rising tide would lift
them even higher than they already were riding, and Pippa drew
laughter and applause with the concluding sentence of her introduction. "Ladies, I am proud to introduce you to my husband,

Tate Weston, who is a self-made man, which means he thinks he knows everything and won't follow directions."

On the return trip to drop me at the *Clarion* curb, I grilled Weston about how a therapy session with Goebbels could end up transcribed and in the hands of the *Defender*. He had no idea. Goebbels was always taking copious notes, he said, but there had never been a tape recorder obviously in use to his knowledge. Goebbels had been with a patient when Weston had called earlier that day.

"I might have a return call by now at the law office," Weston said. "If not I will call again."

I beat Weston to the punch, but a raspy-voiced answering service told me Goebbels had just left the country for a week and offered to book an appointment if I needed to see him.

"Where did he go?" I asked, pleasantly like it was a casual inquiry.

"I don't know," she said, "and if I did, I would not be at liberty to tell you."

If and when I ever got to Dr. Goebbels, I would be armed with questions to which I already had the answers. Both had come from an unexpected source, Weston's driver. Following the Centennial Club speeches, Nate Larson had dropped Tate and Pippa Weston off at the law office downtown and returned to the *Clarion* parking lot. Rather than come in the newsroom, he had gone to a greasy spoon a block away and telephoned a sheepish request that I meet him outside. "You'll understand when I tell you why," he said.

Larson, then twenty-five and a Peace Corps veteran, had been hanging around the apartment I was sharing with Rhodes Newbold. He had been scholarly enough to be named *Law Review* editor and had a lot of interest in politics. When Weston decided he needed someone else to drive the Pontiac, I had recruited Nate for the job. The Westons had taken to him right off. I knew Tate would because the man was a clothes horse never seen wearing anything but white shirts, colorful neckties and well-cut suits that fit like they had been painted on him; and Pippa was charmed by his good humor and perpetual smile. She said he reminded her of Tate when he was that age, "only much quieter."

What Larson had to tell me was stunning.

"I don't know anything about how that transcript got to the *Defender* and I probably ought to keep my mouth shut," he said. "But there is a woman that works for Goebbels that might be mixed up in this some way. Her name is Eva and she is clearly not your normal receptionist. She's the wife of some big shot, and serves as the doc's answering service, too. When they are not in the office, his office phone rings in her house somewhere out in West End."

Goebbels' practice was a little strange. He kept no regular office hours and only showed up for previously arranged appointments, as did she. The elevator to the penthouse required a key, and when Larson first started driving Weston, they used to have to wait in the Pontiac for either Eva or the doc to arrive. But then Weston came up with his own key, and the visits to Goebbels' office became more frequent, sometimes two or three a week. And they were not all therapy sessions either, at least not the normal doctor-patient relationship. Other beautiful women showed up to be with Weston.

"The place was more party house than anything else," Larson said, "Once they even brought one for me."

"Weston made no bones about it: Goebbels and Eva were a red-hot affair until that blackberry business hit the paper. Then the doc broke it off and Eva wasn't at all happy about that. They had a helluva fight in the parking garage. She shot him the finger as he was driving away. I'll tell you this. She's even gorgeous when she's raving mad and yelling 'Fuck you.' Wait until you see her."

The office where the celebrity shrink earned his living was in the penthouse of a high-rise condominium on the edge of the hospital district that separated downtown from the swanky West End neighborhoods. It was pouring cats and dogs so I pulled into the underground garage and parked my ten-year-old Ford convertible, with its ridiculous painted-on signage—"Built and Tuned by Dick Hoffman." While waiting for the elevator, I looked back on it parked amidst what I assumed to be a platoon of "doctor cars"— shiny new Cadillacs, Mercedes and BMWs. How out of place did this East-of-the-River hot rod relic look? Who in the hell was "Dick Hoffman" anyway? If I didn't know, nobody else would either. Even if I couldn't afford something better, I needed to get rid of that car. It was no longer me—or I was no longer it.

The elevator door opened when you pushed the button and closed when you got inside. But it would not move without the key. I went to the condominium office but got no help. Only Dr. Goebbels or his assistant could permit me entry. Calling the answering service number had been futile so I got back in the Ford and headed for West End. Larson had been right on all counts. I only had his word, but in this case, his word might be enough to let me bluff my way through.

Eva was Mrs. Jefferson Madden, wife of a Bluff City moneyman, who in the *Clarion* morgue clippings was described as the biggest contributor to the Republican Party and the second or third largest stockholder in both the Holiday Inn and Kentucky Fried Chicken franchises. They lived in a hotel-size mansion on a cul-de-sac off of West End Boulevard that had its own name—Jefferson Place—presumably after the owner.

The voice I had heard on the phone belonged to a statuesque brunette who answered the doorbell with an attitude just as raspy—and bedroom eyes that could not be disguised by her all-business horn-rimmed glasses. And she was indeed the looker that Nate Larson had told me she was—less like a receptionist than the trophy wife of a billionaire. What a woman like her was doing as receptionist for a psychiatrist was the first question I asked.

"I majored in psychology at Emory and Dr. Goebbels is a close friend of my husband's," she said. "So a year or so ago when his receptionist took a maternity leave, he took me up on my offer to help out. She never came back and I enjoy the work. Besides, it keeps me off the street. And now, what the hell business is it of yours anyway?"

"None of my business," I said, with all the confidence gained in a couple of years of journalistic education from Jack Hickenlooper and Red Whitmore. "I work for the *Clarion*. It's *Clarion* business I am here on."

She did not invite me in. Instead she kept me standing on the stoop and spoke to me from behind a half-open storm door, which I didn't expect to stay open long. I got right to the point.

"When did you start taping Tate Weston's sessions with Dr. Goebbels?" I said.

She looked like I had just thrown cold water in her face. For a second, only her eyes spoke and I couldn't tell whether they were spewing anger or pleading for mercy. For sure, she had been pushed off balance and was trying to recover.

"I...I...I don't know what you're talking about," she snapped, finally. "Ask somebody else."

"Who else is there?" I said. "Either you or Goebbels are responsible for that transcript being in the *Defender*. Either you gave it to them, or he did and you're covering for him."

"You're crazy," she said. "Get the hell out of here before I call the police."

"Go ahead and call them," I said. "I probably will know whoever shows up to arrest me by his first name and the names of his children. That's what you really need right now, isn't it—a public airing of all this? I know all about the affair you have been having with Goebbels."

"That sonofabitch Weston told you," she shot back. "You're that flack that writes all his bullshit publicity. He sent you here to intimidate me, didn't he?"

"The *Clarion* sent me to find out who violated all the privacy laws and Dr. Goebbels' medical oath by identifying his patients and putting what they said to him in the afternoon newspaper."

"Get the hell off my property," she said. "I have no comment."

"Okay, I will," I said. "But when I leave I will go directly downtown to Madden Properties and ask these questions of Jefferson

Madden. He is your husband, isn't he? You talk to me now and maybe we can make all of this just go away."

Her attitude softened immediately.

"Come on in," she said.

Eva Madden never admitted being the anonymous mailer of the transcript straight to the home of Colonel May, who lived only four blocks away in her neighborhood, the estate section of West End deep in the virgin forest with its ancient trees. But she did tell me that as part of her employment arrangement with Dr. Goebbels, she was allowed to listen in on some of his therapy sessions as part of her continuing education as a psychologist and that indeed she did tape them from time to time to prepare herself for later discussions with Goebbels.

"Did you tape that Weston session that showed up in the paper?"

"I may have."

"Did you tape it?"

"Yes."

"Did you send a copy to the *Defender*?"

"I am not answering that question."

"You don't have to. I know you did."

Someone had. One of Red Whitmore's friends said the colonel came in floating on air one day and dropped it on the city desk.

"Bobby says hello," the colonel said, smiling, and pretended to crow like a rooster. "We've got the fucker now. Run it as is with no explanation. I'll have a Straight from the Heart."

I knew that no matter how much detail I got out of Eva Madden, it would never see the light of day in the *Clarion*. And I was bluffing when I said I would have taken the issue to her husband. In those days, newspapers didn't dig into the dalliances of public figures, other than for titillating tidbits of dinner party conversation. A dozen big name reporters knew that JFK had imported the girl-friend of gangster Sam Giancana for trysts in the White House and never said a word about it except to each other. Voyeur journalism did not come into vogue until years later when the chairman of the House Ways and Means Committee drove into the tidal basin with an Argentine stripper and the leading Democratic candidate for president dared reporters to catch him cheating on his wife—and they did.

Informed that Eva Madden's actions stemmed from an extra-marital affair with the psychiatrist who treats his newspaper's candidate for the United States Senate, Hickenlooper buried his face in his hands and covered his eyes. "Hopeless," he said. "We can't touch this without wrecking two marriages. What the hell was Weston thinking?"

Obviously, he wasn't. And he wasn't going to the Senate either. The primary vote was closer than expected, but J. Howard Binghamton went back for another six-year term on the strength of rural voting patterns, and the politically suicidal behavior of Tate Weston. Meanwhile, investors fled Tex's Ham and Biscuits in droves and the feds shut down Community Southern along with twelve other banks. The Packers went to jail for twenty years in the same Florida white-collar prison that held Judge Martin Collins, but the millions they had stashed away were never recovered or fully accounted for. This left the *Defender* to speculate that "Tate Weston and his band of thieves have feathered their bed for the rest of their lives with the proceeds of fraud and corruption perpetrated upon unsuspecting investors left swimming in a cesspool of worthless stock and bankruptcies."

The cloud of corruption and failure would hover over Weston for years to come, but whatever inner force drove his ambition and imagination remained undaunted. After a brief wallow in seclusion and self-pity, he would emerge again, wounds licked clean and healing, with no greater goal than to restore his good name and get even with Colonel Hiram May in the process.

Like any lucky passenger on a derailed train, I walked away from the wreckage, besmirched only by the black eye my career suffered when punched by the *Columbia Journalism Review*, but far better educated than when I had gotten aboard. For the next three months, I had little to do with Weston other than to follow the press reports of bank failures and ultimately futile attempts by the Securities and Exchange Commission to find him guilty of some criminal wrongdoing. The next time I saw him he was putting on his grand arrival act at the Palmer House in Chicago in quest of accommodations superior to those awarded other delegates to the 1968 Democratic National Convention.

Accompanied by his campaign driver Nate Larson and two younger people I had never before seen, Weston was demanding that the assistant manager of the hotel identify the guest the hotel had lodged in the suite he had reserved months ago. And he wanted to know immediately where was the good friend and former college roommate who managed the place, who would certainly straighten out this terrible mistake. The assistant manager had disappeared from view for a few minutes, presumably to phone whomever it was that Weston claimed to have known since childhood—and eventually returned with a key to the penthouse.

"He didn't have any damn reservations," Larson whispered to me. "But they say the place they just gave us is a palace. Why don't you come stay with us? We have plenty of rooms. The tear gas will never get up that high."

Some more of Weston was the last thing I needed. Hickenlooper had brought me to Chicago as part of a *Clarion* team to cover the convention that would have surely nominated his close friend, United States Senator Robert Kennedy, had he not been assassinated earlier in Los Angeles. The ultimate nomination of Vice President Humphrey was a foregone conclusion by then, but everybody that was anybody in the Democratic Party was there, Tate Weston being no exception. He long-armed me around the neck and pulled me into the elevator with his entourage.

"Of course I am heah, David Aahthuh," Weston quipped, obviously for the benefit of Larson and the rest of his entourage. "You were there the day Hubert and I became very close friends. How much money you think I raised for him that day? A million, maybe two, didn't I, David Aahthuh? They were emptying their wallets even before he showed up, weren't they, David Aahthuh?"

"Absolutely, Tate," I said. "You were at your best that day."

"Indeed," he said. "And I am here to help him defeat that degenerate scumbag Nixon. Hubert should put me on the road for him, don't you think? My own little Humphrey campaign."

That did not materialize, at least right away. Because even before the street rioting broke out and the Palmer House was tear gassed, Weston had left his entourage behind and departed as abruptly and expectedly as he had arrived. His beloved Grand—Clara Hancock

Weston—had passed away at age eighty-five of pneumonia and a failed heart—"no doubt broken by grief and stress" as Weston would allege in an impassioned eulogy widely reported by the national press, including a cover quote and picture in *People* magazine.

Meanwhile, back in Chicago, in furtherance of my career and continuing education program, Hickenlooper was introducing me to every media contact, party mogul and political contact among the conventioneers, including Massachusetts Senator Ted Kennedy, whose eulogy to his brother keynoted one of the most raucous and widely reported conventions in the country's political history. Inside the convention hall, Humphrey's establishment Democrats turned back the challenge of the anti-war movement candidate Eugene McCarthy, who had inherited many Robert Kennedy supporters. And outside, Mayor Richard Daley's police cracked the skull of the anti-war movement hippies protesting Humphrey's nomination and the glass on the front doors of the Palmer House.

Hickenlooper also presented me with the challenge of matching my reporting and writing skills against those of Peter Lisagor, the great *Chicago Daily News* Washington correspondent, whose coverage of the convention would be flowing daily back into the *Clarion* newsroom each night.

"If your work is not as good as his," Hickenlooper declared, "Lisagor's byline will be on the front page, not yours."

Lisagor never pushed me off the page, not because mine was better I am certain, but more likely because Hickenlooper wanted his still-green protégé from east of the river to believe it was. Apparently, I must have passed all of Hickenlooper's tests at the Chicago convention because not long afterward I was assigned to cover another, this one the annual meeting of the Southern Newspapers Publishers Association in Atlanta where both he and Weston, as the *Clarion*'s lawyer, were to appear on a panel discussion on the hottest topic in the industry— chain ownership of newspapers. One by one, the traditional sole proprietor newspapers like the *Clarion* were being gobbled up by publicly held corporations as the second and third generations began to cash in on the equity fortunes built by their fathers and grandfathers.

No one held more vehement opposing views to being gobbled up than Hickenlooper, who said so to anyone who would listen. And on the pro side of the panel was the hungriest gobbler of them all, Ike Oldham, known as "Big Ike," founder of Citycorp News Company. A Canadian entrepreneur who had made his fortune as a bone-picker of failing auto parts companies, Oldham was looking for new bones to pick, and was rapidly building an empire of small market daily newspapers.

SNPA always met in Atlanta and I had driven down a day early from Bluff City in a rental with instructions to pick up Hickenlooper and Weston when they arrived the following day at the airport. On the ride into town, it became evident that our side of the panel was girding for a fight.

"I heah this Big Ike character is an egotistical asshole," Weston said.

"I hope so," Hickenlooper replied, "Bob Kennedy always liked enemies who were assholes. What's the old saying, best defined by the enemies you make?"

"How the hell he get to be called Big Ike?" Weston wondered. "He's a short little shit."

"A little Napoleon, they say. But big aspirations, big talker, too," Hickenlooper said. "Least that's his reputation."

The publishers were meeting at a new downtown Hyatt Regency Hotel, an architectural phenomenon because the rooms on each floor were situated around a spectacular atrium served by elevators that were all glass on three sides. Riding up to your room you had the sensation of lifting rapidly straight up off the lobby floor like a helicopter take off. As luck would have it, the door on the glass cage Weston, Hickenlooper and I were about to take reopened at the last minute and in stepped Big Ike.

The only things obviously big about Oldham were a barrel chest contesting the buttons on his white open-collar shirt and an ominous presence suggesting he might be about to huff and puff and blow your house down. Gold neck chains were the rage back then with a certain kind of man, and Ike wore a doozy, glistening through a nest of black chest hairs. Otherwise, he was slick as a puppy's peter, silver, razor-cut hair tight to his cranium, tanned and tailored to a T in varying shades of gray, black and white—newspaper colors. No one had ever seen him wear anything else. With Weston and Hickenlooper already in place, very little oxygen was left in the cage. Big Ike sucked up the excess in his first breath and began siphoning ours while spewing cordial bullshit about how much he admired the *Clarion* and hoped to someday own at least one newspaper like it. He greeted Hickenlooper like a much admired peer or old friend, while carefully measuring the half-foot taller Weston with eyes that appeared to turn green with envy for a half second and then back to cool gray, as if sizing him up as a possibly formidable foe in some future combat.

Weston, by nature, exuded his usual casual charm, equally delighted to meet the president of the United States or the Negro shoeshine boy at the airport. He almost always beat them all to the handshake draw, too, literally capturing their hand in his right, while his left found a shoulder to pat here and an elbow to cup there. He saw everyone as his next big client or if not, at least a voter somewhere down the road, on which to bestow his perpetual smile, revealing more perfect pearly white teeth than ought to be any single mouth. Weston also frequently had the advantage of looking down on whomever he was meeting with the confidence of someone who believed he had the right to do so, someone who knew he was the smartest man in the room and figured everyone else would eventually reach the same conclusion.

On the dais later that afternoon, the fight the *Clarion* side wanted never materialized. Hickenlooper spoke directly to the old owner-publishers, warning that the loss of local newspaper control would turn them into slaves of Wall Street. But Oldham spoke directly to their heirs, many of whom were present, and to the Wall Streeters, who always monitored these meetings, arguing—quite correctly—that most locally owned daily newspapers were poorly managed underachievers robbing their readers and advertisers of quality and their owners of the cash flow needed to improve.

"Of course, there are notable exceptions," he said. "Our objective at Citycorp News is to re-model our acquisitions in the mold of the best local papers among you—such as the *Courier Journal* in Louisville, the *Register* in Des Moines and Mr. Hickenlooper's prestigious *Clarion* in Bluff City."

Hickenlooper and Weston smiled at the guile of "Big Ike" and joked that the SNPA had just heard a speech by "a wolf in wolf's clothing" and returned to Bluff City with no idea at whose door that wolf might eventually appear.

I remembered thinking thirty was old. But no longer, having just celebrated that milestone by sleeping with a woman I shouldn't have and realizing that I will regret it for the rest of my life, which could be a while. Only the good die young.

She had tendered the offer as a deserving birthday gift for a deprived soul who had endured months of celibacy as a result of a job change and relocation to Washington D.C., where sex is apparently restricted to elected officials and the lobbyists who supply it for them. And even though she was the longtime companion of my best friend and benefactor Rhodes Newbold, I accepted it with the pathetic rationalization that since his other friends were fucking her, why not me, too.

Actually, there is a good chance that Greta Swift, the Georgia tart that had been with Rhodes off and on for five years, was acting more out of her own deprivation than mine. Somewhere in the middle of the night she had cried and confessed that through several years of friendship, including many nights in the same bed with Rhodes, they never had intercourse, apparently due to erectile dysfunction beyond her ability to rectify no matter how hard she tried. And that was saying something because Greta had skills that could raise the dead. If she were my pharmacist, I'd get my prescription filled one pill at a time.

More troubling to my porous conscience than the belated shame of cuckolding my friend was learning that impotency was probably the reason Newbold had been drinking himself to death, and perhaps already had. Earlier that morning we had signed him into Johns Hopkins with a belly the size of a small watermelon and the complexion of a banana. The immediate diagnosis was liver failure requiring immediate dialysis, an illness that might kill him within a week.

Nearly ten years had passed since the night I accepted my first sip of whisky ever from the last swig of a half pint of Jack Daniels that he had consumed in less than an hour. From the way his liver looked to the Johns Hopkins experts, his quip that night that his first taste had been through the nipple of a baby bottle may not have been apocryphal after all.

Neither of us was the same person we had been that night. After several years of friendly rivalry and even friendlier revelry on the *Clarion* back row, we had flown almost in tandem from Hickenlooper's nest of rising journalism superstars, me to the *Morning Herald* as a national political correspondent and Rhodes as a desk editor in the Washington bureau of the *Times*, both glad to be gone and sorry to have left. I had already settled in a Watergate apartment and Rhodes stayed with me for a while until Greta showed up and they got their own place.

We had been mostly a threesome ever since, Rhodes and I back to friendly rivalry during the day, caught up in the fierce competition between the two Big Apple newspapers, and at night the same old pals sharing dinner now and then but drinks every night at a newsie bar called "The Rooster is Black." The first one of us to leave the office always left the same telephone message for the other—"Seeya at the Chicken." Greta joined us frequently and I always left before they did. The problem was Rhodes not only saw me at the Chicken, he took the chicken home with him and nursed it well into the morning. And unbeknownst to me, the first thing every morning he'd take up that chicken again. Physically, there wasn't much to Rhodes to start with, but now he was a skeleton with a potbelly. When we first met, he was a good golfer and a better than average tennis player. But the drinking had taken its toll. Instead of singles on a tennis court, his exercise regimen had deteriorated into playing hit and giggle doubles in badminton and Rhodes was not very good at that.

I only discovered what sorry shape he was really in when we found ourselves ensconced in the famous Belvedere Hotel chasing the same sordid story. Only a president as crazy and corrupt as Nixon could pick a vice president as petty and shoddy as Spiro Agnew. And only the smallness of the world we lived in could have put us in that place at that time, Rhodes leading a team of Timesmen and me a lone wolf for the *Morning Herald*, vying to see which one of us could nail Agnew for accepting free tailored suits. Rhodes was staying in the suite the *Times* had rented as a task force office and I had a room on another floor, but we had planned to meet for breakfast the first morning after we arrived.

Rhodes showed up with Greta in tow and a large brown paper bag in the crook of his elbow. The reporter in me should have suspected something was up when Greta ordered the giant "Union Man Special" breakfast and Rhodes only coffee and a large orange juice. I thought maybe he had some carry-out delicacy in the bag he had deposited on the tabletop.

"What's in there?" I asked.

"Lunch," he said, a response that for no apparent reason meant more to Greta than to me because it provoked an immediate smirk and a fit of eyelash batting.

"Aren't you going to eat breakfast?" I asked. "You look like a refugee."

"Thank you," he said. "Greta just ordered a dog's bait and I'll eat hers." Now and then, the rural Alabaman in Rhodes pierced his normal aristocratic veneer. And he was always quick with a humorous double-entendre. "Believe me," he quipped, "she is used to me eating hers."

Greta giggled the way an eighth-grade girl might do at a remark like that and as I suspected she might even do while he was eating hers, but I let the remark hang in the air as their private erotic secret, the significance of which was yet to dawn on me.

Rhodes did grab a fork and pick at the fried potatoes in Greta's Union Man Special but hardly enough to qualify as eating. He only drank half of his orange juice, too, but poured the remainder into a small glass jar he pulled from the paper bag. "Lunch," he said again, and rolled the top of the brown bag down, until it looked like exactly that.

The second morning at breakfast was a repeat of the first, except sans Greta who was "sleeping in," according to Rhodes, who looked like death on a stick and was moving around like a turtle. He had not been that way the night before, when he and Greta became animated and poking fun at me for being befuddled by some strange objects occupying a half acre of trash cans at the Lexington Street outdoor market in downtown Baltimore. Whatever they were looked like deflated softballs with eight squiggly legs and a set of pliers on one end.

"What you do with those?" I asked.

"You eat them, dummy," Greta said.

"You're kidding," I said. "How?"

To my knowledge, there had never been a soft-shell crab in Mill Town.

When we got back to the Belvedere, Rhodes and I discovered that Hickenlooper had sent us a present. Attached to a pay phone in the lobby was the venerable face of the *Bluff City Clarion*, Red Whitmore, who quickly ended his conversation. "I'll have to call you back," I heard him say.

"Jack sent me up," he said, "figured you guys needed some supervision."

Rhodes and I had been friends so long that by then we had similar reactions simultaneously, and immediately glanced at each other. I read the look on his face as puzzlement, which was how mine was intended. Neither of us could remember the *Clarion* ever sending Red out of town to cover a breaking news story of any kind, particularly a national scandal like the investigation of a vice president. There had to be some other reason.

Whitmore was a human vacuum sweeper of local news, who hated airplanes and seldom traveled anywhere beyond the range of his Plymouth. He actually preferred to gather news by telephone or on foot, like a hunter daily checking his traps, tapping sources at the state capitol here, the city hall there and the United States courthouse in between. But he was even more efficient at mining the town's underbelly, places like Uptown Billiards, whose extraordinary number of pay telephones were not there to accommodate large numbers of husbands signaling late home arrivals. It was in fact a hotbed of illegal gambling and widely believed the terminal from which the daily numbers racket bets were laid off to Chicago. And even on his off days, Red found a reason to saunter late in the afternoon through News Alley, downtown's lone strip of nightclubs and stop for a chat with Simon "Bones" Cohen, who, rain or shine, could be found in a chair outside his famed "Starlite Room" taking in the sun and not-so-fresh air with his collection of toy dogs on leashes lashed to his chair. Everybody knew "Bones" was "connected" out of town, but had a different idea to where and to what else other than the bevy of local ladies of the evening for which he was ready reference.

I later learned it was to "Bones" Cohen that Red had been connected by phone line when we walked up on him in our hotel lobby. Red spent the next day hanging around the *Times* and *Morning Herald* headquarters and picking our brains on the Agnew case, which we both knew would constitute the bulk of his "reporting" and that whatever we told him would show up in the *Clarion* the next day attributed to "sources close to the case." But we didn't mind. Both of us owed him for years' worth of education and took him to dinner the following night when Rhodes and the tart had promised to prove that deflated softballs could be eaten. They guided Red and me to O'Bricki's, which they claimed was the best restaurant in town, but which I doubted because it only had newspapers for tablecloths and garage tools for eating utensils.

Whitmore kept getting up and visiting O'Bricki's lone pay telephone and toward the end of the meal, when the tart had gone for a potty break, Newbold said, "Now Red, Arthur and I have given you every piece of information we have. Are you holding out on us? All this phone work you're doing suggests you are working some inside source here in Baltimore that we don't have or you wouldn't be up here in first place."

Red did one of his physical contortions that made him look like Don Quixote tilting at windmills and let out a barrage of high-pitched "hee-hees." "Shit, No. I don't know a soul up here but you guys," he said. "When you walked up last night I was talking to Bones Cohen at the Starlite. He told me last night he was sending a couple of whores over to my room at the Belvedere and they never came. Now he just told me they got their days mixed up and they're coming tonight."

"Well, what the hell are you doing up here anyway?" I asked. "The *Clarion* takes Newbold's paper's wire service and mine. Is Hickenlooper that hot on this story that he wants a *Clarion* byline on it?"

"Hell no," Red said. "He just wanted me out of town for a few days because I got my tail in a crack."

About then, the tart appeared from the potty and slinked toward the table, and Red said he'd have to tell us later, but he never did. I expected him to join the three of us for breakfast the next day, but he left on an early flight and I never found out what crack his tail was in until years later when I moved back to Bluff City.

At breakfast that next morning, Newbold slowly retrieved from his pocket a crusted crab leg from the night before. "You're a believer now, aren't you," he declared. "Just attach this to one of your college diplomas. Continuing education is a wonderful thing."

Again he ordered only coffee and a large orange juice, and when I asked whose breakfast he planned to snack from, he said he could not eat because his stomach was "really bad today."

"From the crabs? What the hell do you mean, really bad today?"

"David, you're beginning to sound like my mother," he admonished. "I don't know what the hell it is, but I've been having trouble in the morning. My belly is so swollen today, I can't even button my pants."

"Jesus Christ," I said. "Have you gone to a doctor? You look awful. You're pale, downright yellow even. Except your nose, which is red as a sugar beet."

"Now you really sound like my mother," Rhodes said, his face breaking into that cherubic angel grin of his. "But Jesus might listen to her. You don't have a chance that he's gonna hear you. Wrong side of the river."

He opened the bag, took out the jar again to deposit the remainder of his orange juice. This time I reached over and pushed the bag open, exposing its contents—an unopened fifth of Smirnoff.

"When did you desert Jack Daniels for Igor?"

"Oh, I haven't deserted Jack." he said. "He is still my pal at night. Vodka is for the daylight."

"What the hell is this?" I asked. "You doing a fifth a day now?"

"Lunch," he said.

Why had it taken me this long to figure it out? The crazy bastard had stopped eating but had continued drinking—a suicidal recipe.

"Hey, Rhodes," I said, sticking my nose in business that was not really mine. "You drink. You don't eat. That'll kill you."

"Excuse me, Mother, and forgive my haste," Rhodes said, aristocratically cool and sarcastic, "but I'm late for my real mother —Mother *Times*." He stood up, rolled down the top of the brown bag and ambled with leaden steps out of the restaurant, a tired-appearing union man on his way to work, lunch in hand.

The only other person I knew at the *Times* was Newbold's deputy, Rob Douglas, who lived in the same apartment building as he did, and often joined us at the Chicken after work, sometimes leaving early with Greta, of which I thought nothing at the time. Douglas had come down to Baltimore, too, to do the desk editing and was probably already at work. I found the nearest hotel phone and called the *Times* suite. He answered.

"Hey Rob, it's me, David," I said. "Our friend Rhodes just left breakfast with a fifth of vodka under one arm, and holding up his pants with the other. His pot is so swollen he can't even button them. I think he's in trouble. You better get him to a doctor. He's in no shape to work."

"I know about it, but he won't listen to me, Dave. You and Greta are going have to do it. He'll listen to you two, if anyone."

"When you see her, tell her to call me in my room SAP."

She never called, but showed up outside my door instead.

"Rhodes is on the road to cirrhosis," I said. "Take that damn bottle away from him and you two meet me in front of the hotel. Tell him I have a break in the Agnew story and he better go along or read about it in the *Herald*."

By the time he and Greta showed up on the sidewalk, I had already given the cabbie our destination and taken the front seat. Rhodes and Greta slipped into the back.

"What's up? Where we headed?" Rhodes wanted to know.

"To meet a guy who called me on the phone. Said he had the goods on the VP."

When the cab pulled into the emergency entrance at Johns Hopkins, the Newbold antennae went up. "Your guy in the hospital? Nut ward, I suspect."

"No, he works here," I said.

If Rhodes had any talent greater than his nose for a good story, it was his bullshit detector. As I was getting out of the cab, he yelled, "Wait a goddamn minute, what are you two up to? Goddamn you, Greta, what have you been telling him? I'm not getting out of this cab until you tell me what the hell is going on."

"Even to save your own life?" I asked.

"Hell, no. Not even for that," he quipped.

I pushed Greta away from the rear passenger door and reached in for Rhodes.

"If you don't get your sick, scrawny little ass out of his cab, I'm gonna drag you out of there and all the way to the nurse's desk. And you know damn well I can do it."

For a few seconds Rhodes considered trying me, then thought

better of the idea. "But just long enough to get something for my stomach, okay?"

"Okay, Rhodes. Okay."

Forty-eight hours later, he slipped into a coma. When he finally came out of Johns Hopkins, it was in a bag on a gurney headed for a shipping box and a plane trip to New Orleans. His family, a mother and a sister I only knew as voices on the phone, said they wanted to see him one more time before cremation. Bodies aren't buried in the ground in New Orleans anymore because they float up again after heavy rains.

In a few weeks, Greta, Rob Douglas and I flew down for a memorial—a "celebration of life" at his mother's house. It was one of those lovely bungalows in the Garden District where she and his sister Naomi had moved from Alabama a decade earlier in what I reckoned to be an attempt to distance themselves from unpleasant memories. Rhodes had told me that his father, the town's most prominent attorney, had put a pistol in his mouth and blown the top of his head off on a sidewalk outside the courthouse. A confirmed but untreated and secretive alcoholic, Rhodes Newbold Jr. had not drawn a sober breath in years. On an end table in the sun porch was his framed law license, Harvard '48, and beside it a picture of him in a three-piece suit and horn-rimmed glasses. The squatty, froggish Rhodes had been his spittin' image.

Mrs. Newbold was a New Orleans native, and by all appearances one of those Iron Magnolias, slim, tall and stately with pewter hair crafted like a skullcap, stoic in her grief, and the sister Naomi a carbon copy, but with rich brunette hair to her shoulders and a model's figure. Both reeked with the graciousness of the well-conditioned New Orleans hospitality. It was obviously from the female side of the family that Rhodes had inherited his aristocratic manners and kind nature.

The memorial was a small affair, with a doddering old brother of Mrs. Newbold, Uncle Somebodyorother, and couple of Naomi's New Orleans friends who had met Rhodes previously. A Bluff City Air charter delivered a group from the *Clarion*, including Hickenlooper, fat Herman, the photographer Billy Morehead, and to my surprise, the airline's gloriously seductive and entertaining manager, Allston Williams, who had gotten to know Rhodes during frequent visits to his apartment where I had lived until I left the *Clarion*. She had a reason for injecting herself into the flight, and the first minute we were alone she invited me out in the garden just off Mrs. Newbold's sun porch to let me in on it.

New Orleans is a dank, sunken basin of odors in fierce conflict—gasoline, burning rubber, petro-chemicals and spilled whiskys. You can smell it twenty miles away by land and its breath hits you in the face the minute you get off the plane. But it is also a freak of nature, at the same time lush with fragrant tropical foliage—banana trees, hibiscus, crepe myrtle and sweet olive—ambrosial fragrances that overwhelm the sewage breath of the downtown swamp once you reach the Garden District.

Mrs. Newbold's backyard was a flowerbed of vivid tropical blooms and red climber roses, green and yellow bananas and peach-colored angel trumpets of bougainvillea, and naturally, a bouquet of aromas, most prominent among them the night-scented jasmine worn by my childhood sweetheart. No longer the Annette of the *Mickey Mouse Club*, she looked more like her stylish beau monde mother Henri, always the real beauty in the family. Henri's step up in the world had layered her with a veneer of socialite polish, some of which had obviously rubbed off on her daughter, who had traveled to the Big Easy in a high-fashion three-piece pant suit, glen plaid in autumn colors topped off by a snazzy black beret.

The true nature of my lifelong weakness and eternal burning in my loins for this woman could only have been love, which I have never been able to define to my satisfaction despite all the musings of poets and philosophers. I knew what familial love felt like because I surely loved my mother Sallie Mae. But nothing else in my limited experience had been so gloriously, miserably and persistently distracting as the urgency of whatever it was I had for Allston. It must have had something to do with love because my feelings for her and my mother had one thing in common. Though in vastly different ways, they both made me feel wanted. And Allston had made me feel wanted in the best of ways and to want her with every bone, muscle and nerve in my body since I was a boy. Always quick to profess her feelings as love, she promised her love to me forever, but for some inexplicable reason I was always just as quick to doubt her sincerity.

And then there was this problem of her marrying other men, and me never finding the right time to ask her to marry the right man—again. We were a tragic comedy all right—of errors. First there was her mother Henri's objection to my low-rent lineage and her vindictive effort to have me imprisoned for kidnapping, then Allston marrying the thug Randy. And then me hesitating to propose because I was too poor to support her and Randy's child, and then moving off to Washington without her because she was reluctant to leave her mother and her good job in Bluff City. And now, she had come to Rhodes Newbold's wake for no other reason than to tell me she was about to get married again so Randy's son would not grow up without a father.

"He could have had a father in Washington that was finally earning a *Morning Herald* salary instead of a *Clarion* rice-and-peanut-butter salary," I said.

"And you could have stayed in Bluff City and not worked at all because I make enough to support us all," she replied.

"That's the problem," I said. "If Woody Arthur has really gone off somewhere and died of a high-blood pressure stroke like Sallie Mae believes, he would turn over in his grave. Being able to support his family was his one source of pride and the only thing he ever taught me except don't ride the clutch. Anyway, who is this lucky bastard you've fallen in love with?"

"Who said I had fallen in love with him?" she said, haughtily. "Besides I can never love anyone like I have loved you."

She moved closer to me and put her arms around my neck, resting them on my shoulders, the jasmine as seductive as the garlic had been nauseating at Blackberry Farm, which was the last time we had been alone together.

"You smell a lot better now than you did the last time I saw you," I said.

"Damn you, Vic," she said, smiling. "Can't you ever be serious?"

"Can't I ever be serious? That is the pot calling the kettle black if ever I heard it. When have you ever been serious in all these years?"

"I am being serious now," she said. "There is only one love like ours in a lifetime. But for some reason I don't understand, we are never going to be together. I am not leaving my hometown. I do not want my son to grow up in Washington or New York, or any place like that. And those places are where you must always be to do the work you love. You have flown the coop, Vic, darling, and you will never come back and I just have to accept that and so do you."

I had no rational argument to put up. She was right. She wasn't leaving and I was never going back, or so I believed at the moment. We were indeed cursed. Cursed by happenstance of time and place and our own stubbornness and ineptitude. What else was there to say?

The celebration of Rhodes Newbold's life turned into a liquored-up litany of Rhodes remembrances. Jack Hickenlooper brought Rhodes' mother and sister to tears with a touching tribute to his extraordinary rise to the top at both the *Clarion* and the *Times*. "As a reporter and a young editor—good as I have ever seen," he said, tweaking a pang of envy I sometimes felt during my years of head-on competition with Rhodes. As critical as Hickenlooper's generosity and encouragement had been to my own career, my Mill Town inferiority complex compelled me to feel that he had favored Rhodes and regarded him the superior talent.

But I had to agree. I told them the story of how Rhodes had steered me through my worst moment of self-doubt and over the first hump in my career by actually crafting with cool questioning the first story I ever wrote for the *Clarion*; how competing against him had honed my own skills, and how unusual it was that my most fierce competitor was also my best friend, an utterance that made me glance at Greta Swift and wonder all over again why I had let the passion of a moment undermine the integrity of a decade of close friendship.

Mrs. Newbold, who nursed a single glass of club soda through the entire evening, watched Greta and Rob closely, particularly when they got up to freshen their drinks, and I could not help wondering what was going through her mind. Was she was putting two and two together, somehow faulting one or the other, or both, for abetting her son's lethal addiction to alcohol? Mothers tend to want to blame others for the failure of their sons. They have an acute sense of betrayal, too, and maybe hers had been at work assessing the obviously familiarity between the two. But she could not blame them for her boy's faulty genetic wiring. His father had been a drunk and ultimately mentally defective, and Rhodes had not kept his own excessive imbibing a secret from his mother or anyone else. But had she any idea of why her husband drank? Or possibly have known that Rhodes might be doing so out of frustration over his impotence? She never let on about either.

The affair at the Newbold home ended with a toast by the sister Naomi, who raised her glass of Chablis to "a brother unique in the breadth of his talent and the size of his warm and caring heart." My first drink of whisky had come from Rhodes Newbold's half pint as we were getting to know each other in my Ford at the curb outside the *Clarion* when I was twenty. And since then I had moved from drinking Jack Daniels straight to Scotch on the rocks and finally to double martinis that for the one and only time had rendered me too drunk to remember an entire day of drinking and driving in the

D.C. traffic. Ten years later the glass I raised to Rhodes in the sun porch of his mother's house contained a swig of Jim Beam from a bottle that Red Whitmore had sent along with Billy Morehead. It would be my last. Sallie Mae Arthur had been right about old John Barleycorn. He had robbed me of a relationship with my father and taken my best friend. I figured I had given him enough.

When I lowered the glass from my lips, I felt the familiar eyes of the teetotaling woman who had told me so many times that "lips that touch liquor will never touch mine." Of course, the lovely bundle of contradiction was staring at me with a glass of water in one hand and a stick of killer tobacco in the other. I walked over to say goodbye, figuring her charter would be heading back to Bluff City.

"Your plane going back tonight?" I asked.

"No," Allston said. "It's too late. We're going back tomorrow."

"Where are you sleeping?" I asked, not an entirely innocent query, though I delivered it as such.

"With you," she said, "wherever you're sleeping. I brought you a birthday present."

Indeed she had. She fumbled in her tiny handbag and pulled out a package of Peanut M&Ms, a delicacy we had devoured together many times over the years. I reached for them but she jerked the package away and returned it to her purse.

"Not so fast, Vic," she said. "You have to wait for it."

For IT, I had been waiting a long time. My love life in D.C. had consisted of a brief fling with Sue Anne, a beautiful government bureaucrat with a perfect face, a perfect body and a lovely apartment in my building at the Watergate, where during our overnights her cigarette cough kept me sleepless and whose pillow talk ranged from "my back hurts and your hands are cold" to "you forgot to move my tomato plant in out of the cold off the balcony" and "don't forget to take out my garbage when you leave."

When I left for the last time, I did not take out the garbage.

The next morning the perfect wife that never would be mine was gone with the dawn, and I lay in the airport motel savoring the night before and bemoaning the future. Who knew if or when I would ever see her again?

A month or so later, Red Whitmore telephoned with the news of Allston's marriage to Hamilton V. Jackson III, a fast-rising junior executive at Equitable Life Insurance, the linchpin of her new stepfather's financial empire. His fax of the wedding picture in the *Clarion*'s "Society Section," showed the happy couple being congratulated by old Brownlee Stokes, who had given his stepdaughter away, and nearby his twenty-five-years younger trophy bride, Henri Ravenel Williams Stokes, smiling her approval. The list of notable wedding guests included the name of the bride's stepsister, Pippa Stokes Weston, but no mention of her husband. I had forgotten to ask Red if Weston had been in attendance and what the initial "V" represented in Hamilton V. Jackson's name. Hopefully, not Victor. Surely, Allston would never call him Vic. Then, in a rare moment of bravado, I asked myself, why should I care and what the hell difference would it make if I did? It was like we had agreed in New Orleans: She would never leave Bluff City and I would never go back.

I sat at my desk at the Washington bureau of the *Morning Herald* and stared out the window at Pennsylvania Avenue, only a half-block from the White House but a million miles away from Sallie Mae Arthur in Mill Town and the river, Red Whitmore and the *Clarion*, and even further from Allston and her new life. All those years, I had been reaching for her and a life like she had wanted and now had finally landed—without me. For what should I reach now—if anything?

Not that I didn't have a life and that there was nothing interesting going on around me. The crackpot president of the United States had committed high crimes in office and was about to be impeached. I was up to my ass in the Watergate scandal, the cover-up of a burglary that had taken place in my apartment building. This was a Friday and on Sunday, I would be going on national television—*Meet the Press*—to talk about it, something Sallie Mae Arthur would not want to miss. I wondered what would be the least offensive, a son neglecting to tell his mother, or the perceived braggadocio of one calling up to say, "Hey Mom, look at me. I'm going to be on television Sunday."

I called to tell her.

It was the lunch hour in Washington—or lunch two hours—and long before the era of cell phones when a buzzing in your pocket can disturb you just as the meal reaches the table. So I did what I had become accustomed to doing when I had no luncheon appointment. I walked out of the newspaper's office at 1700 Pennsylvania up Seventeenth Avenue to the winding stairs that led to the Guitar Shop. There someone as talented as the resident luthier Mike Tobias with his flying fat fingers might be playing Delta blues for all the wannabe blues players like myself. And there I could take down one of the fine instruments from the wall and try to emulate what I had just seen and heard. There is no better therapy for a man who has lost his woman than to play a twelve-bar Delta blues about a man who has lost a woman that done him wrong.

"Got the blues...can't be satisfied...Got the blues...can't be satisfied...

"Lose the blues...catch that train and ride."

The train David Arthur would catch would be a long one on a long run, each car in the procession a precious gift of work... work...work...work...work and more work, exhausting but exhilarating and rewarding beyond the imagination of a Mill Town kid whose childhood memories were from a tiny apartment above a grocery store and a window that looked out on train yards of the Tennessee Central. It would take him on the White House lawn to watch a fallen criminal abandon his presidency and wave goodbye to a stunned and saddened nation... to China with his good guy successor Jerry Ford and the inestimable Henry Kissinger whose forays for Nixon into Communist mainland awoke a sleeping mammoth that would eventually become a roguish giant of capitalism; and then to a year's sabbatical at Harvard University and eventually to the collapse of the Berlin Wall and the Soviet Empire and finally to the editorship of the New York *Morning Herald* in a futile attempt to save a dying newspaper.

Along the journey, there would be mournful looks into his rearview mirror, brief moments of reunion with the roots from which he had broken free but never truly could outdistance, mostly fond memories that trailed in his wake like long crooked fingers stretching to touch him and hook into his clothing and slow his escape, calling after him seductively like the Jasmine Lady of the Night beckoning him from the street into the shadows, always lurking there in his orbit like some forsaken but persistent moon.

The Sunday morning his son appeared on *Meet the Press*, Woody Arthur rose from the dead. The grave where Sallie Mae had wished him turned out to have been a houseboat in Key West, from which the father telephoned the son to proudly congratulate him on achievements never thought possible for the grandson of a moonshiner. And they had reminisced about the one time the son remembered when they had done something together, just them, without Sallie Mae and their bickering about Woody's drinking and lack of ambition that would eventually disrupt whatever they were all doing together.

His father had come to his bedroom in the middle of the night to tell him that Brush Creek had flooded in the Cumberland Mountains and that "your Granny Arthur is trapped in the family farm house and needs help."

Under a heavy, black blanket sky, they had driven the fifty miles to the northeast in sheets of driving rain, straight through the storm that had caused the flood. Normally moody and quiet—"sulled up" in the lexicon of his wife—Woody had talked the whole way, explaining the lay of the land around the hilly farm and plotting out loud how they might have to borrow a motorboat to get through the meadow in the gorge that led up to the farm. That was small talk to the son then, but now in retrospect, it was his one and only glimpse into whatever there was in his father, alone in the frozen Argonne Forest, that allowed him to survive the Germans and help his country kill them.

The boy had visited the family farm in the mountains only a few times ever, and only once since his grandfather Jaybird had died of food poisoning. All he remembered about the place was that it was a hundred acres of rock with only a couple of hillsides flat enough to be plowed and hold corn, and a big old barn that stood on stilts over a muddy stream feeding into Brush Creek. His father had done his talking while hunched over the wheel of his base model 1956 Ford, the only new car he'd ever been able to afford, its only "extra" a radio that went in and out and mostly to static in the storm. Never taking his eyes off the road, his father had gripped the steering wheel with both hands like it might be trying to get away and fight the curves and strong winds on its own, in a survival struggle of some kind against the storm and against the driver. Now and then, the boy would see his father's hawk nose dip forward as he appeared to study the neon gauges reflecting his speed and his gas supply, more than once wondering aloud if he had enough fuel to get there.

The place they were headed was called New Middle Town, hardly more than a wide place in a narrow road, with a single store stocking both groceries and hardware, a two-pump filling station, one gas and one diesel, and a garage where a guy named Napoleon, and called "Poleyun" by his father, worked on cars and farm equipment. Poleyun would have a motorboat if they needed it, Woody said. But when they got there, the storm had passed. The water had receded back into the creek bed, and the dim light of dawn revealed only a few ponds scattered across the meadow like big, silver coins between the main road and the Arthur house, which stuck out from the side of a rocky hill so sharply that it looked like it might fall off. The boy remembered it having no backyard to speak of, and that his grandfather had once told him the front porch was exactly five football fields from the main road.

A gravel lane to the house ran down the side of "Poleyun's" garage, which sat on a half acre he had bought from the Arthurs. And as the boy and his father walked by the building, Poleyun stuck his head out a side screen door and said, "You'ins come to check on Miss Ellie, didya? I done checked and she's okay."

"Thankya, Poleyun," Woody said over his shoulder, and they kept trudging through the mud. Already they could see some movement on the porch, something white, up and down, left and right. The closer they got, the more white movement they saw and finally they saw that it was Granny Arthur waving a big towel or a sheet.

"Your Granny Arthur is raising a white flag," Woody said. "Reckon she's surrendered." David Arthur remembered the remark as perhaps the most humorous thing he ever heard his father say.

No longer in need of rescue, Miss Ellie did appear to be in need of a good meal. She was a tiny, wizened figure of eighty years, skin and bones, hair the shade of slate and twisted up in a tight bun. She had a black shawl pulled close around her neck. Clearly the genetic source of his father's hawk nose, she was, in the words of her daughter-in-law, "so tight everywhere she squeaks when she walks." The first words out of Granny's mouth were an apology for calling for help in the middle of the night.

"But Lordy mercy, son. It was raining pitchforks and nigger babies and I didn't know what else to do. That sorry Poleyun didn't answer when I called him. He couldn't hep a hen and chickens anyway. Then you come all the way up here and I didn't need no rescuing, I declare."

"Well, while I'm here," the boy heard his father say, "I might as well take care of that other thing."

"What are you going to do with it?" Miss Ellie said.

"Brush Creek is rolling so hard now I'll just pitch most of it in there and let her float on down. Nobody'll ever know where it came from."

"All that copper is worth something, ain't it, son?"

"Yeah, I'll roll that tubing up and take it home in the trunk of my car. I can sell it in Mill Town. They use it in construction, lights and plumbing and stuff."

After Miss Ellie fired up her woodstove and made them all a fried-egg sandwich on light bread browned in a skillet, the two of them went out to the big barn, which sat off to the side of the house and backed up to the same wooded hillside.

"You better watch that telephone pole now," his father warned. "It'll be slick from this rain and you'll fall in the pigsty again."

Woody was talking about the thick pole that served as a walk-way from the rear of the barn to the hillside and stretched over a muddy creek that once was the home of his grandfather's sows and piglets. When he was eight, the boy had slipped off the pole and landed in a muck of mud and pig shit and was threatened by a 200-pound sow that figured he was either a threat to her piglets or dinner, either of which deserved the same lethal response. He had been jerked from her path by one strong arm of Pappy Jaybird and escaped unharmed except for the taste and smell of hog manure that resided in his senses so long he feared it was permanent.

At age fifteen, the trip over the pole with his father had been completely uneventful. Once across, an immediate right took you down a path behind a line of pines that stayed green and thick year round to a small clearing that was the site of Jaybird Arthur's manufacturing plant. They spent a good part of the morning dismantling the tangle of tanks, tubes, washtubs and woodstove that had been the source of Arthur family income over the years. The pathetic corn crop made no greater contribution than for cornbread and cover for the ceramic jugs of silver firewater in a farm wagon journey to the New Middle Town "corner grocery," from which it was sold outback to a stream of steady customers from surrounding counties and given out freely to county sheriff's officers and the state highway patrol.

Once, in a failed attempt to slide down the banister of a stairway to the second floor of the farmhouse, young David Arthur had slammed into the big decorative knob atop the bottom pole, knocking it to the floor. Three roles of cash and a small caliber pistol came out of its hollow.

"Lordy, mercy," Miss Ellie had wailed. "Bird Arthur had that stuff hidden all over the house, didn't he?"

When the tubs, tanks and woodstove had been pushed into the roaring Brush Creek and the copper tubing had been twisted into rolls and stashed in the trunk of the Ford, Miss Ellie packed her bag and rode back with them to Mill Town to the new house in Belair. Sallie Mae had baked an apple pie and had coffee hot on the stove for the arrivals.

Though she didn't care much for her mother-in-law, Sallie

Mae was a gracious hostess for any visitor and so played the role for the diminutive, hungry-looking old woman from the hills.

"Miss Ellie," she asked, "how do you like your coffee?"— meaning served black or with cream and sugar.

Totally unfamiliar with the nature of the entreaty, Miss Ellie responded with her perpetually tight smile. "Why Sallie Mae," she said, "I like it just fine."

10

Jack Hickenlooper was one of the three moons in my orbit of which I never wanted to lose sight. Next to my mother and long-gone Allston Williams Arthur Sikes—and now Jackson—the publisher of the *Clarion* had been the most important person in my life and would continue to be as long as he lived. None of his contributions was more valuable than his clout in the world of books and newspapers.

By the time I came to work for what was the most admired if not the best newspaper in New York—the *Morning Herald*—I only knew of the city's movers and shakers and stars of the literary world. And they knew of me only by my Washington bylines. But having already pulled me across the river from Mill Town to the edge of West End, Hickenlooper continued to drag me up the career ladder, rung by rung. One glorious day in 1970, he called with news that would change my life again for a second time. Seemingly exceptionally connected everywhere, he had advance knowledge that I had been awarded a coveted Harvard Fellowship that had been established and endowed by the Kennedy family where his support obviously had been far more important than my qualifications.

"And while you're up there," he said, "Why don't you write that book we've been talking about? I'll write the introduction. I think I know somebody at Little Brown who would be interested."

The book was a tome about the politics behind the assassinations of the Kennedy brothers and Martin Luther King. Crafting it took up most of my sabbatical time in Cambridge, that time not spent in all-night bookstores and the law school learning the ins and outs of the legal history of the First Amendment. Hickenlooper's "somebody at Little Brown" turned out to be the intriguing Phoebe, one of the bright "boiler room" women from one of the Kennedy campaigns. She became a brief romantic interest and the book a modest success, the whole affair best summed up by the lyrics of Guy Clark's classic song—*"This book was given me by a girl I used to know...I guess I've read it front to back fifty times or so...it's all about the good life and getting along in the world... Funny how I loved that book...but never loved that girl."*

Fellowships at Harvard are fishing grounds for media moguls trolling for young talent. When mine was completed in the spring of '72, I had more career options than I ever thought possible. But one of the requirements of the award was that I return to the paper from whence I had come. And none of my prospective new employers wanted me more than the owners of the *Morning Herald*. Just like the *Clarion*, it had passed through generation after generation of family ownership, finally landing in the hands of two elderly Blandford sisters. Both were spinsters and being devotees and financial supporters of the Kennedys, they had gone for management advice to Jack Hickenlooper, who told them their thirty-three-year-old political editor just finishing a stint at Harvard's Kennedy School of Government was the perfect choice to try to rescue an unprofitable newspaper on its last legs.

The vaunted *Morning Herald* had a glittering history of international reporting and fine writing. Ernest Hemmingway had filed dispatches to it from the cafés of Paris and the battlefields of Africa. But like many good newspapers at the time it was besieged by two mortal enemies, the growing dependence on television news and Big Ike Oldham's obsessive march toward monopoly. His Citycorp News Company was gobbling up small town dailies right and left and beginning to eye those in larger markets. The day my name appeared on the *Morning Herald* masthead as editor, he was among the first to call with congratulations. He called me David as if we were long acquainted and wasted little time getting to the real point of the call.

"I'm sure the Blandfords have told you that Citycorp has a serious interest in papers like the *Morning Herald*. We've had several conversations already. Up until now, we've been growing by acquiring small dailies with high profit margins, but not all that much quality. I believe you were there in Atlanta when I mentioned our goals of adding bigger and more respected journalism to our brand, papers like the *Clarion,* for example, and the *Morning Herald.*"

The sisters had told me of Oldham's overtures, but in dismissive tones under raised eyebrows. They had watched Big Ike's cost-cutting and profit-making frenzy over the years and found appalling the idea of their beloved *Morning Herald* falling into his hands.

"I have heard about that, Mr. Oldham," I said. "But you surely know that our cash flow and profit margins do not fit the business model of Citycorp. No doubt we would show up as a drag on your bottom line. Your friends over on Wall Street might not like that."

There was a rustling on the other end of the line, like he was switching the phone to another ear, and I could hear paper rustling.

"Of course, we haven't done any serious due diligence because you guys are private and we don't have the numbers," Big Ike came back. "But we are pretty good at estimating costs and revenue. Even if we couldn't improve your bottom line—and I believe we could—we could live with what you're doing now, a couple of points at best if that, is what we've figured. And what we can do in a case like that is put newspapers like yours and the *Clarion* into a different division. The greater financial performance of the bottom group can support the higher quality of the top. Wall Street doesn't care where the growth and profit comes from, as long as it's there. Think it over, David, and the next time I'm in New York maybe we can get together over a meal. I'll call."

"Well, you do that, Mr. Oldham," I said. "People who work on small margin papers like ours always look forward to a free lunch."

The New York market was being fought over by five dailies. Besides the *Morning Herald*, there was the powerful *New York*

Times, two large circulation tabloids—the *Post* and the *Daily News*—and out on Long Island a fast-growing and phenomenally profitable *Newsday*, which published both morning and afternoon, was moving on Manhattan. Efforts by the *Morning Herald* to even maintain our break-even business model failed. There simply were not enough politically progressive and socially liberal readers to be shared by the *Herald* and the *Times*, which had much broader reader and advertising bases. After bleeding red ink every month of my stewardship, I was compelled to offer the sisters the list of options I had compiled in long-distance consultation with Hickenlooper—options that neither I, nor my far more experienced mentor liked.

The *Herald* could abandon its erudite boutique culture, cut back staff and overall content, and jump into the sensation and glitz competition with the tabloids; look for a partner willing to infuse enough cash for expansion and marketing that might allow us to at least keep pace with the *Times*; or hang a "for sale" sign on its masthead.

The sisters Blandford would have none of it, so we struggled on, and two years to the day after my appointment, the sisters shut it down, rather than watch the quality deteriorate from cost cutting, or sell to a bone-picker like Ike Oldham. Though *Morning Herald* journalism was still winning accolades and remained the darling the progressive arts and literary segment of the biggest newspaper market in the country, I earned the distinction of presiding over the death of a great newspaper—while it was still great, and turned out on the street one of the most talented and diverse staffs of journalists ever assembled, to be gobbled up by *Herald* competitors.

The last call I took as editor of the *Morning Herald* was a long-distance condolence from Hickenlooper. On the speaker with him was the newspaper's chief counsel who began talking over Hickenlooper from the first "Hello."

"David Aahthuh, Weston heah, I hope to hell by now you have matuhed sufficiently to dress propahly foh New Yawk. They don't cotton to rustics in the Big Apple, you know."

"As a matter of fact, Tate, I am wearing a piece of Brooks Brothers' cloth so fine that it would give the tailor Tony an orgasm if he touched it," I said. "You have been replaced as my wardrobe advisor by a stunning Jewess to whose influence I have happily surrendered."

"I hope the bitch is rich, picks them out herself and has them sent over to the *Morning Herald*," he yelled. "You are too tight and onery to buy 'em, and too unfashionable to pick them out for yahself."

Hickenlooper finally got a word in, business as usual.

"I'm calling to tell you first how sorry I am and second that I hear Big Ike's sniffing around your carcass before it evens gets cold," he said.

Indeed he had been. He had called the sisters in a last-minute effort to buy the *Herald*'s famous name and brand, but they had rejected it.

"All he wanted was the masthead and me," I said. "Some cock-amamie idea about launching an *International Morning Herald* daily. But Amy Blandford can't stand him. Says he looks like a pimp and that never would she let the *Herald* name fall into the hands of a man 'who wears funny leisure suits and jewelry around his neck.'"

When the guffaws subsided on the other end of the line, I asked, "How'd you know what Citycorp was up to? It hasn't been two hours since he called."

"Weston was just on the phone with Ike," Hickenlooper explained. "The *Clarion* lawyer has started sleeping with the enemy, you know."

"How could he do that after that panel discussion you two had down in Atlanta?"

"He's a lawyer, which is diagnostic," Hickenlooper said. "They're all for sale."

I could hear Weston howling.

"That man's a beah in bed. But he weahs all that jewelrea and it rattles around and keeps you awake. But theah is always a method to my madness, David Aahthuh, you know that...a pot ah gold at the end of evah rainbow."

"Weston's is now Big Ike's point man on acquisitions," Hickenlooper said, obviously jovial at the prospect. "How about that! The *Clarion* attorney a scout for Sitting Bull."

"And every time a General Custer loses his scalp," Weston said, "Weston and Clark collect a commission and fees on the kill."

Then Hickenlooper led us off into a discussion of the dim future of newspapering. In cities where they were competing dailies, both were suffering losses in readers and revenue. The weaker of the two found the going hard and ended up looking for buyers. In the more promising markets, Citycorp was buying them and then negotiating joint-operating agreements. The one between the *Clarion* and the *Defender* had become Citycorp's model.

Times, they were a-changing, as the saying goes, and the last visitor to my office that evening, the *Herald*'s business editor, Melody Kane, offered no better proof. She had also been my first visitor two years before—but then in an earlier edition named Martin, bringing me my initial management crisis. He showed up at my office wearing a pair of black men's trousers and a frilly feminine blouse. He wore serious horn-rimmed glasses but had diamonds pierced in both ears and a touch of rouge on his cheeks. He was affable and professional but the two female members of his staff accompanying him were both stiff and sour—a demeanor Sallie Mae Arthur used to describe as, "looking like they'd just had a vinegar douche."

I motioned to the three chairs across from my desk set in a row and asked them to be seated. Kane took me up on it, but the women refused and remained standing with their hands on their hips in the classic mode of tired or pissed-off combatants. One of them, a columnist specializing in women's issues, said, "This won't take long. As you can see, Martin is undergoing a life-changing experience. He has had a sex-change operation. And after all these years of using the men's room, he is now using the ladies' room and all of us ladies are mad as hell about it."

My response had been to send the entire matter to the human resources department, a new corporate business invention at the time that had taken the place of personnel departments. The *Morning Herald*'s human resources director was one of the most beautiful and intelligent women I had ever encountered, Gloria Bernstein, whose father owned a Connecticut hosiery mill. Independently wealthy, she lived in the famous Dakota apartment building at Seventy-second Street and Central Park West, where among her neighbors were John Lennon and Lauren Bacall. Gloria eventually introduced me to the New York Ballet and the Metropolitan Opera and Sunday morning strolls in Central Park. An executive rocket on her way up, she was as good as she looked and ended up running the family business and selling it for a billion before the textile industry died.

She sat Martin and the women down together and asked him pointblank in their presence, "Are you now boy or girl?"

He replied, "I'm in between. In transition."

Gloria said, "It's simple then, Mr. Kane. Until you are all girl, you pee with the men. Then you can become Ms. Kane and squat with the twats."

By the time Melody Kane Freeburg dropped in to say good-bye, she was an attractive, tall, athletic-looking blonde, entirely comfortable in her spike heels and sundress, with spaghetti straps and large flower blossoms on the skirt. She broke into tears when she introduced me to her husband, ironically named Marty, and explained to him what a comforting and supporting soul I had been during the most stressful time in her life.

Surviving a dying newspaper is an exceptionally trying time for whoever has to bury it, especially for the failed leader charged with turning out the lights. I walked out of the *Morning Herald* building with a bleeding heart and the weight of the world on my shoulders.

Fortunately I had a half million-dollar check in my coat pocket, more money than I had ever hoped to see in a lifetime—and a place to go. I bought dinner for Gloria Bernstein at a neighborhood café restaurant across the street from the Dakota and we went down to watch Baryshnikov dance. His live-in, actress Jessica Lange, was in the next box over. Later I drank Remy Cognac with Gloria in her apartment in a room full of French impressionists, and croaked a couple of country love songs on my guitar. That night I dreamed of myself in a tunic and black tights whirling across the stage of the American Ballet Theater performing a grand pas de deux with a shorter and much lighter Gloria Bernstein. The next morning, astounded by my agility, athleticism and prowess at pirouettes and loup promenades, and after hearing her hearty laughter at the absurdity of the idea, the load of my failure as a newspaper executive had lightened considerably. What others might have viewed as the worst day of their lives, I would look back on it as one of the best in mine. The Dakota is a long way from Mill Town.

Ten years as a boy wonder—in my own mind anyway—speeding through a world I never knew existed had left me immune to illusions of any kind, or so I believed then. And among those illusions to which I claimed immunity were jet streams like Gloria Bernstein. She was rich, lovely and going places that were mostly concrete, glittering and predictable. I could see myself in a series of Park Avenue high-rises or stalled in traffic somewhere on the way to Connecticut. After two years in New York, I had already had my fill of both.

Watching myself on Pennsylvania Avenue and Broadway from a perch atop the old Mill Town Bridge in my jeans and red windbreaker had become the only throttle on the pace of my life. Watching some stranger that looked like me, wearing Tony the tailor outfits, climb one mountain after another, touching the shoulders of celebrities and the cheeks of beautiful women, moving faster than I ever could, is what kept me out of the ditches. But when you got right down to it, the nature of Gloria's fast track was not really the problem. It was just that she was not the hilarious, challenging cornbread version of Annette Funicello who had made off with my heart—but who was not finished breaking it and whose voice I would keep hearing in my head.

Allston telephoned during my last week at the *Morning Herald*, a "just thought you ought to know" message that her stepfather, old Brownlee Stokes, had gone to sleep the night before and never woke up. He was eighty-two.

"And he left half of everything to mother, Vic, split it up between her and Pippa. His ex-wives and other children are beside themselves. I bet they are going to sue. Who's the best Jewish lawyer in Bluff City?"

"Hell if I know, but there are plenty of them up here. So Henri's a zillionaire now," I said. "How's she taking it, his death, I mean?"

"Well, you know her. She's buried two husbands and she's not even fifty. And you ought to see her now. Had me when she was only eighteen and looks younger than I do, slimmer, too, damn her. Miraculous what spas and a little tightening here and there can do. And you know how I have always hated that she was taller."

"She should be the toast of the town now."

"She's Eggs Benedict."

"But how about you, Allston Jackson the third? This is the third, is it not?"

"Don't be ugly, Vic. Counting you, yes. But you don't count because you were annulled, remember?"

"I don't mean to be ugly. But you are all set now, aren't you... happy?"

"All set, Vic, you got it...except."

"Except what? Don't tell me you don't like the banker already."

"No, its fine. Well, you know what as well as I do. Just thought you ought to hear the news from me before you read the *Clarion*. I gotta go now."

And she was gone again.

For the first time in my life, I was at loose ends. But the former editor of an important New York newspaper has options aplenty, including numerous offers to run newsrooms, in which I had zero interest. The newsrooms I would enjoy running, although they were all under siege from bean counters trying to turn failed business models into profit centers. I had had the bean-counter job, too, at the *Morning Herald* as well as the newsroom. But editor/publisher had become a redundant term for conflict of interest. What I decided to do then was write and there were opportunities galore. The New York magazines loved celebrities, even failed ones, and I signed a contract to cover the 1976 election for *Rolling Stone*.

My first cover story for the *Stone* was a profile of a peanut farmer named Jimmy Carter who was quickly taking over the Democratic Party. Naturally, my friend Jack Hickenlooper found it of interest and excerpted a piece of it for his *Clarion* readers. My identification blurb at the end of the story promised a second *Stone* profile by me of President Jerry Ford. Otherwise, I might never have gotten that second call from Allston that I wished had never come.

It was late in October of 1976, only weeks before the presidential election. I was in Colonial Williamsburg, preparing to cover the head-to-head debate between Carter and President Gerald Ford for the second profile. The *Stone* telephone receptionist found me at my motel early in the afternoon with a message to call Allston at work. I still had the Bluff City Air phone number, which I had transferred from one little black book to another over the years, a treasured relic I suppose, because it represented my only link to her.

"I have to see you," she said, when I called. "Where are you going to be tonight?"

"Here," I said. "In the King James Suites on the bypass watching the president trying not to say something stupid and 'Jimma Peanuts' trying to say anything without grits on it. Why?"

"I have to see you right away."

"How are you going to do that?"

"Vic, I run an airline charter owned by my mother. Remember? I have planes and pilots."

"You're going to fly to Williamsburg, Virginia, today?"

"Yes. Tonight. Absolutely. That's no step for a stepper."

"Can't you give me any idea why...why it is so urgent?"

"I'll explain when I get there. But I think I am going to get a divorce. What time is the debate?"

"Eight Eastern."

"I ought to be there by then. See ya."

The prospects of Allston getting a divorce and being on her way to sleep with me in Williamsburg held a great deal more promise than a debate between two of the nicest guys but dullest politicians who ever sat before a microphone. Now I had something to look forward to, and I had decided that looking forward to something was what had made my life go by at warp speed since the first day I walked into the *Clarion*. I was always in a hurry for the next day, the next story, the next deadline, the next airplane to a place I had never seen or a truth needing to be told. But I could still recall the days before the *Clarion*, when I was growing up waiting for puberty, waiting to put the drudgery of high school behind me, those endless Sunday evening hours in the drugstore when the customers had stopped coming but the opening and closing times on the door kept me there, my only company pill bottles and packaged analgesics. However incessant and unstoppable its march, time still can be one schizophrenic sonofabitch, which it became for me that night in Williamsburg.

Debate began and no Allston. Halfway through it, I called Bluff City Air to make sure she had left on schedule. She had. And someone there gave me the number of the charter service airport in Jamestown where she was supposed to land. No one answered. Carter and Ford droned on and on and on with the president forgetting that Eastern Europe was under Soviet domination being the only memorable contribution to the history of presidential debate dialogue.

Two hours came and went but no Allston. When the Newport News channel that had been airing the debate switched to the local report, the newscast opened with a brief about a "serious accident at the private airport in Jamestown from which a lone victim had been transported to the hospital." They didn't mention a plane crash of any kind, but I called the airport again. This time I got a response. No, there had been no plane crash, but a passenger leaving their terminal had been struck by car and been rushed to the hospital. They had no name. They did yield the name of the hospital, the Williamsburg Community, but all of my prior police reporting experience was of no avail in trying to pry the name of the victim from the nurse at the emergency room. So I left for the hospital, a normal ten-minute drive that I made in five. All the time I had been waiting, Allston had been less than three miles away.

In the emergency room, the same tightlipped nurse I had contacted by phone greeted me at the reception desk with the same taciturn demeanor. I asked the name and condition of the accident victim just transported from Jamestown.

"Are you a relative?" she wanted to know.

"Sort of," I said. "Will an ex-husband do?"

"Yes, but I still do not have permission to release the name. I can tell you she was not from here. She was a lovely woman from out of town. And she was DOA."

11

I went home for Allston's funeral, which was not a funeral
at all, but another celebration of life like Rhodes Newbold's
had been in Louisiana, even though he'd had no life there at all,
except for the matter of days his ashes had set on the mantle
above the fireplace in Mrs. Newbold's home. And likewise,
Allston's life was not to be celebrated east of the river where she
had lived most of it, but in the most popular and prominently
located Episcopal church in West End, only a few blocks from
the mansion in which she had lived for less than two years after
her last marriage.

My initial instinct had been to not attend the event, but rather
to send a note of condolence to her mother, Henri. But Sallie Mae
Arthur, who felt obligated to go, persisted that I escort her. "Son,
some things you just have to do."

So I swallowed whatever it was—grief, anger, pride or a choking
combination of all three I suspect—and flew back to Bluff City.
Showing up at the memorial with my mother, who had known

both Allston and her mother all those years, made it less uncomfortable for me. Perhaps it would do the same for Henri and the new widower, whose comfort was not high on my list of concerns, but who surely had been made aware of my history with Allston. Ex-spouses showing up at weddings and funerals need tread lightly—and briefly.

St. John's Episcopal is the richest and most prominent Protestant church in Bluff City, its elegance and architectural splendor surpassed only by the century-old Catholic Cathedral of the Blessed Mother downtown. When Sallie Mae and I arrived, the gargantuan vestibule was swimming with West End society and business elite, a tribute to the wealth and connections of the late and venerable Brownlee Stokes, whose widow they might not have had a chance to meet at his funeral earlier in the year, but who, according to the newspapers, now sat atop his vast financial empire.

At each end of the walled-off section of the vestibule, large video screens looped pictures of Allston in every stage of her life, from crib to toasts at the Jackson matrimony. There was Allston in a toy-laden stroller, on a merry-go-round, a tree swing, a tree house, playing softball, shaking pompoms in numerous cheerleader poses, relaxing on the beach in Hawaii, pushing her son in her old stroller, lifting him above her head, delight written on both their faces. Bigger than life she was, laughing, cheering accompanied by her favorite songs while in animated conversations with celebrity customers at Bluff City Air and feeding wedding cake to Hamilton V. Jackson III. There was Allston with gold fish, with a myna bird, with several different cats and the camera-loving dog name Gopher she had been holding on a leash in Belair the first time she ever rode in my car. About the only living creatures not included in the memorial menagerie was Randy Sikes, who was dead, and me, who according to my mood at the time, might as well have been.

Beneath one of the screens on an ornamental five-foot masonry pedestal was the urn from Allston's cremation. Putting a person's remains in jars rather than the ground was, well, getting off the ground as a trend at the time, being sold ostensibly as a more civilized and less macabre way of traveling to the other side, but which more likely resulted from limited available space and rising real estate prices. It was there in front of the urn and under the moving video tribute that the widow and son-in-law of Brownlee Stokes were stationed to receive condolences over the death of the woman I loved.

Henri Ravenel Stokes did not look like a woman who, in six months, had lost both a husband and daughter. She looked like a movie star there to sign autographs and welcome hugs from strangers. Enough time had passed since the speeding pickup truck had killed her daughter that the warm smiles and animation of her greetings appeared exaggerated and overdone only in the eyes of the one visitor who felt even more cheated by her loss—me. And Hamilton V. Jackson III did not look like someone Allston would marry. I had anticipated a corporate Adonis, six foot four and 220, tanned and athletic. Even Randy Sikes rated the turn of a woman's head. In her world of brilliant colors, odorous scents and pungent flavors, Allston was a savory, jasmine-scented, chocolate-dipped raspberry, and this Jackson guy was plain, odorless vanilla—a chinless squirt of a man, almost effeminate, with thin, receding hair and the countenance of a funeral director. If he was a rising star in the Brownlee Stokes realm of high finance, he had to be an executive calculator of columns, monitor of heating costs and extinguisher of lights not in use. Well-dressed and courtly, he nonetheless appeared a mere flicker in the aurora of the Amazing Henri, in whose presence he was entirely overwhelmed.

Allston's description of her mother's new look, if anything had been an understatement. Henri's transformation from hard-working, overachieving single Belair mom to West End socialite heiress and chief executive was astounding. Her raven hair hung delicately to the slightly padded shoulders of an exquisitely tailored black Armani suit set off by a pale gold silk blouse and sparkling gold-set diamonds, including a rock on her left hand with a face the size of a dime and heavy-looking enough to tilt her balance. Any Madison Avenue advertising genius looking for the perfect middle-aged model to sell style and elegance need look no further.

The Amazing Henri greeted Sallie Mae with open arms, and even though she was only a few years younger, my mother looked a generation older. Henri offered me a perfect toothpaste ad smile and a soft cheek to peck, while putting her hand on my shoulder and for an instant brushing her fingers across the back of my neck, accidentally I supposed.

"Well, prodigal son returns, dear David, wow," she said. "I have been reading about you. Thank you so much for coming. I know how much you meant to my daughter." She then leaned closer and whispered, "I know she was on her way to see you."

While her cheek rested on mine, I imagined her looking to see what truly important visitor might be in line behind me, and at the same time I felt some strange degree of comfort from her touch, familiar, like something felt before, no doubt from Allston since I could not remember Henri ever before laying a finger on me. And exactly which definition of prodigal had she had in mind? If, in fact, she knew there was more than one? If she meant that of a son driven away, she was being more candid than I ever thought possible, and perhaps even repentant. She had indeed not only driven away the son of a woman she had just embraced in a familial greeting but had tried to put him in jail for kidnapping. If she was labeling me with the wastrel or wasted definition of prodigal, she was dead wrong on the first, for up to that point I had lived a frugal existence. But she would have been right on the latter. I had been wasted all right, at least my value as a husband for her only daughter, whose presence in the urn was evidence that a great deal more than a teenaged forty-eight-hour husband had been wasted.

Fortunately Hamilton V. Jackson III was preoccupied in a conversation with some of his own relatives and paid no attention to my mother and me as we passed. Nothing lost there, and Sallie Mae was already heading to greet her favorite politician, Tate Weston, standing head and shoulders above an adoring crowd just ahead. Sallie Mae had long ago put Weston in the same category of celebrity worship as Elvis and television cowboys James Garner, star of *Maverick* and James Arness of *Gunsmoke*.

Weston saw her coming and left the crowd to greet her. She

had been the hostess and ramrod of his headquarters in his failed Senate race and was still convinced he should be leader of the Western world.

"What about you, Sallie Mae Aahthuh? How's my most valuable player?" he bellowed, and swept her into his long arms, awarding her loyalty with what surely was one of her grandest moments, considering the unlikelihood she would ever be hugged in front of a celebrity laden crowd by Maverick or Matt Dillon, or Elvis, who only recently had departed the planet.

A full foot shorter than Weston, my mesmerized mother stared up into the most handsome face she ever saw—"except Clark Gable of course" and received one of those looks Weston usually reserved for some television babe he might hit on someday.

"Sallie Mae, I hope you kept your running shoes," he said, "because we ain't done yet. I'm still going to Pennsylvania Avenue and I'm going to need you to get there. One day you and me…we'll be laughing and talking in the Oval Office."

A Mill Town girl with a tenth grade education, my mother might as well have been accepting the Hope Diamond. Sallie would volunteer for every campaign he undertook for the next twenty years and would defend him to her death even after he became a spectacle on the street.

"And who is this wandering vagrant tagging along with you?" he asked, turning to me. "Home from Times Square and the Great White Way. The distinguished David Aahthuh. How is the Big Apple these days anyway?"

"Still big and juicy, Weston," I replied. "You should come up some time and take a bite."

He was still holding my mother's hand. "What do you think of this guy?" he asked her. "Did you see him up there the other day on *Meet the Press*? Of course, you did."

Just then, Pippa Weston, radiant as ever and for whom my mother had often served as babysitter as joyfully as she had Weston's campaign employment, joined us. The minute his wife attracted my mother's attention, Weston dropped her hand and put his on my shoulder.

"Come ovah heah, David Aahthuh, I been meanin' to call you. There is something you oughta know."

He hustled me over into a corner of the makeshift room, turned his back to the crowd and put his arm around my shoulder, corralling us into a tight huddle. There in his eye was the same gleam I had seen many times before, in the Pontiac planning his Senate campaign on the way to the tailor shop, in his office theorizing Tex's Ham and Biscuits, and in California when he was about to hijack the stage at the Humphrey rally. The man's imagination seeped out of him through his eyes and coated his entire presence with shiny anticipation. At times like these, he was bursting with the energy of whatever idea had consumed him, the words impatiently lining up to be spilled out in a golden flow of conviction meant to seduce and consume whatever target he had cornered. I knew he was coming in for the kill.

"Big doings in Bluff City," he said. "I am about to buy the *Defendah* out from under the fucking colonel and retire his sorry ass to the trash pile he deserves."

Of all the schemes I had heard from that golden throat, this one took the cake. I could not imagine Weston having the money to buy out the entire May family, of which there were dozens with an interest in the newspaper, or being able to raise such a sum after the ham and biscuits debacle. One of the colonel's brothers had married a French prostitute and sired a passel of children. They lived in Monaco on the French Rivera and couldn't speak a word of English. We were talking millions. Nor could I fathom him owning the *Clarion*'s afternoon rival. What could he be thinking and where was Hickenlooper in all of this?

"What about the *Clarion*?" I asked. "What does Jack think about this?"

"Not much," he said. "But he'll get over it. We're still pals though."

"Aren't you still the *Clarion*'s lawyer. Is that some kind of conflict?"

"Yes, but not for long. We are about to cut the cord. Hickenlooper might keep the firm as chief counsel. But I am leaving it—temporarily, of course. You know Miller is back. He quit when Nixon got elected and is a First Amendment whiz. He does all the *Clarion* work anyway."

"So what are you going to do?"

"Can't say. This is all still hush hush," Weston said, crossing his lips with an index finger. "If that fucking May knows I'm involved, he will resist this until the cows come home. But he has to sell. All the younger generation heirs have grown up and like all these newspaper families, they don't give a shit about journalism or politics—or even power. They just want their money. I know he has to sell, so I am going to see that he gets an offer he can't refuse."

"From whom, Tate, who is going to lend you that kind of

money? What are we talking about, 20 million? Or thirty?"

"Oh, I've got the buyer with the money," Tate said. "My people are doing their due diligence right now. And they know what I know: That the *Defendah* is a losing proposition that cannot be sustained. It is not pulling its weight in the joint-operating agreement. The *Clarion* is carrying the whole deal, which was a sixty-forty proposition to begin with. And the way that JOA works, the *Defendah*'s interest is gradually diminishing with its performance. If he doesn't sell, pretty soon there won't be anything to sell."

For all the persuasive rhetoric behind his pitch, I was still skeptical. It failed my reporter logic test. Who would buy into a failing afternoon newspaper when they were dying like flies all over the country? And why?

"Who is crazy enough to do this, Tate?"

"The privacy laws prevent me from disclosing the identity of an insane person," he said in his best courtroom voice. "Surely a journalist of your eminence knows that, Mr. Aahthuh. Besides it's a client who is guaranteed anonymity by the ethics of my profession that cannot be violated even for a pal like you. But I cannot pull this off while representing the *Clarion*, which is one of the reasons Jack is insisting on the keeping the firm as his lawyer. By doing that, he is in fact forcing me out. Not surprisingly, my young partners are choosing the *Clarion* retainer over my frivolous adventures. Miller is no fool and he brought in all the young ones we have now. Jack is playing chess and the smart sonofabitch has me cornered. He doesn't think I will break from the firm. But I will."

"Well, why are you telling me this, Tate? I think it's crazy."

"Ah, David Aahthuh, you must not be as smart as I thought you were. When I get this done and I don't mean if I get this done, I mean when. When I get this done, I am going to need someone to run the *Defendah*. I'm a lawyer. I know how to defend newspapers in court. I am an expert on the First Amendment and every other aspect of the Constitution of the United States. But I don't know a fucking thing about running a newspaper. And you know everything."

"You think I am going to come back home and compete with Hickenlooper. You've got to be kidding. He made me. He's my mentor, the big brother I never had. I would never have made a wave in this ocean without him. I could not and would not ever compete with him."

"Of course, you will," he said. "What you just said is the very reason you are the man for the job. You two pee through the same quill. You think exactly alike on the very issue that has united the three of us—equal justice under the law. That's what Hickenlooper is all about. I believe in it. You believe in it. I can see the day coming when we have the same editorial page in both papers, your name and Hickenlooper's right up there together...and we will have consolidated the two newspapers into the single most powerful voice of reason and justice in the South."

Weston's voice always grew louder the more wound up he got. I began to look around to see if anyone was listening. He noticed my inattention.

"Listen to me, David Aahthuh. Yes, we have the Civil Rights Act, the Voting Rights Act and the one-man, one-vote decision by the Supreme Court. But laws unimplemented and un-enforced are worthless pieces of paper. And they will only become meaningful when the people demand it. And unless the people are educated about the critical nature of these laws and alerted when they are being ignored, they are not worth a plug nickel. Who is going to do that but newspapers? The *Clarion* has always done it, at least in my lifetime, and now the *Defendah* will do it when you and I control the sonofabitch.

"Colonel Hiram May is an old man. He's gonna die soon. And I intend to see that the old racist bastard spins in his grave for an eternity when he sees what his *Defendah* has become. If it turns out that there is no hell—that the whole idea of it is some writer's science fiction, the colonel will have his own private inferno."

Fantasy. Weston was off on another obsession, unlikely as his quest for the White House, as mystical as Satan's Palace and the River Styx. But somehow, he made it sound plausible, even for someone ten years grizzled by the skepticism endemic to my craft. Good journalists learn to doubt every word they hear—and for the sake of perspective, place every picture they see into a larger frame of reference. But in the end they are like everyone else. They want to believe what they like to hear. That was Weston's genius. Like a superb craftsman with clever hands and deft fingers, he was an artist with words, perpetually saying to someone what they would like to believe. He somehow had the ability to make crazy sound sane. That was his great gift—rationalizing the absurd.

"You're nuts, Tate," I said. "Are you still seeing Dr. Goebbels?"

"Heavens no. Unfortunately he's gone to Birmingham, where they don't know his therapy sessions can end on the front page," he shot back. "Do not get yourself entangled. Hang loose, Aahthuh. You'll be hearing from me soon."

I rejoined Pippa and Sallie Mae, and Tate wandered off to become an attraction in the crowd. Henri and the widower were nowhere in sight.

Before my mother and I departed, we took one more stroll by the urn, now abandoned on its pedestal. She and I had spent much of our lives around the dead, back when they buried most people in the ground. The east-of-the-river political machine of which she and my granddaddy were a part was rooted in a chain of funeral homes owned by the Lermon family, the headquarters forever rooted in their Mill Town mortuary, which was their first.

It was a two-story building and a basement, the rear entrance to which was hardly more than a dugout to which an ambulance could back up and disgorge bodies. The basement was for embalment and preparation for laying out the deceased on the first floor for viewing and visitation. But all the business, both commerce and political, was conducted on the second floor where the sample caskets from basic to ornate were situated in front of large bay windows that looked out over a beautiful meadow, the Southern and Pacific Railroad train yard off in the distance.

As Granddaddy Crockett's only daughter, Sallie Mae worked there fifteen hours a week, mostly in the evenings after her day job was done, selling coffins, consoling the bereaved and listing them as potential voters in the next election. From even before I learned to walk, she had taken me along. By the time I was ten years old, I had seen more dead bodies, smelled more sickening sweet stargazer lilies and heard more widows wailing than most people experience in a lifetime. By the time I flew to New Orleans for Newbold's wake and strolled by that urn of Allston's ashes, the naturalness of death and reconciliation with its inevitability had been etched into my DNA. Both deaths had thumped me in the chest like a meteorite crashing to earth. I never cried nor lost a wink of sleep, but no day had passed since without Allston and Newbold crossing my mind, each memory bringing a well of tears behind my eyes that somehow dissipated before emergence, only to be retained to soak my soul with grief.

I wanted to go over and pick up the urn, stash it under my blazer and take it back to my Manhattan apartment. If there was ever anyone that could entertain and keep you company from the grave, it was Allston.

Hickenlooper had been out of town and one of the few movers and shakers that had not shown up at Allston's memorial, which was essentially just another Amazing Henri coming-out party. So I called Mrs. Earnhart the next morning to find out when he might be in.

"Whenever he shows up is all I know," she snapped. "You'll have to come down here and wait like everyone else."

When he had not shown up by lunchtime, I took Red Whitmore to the Crisscross Cafeteria where we had eaten dozens of times before, and that had made national news as the target of the first street disruption by Martin Luther King's brave kiddie corps. He and I always ate the same stuff: a chopped steak smothered in A-1 sauce, green beans, a baked sweet potato and apple pie for dessert. On the *Clarion* pauper's pay back then, we each picked up our own tab, but the wealthy Newbold was often along and always tried to pay for all three, although regularly upbraiding us for ordering a plate of cholesterol. His tray was always filled with shrimp and salad, the memory of which prompted Red's comment that "If the little bastard hadn't run off to the *Times*, he wouldn't be dead. I would have made him eat."

Over the years, the menu had changed, but only slightly—no sweet potatoes. But Red and I had not—so we both got a baked Irish potato instead. But this time, still flush with my goodbye money from the Blandford sisters and a book advance, I grabbed Red's check. After all, besides being a pal, he was about to be a source. And if there was anybody besides Hickenlooper that I owed, it was Red.

I didn't mention what Weston had told me, but I made sure his name came up in case Red had some beans to spill. Now I always wanted to know beforehand the answers to questions I planned to ask, and I had some for Hickenlooper, who was not exactly an easy interview. But fishing Whitmore only snagged a lot of inside dope on the wreckage left behind by the Packer brothers banking scandal.

According to Red, after the death of Weston's grandmother, the Community Southern had emerged from Chapter Eleven in the hands of the mammoth insurance company, Equitable Life and Accident, owned by the late Brownlee Stokes and that had passed to Pippa Weston in her share of the estate.

"So now, instead of Tate's grandmother owning a bank, his wife does," I said.

"I'm not sure. Some of the Equitable subsidiaries were lopped off into the widow's share. But I know the bank is now being run by this nerdy guy that was married to her daughter, your friend Allston. And get this, the bank president was written in by law way back in the original Wainscott Trust, so he has to be dealt with on anything having to do with the *Clarion*. Hickenlooper has control of what the newspaper says and does, but this Jackson guy has the say on the trust, which includes more than the *Clarion*. So you know where the real power is. Jack says the guy's a prick. And from what I hear, Tate Weston still runs his life on a perpetual quarter of a million-dollar loan from Community Southern on which interest hasn't been paid for years. They just roll it over, or used to anyway. I don't know what they are doing now."

Hickenlooper's plane was late. He had been to Washington on one of his goodwill missions for the underclass, writing a plank in the convention platform of ASNE, the American Society of Newspaper Editors, which had decided it needed a formal goal moving women and minorities into the leadership of the printed press, historically an all-white male bastion. Only a few newspapers had women on their masthead and even fewer had African-Americans in management positions. Hickenlooper's work in the Robert Kennedy Justice Department had been on the civil rights battleground on behalf of the Freedom Riders, specifically the famous heroine Rosa Parks, whose refusal to sit in the back of a Birmingham bus had ignited nationwide sympathy for the integration of the South.

After taking over the *Clarion*, Hickenlooper had hired as an assistant to Earnhart a young female relative of Parks, whom he had met while in Alabama the day he had taken a rock on the head while trying to protect her aunt. Erma Thompson, who was that very day seated alongside Earnhart, would become a pipeline to him directly from the leadership of the continuing Civil Rights Movement to the nation's newspapers, the justice department and even to the White House.

Under Hickenlooper, the *Clarion* had been the first to jump on any civil rights story in the region, with Rhodes Newbold and me his eyes and ears on the ground in Birmingham, Detroit, Jackson, Charlotte and Memphis. His commitment to the story and connections inside the movement had made both my career and Newbold's, and earned Hickenlooper lifetime status as a civil rights icon in the mind of African-Americans.

His latest mission to integrate the hierarchy of the nation's press was all he wanted to talk about when he finally showed up late in the day, only a few minutes before his news meeting time.

"We are finally getting through to the old bastards," he said. "The press has to preach the gospel of this cause and they can't very well do it in dirty skirts from shaky ground. Every business in every community can look them directly in the eye and say, practice what you preach, buddy, or don't preach to me.

"Getting newspapers out front on this issue is critical and damn it if it isn't harder than getting the laws changed. What good is changing the laws and continuing to go down the same old back roads? You know there is only one black publisher of a major daily newspaper in this country—Bob Maynard in Oakland. And you know how many members of ASNE were in Washington today writing this equal opportunity employment platform plant—Maynard and me."

Most of my meeting time had elapsed before I finally got a word in edgewise and asked, "What the hell is going on with Weston and this *Defender* business? Is this all just bullshit?"

Hickenlooper let out a deep and troubling sigh.

"I'm afraid not. But I don't know everything," he said, shaking his head and running his fingers through his hair. Then he raised both hands a foot above his head and leaned back in his chair.

"And frankly, I am up to here with him. Don't quote me on this. But I think he's off whatever medicine Goebbels had him on. You know that clown therapist ran off to Alabama or someplace. I believe Tate is actually considering leaving his firm to avoid any hint of conflict of interest in this deal."

"I don't understand the conflict-of-interest business."

"He's got a partner in this who is also a client, you know, so there's an attorney-client privilege."

"Yeah, he's already invoked it to me. Where would they get the money? His wife's bank?" I asked, getting the question in just as the noise of his regular news meeting assembly crowd began outside his cubicle.

"Hell, Pippa didn't get the bank," he said. "That's one of the problems. If she had the bank, he wouldn't need a partner. The widow got the bank. Old Brownlee gave Pippa the goldmine, which is the insurance company, but he cut out the bank, the barge company and television stations and everything not risk averse and that needs managing, and gave all that to Henri, who I am told is one helluva a powerhouse manager."

I nodded in agreement, smiling.

"You know her better than I do," he said, smiling back, "your mother-in-law once, briefly, wasn't she?"

"Only for a few hours," I said, "and that was enough. Amazing Henri is something else all right. Does Weston think he can get the money from her?"

"Doesn't need to," Hickenlooper said, standing now, his signal that the meeting is concluded. "This new client who is the source of his potential conflict of interest has plenty of money."

Not knowing the identity of this mysterious client was getting under my skin. There had been a time when I would not have pushed the issue with Hickenlooper. But he no longer intimidated me like he once had. As I had grown from boy to man, my awe of him had morphed into simple respect. He had quoted to me many times the words of the irascible *Washington Post* Editor Ben Bradlee, who said he wanted reporters "with balls that rattled when they walked." Mine now rattled, so I pushed.

"Who's that? Or are you invoking the client privilege, too?"

Hickenlooper's thus far solemn countenance collapsed into a wide grin and he began shaking his head, in apparent amazement or disgust, I could not tell which.

"Not hardly," he whispered. "It's Citycorp News. Big Ike has got his sights set on Bluff City."

12

O n a cold, gray December morning in 1978, in the lobby of the New York Stock Exchange, Big Ike Oldham, dressed as always in an ensemble of printers' ink black and newsprint white, announced that Citycorp News had just the day before closed a deal to acquire the Bluff City *Defender* for $25 million. It was City-corp's seventeenth newspaper acquisition in the last three years.

When somebody in the crowd of Wall Street analysts present asked why Citycorp wanted a newspaper that had not turned a profit in nearly a decade, Big Ike stuck out his barrel chest and said, "Well, gentlemen, it will now. Citycorp does not own or operate losing propositions. The market is one of the fastest growing in the South. We have a good solid JOA partner in the morning *Clarion* and for the first time we have reached out to the community and attracted some local investors who now have some skin in the game."

Asked to identify them, Ike turned to a tall, dark, blue-eyed handsome man in a three-piece, pinstriped suit with a gold watch chain dangling from his vest and a golden voice, the likes of which they had never heard.

"Ladies and gentlemen," Big Ike said, "I gladly refer that question to the new chairman, CEO and legal counsel to the *Defender*, Mr. Tate Weston."

"Good morning," Tate intoned in his best Virginia planter's voice. "I represent a group of Bluff City businessmen and women who have raised the money to partner with Citycorp in this exciting venture. We did it because Bluff City is a leading market in a region of this country that is on the rise again. People are moving in droves to the Sunbelt, and while we ah not exactly Sunbelt, we ah the main road headed theah.

"Whetha you are bound for Florida or Texas, you will most likely have to pass through Bluff City. And when people see Bluff City, they don't want to leave. We are a city on the rise in a region on the rise with great as-yet untapped potential. A city cannot have too many clear voices of leadership and the *Defendah* has been filling that role for nearly one hundred yeahs, and will continue to do so with renewed support of our growing population. Ladies and gentlemen, thanks to the wisdom of the Supreme Court of the United States and its decision on the one-man, one-vote principle, we now have a two-party South. What has happened is that Republicans pretending to be Democrats all these yeahs now have their own party that deserves its own voice. What Citycorp's confidence in Bluff City has given us is a chance for that voice to continue being heard. Thank you very much."

Before Big Ike could retake the microphone, someone yelled from the back of the crowd, "Mr. Weston, what do you know about running a newspaper?"

Weston collided with Big Ike and leaned over his shoulder to answer.

"Not a damn thing," he said, smiling and evoking sustained laughter from the analysts and press. "But the new editor and publisher is here and he knows a helluva lot about how to run one."

Big Ike gave me an elbow in the ribs.

"You New Yorkers already know this guy," he announced with his usual casual flourish. "He needs no introduction here. David Arthur, the last editor and publisher of the great New York *Morning Herald*, has signed a two-year contract to run the *Defender* for Citycorp."

How what never should have been but somehow came to be could only have been the handiwork of one man—Jack Hickenlooper. No one else could have talked me into it or survived my friendship afterwards, considering how it all turned out. The truth is, Hickenlooper convinced me it was the right thing to do—for me, for the *Defender*—and probably most important—for him, or at least we all thought so at the time.

The success of Weston's vendetta against Colonel May was the result of a perfect storm of circumstances to which I would never have been privy had I not been suckered into it myself. As lawyer for the *Clarion*, Weston had inside knowledge of the *Defender*'s precarious financial condition within the joint-operating agreement with the *Clarion*—diminishing percentage of ownership to coincide with diminishing contributions to the bottom line.

Contained in that agreement, originally prepared by Colonel May's law firm years before, was the name, address and telephone number of every beneficiary of the May Family Trust, the specified date on which it would expire and be open to renegotiation with the *Clarion*, which happened to coincide with the colonel's eightieth birthday and the end of his term as the sole trustee, for which he would have to stand for re-election.

The day the *Defender* reprinted the picture of Pippa and their daughter's surprise visit to his room at Blackberry Farm, Weston had pulled a copy of the JOA from his files and mined it for all its critical information. Then he flew to the headquarters of Citycorp News in South Miami Beach carrying a proposition that Big Ike Oldham could not refuse, the nature of which was so ingenious that the giant egos of both men compelled them to share it with others, the same way big game hunters must recount their successful stalks.

If Citycorp would agree to pay an above normal premium price for the *Defender*, Weston would raise an additional 3 million from local investors to sweeten the pot for the heirs, who would then also be fed the news of the rapidly diminishing value of their inheritance. The sad story and offer of rescue by Citycorp News had been personally delivered to most of them by Big Ike himself, who often arrived by limousine motorcade, and, in the case of the sizable French Riviera clan, via helicopter, which was used to ferry the stockholders' children up and down the Mediterranean coastline while Ike motivated the adults.

All of this, as well as Big Ike's surprise appearance at the May Family Trust annual meeting in Boca Raton later in the fall, took place without a single hint of involvement by Tate Weston. But his appointment as chairman of the *Defender* was said to have been a contributing factor to the devastating stroke that felled Colonel May the day the newspaper changed hands. Red Whitmore's contacts within the *Defender*'s staff claimed the old warrior had never spoken a decipherable word since, and spent his final days in a wheelchair with his Civil War sword crosswise on his useless knees.

To what extent Hickenlooper had knowledge of Weston's activities was forever clouded by their period of estrangement that followed and each man's reluctance to talk freely about the other. But Hickenlooper pleaded ignorance to me during the series of conversations that resulted in my accepting Big Ike's offer to be Citycorp's man in Bluff City, the details of which at my insistence had me reporting directly to Big Ike's editorial vice president in Miami and not to Chairman and CEO Weston, whose titles were more honorary and ceremonial than operational. Weston was on the hook for the money, however, which eventually played a critical role in his coming apart.

There is no doubt whatsoever as to the degree for which Hickenlooper was responsible for me taking a job I did not want. His initial pitch was expertly aimed, deadly accurate and not all that different from what Weston had told the New York analysts: A city is better off with two newspapers than with one. Bluff City was becoming big and diverse enough to have two voices, and the one the *Defender* would have with me at the helm would be a helluva improvement. That was what Hickenlooper would tell the community in his *Clarion* editorial on the sale and what he would repeat publicly and privately as long as he lived. But the compelling argument that eventually brought me back home told me more about him and people like him—me for instance—than I really wanted to hear or that I would want anybody else to hear.

"Look," he said, "take yourself out of it for a minute. Pretend someone you care about has come to you for career advice...."

"Like I have come to you now," I said.

He shook his head. "Don't complicate this. Listen," he said, "look at it like you don't have any skin in the game beyond helping the other guy. It boils down to somebody trying to save a newspaper that is on its last legs. You've already been through that. You kept the *Morning Herald* alive and it did good things before it failed. Keeping one alive as long as you can is a public service. You just saw a good one die, so you know what I am talking about. Even a live bad one is better than a dead good one. Okay?

"So then you look at this guy who has asked for advice, and you consider the circumstances. The paper's half assed and Big Ike is no good. He's gonna run newspapers on a shoestring just to make money. So why does he want you? Because not only does he want money, he wants respect. Nobody even wants to go to dinner with him at the conventions and big events because they know what he is. You have what he needs. Hiring you will raise his esteem in the eyes of his peers. Everybody knows how good you are. So you will become a jewel in his crown. Rejecting his offer is what people would expect you to do. Trying to hire you is not something they would expect him to do.

"Lyndon Johnson always said when you are dealing with another man you need to have his balls in your pocket. You've got his.

Make him pay for the privilege of you being associated with Citycorp. Not only can you extract a big piece of change for two years—and you know that all but a few people in this game work for a pittance—but you can hold him up for other stuff, guaranteed budget for instance, total independence. Say I'll take the job but don't fuck with me and that you want it written down, big severance and no complaints if it doesn't work."

Hickenlooper leaned back in his chair and smiled, as if waiting for a response. But before I could construct one, he continued, a bit sheepishly like he had been putting me on and was not about to give me the straight scoop.

"Now all I have been saying is hypothetical. Remember, I am not advising you one way or another. All I'm doing is postulating what you might in all candor tell someone if you were in the position that I am in today. But I will say, what have you got to lose? You're young and you've got Big Ike by the short hairs. So down the road maybe all you've done is keep a newspaper alive longer than it would be if you don't come and earn yourself a big piece of change.

"I could even argue that running a newspaper that Big Ike Oldham has to refrain from pillaging in order to keep you from resigning and writing a book about how shitty Citycorp News is a...a...uh...well, a worthwhile public service. Besides, I'd like to have you over on the other side of the building even if you reported to the devil himself."

Had Hickenlooper restricted his opinion on my career path to the last sentence he could have had the same influence and saved a lot of breath and hypothesizing. Idolatry can be mesmerizing.

Looking back on that conversation, I realized that what I had witnessed was the regurgitation of how the Kennedys rationalized every twist and turn in their journey from shanty Irish to America's royal family, which is a microcosm of how to make it in America. Hickenlooper had just given me a blueprint of a chess player's route to checkmate, ruthlessly and even selfishly Machiavellian in the plotting, yet miraculously honorable and justifiable in intent.

His lesson was very effective in prying from Citycorp News a $300,000 annual compensation package, a guaranteed 10 percent editorial budget increase each year and—on paper anyway— shielding from meddling Miami corporate executives or the mercurial CEO Tate Weston. The next eighteen months appeared at the time to be only a small-time repeat of what had happened to me in New York—a newspaper struggling on its last legs. But looking back on it now, I was watching the acceleration of a virulent cancer that would kill relatively overnight the free press, an institution that had been critical to American democracy since its inception, and would make the profession of newspapering and the people who devoted their lives to it seem irrelevant to history. Both Hickenlooper and I would retire before it died, but we would eventually have to acknowledge—and did—that perhaps the best of us had been buried with it.

"Once the camel gets his nose under the tent, it's over," Hickenlooper, consummate reader of handwriting on the wall, is saying to me in one of the many gripe sessions in the tent we are sharing with Big Ike and Citycorp News. "The only question is how long can we survive before the stinking sonofabitch pushes us out the other side."

This is about a year into my brief Board Street act as star publisher and editor of the *Defender*, a point at which it became apparent there was no light at the end of the tunnel. I had not been foolish enough to make any radical changes that might drive off the newly minted Republican minority that was growing with leaps and bounds in the suburbs beyond the West End. The *Defender* was still the *Defender*, only without the insanity of Colonel May editorials and the berserk front-page lurches for and against stuff that made news. I had even restrained myself from implementing the editorial budget increases guaranteed in my contract, which I had intended to use to compete more equally with the *Clarion*.

Still, the only people truly happy with the arrangement were Tate Weston, who loved his new high profile as a Bluff City business tycoon, and Sallie Mae Arthur who believed her son now living in the West End as a peer of Jack Hickenlooper was really neat. Her single-mom success having been validated in public, she had even retrieved Woody from the grave and the houseboat, let him back in the house on probation and had gotten him a part-time job as a sergeant at arms in the state legislature. With me running the *Defender* and her now babysitting from time to time for the Westons and helping plot his comeback, she had settled in as political power broker.

But Hickenlooper and I both recognize that status quo is endangered when the camel starts walking circles in the tent. Citycorp bean counters in Miami, weary from weeks of *Defender* red ink, due largely to Big Ike's budget concessions, which they believed he must have been on something when he signed, had become restless. In their mind, he had grown soft in his old age and was already looking toward retirement, and they began girding for a return to their normal rape-and-pillage business model.

Meanwhile, the *Clarion* had problems of its own. *Defender* losses were cutting into the bottom line of the JOA, which did not set well with the new trustee, Allston's nerdy widower, Hamilton V. Jackson III. Not only did Jackson have a fiduciary responsibility to all the Perry family members of the Wainscott Trust, Community Southern was hung out on a personal half million loan to Weston, and a couple of million more to the investors he sucked in with him in the local group that partnered with Citycorp. None of them were making their interest payments and Jackson's bank had an independent board that was on his case. According to Hickenlooper, at least one member, a crotchety old descendant of the esteemed Caldwell family, had already publicly rebuked Jackson for not calling Weston's loans, and asked him in an open meeting if he had been an investor in Tex's Ham and Biscuits, which indeed he had.

Typically, my source on all this was my old pal Red Whitmore, who was getting most of his information from the *Clarion* lawyer, former U.S. attorney Miller Clark, who had signed on as guarantor for Weston's personal loan. Clark was of the opinion that some of the local partners were stalling on their loan payments in the expectation that Weston was about to pull off another deal that would square things. Whatever was in the works, Clark had no idea, and according to Red, neither did Hickenlooper. It was another of those secrets hidden behind the lawyer-client privilege.

Before the nature of Weston's conniving became known to any of us, there was the infamous "the dinner party explosion," the widespread consequences of which are still being calculated all over Bluff City these many years later.

The stunned hostess was the new star of West End society, the Amazing Henri Ravenel Stokes, whose invitations to her small dinner gatherings were rapidly becoming the hottest ticket in town. However competent she might turn out to be as a chief executive, she had become an overnight sensation with her intimate ten or less soirées at the elegant but relatively modest old Stokes mansion in the oldest section of the best neighborhood, where only the forest was still considered virgin.

Prior to the eruption, which occurred before a single crystal goblet held a drop of Pinot Noir or a single piece of silver raised, the most surprising aspect of the event was my own invitation, which I received in a lovely embossed linen note at the *Defender* stating that Mrs. Henri Ravenel Stokes requests the pleasure of my company at 7 p.m., October 15, 1980, at her home at 1000 Warner Park Hill Road. Since a messenger to my office delivered my invitation only forty-eight hours earlier, my persisting East-of-the-River complex pegged me as a last-minute fill-in, which turned out to be the case.

There was something familiar about the big silver Mercedes already in the parking circle. And as I was getting out of my car, Hickenlooper's beautiful emerald green, but often unreliable, Jaguar careened into the circle. I waited outside long enough to congratulate his wife, Deidre, on having arrived unharmed despite having let him drive.

Hickenlooper had definitely married up. Deidre was a Beacon Hill Saltonstall whose promising career had landed her at the New York Metropolitan before she gave it up and moved south to marry a young reporter who made sixty bucks a week and kept forgetting to wear a belt. The frequently asked question of why she always answered the same way: "Because Jack is irresistible and most divas die from overweight." A champagne blonde physical fitness buff an inch or two taller than her husband, Deidre was as sleek as the Jaguar.

"I thought you ran everywhere you went," I said, as she offered me a cheek. "I would have," she said. "We live close enough but I didn't think Henri would appreciated me wearing Adidas on my first visit."

"I see the Goebbels are already here," Deidre said.

She glanced again at the Mercedes, and said, "Jack said the Miller Clarks are coming. Is there anyone else?"

"Don't ask me," I said, "I'm pretty sure I'm an afterthought."

Deidre shook her thick mane back into place and drew herself up to a degree of perfect posture seldom attained by normal humans and as we approached the door, Jack, late behind us as usual, said for Deidre's benefit, "You know Henri, don't you, David?"

"Since I was a kid," I said. "But we have never been close."

Before Deidre touched the bell button, the door opened before us and we were greeted with the slight bow of an elderly black man I knew as the retired former butler at the governor's mansion. He and his wife Lorene, a widely admired gourmet chef, now ran a wildly successful catering and a rent-a-butler business.

"I see Mrs. Stokes has gone all out for this one, Lenny," I said, "or you and Lorene wouldn't be here. God, I'm glad I got invited."

"Thank you, Mr. Arthur," he said. "You are very kind," and then in a whisper, added, "and as usual, full of you know what."

Lenny was from east of the river, and he and I went back a long way.

"Mrs. Stokes is back in the kitchen with Lorene," he said. "She will be out directly."

In fact, she was already out en grande tenue, an exquisite hourglass of chic, a simple little black dress set off by a sphere of glitter. Steffie Goebbels had chosen black for the occasion as well, another simple wrapping but for a plain matronly grandmother with a kind face and limp brown hair done up in a bun. She smiled meekly at us but said nothing. Henri and Deidre Hickenlooper exchanged hugs and Henri offered me her hand and a cheek to nudge.

"So glad you could come," she said, squeezing my hand. "I have been wanting to talk to you."

I bet, I said to myself, and then to her, "Good. What a nice surprise, Henri, thank you for including me."

Just then, Miller Clark arrived with his wife Denise, a prim and proper domestic relations court judge. Henri graciously led us all into a cozy sitting room, its walls lined with museum-quality art, including what looked like a Van Gogh. On one wall, a small fireplace was gently ablaze and through a wide walkway at the other end, the candelabras on Henri's widely coveted dinner party setting were visible. The hands clasped behind the back of the tall man perusing the table like a butler inspecting silverware belonged to the esteemed Austrian celebrity psychiatrist, who had been virtually invisible since the embarrassing leak of his therapy session. Apparently an invitation from the Amazing Henri could lure even a humiliated fugitive back from his Alabama hideout. Goebbels had the striking military bearing of a Prussian officer and always spoke in a quiet, accented baritone that reminded me of Henry Kissinger, also a ladies' man.

I caught Deidre peering into the dining room, and she caught me watching her count the plates. "Ten," she said, "Wonder who is not here yet."

We were not long in finding out. Again, Lenny had opened the door before the warning bell, so we did not know until they were escorted into the salon. At first, my view was blocked by the Amazing Henri who had rushed to greet them. When she turned to bring them in my direction, I could not believe my eyes.

"Deidre Hickenlooper and David Arthur, meet my neighbors, the Maddens, Eva and Jeff."

Eva's eyes met mine and darted away like they were avoiding a sunburst.

Jefferson Madden was congenial, pot-bellied and balding, twenty years older than his wife. He'd made a fortune in commercial real estate development and then bought up as many record companies and talent agencies as he could assemble and taken to the casual attire of their executives. The only man in the room without a necktie, he reminded me of Big Ike, only less natty and more like a used car salesman than owner of the dealership. I could see now what Eva had seen in sterling

Gunther Goebbels, everything Jefferson Madden was not.

Fortuitously, Henri quickly led them off to meet Hickenlooper and the famous shrink. I watched Goebbels smile and nod like he was greeting old friends, then summon over his wife who had been admiring the Van Gogh. Steffie Goebbels, I am told, was meeting the Maddens for the first time but already knew precisely who they were and I watched her give Eva the once over. Distinctly beautiful women rate closer and more obvious inspection from men but less attractive women pretend little interest upon introduction, only to size them up later with longer looks when their backs are turned.

Men check out potential rivals that way, too, and I now know why: because they might somehow someday meet in them in some kind of combat. Why women do it, somebody else will have to explain. My assumptions about why women do things end up being wrong. When it came to Mrs. Goebbels and Mrs. Madden, however, I had a pretty good idea.

When Lenny lit the candles and we found our places at the table, Henri had arranged us boy-girl, with her at one end and me at the other, properly but clearly obviating our need for any conversation between us. Denise, the judge, was on one side of me, and Deidre on the other. Dr. Goebbels was next to Deidre with Eva Madden on his right and then Hickenlooper next to Henri. On Henri's right was Miller Clark and seated next to him was Steffie and at her right, Jeff Madden. Innocently I assumed, Henri had placed Steffie and Eva directly across from each other.

Before taking my seat, I slipped Henri's chair underneath her and headed for my end of the table. When I got there, Steffie Goebbels was still standing as was Miller Clark, waiting for her to sit. But she never did. Instead she fixed her eyes on Eva Madden, who was already seated, and said calmly:

"Mrs. Madden, would you please tell us when you stopped fucking my husband...if you really have?"

"Oh, my God," said Denise the judge, and I heard Deidre's water goblet thud on the table and felt the ice water draining into my lap.

Gunther Goebbels was on his feet now, glaring. "For Chrissakes, Steffie, what in the world...!"

"The hell with you, Gunther Goebbels, you lying bastard!"

The Amazing Henri had turned to stone in her chair and didn't even respond when Steffie passed, briefly touching her arm, and saying, "Sorry, Henri, I'm going home now."

Eva sat staring into the center of the table like she had looked back at Sodom and been stricken a pillar of salt. Jefferson Madden was glaring at Eva like he could kill her and might before the night was over.

When finally I got a look at Hickenlooper, he had his sheepish, "Can you believe this" grin on his face. Then he shook his head, closed his eyes, and leaned back in his chair like a man slipping into a coma.

Henri was the quickest to recover and tried to save her dinner party by saying, "That was only the entrée, people. Wait until you see the dessert."

Everybody that had wanted to cry seconds earlier joyfully broke into uproarious laughter that dissipated as quickly as it began. There was no saving this dinner party—or the two marriages it had just destroyed.

Either Steffie had driven to the Stokes' house that night or Gunther had left the keys in the car because the Mercedes was gone when Lenny opened the door for us to leave.

"Guess I need a ride home...or to somewhere," Goebbels quips sheepishly, looking around for offers.

"I'll drive you somewhere," said Henri, who had been smothering him with unnecessary apologies.

She kept saying, "If only I had known, they would never have been invited."

Apparently, Henri, Deidre, Denise the judge and Jeff Madden were the only ones who did not know that from the first minute Eva Madden entered that room, the fuse to a bomb was there for the lighting. Weston had been so indiscreet and boastful about his conquests that Hickenlooper and Miller Clark had to know what I knew. How Steffie came to know never came out in the reams of depositions or the ultimate divorce proceedings, but she finally divulged to Henri that she had learned of the affair from Pippa Stokes who had browbeaten the information out of Nate Larson before he left the Weston firm to succeed Miller Clark as the U.S. attorney for the Bluff City district. Having been exposed over the years to the artful and wily inquisitorial skills of Pippa Weston, I know that even Larson would have wilted under her cross-examination. Although Pippa never took the bar, she could have been as good a prosecutor as Larson or Clark. I would have wilted, too.

The divorces that followed—and the wealth involved—took five lawyers, thirteen meetings at seven, separately negotiated locations so neutral they included the public library, and six months to settle. Eva Madden, Gunther Goebbels and, eventually, Tate Weston came out on the short end. She got a condo in Fort Lauderdale and a Cadillac that Madden abandoned on Interstate 40 rather than deliver. Goebbels skipped town and Weston got zilch, zero, nothing but visiting privileges with his daughter and the debt he was carrying, but the implications of his sudden thrust into poverty reached long into his future, and also into Hickenlooper's and mine and the people our newspapers served.

Of all the things now broken about Weston—marriage, home, reputation as a family man and entrepreneur—his will and energy was not among them. His resilience was extraordinary, the skills he needed to recover still sharp and plentiful. He went underground for a while, reportedly at a Florida resort where he was shielded from creditors, his unhappy former local partners in the *Defender* and the snide comments that followed the dinner party fiasco, from which snips and quips about had spread through West End like a virus. Even gossip and subpoenas have trouble catching up with someone who cannot be found.

There were rumors he had suffered a mental breakdown and was in a Winter Park rehabilitation center, and that he had been arrested for driving under the influence and was in jail in Key West. Both turned out to be false. Another had him reconnected with Dr. Goebbels in Alabama and undergoing treatment there. I found Goebbels in the Birmingham white page listings and called several times, never getting anything but an answering service with a voice that sounded like Eva Madden's, probably an old tape.

Hickenlooper assured me he had not heard a word from Weston. Red Whitmore doubted that, giving me reason to do so as well. He had reports that Weston had been seen regularly in and around Citycorp News headquarters in Miami Beach, information he had surely passed along to Hickenlooper that he had not been inclined to share. This, of course, only tweaked my long suppressed but always latent suspicion that Hickenlooper's love of chess playing in relationships trumped his commitment to candor. But then there was the distinct possibility that during a decade of existence within the spheres of Tate Weston and Jack Hickenlooper, my simple neurosis had advanced to complete paranoia.

About this time, there was a movie actor turned politician afoot in the land whose motto—trust but verify—was the only thing about him that I respected. So I checked with Miller Clark, who confirmed that he had been the source of Red's reports and that both he and Hickenlooper believed that Weston was up to something in Miami Beach. The only thing certain was the newspaper of which he was part owner was dying underneath me.

In what I viewed to be damage control cued by my call to Clark, Hickenlooper invited me to lunch and shared with me the rumors of Weston's possible presence in Miami Beach that Red had already slipped me and that Clark had verified. Had I heard anything from Big Ike about Weston, he asked?

"Of course not," I assured him. "You would have been the first person I told." This I intended as a dig.

"I didn't think so," Hickenlooper said. "What do you think he's up to?"

I had a good idea but chose not to advance it.

"Well, whatever it is is not good news," Hickenlooper said. "The bank told me Big Ike has been messing around with the Wainscott Trust beneficiaries. The trust is up for renewal soon. I know all the Perrys and they are just as vulnerable as the May family. I think Big Ike is coming after the *Clarion*."

"With Weston's help. God, that's hard to believe," I said. "As close as you two have been."

"I can believe it," Hickenlooper said. "Tate is desperate and he has always been a little unstable under pressure. He's got some tics. You saw one of them flying in that small plane with him. And he is vulnerable. Remember, the Packer boys had him rolling around in cash on the floor of a hotel room. And he still had Pippa then. He has the brains and the skills, but she was the rock. Without her, he's a different guy. No telling what he'd do."

Two days later, Hickenlooper walked into my office unannounced.

"You are about to get a call from Big Ike," he said. "He wants to see us in Miami. I've got Earnhart working on our reservations."

13

Big Ike had sent a long white limousine for us at the Miami Airport. The uniformed driver, a former Miami cop named Earl, who met us at the gate holding a large printed Citycorp sign, informed us that our meeting was not at the Citycorp News Building in Miami as we expected, but out on a peninsula in Biscayne Bay. He drove us across the main Biscayne Causeway, turned south toward the swanky neighborhood that Richard Nixon frequented while president. The Nixon houses were hardly more than simple vacation homes but Earl delivered us to a sprawling, gated estate, at the center of which was a large concrete box of a house that, thinly disguised by some architectural gingerbread, still looked like a fortress constructed against a hurricane.

Big Ike, in a black-and-white jogging suit and red Michael Jordan basketball shoes, met us at the curb and led us through a room with a twelve-foot ceiling and big enough to host a state dinner, featuring a completely glass exterior wall looking out in the direction from which a storm would most likely approach. The former owner of the place, he said, was a guy who raised funds for Richard Nixon and the president often came there to plot domestic crimes and secret foreign policy forays to China. The glass-walled room facing the Atlantic, he quipped, was "Nixon's idea of transparency in government."

"We wanted the negotiations the three of us are about to have to be completely transparent," he said, and led us out through a sliding section of glass to a veranda with an umbrella table and four chairs. "Have a seat, gentlemen," he said. "Here's the deal."

In fact, earlier that morning while we were in the air, the deal had already been done. Citycorp had tendered an offer to purchase the *Clarion* from the Wainscott Trust for what was then a whopping $60 million.

"Our offer is so generous," Big Ike said, "that the Street will beat me up for overpaying. This banker guy Jackson who deals with them predicted unanimous approval, barring some unseen and unseemly developments."

"Like what?" said Hickenlooper, who seemed not the least bit shaken by what he had just heard. "Sounds like you've nailed it already."

"Not quite," Big Ike said. "Two important humps we have to get over. First of all, as you both obviously know, antitrust laws prevent us from owning both newspapers in the same town. That legal barrier is short-lived, but it is still there today. We have to either sell the *Defender* or close it, which is not that big a deal. We sell or close newspapers somewhere most every day. The other is more problematic—and delicate."

Up to this point, Big Ike had been speaking toward some

unseen audience out in the Atlantic, his eyes somewhere on a goal in Utopia, but suddenly he started looked directly at me while he talked. "The fact is I don't want the *Clarion* without Jack Hickenlooper." Then he moved his eyes to Hickenlooper and nodded, "I valued my offer based on the idea that you stay and run it exactly like you have been doing and at the same time help me with an exciting new project."

Then Ike stood up and unzipped the jacket of his athletic suit revealing a red T-shirt emblazoned with what appeared to be a blue and white newspaper masthead—THE WORLD TODAY— complete with a script underline promising, "Global Voice of the West."

Then Big Ike turned to me again, this time with the sly look of a carnival barker.

"And Mr. Arthur. It is not without good reason that you are here. Whether the *Defender* is closed or sold is yet to be determined. If we can sell it, I feel sure any new owner would want you to remain in your post, that is, if they have a brain. If it has to be closed and folded into the *Clarion*, which is the most likely scenario, you would obviously have an executive role in the combined operation. Or…and this is my hope…that you would be willing to leave and become editor of…" Here he stopped and pointed an index finger at his chest…"THE WORLD TODAY, Global Voice of the West."

I glanced at Hickenlooper who was grinning sardonically into his lap.

Of the mental list of all the HOLY SHIT moments in my life, that meeting is clearly at the top, but it got even more bizarre. Behind us, the glass door opened and out strolled Tate Weston, wearing the seersucker suit in which I had seen him lounging around Bobby Kennedy's pool, topped off by a Panama Stetson, under which he was a tanned picture of health. I had never seen him look better— or more unwelcome. The entire scene began to look scripted, and Ike's response to Weston's appearance underscored the accuracy of my suspicion.

"I figured you two would not bring your lawyers with you," Ike cracked. "So I imported one for you."

When I looked at Hickenlooper, I saw a face I hardly recognized, contorted with the pain of disgust. He stood up, gave me what I interpreted as a "knowing look" requesting my close attention to what he was about to say, and then he flashed a hard one at Weston, but spoke to our host.

"Ike, I don't like any of this," he said. "I wish you'd get your driver to take us to wherever you have put us up, and let's get together later to discuss this. I've had Weston as my lawyer before and I know I don't need him now. As far as I am concerned, he has no place at the table except where it concerns how he plans to handle the debt with which he has saddled the *Defender* and that he has all but abandoned. If you want to talk to me again, I would appreciate you leaving Weston out of it. He is rife with conflict of interest."

With that, he walked back into the big room and stood pouting as if waiting for transportation to anywhere else. That was Hickenlooper's opening move in a bare-knuckled chess match, if there could be such a contest, the likes of which could be Diplomacy 101 for any foreign diplomat trying to avoid a shooting war.

Big Ike ultimately convinced Hickenlooper that the estate was plenty big enough for all the participants, that the limousine had gone and would not return until dinner that evening and that all we really needed was a break for lunch. Hickenlooper said he would take his in his room, a suggestion I seconded on my own behalf.

Together we took lunch of pea soup and chicken salad in a suite on the floor above with a wall of windows that offered the same view of Biscayne Bay. Once alone together, Hickenlooper's harsh demeanor disappeared. It was as if Ike had just delivered good news.

"If a hurricane did hit this place, you surely couldn't complain you were surprised," he said. "You could see it coming for miles."

"I wouldn't want the job of boarding it up," I replied.

"I saw this coming, too," Hickenlooper said, back to business as usual. "Once the bank changed hands, I could feel the wind blowing. Somebody, maybe it was you, or Deidre maybe, someone told me the day Citycorp closed on the *Defender* that the *Clarion* was his real target. And I'm not sure Weston had any idea what he was getting us into. Getting the *Defender* away from Colonel May had become an obsession."

Like any good reporter, I wasted no time getting to the burning question.

"What are you going to do?"

"If I owned the paper or any significant part of it, I'd fight this bastard to the end," he said. "But I'm just a hired hand. I could make a run at the board but it would be an exercise in futility. So what would I do then? Resign and issue a statement about how the free press is being eaten alive by big corporations and then go run a journalism school somewhere?"

He paused for a minute, then got up and looked out at the Atlantic.

"Perched up on there on principle is rewarding for a few minutes," he said, "but that's a temporary high and not very practical. I have to talk to Deidre about it, but my inclination is do exactly what I suggested to you when you were considering taking the *Defender* job. Try to make a pact with the devil I can live with.

"You heard him. Ike wants me for the same reason he wanted you. We have something he does not—respect. The *Clarion* has a gilded history. It is a newspaper known for persistent pursuit of the truth and for its long and courageous battle against Jim Crow and segregation. The rock it stands on is simply equal justice for everybody. And for all this, we have earned that respect. That is what Ike Oldham and Citycorp News lacks and he has now decided to try to buy. This time he's not just trying to buy another newspaper. He is trying to buy respect and I am going to show him just how expensive that stuff can be."

I never knew the exact terms of whatever agreement Big Ike and Hickenlooper eventually came to, whether it was oral, a written contract, or sealed by a blood-drawn handshake. But it was clearly ironclad and remained unbroken for the next twenty years, and by the chance of circumstance, I had been present at the very moment that checkmate occurred. Hickenlooper seized the upper hand in what had to be the burying of the sharpest of hatchets and the lying down together of the strangest of bedfellows.

Neither of us knew before flying to Miami that on the evening of our arrival that Ike had scheduled a late-night appearance on

ABC News' *Nightline* with Ted Koppel to unveil a prototype of *World Today*. The plan was to have dinner at Joe's Stone Crabs in Miami Beach and then move on to Miami's ABC affiliate where Koppel was taping at ten one of his road show segments for an eleven-thirty broadcast.

Earl, whose full-time Citycorp employment consisted of driver and bodyguard for Big Ike, was late arriving at the Key Biscayne compound and had not bothered to call. So Big Ike was already on edge when we exited the concrete box and, there, in place of the long white Lincoln limousine to which he was accustomed, was an aging blue Chevy sedan with a crumpled fender and sporting one of those tiny emergency use-only spare tires that made it sit at a decided tilt.

"Goddamn, Earl, where's the car?" Big Ike demanded.

"Wrecked," Earl said. "Some guy ran a light and I got T-boned trying to turn onto the causeway. I believe it's totaled."

"What's this bucket of bolts? Worst rental I ever saw."

"It's not a rental, Mr. Oldham. This is my personal car."

"Why the hell didn't you get a rental?"

"I didn't have time, Mr. Oldham. I was already late by the time I got the limo towed, so my son brought me my car and my wife followed him over and they had a flat on the way."

He pointed to the right front of the Chevy. "That's why my little spare is on there."

Hickenlooper and I climbed into the back seat with a bag full of half-empty fast food cartons Earl had obviously had had no time to dump. Now the driver, a half-foot taller than his boss, was standing outside the open door on the passenger side, stoically waiting for Big Ike to take the shotgun seat. But Ike kept standing outside the car jawing at him, his refusal to even enter the vehicle some kind of augmentation to the punishment of his tongue-lashing.

Hickenlooper, looking frustrated, leaned forward. "Hey Ike," he said. "We're already late. If you don't get in, we'll have to skip dinner."

Ike didn't respond, but got in and kept up his tirade, only louder so Earl wouldn't miss a word as he circled around to get in. And the boss continued to pelt his driver with questions about the accident, the condition of the Lincoln and was he sure it had been totaled. Then he began to denigrate Earl's decision to substitute his own personal car instead of getting a rental, which he said would have "been as easy as falling off a log."

I kept my mouth shut in deference to my relative junior varsity status, but Hickenlooper kept trying to deflect the flak from Earl by pointing out how much better the Chevy was as transportation to Miami than walking.

"It would be a long ass hike, wouldn't it, Earl?" Hickenlooper said. "How long is that Rickenbacker Causeway anyway?

"About seven miles," Earl said. "We're about to hit it right up here."

Ike was about to level another blast, but Hickenlooper cut him off with more small talk about how stuff all over Florida had been named Rickenbacker after the aviation icon that founded Eastern Airlines. But each time Hickenlooper took a breath, Ike bored in on Earl, explaining in harsh tones that all he had to do was call Hertz or any one of the other executives at Citycorp and they would have sent him a luxury sedan right to the scene of the accident. When Earl said the only way he even got a call through to his wife was via the police dispatcher, Ike yelled, "Goddamn it, Earl, quit making excuses. You could have asked the cops to call our company or Hertz."

At this point, we were about five minutes into the trip and half-way across the Rickenbacker, normally a six-lane racetrack of heavy traffic. But it was nearly nine at night and as dark as South Florida's perpetually neon lit sky ever gets. A few raindrops had begun to glisten on the windshield, and there was not another car in sight in the northbound lanes, which Earl suddenly abandoned altogether and screeched to a halt on the shoulder. He turned slowly to Big Ike and said, "Get out of the car, Mr. Oldham."

Ike glared at Earl in disbelief. "What the hell you talking about, Earl? What did you say?"

"I said get the fuck out of the car—all of you."

He sounded serious enough to me that I started to get out, but Hickenlooper caught my elbow with his hand. Ike had begun to curse and stammer obscenities reminding Earl where his "goddamned bread is buttered."

"Get hold of yourself, Ike," Hickenlooper said, "It's Earl's car and he is using it to get us to dinner and your television show."

Then Earl spoke up. "It's no use, Mr. Hickenlooper, I know y'all ain't at fault. But my shitty old car ain't taking this no-good asshole another inch. All of you get the fuck out of my car."

Hickenlooper, whose presence on the passenger side in back had prevented me from leaving at the first request, opened the door and got out on the shoulder, but Ike stayed firmly planted in the passenger seat. Hickenlooper opened the door.

"Come on, Ike, get out," he said. "Earl wants us out."

"He'll get over it, won't you, Earl?" Ike said, an entirely different tone now that he considered all the other options. "Everything will be okay, Earl. I just lost my temper. Let's just go on."

"Ain't nothing gonna be all right," Earl said, sternly. "We ain't going on. I'm going on. Get out my fucking car before I pull you out."

The rain had picked up now, one of those little Florida squalls that pop up without warning. Ike stepped out into it, a few folded copies of his *World Today* prototypes in his hand. Hickenlooper grabbed them and stuffed them into a zippered business case he was carrying. Earl hit the gas even before the passenger door could be closed and squealed off into the night. Through the thickening downpour, we watched the Chevy's taillights until they faded into the glare from the Miami skyline.

I kept looking back over my shoulder for traffic coming from Key Biscayne. But the cars were few and far between, and they were usually traveling so fast when they reached us that flagging them down was impossible. It was doubtful they even saw us trudging through the downpour.

We had endured a mile-long soaking by the time a Key Biscayne Village police cruiser flashing blue lights pulled up behind us on the shoulder and let out a little belch of siren. A young blond officer with a big Glock on his hip and a flashlight in his hand got out and approached us in good humor.

"Some guy called the station and said there were three gentlemen walking down the Rickenbacker creating a traffic hazard in the rain," he said. "You must be them."

"We plead guilty," Hickenlooper said. "Can you help us get to Miami?"

He could. His dispatcher called ahead and had a cab waiting for us when we reached Highway 1. Dinner was out of the question and we were soaked to the skin, so the cab took us directly the ABC affiliate station in Miami. In those days, Ted Koppel's *Nightline* was a must-see for anybody in the news business. He often abandoned its New York home to tour big cities around the country where he brought in locally prominent residents to talk about how they viewed stuff happening in the insulated Washington/Big Apple corridor.

It was the perfect venue for Big Ike's announcement. But the normally confident, overbearing Big Ike was a mess. His printer's ink and newsprint costume of the day had faded into colorless, indecipherable oblivion. The starch was not only out of his shirt collar, it was gone out of him, too. His curly, carefully constructed silver coiffure had melted into ugly mop strings that now clung to his forehead and eyebrows, exposing a large, bald pate it had once concealed. He looked at the reflection of himself in a makeup room where some poor hairdresser and fix-it artist was trying to prepare him for the cameras. Like some old, spent vainglorious stage actor giving up the ghost, Big Ike took a good look at himself and announced, "I can't go on television like this, Hickenlooper. You will have to do it."

Neither Hickenlooper nor I looked much better. But of the three, Hickenlooper had survived best. His suit, a little baggy as usual, must have been wash and wear, and his shirt collar had dried back perfectly to a reasonable facsimile of its original self, as had his hair. The leading-man blue eyes were clear and sparkling. He even had on socks.

"Why me?" Hickenlooper asked. "I haven't even decided to stay with the newspaper you are buying out from under me. I surely have no connection to *America Today*."

"*World Today*," Ike corrected. "But you will have. I want you to manage the start-up. Get it off the ground. Design what kind of editorial policy it has. Having you there will give it instant credibility and quality."

Knowing what I knew about Hickenlooper's intentions, I could hear the sound of Big Ike's balls plopping into Hickenlooper's pocket.

"How could I do that and still run the *Clarion*?" Hickenlooper asked. "How in the hell could that work?"

"With the Citycorp airplane and with my money and insistence," Ike said. "Just go back and forth. You can have carte blanche both places. I'll see to it."

"Damn, you want me to do two jobs?" Hickenlooper sounded legitimately incredulous.

"I'll make it worth your while," Ike said.

"I'll hold you to that," Hickenlooper said.

Then, he reached into his zippered case and removed the perfectly dry prototypes of the *World Today*. "I better take a look at these," he said. "So I know what I like and what I don't and what I should say to Koppel."

What I had taken as outright betrayal, Hickenlooper blew off as the desperate act of a basically good and well-intentioned man. His friendship and affection for Weston never waned, another life lesson for me. The anger he had displayed on the veranda had been solely for the benefit of future negotiations with Big Ike. He explained it all on the plane ride back home.

"Weston knew there was no future for competing newspapers in markets the size of Bluff City and that his deal with Citycorp was falling apart," he said. "His partners were about to take a bath in the deal. They all owed more money than they could ever pay back. He had been brainstorming with Miller Clark about how he might save them from a financial wreck and himself from another business embarrassment. The blowup at the dinner party and the divorce from Pippa had left him with no options. He knew the bank was going to move on him and that I would eventually face from the Wainscott heirs what the colonel had experienced with the Mays."

Hickenlooper went quiet for a few minutes and seemed to be studying cloud formations out the plane window. After a while, I asked him the same questions I would have had I been doing a story about us for the *Rolling Stone*.

"Do you think Weston instigated the move on the Wainscott beneficiaries?"

"No. Ike had that in mind when he bought the *Defender*. He didn't really want a fading afternoon paper. He wanted the *Clarion* and me. Tate only accelerated it because it looked like the best way to avoid another public humiliation and he figured in the long run it would be best for the *Clarion* and me—to be owned by a big corporation with all the resources of Citycorp rather than the newspaper being at the mercy of a bank trustee and some third-generation heirs hungry for a payout. I knew I would be bought sooner or later, just not by whom."

Far as I can tell, until the day Hickenlooper left the building on Board Street, the *Clarion* never missed a beat or changed its tune. While other Citycorp papers faced repeated belt tightening year after year, the *Clarion* was somehow spared the pain. Meanwhile, *World Today* took some doing, but it was eventually a major success, and remained somewhat of a beacon of truth-seeking even as newspapers slid toward oblivion. And despite vast differences in political opinions, lifestyle and the worth and duties of newspapers, I believe Big Ike and Jack Hickenlooper even came to like each other.

Oldham hit the magic corporate mandatory retirement age of sixty-five several years before Hickenlooper did, but whatever arrangement they had lasted until the calendar clicked on Hickenlooper—and even beyond when the two became industry elder statesmen without current portfolios. Because the company age requirement did not apply to the Citycorp Charitable Foundation, in which Oldham was able to stash much of the company's assets before he retired, Big Ike in effect took the foundation with him when he left, which enabled him to remain an important figure due to the vast millions he had to spread around. Some of that largesse landed directly on Hickenlooper who would eventually die a wealthy man, and more indirectly on Bluff City in the form of a multimillion addition to the Bluff City Metropolitan Library with Hickenlooper's name emblazoned on it in perpetuity.

14

Before our flight from Florida landed, I had asked Hickenlooper a question that I wanted to ask him for nearly twenty years.

"Do you think Weston is a sick man, mentally I mean?"

"I do," he said without hesitation. "I don't know if he is just severely neurotic, bipolar or maybe even borderline schizoid. He's got some genius in him for sure, and sometimes there's a very thin line in between. What I'm really worried about is how losing Pippa is going to affect him. He is not someone comfortable with being alone. This might put him over the edge. And Miller says he's no longer taking whatever medicine Goebbels had him on and now he is on some other mood medicine, Prozac maybe or something similar."

Whatever substance sustained Weston, pharmaceutical or the product of his own glands, it was doing wonders for him. The very next day he was back in full pinstriped Philadelphia lawyer regalia, complete with gold watch fob and the straw Panama he was sporting in Florida. I found him in the office at the *Defender* where he had seldom shown his face the whole time he'd been part owner and so-called "chairman." It was Colonel May's old publisher's suite, which I had rejected as too remote and claustrophobic for me. Having learned early the benefits of publisher transparency, I had chosen to build myself a small glass-walled cubicle in both the *Morning Herald* and *Defender* newsrooms. So Weston had claimed the colonel's old haunt for himself, but had only used it sparingly to entertain people he wanted "to impress but suspected were closet Nazis."

"This place is full of ghosts," he complained, and rattled off the names of Hitler, Stalin, Chairman Mao and Attila the Hun. These Cretans who like the *Defender* will all be right at home in there. Bedford Forrest's painting is still up over the fireplace."

If Weston had been flattened by Pippa's divorce filing, or any way shaken by Hickenlooper's dismissive behavior in Key Biscayne, you could not tell it.

"I guess you know our goose is cooked," he said. "Big Ike told me last night he'd rather close the *Defender* than put up with another partner that can't hold his own. You believe he said that about us, that we can't hold our own? I don't know about you, David Aahthuh, but I can still hold my own with the best of 'em."

He was quiet for a minute, then rose from the colonel's rich walnut desk and stood as erect as a six-foot-four man can and with the fingers of one hand began twirling the Panama around the fist of his other. "Truth is, I won't even let anybody else hold mine," he said, flashing that movie idol grin. "Not even the lovely Eva Madden, damn her soul. David Aahthuh, you know

what the playwright Larry King said about the late, great Hank
Williams, don't you?"

"A lot of things," I replied. "What in particular did you have
in mind?"

"That Hank Williams died at the tendah age of twenty-nine
yeahs and never had a piece of pussy that didn't go bad on him.
Reckon old Hank and I have more in common than just talent and
good looks."

Then he placed the Stetson at an angle that suited his jaunty
mood, and headed for the door.

"Where are you staying?" I yelled after him.

"I have a very small room at the new Downtowner Motel just
up Board Street right near the Capitol," he turned and said. "It's
temporary of course, while I am waiting for my new condo in
the West End to be painted, but the location is very fortuitous
considering that the Community Southern has this very aftahnoon
replevied my Pontiac, as well as the rest of my assets. I will be in
court shortly to recover them. But tell our friend Mr. Hickenloopah
that I am temporarily afoot—down in town perhaps—but definitely
not out."

I couldn't have imagined it at the time, but Tate Weston was
plunging off into a decade of near homelessness on the street,
pandering if not for food and funds, for attention and reclama-
tion of his self-esteem. From what I gathered later from Miller
Clark, with whom Weston remained in touch, and from Red
Whitmore, the prodigious human street sweeper of information
from the gutters and corners of Bluff City, there was never a West
End condo to be painted or a chance in hell of him recovering his

Pontiac. He indeed remained afoot, amassing thousands more debt in unpaid Downtowner room rent and telephone charges, an inordinate percentage in wasted long-distance, fundraising quests with political and business acquaintances unfamiliar with his fall from wealth and prominence. Unable to sell his charade in person, he had become dependent on the façade of a telephone line.

Within a short time, the Downtowner shut off his phone and began proceedings to have him evicted. The visual of him with his belongings in a wheeled grocery cart was so disturbing I called Miller Clark, now senior partner in a new firm called Clark & Larson, who had resigned as U.S. attorney after a rock star stint in which he brought down an incumbent governor for taking bribes.

"Don't worry, we're not going to let that happen," Clark assured me. "Pippa and I are leasing him a condo beyond walking distance of the Capitol and the courthouse. Maybe it will keep him off the streets."

It didn't. Sallie Mae had used her Sheriff Lermon/Captain Crockett political connections to trade her drugstore job for a spot as deputy registrar in the County Election Commission from which she called one day in tears.

"David, you won't believe this, but Tate Weston is at this very minute standing out in the hallway dressed up like Ben Franklin in a frock coat and a wig. He looks like a fool. Is he sick or what?"

"I'm afraid so," I said. "People think since Pippa divorced him he has gone off the deep end."

"My God," she said. "That is so sad. I just want to go out there and give the poor thing a hug and take him home. He needs a haircut and even looks like he might need a bath. And he has always been so clean cut and good-looking."

It was shortly after that, when I was in Bluff City and had stopped by the election commission intending to say hello to my mother, that I saw Weston in his ridiculous garb turning in his qualifying petitions and shamefully avoided ever speaking to him. The year I spent in Cambridge I had often encountered a bearded street screamer, costumed as a Viking, horned headdress and all, waving a staff. He frequently stalked Harvard Square, screaming angrily at the top of his voice to no one in particular. He had Tourette's syndrome, a disease of the nervous system that manifests itself in an uncontrollable tic of intermittent explosive behavior. I wondered if Weston was headed in that direction.

At the time, Hickenlooper was still running the *Clarion* and I stopped by to talk to Whitmore, who I knew was still keeping an eye on the county courthouse and the Capitol and surely would have run across Weston on the street collecting names. I asked him if Weston had lost it completely.

"No, not really, he's off on this Constitution obsession, which is why he is all costumed up like a founding father, Jefferson or somebody he regards a constitutional hero. It's all just a show. He wants people to ask him why he is masquerading as a founder of the country and he launches into a sermon about how Jefferson did this and Lincoln was the greatest president ever and the first to interpret the Constitution as guaranteeing us all the same rights equally. And now he likes this definition of the perfect democracy that the Czech president used in his speech to Congress, about how elusive it is and that you only move toward it like a horizon you never get to."

"I know exactly what you're talking about," I said. "I like it, too."

"Well, Weston's in love with it. You know how he used to quote Kennedy's speech all the time about the rising tide raising all the boats. Well, now he's all about trying to float toward a horizon while fighting 'the stiff winds of reactionary resistance.'"

"I thought they were trying to keep him beyond walking distance," I said to Red.

"Fat chance of that," he said. "First, he started taking cabs downtown. Now he rides the bus. Can you image that? Thomas Jefferson on a bus. He comes in every day like a panhandler. He usually picks out a corner and stakes it out as his own office. Weston just walks up and down the street talking to people and asking them what they think about some court decision or tax referendum. He's as pleasant and charming as ever, only dressed like a clown. A couple of times, I have seen either Miller or Pippa come by and stop their cars. He gets in and they take him home. Two hours later, he's back."

My new life in rural obscurity, financed by frugal handling of two relatively sizable inheritances from two newspapers that ironically had starved to death under my guidance, included significant time lapses between freelance writing jobs and my guitar playing gigs in cheap roadhouses. So I decided to use some of it to try to find out what had caused a brilliant, highly educated constitutional lawyer to become a laughingstock on the street.

Back in corduroy and denim and with a new set of wheels, I fired up my Ford pickup and headed for Birmingham in search of an answer. Dr. Gunther Goebbels had set up his practice in a suburb that looked like Birmingham's answer to West End. His receptionist, who bore an uncanny resemblance to Eva Madden, confirmed that the doctor was in but was available only by appointment.

"I understand," I said, "but I am not a prospective patient. Is he in the building at the moment?"

"Well, yes," she said, "but he is preparing for his next therapy session."

"Good, just take him this message for me, please. David Arthur is here from the *Rolling Stone* to ask how the ethical breach that has driven Tate Weston insane came to take place."

Goebbels then came out and led me back into his office. Up close he appeared 10 years younger than the wife who had bounced him, a dead ringer for Alexander Haig, the officious Army General who had replaced the German criminal elements in the Nixon White House during the Watergate scandal--and a perfect example of Weston's cookie cutter brand of physically attractive associates. No wonder they were play pals.

After a bit of small talk about the relative size of Birmingham to Bluff City and how his new practice was off to a terrific start, he folded his hands in front of him on his desk like he might be about to pray. "What's Weston doing that makes you think he is insane, Mr. Arthur?"

"He's walking around in a Thomas Jefferson outfit making a fool of himself," I said. "He's become a street person."

"That's terrible news," he said, "but no reason to assume insanity. Perfectly sane people do that every day, some as a means of making a living. But even though Mr. Weston is no longer a patient, I cannot discuss his case at all."

"You've already allowed his case to be discussed in great detail on the front page of a newspaper, Doctor," I said. "And that disclosure has apparently wrecked his mental health and his life. Don't you think it's a little late to hide behind doctor-patient confidentiality?"

"That could not be helped. It was a vengeful act by one of my employees. I had no part in it."

"I'd be sure to report it that way," I said, "but if you will help me understand what I need to understand, there might be no need for another story in the *Rolling Stone* or anywhere else. I came from the era when journalists believed a public figure's mental illness, alcoholism or sexual behavior was relevant only when it affected the performance of his duties in whatever public office he held or was seeking. We also believed in anonymous sources and had the law on our side when it came to protecting them. All of that has changed now, but I haven't."

Goebbels appeared to relax for the first time. He removed his spectacles and studied the desk before him. "Well, perhaps if we put this on a hypothetical basis, you know, talking about a hypothetical patient's case, perhaps we can do it that way. What is it you want to know, or understand, as you put it?"

"I want to know what you think a hypothetical patient is experiencing after his franchise business fails—largely due to your leaked therapy session transcript—and when he loses an election to the United States Senate and then being caught up in an embarrassing, infidelity-laced divorce scandal in which he lost a rich wife who also happened to be one of the most desirable and beautiful women on the face of the earth?"

A stern-faced Dr. Goebbels took a deep breath and let it out in a sigh.

"I would guess that someone dealing with that set of circumstances would have cause to have lapsed into a deep depression."

"I mean clinically, what does that entail?"

"It would entail a decline in the level of serotonin, a complex amine found in the blood and the brain. Serotonin can be produced naturally or synthetically. Among its effects are the constriction of blood vessels and contraction of the smooth muscles. It is important as a neurotransmitter and a hormone that controls mood. No one knows how to exactly measure the amount present in the brain, only that the less you have in your system, the more depressed you are likely to be and that more can make you happier."

"Can the kind of depression you're talking about make someone suicidal or dangerous to others or drive them into Tourette's syndrome or some other nerve system disorder?"

"That depends."

"On what?"

"On the individual."

"What about an individual like Tate Weston?"

"I told you I cannot talk about him."

"You can unless you've got a receptionist listening out there, who in an act of revenge, leaks the transcript to the *Birmingham*

News. What you are saying to me is going nowhere. It is just for my education. So what about some hypothetical patient of high intelligence, high self-esteem, maybe a close to genius level IQ? We all know someone like that, don't we, Doctor?"

"Well, a patient like that might be a well-adjusted individual, legitimately secure in his or her own skin and though they might suffer depression as anyone would from a set of circumstances you have described, they can recover. At the bottom, they would be nearly catatonic, unthinking, prone to sleep and insulation from everything around them. But then, they would either naturally or through proper regulation of artificial serotonin enhancement—drugs—begin to climb back. The critical point would be some-where in the progress back to normal, when they began to think clearly again. The well-adjusted patient might consider suicide and then likely reject the idea and go on. But someone whose apparent stability, security and high self-esteem is actually a façade for a truly fragile and vulnerable inner self. Well, that's different. They are like an egg with onionskin for a shell. Likely to come apart and do anything. The morgues and hospitals are filled with them, and in some cases, their victims."

"Doctor, you have been using the plural pronoun in your expla-nation. I am trying to find out about one particular patient who is obviously going through what we have been talking about. What category should he be in?"

"Again, we are talking theoretically, remember. I take it that you are most interested in the egg with the onionskin, right? But my guess is that if your onionskinned egg has not burst by now, it is past the danger point and, barring some even more devastating disappointment, will never harm him or herself or anyone else.

"I had a patient like that once who, as I have been saying, cannot be identified, but who defied every norm and category we have developed as a means of case discussion in my area of medical science. He—or she—first came to me because, in addition to a fear of flying in small airplanes, had from adolescence suffered panic attacks, marked by severe heart spasms and shortness of breath, even though there was no evidence of heart disease.

"This patient was a successful young lawyer with a healthy sex life but was deathly afraid of suffering one of these panics while addressing a jury or making a speech or during a closing argument—or God forbid—while having sex when blood pressure was elevated. So, Mr. Arthur, though normal brain has approximately 40 million cells, I am convinced this patient had more. The degree to which this person was capable of focusing on something or loving and hating him or herself—sometimes simultaneously—was such that a score of Nobel Prize winners from several disciplines should be empanelled immediately just to study it. And I have reams of taped therapy sessions I would gladly contribute with every confidence that they might well result in a complete rewrite of everything we think we know about the human psyche. This person could reach the limits of depression one minute and the height of wellness the next. I could not even keep up with whatever level was being experienced. But I can tell you this, this patient had one of the strongest instincts for survival that I have ever come across or read about. And if the person you are asking me about was my patient or like my patient, you have nothing to worry about. We are talking about someone who is the ultimate survivor."

"Well, Dr. Goebbels," I said, wrapping up my interview. "We both know a man who fits that description of your patient and a woman who might be looking for work about now who is experienced in transcribing those tapes for you. Thank you very much for your time."

From that moment to this, I ceased worrying about Tate Weston going postal and every election since when his name appeared as a candidate no matter the office, I made sure to pull the lever for him. And when his name did not appear, I requested a paper ballot and wrote it in, and reminded myself that someday I should write a book about the brightest, most interesting, charismatic man I ever knew. He never won an election to public office, but he never stopped trying. And he remains a familiar and imposing figure on the streets of Bluff City, gathering names and filing one lawsuit after another challenging the crazy laws pushed through the state legislature and the Congress by the third-party wing nuts and reactionaries that dominate public policy today. His goal is the same as it has always been and was for his pal Hickenlooper, with whom he ultimately buried the hatchet if one ever really needed burying. Both men can truly claim that they have spent their lives in quest of equal justice under the United States Constitution, copies of which will still bulge from Weston's pockets the day God calls him home.

VIC AND ME

I am now one of those men who other people look at and ask, "What the hell does he do?"

Good question. If directed at me, a truthful answer would be, "pretty much any damn thing I want to." Which would be an embarrassment to my late father Woody Arthur, who did not respect anyone who resembled a "kept man." But Woody and Sallie Mae both died in ninety-five, one two months after the other, as old married couples tend to do. And though they never spent all that much time together, they did get married twice and lived together some between marriages, so they qualify. Both are now in matching urns in a decidedly upscale Lermon Mausoleum on the downtown edge of West End, a decision by me to move them up a class or two in case there is another side and we meet there and I have to explain anything.

Actually, I am only partially kept, for I did manage to retain and enhance enough from the million dollar-plus final settlements of dead newspapers to preserve at least a cornerstone of independence. And I can sell a book or a story now and then or consult on a political campaign, both of which keep me marketable on the speech circuit. People now actually pay to hear in person the talking heads they see on television.

But mostly I just take care of three quarter horses and ride around my twenty acres on the South Harpeth, play my guitar when it suits me, write a song when one strikes me, and hang with an older woman and her grandson. How all this came to be is a long story, but having spent so much of my life writing stuff for newspaper readers and politicians with short attention spans, I'll cut right to the good stuff.

No matter how hard Hickenlooper tried to keep me a newspaperman, even offering me the editor's cubicle at the *Clarion*, I'd had enough. If he wanted to spend the rest of life dealing with the Ike Oldhams of the world, more power to him. I walked right up Board Street and rented me a little office from old Tom Farwell, the madman who had entertained me through my entire six years in the Air National Guard and who had channeled his audio and video genius into a fortune as a media consultant for politicians. Then he drove me twenty miles south of Bluff City to the little Harpeth and sold me the back twenty acres of his farm, a gorgeous river bottom, including a cabin and a barn on a hillside steep enough to protect me from high water.

Then, two months after Woody succumbed to a hypertension stroke in the nursing home, Sallie Mae up and died suddenly of a heart attack, probably dictated by years of chain-smoking unfiltered cigarettes, which is also what finally claimed her daddy Morgan Crockett. Her visitation and funeral broke all records for attendance at Lermon's Mortuary, attracting what had to be the longest motorcade from West End ever to cross the river for a social event in Mill Town. Had Sallie Mae been watching from somewhere supernatural, her critique for the other angels would no doubt have been emblematic of her inimitable storytelling prowess:

"Pee ran down my leg like dew when I saw Tate Weston stand up and start saying all those nice things about me. And he looked so much better than he had been looking before I died. And the Hickenloopers were there in droves—even Jack Hickenlooper himself and that still pretty Deidre, who is sixty-five at least and didn't look a day over forty.

"Speaking of pretty, Pippa Stokes came, too, and brought that sweet daughter of hers and Tate's. I can't think of her name right now. Brooke or Brock or something like that. And she is nearly as beautiful as her mother and you know Pippa's a professional model with her face on makeup billboards all over the country, and she don't even need the money. Nuns and priests were everywhere, some I didn't even know. You would've thought it was a spaghetti supper at the Saint Paul Guild.

"And Godamighty, politicians came from all over. All those people from all those campaigns. You know I can't be sure, but I swear I thought I even saw Judd Packer there, too, and that sorry brother of his that got him into all that trouble. I thought they were both still in jail.

"And I felt so sorry for my only son David, who kept choking up trying to talk about me. Bless his heart. He should have just shut up and sat down. And for the life of me, I did not recognize that lovely older woman who kept talking to him all night. But there was something really familiar about her."

My heart did indeed get blessed that day, and yes, it was an older woman barely recognizable I admit, who came up behind me and poked me in the ribs with an index finger. When I turned around, lo and behold, there was the Amazing Henri Ravenel Stokes and by her side a handsome teenage boy taller than she. Both were dressed to the nines.

"David, I would like you to meet my grandson, Al Ravenel," Henri said and offered me a cheek soft as a rose petal. "Allston insisted on giving him her first name and my maiden name, which is very old Charleston—you can understand why she did that—but it does constantly require explanation at times like these."

"Al, it is a pleasure to meet you," I said, turning to him and sticking out my hand. "Your mother and I grew up together, you know."

"Yes, sir," he said with a firm handshake. "My mom talked about you a lot. You are Vic, aren't you, the one I am named after? My middle name is Victor. I am Alan Victor Ravenel."

The look on my face and some emotion that I guess was so obvious that Henri quickly seized both of my hands in hers, drew them to her bosom and held them there tightly for a minute. Then she released them and pulled me tight into a hug that did not feel like a grandmotherly condolence but I hoped looked like one to anybody watching.

"I am so sorry for your loss," she whispered, her lips nearly touching my ear. "I know how close you were to your mother. Sallie Mae came to my first husband's funeral and was there at our celebration for Allston, so I just had to come and I thought it would be a good time for you to meet her son. He's been with me at the Stokes' house ever since her accident. Now I am all he has—and with Brownlee gone, too, he is all I have. So it has worked out fine. Al, or Vic, I am beginning to think he prefers to be Vic, wanted to meet you. I hope you don't mind."

"Of course not," I said, and for the first time felt a twinge of sympathy for someone I never even considered as needing any.

The Amazing Henri never left my side the entire evening, taking a place beside me with her grandson, forming a kind of receiving line, as if she were my companion or a family member, reminding me that except for some Cumberland Mountains Arthurs that I'd never even met, there was no family; not one blood relative I could name. At first I resented it a little, thinking maybe that, out of habit, Henri simply needed to stand at the center of attention, which as Sallie Mae's only surviving relative I had naturally become. But as the evening wore on, I began to enjoy her support and company. An attraction on her own, she also moved the well-wishers along and made the evening go by faster. She and the young man left promptly with the crowd, but not without another full body hug that, like the one earlier, did leave me feeling it had come from a family friend simply trying to give ease to a grieving heart. And as she left, she reminded me that "we never got to have that talk" she had mentioned in the turmoil of the dinner party. "I'd like to call and try again if you are interested." I gave her a card from the ad agency.

That night when I left Lermon's, I drove through Mill Town past the smoke-belching old DuPont plant where Woody worked most of life away, which now polluted the air with a putrid purple smoke, and down by Crockett High where Sallie Mae had dropped out in the tenth grade after she had been caught and expelled for smoking in the girl's bathroom. Then I headed toward the river circling off the highway, first to the left down the Rayon Drive, the right side that abutted the Tennessee Central and NC & STL railroad tracks. Midway in the block of shingled bungalows was the postage-stamp yard of Woody's first household with the oak tree in the center where I had rolled around on the protruding roots with a black-and-white collie cur named Bob. It still looked as awful as I remembered. Down at the end of the block, I took a sharp U-turn back up the alley that separated the row of houses from the backs of those on the next block. And still standing was a dilapidated old garage where, when I was six, my eight-year-old friend Aileen let me peer down the front of her underpants to prove she had no "dickie" in the spot where I had one.

The alley emptied back into the highway directly in front of the crumbling brick building that once housed Moser's Grocery. When I was four and Woody Arthur fresh home from overseas, the two-room apartment on the second floor became the first home he ever made for his family. It had a rickety porch on the back then that looked out over another alley from which a neighbor boy had hurled the cinder that left a scar I still carried in my hairline. Beside the store was a level vacant lot where a shoddy, little carnival set up in the summer time and I rode circling ponies every time I got my hands on a dime.

Though it was dark and the streets were weak and dingy, it was obvious that everything I had seen, not much to start with, had deteriorated to even less. I was glad it was the middle of the night and I had not seen the people who lived there now because they, too, would have reeked of next to nothing, and I doubted that any of them would find a way out as easily as I had. People may still be born equal in Mill Town, but from all appearances, their first breath would likely be their last taste of equality.

I took some comfort knowing that Sallie Mae Arthur had spent her last night East of the River. She was there with me in the front seat, her urn belted in tight in case of a sudden stop, on her way, thankfully, to the West End.

A few days later, the Amazing Henri called with an invitation to a brunch at the Stokes' house the following Sunday. I figured it for another West End social gathering but only Henri and the boy were there. No butler, no cook, no caterer. Henri had done the cooking and though it was a simple Southern country fare—ham, biscuits, gravy, scrambled eggs and fried potatoes and onions—I had never had better.

"I should have known your grandmother was a superior cook," I said to young Al Ravenel. "She is an expert at whatever she does. Your mother was my first evidence of that."

"Of course I can cook," Henri said. "My mother was a great cook. She was an Allston and her kitchen was the best restaurant in Charleston. She taught me and I am a good learner. I can sew and clean house and patch the damn roof, too, if I have to. I am not the silk-stocking socialite people think Henri Ravenel Stokes has become."

"Seems to me you're doing great at whatever you do," I said. "And from what I read in the *Wall Street Journal*, you're doing a darn sight better than okay as a Fortune 500 CEO."

"That's been a sharp learning curve," she said. "And I am still in the middle of the bend, but I have pretty good help mostly, and I am getting there."

Later we walked around the Stokes estate, which had small but exquisite stables and was manicured to the level of a golf course. I saw a couple of Thoroughbred geldings in a paddock nearby and walked over to check them out.

"Do you ride?" I asked.

"As a girl I rode a lot," she said. "Mostly hunt seat, chasing the hounds. But I've never been on any of these. I have no idea what they are. But I do own very nice riding pants—you know, for parties at horse venues."

"What about your grandson? He ride?"

Young Ravenel had stayed inside, having volunteered to clean off the table and straighten up after brunch.

"I don't think he's ever been on a horse," Henri said. "I know he'd like to learn. You have horses on your place I understand."

I didn't know how she knew that, but figured maybe Miller Clark or the Hickenloopers had mentioned it to her. Miller and Hickenlooper's boy Jack Jr. had been over to ride with me. All three of my quarter horses were push-button former Western riding show competitors with years of training. Even little kids were safe on them.

"Bring him over sometime," I said, never expecting it to happen. "And we all take a turn around the farm together."

Well, that's how it started. They did come over, Henri in a pair of painted-on jeans and Ostrich cowboy boots. She had not forgotten how to ride and the boy took to it with relish. Soon it was a regular event. I had guitar cases strewn all over and they talked me into opening one. Next thing I know, I'm showing him a few chords and I'm up on a stool doing "Faded Love," of all things. And when they had gone home, the kid driving Henri's $75,000 Mercedes, I would sit there and marvel at the absurdity of it all—me at nearly fifty years old, pretty much alone except for the mother and illegitimate son of the love of my life and the dead thug who stole her from me. There had to be a country song in there somewhere but I never found the hook.

But what I did find out was that the Amazing Henri was amazing all right, but not the uptight bitch I had figured her to be when she had looked down her nose at me and tried to punish me for running off with Allston twenty-five years earlier. Nor was she the highfalutin' phony, ladder-climbing gold-digger I figured had married old man Stokes for his money. What was amazing is that she was okay, a down-to-earth, better educated, more erudite version of Allston—and I was becoming as comfortable around her as I had been with her daughter.

I had come to expect Henri to be the aggressor in the relationship, which I figured she was doing for the benefit of the boy. She would call and initiate the outings and when out of his presence, she often thanked me for the time I had been willing to give him, teaching him to ride and care for horses and a few riffs on the guitar. She had even fingered me as his best possible advisor about where to apply for college and how to choose a career path.

"You would have made a great father for my grandchildren," she told me once. "I totally misjudged you then. It was the worst mistake of my life."

I never pushed her to admit what underlined her misjudgment because I knew and no longer needed her to say it to square things, which I once would have demanded. She had judged me by my roots and my neighborhood and the way my mother dressed and talked and how my father earned his money standing waist deep in DuPont textile mill water. Henri Ravenel of the Charleston Ravenels and Allstons had somehow ended up the young wife of an alcoholic musician from nowhere named Williams, and by the time I crossed her path, was on the road to better things and was determined to take her only daughter with her. And I was then undoubtedly only a walking, breathing symbol of everything she was determined to leave behind.

"How Do You Like Me Now?" is the not only the title of a hit country song, but the tune I was playing in my new role as mentor to her fatherless grandson. A Vanderbilt and Harvard man, author of five books, editor and publisher of a famous New York news-paper, advisor to potential presidents, pal of celebrities and lover of women from Smith and Wellesley and the Junior League. I had crossed the river to be something else, to be at ease in West End and so had she, and each of us, having become whatever we were hell bound to be, were finally free to be ourselves. So how did she like me now? A helluva lot better.

Al, or Vic, as he kept wanting to be called, had turned out pretty well for a kid who had the good fortune of never knowing his real father and having less than two years exposure to the nerdy banker Hamilton Jackson, who Henri finally had to fire for not paying attention to Community Southern and letting some underling fuck it up. The kid was lucky to have been raised by two good women, because as a group, women are a lot better human beings than men. And I am just as lucky, having been raised by a good woman, by finding and knowing a few more, and for responding to an invitation one evening in 1982 to visit one of them while her grandson was off on a road trip with the West Mont Academy golf team.

The dinner was simple: No Lenny the butler, no Lorene the cook, no caterer; and nostalgic, at least for me—pasta salad, tiny pimento cheese and chicken salad sandwiches, low-fat potato chips and Pinot Grigio—and for dessert, a large bag of Peanut M&Ms. Allston had fixed the same for me a dozen times over the years in parks, on boats, in motel rooms and automobile hoods. Only Henri's had been served before a roaring fireplace on a glass-top coffee table between matching $5,000 sofas.

Our attire was casual: Henri in a fluorescent pink running suit with painted toenails the same shade peeking through bedroom slippers; me in my usual cowboy boots, black T-shirt, denim jeans and wheat corduroy vest.

When we had popped the last M&M, she got up and came around to my sofa and—as casually as if she had done it a thousand times before—sat down on my lap and put her arms around my neck, bending her face down an inch from mine.

"Allston told me all about how you came to be known as Vic, all the other qualities, uh…let's call them qualities that were the reason she was crazy about you when you were a boy. I assume that you may have even enhanced them on the way to becoming the extraordinarily accomplished man that I have come to know." And then she bent closer and kissed me on the lips, once lightly, then slightly harder and then a third time when I felt her mouth open and the tip of her tongue on my teeth. What happened next was remarkedly similar to what happened on her den sofa in Belair when I was seventeen and her daughter had suddenly stood up and ripped off every shred of her clothing and started on mine while her mother was still making noise in the kitchen.

Shedding clothes in a hurry must have been a skill passed from mother to daughter, in their DNA. In a heartbeat, the Amazing Henri was standing stark naked in front of me. Whoever had assisted her in the makeover had done a marvelous job. Allston had not looked that good when she was twenty-five years old.

Henri began removing my clothes with the same aplomb her daughter always had, and I began to consider what was about to be expected from me. I knew what I was supposed to do, but for the first time in my adult life, I was not sure I could finish what I had not started. My equipment had been parked for some time, like some old tractor in a garage with the battery down. Would it start? Of all the women with whom I had previously found myself in the same situation, none had ever presented as intimidating challenge as Henri—and I was no longer the man I had once been. I had been with beautiful women before but none that towered over me naked as the day they were born and disrobed me at a speed that I feared my manhood could not match. A threatening cloud of embarrassment hovered danger-ously closer, and the awful specter of erectile dysfunction reared its ugly head. But then the instant I felt the warmth from the inside of her thighs against my skin and watched a somewhat familiar thatch of ebony pubic settle into my lap, miraculously, so rose what I had feared would not.

"I hope you don't mind," she said. "But I like it on top. It's where I do my best work."

Astride me with her knees on the sofa, Henri gently guided me into heaven, captured my full attention and held it there, moving slowly at first and then gradually accelerating until she settled into the steady rhythm of a quiet effortless, long ride to ecstasy as elegant and genteel as the lady at the wheel. There were no acrobatics, or moans or screams or even labored breathing, and after two orgasms slid her slim body off of mine and came to rest, nuzzled against my shoulder. I looked at her and smiled, and managed to say, weakly. "You are indeed the Amazing Henri and yes, on top is exactly where you belong."

Young Al Ravenel is off at Duke now and Henri is pushing me to have a blood test to legally determine his true parentage, hoping of course it will prove he is not the son of a petty criminal shotgunned to death in his parking garage. So quick to her back was Allston in those days that her mother believes—as I sometimes wondered—if she might not have been ripping the clothes off Randy Sikes and me during the same period of time. He became prominent in Allston's life and on Henri's radar screen just as I was being wiped out of both.

"What other reason could Allston have had for wanting to name her son Vic, Vic?" Henri says. "I think she might have believed you were the father."

I am considering the possibility and the test but am not sure I am all that anxious to know because Al—or Vic as Henri now prefers—would have to take the test, too, and the results might tell us both something we don't want to know about his mother. I keep asking myself that if by some stretch of the imagination Henri and I were to get married, I could be considered both father and grandfather to Vic.

There has been no talk of marriage, or of the seventeen-year difference in our ages. When the male is by far the oldest in a relationship, no one gives it a second thought, and Henri frequently asks rhetorically, "Who cares how old we are?" But she quickly followed that she had already dispatched one husband in the courts, buried another, and had "no interest in taking care of another old man"—as if I were the older and she expected to outlive me.

Henri says, "People are only as old as they feel," and I can assure you that as the man who does the feeling, Henri does not feel old. Like her daughter, she is fond of sex and lavish with both gifts and kisses. I cannot say that either has kissed me like they meant it.

When invited, I accompany Henri to all of her CEO commitments and board meetings where a companion is in order, which takes me to a lot of Fortune 500 gatherings at the Biltmore at Jackson Hole and the Greenbrier in West Virginia. We are also regulars on the Bluff City social front and travel frequently to Chicago and New York because Henri prefers their symphonies, ballets and operas to those in the West End, even though she is listed among the donors to them all.

All this air travel would normally be too onerous for me if we had to put up with the cramped seats and absurd security connected with commercial airlines. But now I only travel by Bluff City Air private jet, which Henri also makes available for my book tours, speeches and consulting jobs. And she appears more than happy to chauffeur me to my roadhouse gigs in her Mercedes and sits in the front row and applauds my performance.

Life seems to have so many more rewards when lived on the West End side of the River.

16

Red left the *Clarion* the same day Jack Hickenlooper retired, his high-wire act closing with the disappearance of his safety net, which it turns out was exactly the nature of their relationship.

The basis of that conclusion came from a source of previous enlightenment, Weston's old driver, Nate Larson, who had first warned of the potentially combustible relationship between Dr. Goebbels' and his receptionist that brought Tate Weston down. That Larson went on to become a feared federal prosecutor and admired member of the judiciary is a testament to his persistence in search of truth regardless of its consequences.

For all the deference and loyalty he exhibited, Red was always more of the Perrys' *Clarion*, more an old rival of Hickenlooper's than one of his New Frontiersmen. Like Lyndon Johnson in the Kennedy administration, Red was trapped in Hickenlooper's Camelot. Oh, he bravely fought on the frontlines of all the Hickenlooper wars, but not because his heart was in it like ours, but because his ass was in harness—and unlike ours—constantly at stake.

About the time that Rhodes Newbold and I were chasing the Spiro Agnew scandal in the early 1970s, Larson was deep into an investigation of influence pedaling by some public officials in Bluff City. An undercover FBI agent assigned to the case had documented regular visits by the main suspect to the *Clarion* offices, yet no records of his visits appeared on the security logs kept at the front entrance of the newspaper building (a procedure instituted back when Colonel May owned the *Defender* after a prankster-loving *Clarion* reporter set off a box of giant firecrackers under the colonel's car).

Subsequent undercover FBI work determined that the bribery suspect was signing in under a false name because he was delivering substantial sums of money to a *Clarion* employee—Red Whitmore—presumably in exchange for Whitmore's efforts on his behalf to keep a lucrative annual contract providing recreational services to both the city and the state governments. For years, elected officials interpreted what Whitmore said as being what the *Clarion* wanted.

Rather than arrest Whitmore or begin electronic surveillance on *Clarion* executives, Larson had taken both his suspicions and evidence directly to the publisher's office. He said Hickenlooper appeared stunned by the disclosures and promised to get to the bottom of it. Not long after, however, the target of Larson's investigation was assassinated. The bribery case died with him. His murder was never solved and the motive remains a mystery to this day. Equally mysterious to Larson was that Hickenlooper never reported back and Whitmore's role at the *Clarion* remained the same until his retirement.

What had puzzled Larson was no mystery to me.

Whitmore had been the political henchman and point man for two generations of Perrys. He came with the building, carrying twenty-plus years of *Clarion* baggage with a treasure trove of knowledge of what had gone before—both good and bad—and the merits and scars from having done both. To Hickenlooper, along with the titles of editor and publisher, Red had come a human tool too useful to waste but perhaps too dangerous to use, somebody who knew all the past rights—and wrongs. Whitmore reported ready for duty to Hickenlooper just as he had to Wainscott Perry and his father before him, willing to do whatever needed to be done.

Hickenlooper had used him to do what needed to be done, just as the Perrys had and as Red had used me that night he sent me out to watch the home of Councilman Culverhouse. Red was only a few days shy of his deathbed at the Daisy Hill nursing home when he finally told me what we were doing there.

Maddux had been forced to resign based on evidence gathered by a *Clarion* photographer inside the home of Councilman Culverhouse minutes before Red showed up at my car door.

"Sure, Colonel May wanted his man Maddux to stay in office so he could whitewash Judge Collin's jury tampering trial, but there was another, even more compelling reason for him not to resign," Red said. "Maddux was getting rich from payoffs from the Negro numbers bosses. Second Friday of every month on his way home he stopped on Lincoln Avenue to collect. We're talking at least ten grand a month for years. And that wasn't all he was getting. He was fucking the councilman's daughter who lived in the house, which I suspect was part of the deal all along. Savannah Culverhouse was gorgeous and would fuck a snake if somebody would hold its head.

"So that day, I rode out there in broad daylight with the photographer like we were on a routine assignment. Billy Morehead would do anything the *Clarion* asked him to and wasn't afraid of the old devil himself. We went in to see Savannah and set the whole thing up. Either she cooperated or she goes to jail with her old man. When I left, Billy stayed behind and hid in Savannah's closet. When Maddux stripped and climbed into her bed, Billy busted out of the closet, camera flashing, caught both of 'em naked as jaybirds and was out of there before Maddux ever knew what the hell was happening. I was parked in the alley and we came right around to meet you. Billy had a darkroom at home, which is where he went to develop the film and make the prints. Then he brought 'em to me in the parking lot of the newspaper and never said a word about to this day far as I know. There was a plane waiting for me at Bluff City Air with an FBI agent from Washington on it. Next day, that plane is back with a package from the attorney general. First thing Maddux saw when he opened it is his bare-assed self on top of Savannah Culverhouse looking around at something like a deer caught in headlights—and right under it was a letter of resignation for him to sign. That's how our boy Miller Clark got appointed U. S. attorney in time to handle the jury tampering trial and I doubt Miller ever knew how it all got done."

By the time Red told me all this, I was pretty well steeped in figuring out the answers to my questions before I asked them, and the shape Red was in from lung cancer, he had no body language to read. "How in the hell did we know about the payoffs and how did you get Savannah Culverhouse to cooperate?" I demanded to know.

Red responded first with a sly smile, then a weak little "heh... heh."

"Well, Miller Clark never went after Maddux, Savannah or her daddy for conspiracy and bribery, so you gotta figure there was never any case file on anything when he took over—or the Kennedys told him all about it and not to prosecute. I don't know which. But all three of 'em could have gone away for a long, long time... and as for how we knew, the *Clarion* I mean...let's just say Savannah had hootchie-cootchie ways with a lot of white men who could do things for her. Back then, well, she and I were real close...a lot of extracurricular business together, you might say. She came by here just the other day to say goodbye. Still looking real good, too, I mean for a woman her age...heh...heh."

I cannot say for certain what my reaction would have been had I known all the gritty and disturbing details of what I was involved in at the time, or what Red was doing on his own. Surely, it would have raised hackles on the back of my neck and tempered my infatuation with Hickenlooper and the *Clarion*. Sallie Mae Arthur would have hoped as much. But the enduring human nature principle of end justifying means was still light on my tongue from the reading of *All the King's Men* and *The Last Hurrah*, and yet to be comfortably digested. But it came to be, eventually forced to rest comfortably in my gullet by my own failures to save the *Morning Herald* and the *Defender* from extinction. By the time I had witnessed the burial of both Red Whitmore and Jack Hickenlooper, I understood completely the nature of their relationship as endemic to the circumstances.

And after hearing of Larson's experience with the FBI case, there was no question in my mind that in addition to furthering the *Clarion*'s interests without question, Red had an agenda all his own. And I brought up the Larson case in our final visit.

"Oh, that," Red said. "Nothing to it. But that's the reason I showed up in Baltimore on the Agnew thing. Jack ordered me up there, just to get me out of town for a few days. I never heard another word about it. But that was a damn good story you all gave me while I was up there. I really appreciated all the help."

At the intersection of the press and politics there is collision after collision of competing interests, choices between bad options and worse, decisions between embracing the devil you know or the devil you don't. Often the lesser of two evils is the best bet. Obviously, Hickenlooper had bet that throwing Red Whitmore under Nate Larson's steamroller was the worst of options—the devil he didn't know. What would damage the *Clarion* more? Its best known reporter going to prison as an influence peddler, widely regarded no doubt as a scapegoat for the newspaper's wrongdoings. Or Whitmore escaping prison by ratting out years of previous and even current *Clarion* backroom political shenanigans?

Lucky as usual, Hickenlooper was saved by the apparently unrelated death of Larson's main witness. And in the end, Red's service to three generations of newspaper publishers had not gone un-rewarded.

HICKENLOOPER

17

Hickenlooper's proposition of equal justice for all still lay before the country, a work in progress, slowly moving toward the horizon of a perfect democracy in ways better or worse—decidedly worse now that the old publisher's passion for it is as cold as his bones in his stone-colored coffin there before the altar in his beloved cathedral, which will hold only a tiny fraction of the three thousand who attended his wake the day before. Not only was the man widely admired for all the things he did for his city, he had earned the gratitude of many for things he didn't do.

As usual the most loyal of those who had labored in his causes are close by, in pews marked in purple for VIPs and in blue for the inner circle that had earned his greatest trust—the honorary pallbearers—now a klatch of mostly white-haired men in dark suits whose power and influence had waned along with their testosterone. Long rendered politically impotent by the blooms and fruits of seeds they had once planted, now—for the moment anyway—they had been reinvigorated by the exclusivity of their proximity to Hickenlooper's bier.

The honorary pallbearers had been listed by name in the cathedral's celebration program along with his immediate survivors, ceremony participants and a collection of family photographs of Hickenlooper from young to old. We are forty in number, and by sight a group spared ghostly countenance only by bulbous red badges of alcoholism or hypertension on our faces; or in the case of some, the more colorful presence at their sides of once-glittering trophy wives who had been plucked in broad daylight from high society for the blue of their blood, or women of the night honed in on due to the summoning heat in theirs.

None is more visible or animated than Tate Weston, a full head of silver hair, still ramrod straight and strutting at eighty-five, somehow seemingly shed of recent decadence and nearly elegant again in his trademark costume that a half century earlier he had hoped to wear to the White House—a newly tailored, blue three-piece pinstripe, red-and-blue striped tie and gold watch fob across the vest. Never comfortable below any horizon, Weston would be the last to take his seat, then up again and again to greet some later arrival, patrolling the center aisle, bending to kiss some old friend's grandchild and finally settling in the second row pew behind me alongside a member of Hickenlooper's Catholic mafia, Tommy Egan.

Car dealer and former nightclub owner, Egan was a childhood friend and a golfing partner of the deceased until failing knees drove them both to the clubhouse to play pinochle instead. Nearly twenty years earlier when I had been in their foursome as Egan's partner, my putting caused us to lose to Hickenlooper and Weston. The next day, Egan dispatched by courier a new $200 putter to my little farm. It was still in my golf bag and I told him so.

"Hope you learned how to use it by now," he growled.

At least as old as Weston, Egan was one of few non-bald among us whose hair showed no gray, to which the ever-observant Weston took note.

"Tommy, you look too damn young to be who you are."

"It's my new hair," Egan retorts. "From a bottle. At my drugstore, they give it to you when you get your Viagra prescription filled."

Weston's face breaks into the grand smile that had accompanied thousands of lies. "What, you got a girlfriend now, Tommy?"

"Hell, no," Tommy says. "I just take enough Viagra so I can pee over the edge of my shoes."

Obviously, people who knew what they were doing had planned the seating arrangements. Each of us had been notified of what time a designated entrance to the cathedral would be opened through which only those on a list would be admitted, as were the invitees to sit in the VIP section, among them divorcee Pippa Weston and her stepmother, the Amazing Henri Stokes.

In the old days, Hickenlooper always assigned me these logistic jobs. I suspected this one had gone to one of his nieces, Cathy, who had assumed the leadership of her father's advertising agency, and who had once worked for me at the *Morning Herald*. My suspicions are born out when my front row companions arrive, both former Bluff City mayors whose campaigns Hickenlooper had sent me to shepherd when the *Clarion* was earning its kingmaker reputation.

William "Billy" Andrews, who had gone to Congress as a result of the reversed election in 1962, is at least eighty years old, frail and with hearing no better than mine. Though side by side and contorting to turn our best ears toward each other, we have trouble communicating in the din of the cathedral, for it is rapidly filling with people like us long in love with the sounds of their own voices. After serving three terms as its congressman, Andrews had returned to Bluff City to serve as its mayor for the next twelve years, a critical period in its growth and economic development. He had been followed in office by a clown whose name escapes me that the *Clarion* had supported as the "lesser of two evils wanting the job." But it was not long before the *Clarion* turned on him and drove him from office. He was succeeded by Russell Billings, a financial wizard and egg-headed, ex-college professor from Princeton who had made a quick fortune spearheading development of downtown Bluff City. As a politician, he was a total Hickenlooper creation, recruited by the *Clarion*, and though colorless and saddled with an image as a carpetbagger, easily sold as a competent alternative to a clown. For three terms, he led the city so well he was twice elected governor and sometimes included in media talk as a potential candidate for president.

I had seen neither man for a decade or more, during which Bluff City had a reputation as a model of urban governance and development, repeatedly chosen as one of the best places in the country to live and do business. I sincerely believed that their combined quarter of a century in office had been largely responsible and offered the compliment.

Next to me, Billy Andrews raised a gnarled index finger and pointed to the casket. "The one thing we had in common," he declared, "was that guy there in the box." To which Billings nods, "Amen. Never would have happened without him."

Looking frequently back over my shoulder to keep track of arrivals, there was a former vice president of the United States and Nobel Prize winner, two current United States senators, several governors, and the son and widow of Robert F. Kennedy, the man Hickenlooper had loved like a brother and who had called on him so many times in the past to help spawn something new in the country. Hickenlooper had reassembled us one last time to a glorious parting benediction that marks not only his passing but in my mind our own relevance and the end of an era. For four decades, we had ridden a gentle but persistent tide that washed away old legal barriers and leveled the political landscape, effecting historic change, nowhere more evident than on this day in the old cathedral.

Funeral planners—the sharp niece maybe or even Hickenlooper himself in one last show of political cleverness—appear to have crafted the ceremony into a reflection of the aggravating status of our long battle—equal justice for all almost—but stalled now short of the horizon by stubborn reactionary forces.

The recollections fly through my mind like autumn leaves stripped and scattered by a swift wind foreshadowing the winter of our lives, fleeting past one by one, there for an instant and then replaced by another, all blown in a flurry to a resting spot where they settle and pile, one memory blotting out another.

The gust subsides only when quieted by sight of the widow

Deidre, only a few years younger than her husband but still sunny, fit and unbent by either years or grief, who appears in the near alcove to lead her family to the pews directly across the aisle. At her elbow is the Hickenloopers' only son, Jack Jr., his father's pride and joy, who is a Broadway producer and behind his actress wife and teenage grandson.

By sheer numbers alone, Caucasians dominate the altar, the imperious and flamboyant Catholic Church liturgy prevailing as usual. Archbishop Flannery, enthroned in red and purple, the nine mass celebrants in their muted lemon vestments of Lent, moving authoritatively about the altar beneath the gilded ceiling of the vaulted apse, lighting candles, one flicking Holy Water over Hickenlooper's box, symbolically to germinate the seeds of Resurrection, another swinging a thurible spewing incense to spread the fragrance of new life.

But this is not your grandmother's regular funeral mass. I have seen enough of them to know. On a bench off to one side are two black Bluff City preachers I recognize as fundamentalist Southern Baptists, who, over the years, have spent enough time in Hickenlooper's various offices that their asses imprinted his chairs. And their presence near the altar is not mere tokenism. They are not here just to be seen. That black knot on the other side of the altar, nestled not a Holy Water sprinkle away from the Archbishop, are the all-black choirs from their inner-city churches, twenty-five singers by my count, a coil of pent-up energy that when loosed will become a vocal monument to Hickenlooper's life. The rhythm of revolution, music oils the heart and soul of its engine—superior numbers—the defining element of a majority ruled democracy. From their opening a cappella rendering of "The Battle Hymn of the Republic," the choir and accompanying music of a quartet from the Bluff City Symphony took over Hickenlooper's funeral and held it captive through every stage of the liturgy. Perhaps never before anytime anywhere has a Roman Catholic faithful traipsed hands folded to the Communion rail to the tunes of "On Eagles' Wings" and "This Little Light of Mine."

What we were witnessing was eventually explained by the suggestion of the lone eulogist that the life we are celebrating was that of a truly spiritual man. That Hickenlooper was spiritual never occurred to me. He never wore his religion on his sleeve and was contemptuous of any who did, privately anyway, as he was forever in league with some priest or preacher in one cause or another, almost always along a political angle. Maybe it was his association with the Kennedys whose power sprouted from shanty Irish Boston, where religion and politics are one and the same and the definition of patronage is family, church and neighborhood in that order. The Hickenloopers are not Irish. They came from Germany in 1754 as Hickenlivelys, an American bastardization of Heckenliables, which one of Hickenlooper's enemies once researched and told me translates to "hedge hopper/thief"—a description he obviously favored.

The eulogist, however, an ordained Catholic priest and brother-in-law, sings a different tune, and it is convincing. Father Pat Watson had chosen to sit with the Negro preachers and to wear a sport coat and collarless T-shirt, green in color to signify the beginning of heavenly afterlife rather than the normal black garb of his order.

Black faces are abundant, more than I have ever seen at the funeral of a white man, but blackness of clothing—a symbol worn by the grief stricken in mourning—is nowhere—no doubt because it would clash so sharply with cool Lemon of Resurrection.

It is from Hickenlooper's Catholic upbringing by an Irish mother, an O'Brien, and the influence of nuns at Cathedral School that Father Watson has written the verses of his song of spirituality, which makes sense. In its long quest to become the only worldwide religion, the Catholic Church had been persistently colorblind, a refrain from which the brother-in-law clergyman believes Hickenlooper developed his passion for equal justice under the law and earned this eulogy as a spiritual man.

Father Watson's message is hardly the last amazement. The choir members are not the only singers present. Lurking at the edge of the black knot from the outset is a gray ghost, distinctively tall, slim and stately, now a matron over sixty, wearing a pewter dress and shimmering hair of the same shade to her shoulders. Her face is a white powder and her infamous riveting eyes hide behind coal black shades. I had been among her fans for years, once even having the privilege to play on the same stage with her. The folk music aficionados could probably have recognized her simply by the big blond Gibson guitar hanging from her neck. Even the Negro mourners must have suspected she is someone famous. I check the program to be sure. Indeed, she is Emmy Lou Harris. One legend has come to celebrate the life of another, her presence alone clearly another threat to the grief and solemnity that burdened Hickenlooper through the plethora of Kennedy tragedies. Emmy Lou waited her turn by

adding her voice to the choir at every opportunity and sway-
ing to the strains of the symphony quartet like some hooded,
raccoon-eyed serpent seduced by the melody of the charmer's
flute.

The minute she finally rises and stands alone with the big
Gibson before the microphone produces the first tomblike silence
of the day, like when a conductor first raises his baton before his
orchestra. Everyone who has read the program knows the core
message is coming. She sings their anthem—"We Shall Overcome"—whose lyrics have been the voice of protest and hope
all the way back the pre-Civil War days of "No More Auction
Block for Me."

We shall overcome...We will walk hand in hand...We shall
all be free...We are not afraid...We are not alone...We shall
overcome...We shall overcome someday.

Even when delivered in a haunting voice by a pale ghost with
black holes for eyes, the anthem is an indisputable message of hope
and a fitting closure to the celebration of a lifelong struggle for
equal justice for all, a clear statement that even though segregation
in America was doomed by the evil nature of its beginning and the
inevitability of miscegenation, the challenge of racism remained.
But the song's melody, if there is one, is faint, hardly discernible
and hardly the kind of uplifting note preferred by Hickenlooper—
had it not been for its absolute appropriateness.

Overcoming is inevitably a journey of fits and starts that careens
into ditches, over cliffs into an abyss after abyss only to rise again
like a Phoenix from ashes, back in flight to take another crack at
the horizon.

The night in 2008 when Obama cleared the most formidable barrier facing a black American, Hickenlooper and I somehow found each other amidst the flood of telephone congratulations being exchanged by the veterans of the long pursuit. Our joy was tearful and giddy and bursting with emotion, and we'd both repeatedly had to go silent and cover the phone to avoid the embarrassment of one old man hearing another cry out loud over the results of an election that might never have occurred had it not been for Hickenlooper and his friends like Bob Kennedy.

The second Obama election was even more important as validation of the first. Turning America's first black president out of office after one term, when the same voters had given two to the bungler Bush, would have been a tragic retreat backwards in the worst possible way for the world to see.

But our elation already had been crushed earlier in the campaign by tragedy more painful and personal, on an infamous day for us both, the day one on which I suspect Hickenlooper's once indomitable spirit began to die. Long gone to whatever afterlife reward he deserved, Big Ike Oldham's newspaper culture still dominated the pathetic remains of the business. With Hickenlooper retired into academia to spend his Citycorp Foundation legacy in search of a glorious past, the *Clarion* had been repeatedly raped and pillaged by the Miami bean counters and reduced to fluff and drivel, the only remnant of its former prowess being the name "Chairman Emeritus Jack Hickenlooper" still on its editorial page mast. By 2012, the paper was being managed by two of corporate America's young female ladder climbers on the way up, not because Hickenlooper had been a pioneer in pushing women to the top, but because the glass ceiling against which female executives still bumped pushed 30 percent more compensation expense down to the bottom line. With little knowledge or concern for the *Clarion*'s history as a beacon of civil rights and equal justice, the women had endorsed silk-stocking conservative Mitt Romney's bid to push the first African American out of office.

The morning that happened I called Hickenlooper's cell phone to commiserate but could only leave a message, "God damn their heathen souls." It was the first time in our long history that my call was not returned. Later he apologized and said the *Clarion* editorial calling Obama a failure had been too personally devastating to discuss at the time, a disappointing note in history as discordant and unfathomable yet somehow as appropriate as the melody missing in the civil rights anthem. As close as we had become, Hickenlooper could not bring himself to tell me that his emotional injury had been inflicted with insult. The modern Clarion leadership, now dedicated to the delivery of only good "news," had neglected to inform him in advance of the bad news that they were abandoning the editorial policy that had been the heart and soul of the newspaper for a century and to which he had devoted most of his life. The Chairman Emeritus had learned of it almost casually in a phone call after it had become common knowledge in the newsroom.

Just as the long march will surely do, Hickenlooper's benediction veered back on track. After one of the liturgical Lemons mumbled a few final prayers of Godspeed, Emmy Lou and her Gibson, the choir and the symphony reeled back in tune and high spirits. Instantly the normally silent family funeral procession toward the hearse waiting on the sidewalk outside becomes a rocking, roof-raising, Protestant Negro church "Hallelujah."

I'll Fly Away, O Glory...I'll Fly Away...When I die...Halle-lujah Bye and Bye... I'll Fly Way...To a home on God's Celestial shore, I'll Fly Away.

...When the shadows of this life are gone, I'll Fly Away... Like a bird from prison bars has flown... I'll Fly Away.

On the way to my car, I finally got around to reading a poem the cathedral program had deemed Hickenlooper's favorite, "Miracles," by Walt Whitman, who knew nothing but miracles from "every hour of the light and dark" to watching "honey bees around the hive of a summer forenoon" or "animals feeding in the fields."

Maybe the soldiers in Hickenlooper's war on inequality had witnessed one as well, the once unthinkable miracle of an African American being twice elected president of the United States, rendering forever futile two centuries of racism and oppression.

Though this miracle had engendered a backlash of resistance that left us stalled temporarily like empty shells strewn on the very beaches we had conquered, we had indeed overcome—and like birds from prison bars had flown, still free. And I felt a welling of gratitude for the life of Jack Hickenlooper, as I had for the lives of Rhodes Newbold, and Allston and Captain Morgan and Sallie Mae Arthur, and yes, Tate Weston, too. For they had made my life and time so full and rewarding it would be shamefully selfish to dread my own death.

AUTHOR
INDEBTEDNESS

This story was years in the writing and without the contributions of many people would never have been told. I am most grateful to my agent Deborah Schneider for her patience, confidence and encouragement; to readers Larry Woods, Chris Tokarek and Ralph Squirrel for their knowledge, contributions and support, both moral and otherwise; to Bethany Brown, Gwyn Moores and Melanie Zimmerman for their expertise in making it happen; and most certainly to my literary hero Robert Penn Warren and his characters Willie Stark and Jack Burden for the inspiration.

CPSIA information can be obtained
at www.ICGtesting.com
Printed in the USA
LVOW01*0015131215

465913LV00002B/2/P